Four Psychos

Book I of The Dark Side Series

C.M. Owens writing as

Kristy Cunning

Thank you to the ones taking this fun little leap with me. <3

TABLE OF CONTENTS

CHAPTER I

"Oh! Oh yes," the woman with the perfect *purr* says around an exaggerated moan.

Really, can't he tell the girl is quite dramatic with the theatrics?

But Three doesn't care.

Three is a rather selfish fellow, I've noticed. He lets One, Two, and Four do most of the heavy lifting, then he steps in and does something very scandalous it seems, if her breathy pants and moans could be trusted.

It's not really scandalous. He's just fucking her nice and hard, chasing his own release, and she's fake moaning like she's working for a Grammy.

It's times like these I'd really like to be able to eat popcorn. It seems like the perfect time to have a bowl. The damn stuff slips right through my non-tangible hand.

Frustrating. As. Hell.

Anyway, Three gets his and moves aside for Two to step in. Two likes the nipples. He always works the nipples, and that's when her moans will get raspy, more genuine. Two is who I'd like to meet first. Three would have to sit out if I ever get out of this half-here, half-not phase and touch some skin.

I'd make him watch, while Two took my nipples just like he's doing to her now. As he was doing that, I'd make One and Four change their routine from going first to going second.

As soon as Two finished my nipples, I'd have One and Four do that delightful little blindfold game they do. I wouldn't know which one had his face between my thighs, humming whatever tune he wanted. I wouldn't know which one was behind me and running his hands all over my body.

Those two like to share a lot.

Three would usually step in and steal all this glorious thunder so he could deliver some anticlimactic lightning. *Pew. Pew.*

Not with me. He'd have his very impressive-looking ass on the sidelines, stroking himself for my viewing pleasure, as Two stepped back in and took me slow, then hard, then slow…

Oh yes. This is exactly what I've been doing for the last few years since I became whatever this thing I am.

We went dancing tonight. The four of them often go to clubs to find a willing participant interested in a scandalous night of debauchery with four sexy men.

I love dancing. I always pretend like it's me they're surrounding as I stand in the middle with the woman of their choice, while they close ranks, boxing her in on the dance floor and making her feel like the sexiest, most desirable woman in the world.

It's breathtakingly erotic and empowering. Obviously it's just make-believe on my part, since they're not aware of me.

I'm neither here nor there. Alive nor dead.

I don't even quite know who I am. I know what century I'm in, and who the American president is. I assume that means I'm American, especially given the fact English is the only language I know.

But me? I have no clue *who* I am. I know all that other seemingly less important information, but not where I live, or what I do, or even my name.

And I have no clue who these four are, other than the fact they're not entirely human, though they look like the finest specimens in the world.

Well, I've learned their names; I just had them numbered first, so I considered them pet names after that.

Jude—Four—is the dark and tempting type. Not generally brooding, but certainly foreboding. A sinister twinkle sometimes flickers in his eyes. Dark hair, dark eyes, beautifully tan skin, and a body that would set my panties on fire if I could wear physical panties.

Yeah, he's the one that drives you to the fine edge of pain, and that's when those moans become disbelieving, as though they can't possibly fathom anything is quite so good.

Four is definitely my favorite.

Two is a close second though, because he takes his time. His blond hair is a stark contrast to Four's inky black hair. The two side by side have no visible similarities, besides the fact they're carved like sexy stones.

Three is probably the most attractive—blindingly gorgeous, to be honest. But it's wasted because he's so selfish with his body, only touching but never letting anyone else touch.

His hair is almost as dark as Four's, but it's just a little lighter, always messier. But it's messy in a deliberate way that only spikes his appeal. And again…that body.

One, who is built just as freakishly perfect, has very light hair, but not quite blond. It also looks the softest, and I really want to get my fingers tangled in it one day.

Now, I know what you're thinking. I'm terrible for watching these people in their dirtiest, darkest, most intimate of times, when they're utterly clueless of my presence.

Yeah. I felt that way for the first little while.

During that time, I would flicker in and out. It seemed the longer I had my eyes on them, the longer I was able to stay in this place. Their world.

But when I would seal them out during these intimate times to give them their privacy whilst I called that nasty skank a string of names, I'd slowly start to fade.

What sort of self-respecting woman would allow four men touch her like that? How sickeningly filthy would one have to be to partake in such acts of debauchery?

After years of *no one* being able to see you, hear you, smell you, feel you, or even sense you? You stop giving a damn about what other people might think of you, and you face the truth of who you really are and what your moral compass truly is.

Because your opinion becomes the only one that exists. No one else even knows *you* exist.

Turns out, I'm a shameless hussy.

I watched, I coveted, I even did some really questionable things to try and actually possess whatever woman they brought home with them. I'm apparently not the possessing type of ghost.

Or poltergeist? Am I a poltergeist?

If so, I'm terrible at it. I can't even rattle the electricity or change the channel on the television. Power surges are obviously way out of my league.

Anyway, I've since perfected my own personal fantasy. Living. Watching. Learning. I know all four of them as if they're my real life family.

Well, not family. My people. There.

But they have no clue I even exist.

When I'm watching them watch TV—*okay, that sounds creepier than it is*—I like watching their different reactions to the same thing. Four always likes the gory stuff. He actually grins when blood is slashed.

Three lights up like a horny teenager when anything to do with sex is on. Ironic, since he's the worst one at the act.

Two likes to watch with heat in his eyes instead of eager, unlike Three. He also likes to watch his friends—definitely not brothers, learned that—have fun with the girl of their combined choice.

One is the type to react differently the most to things. Sometimes he's into gore. Sometimes the sex.

Jude is my favorite, of course. He's the one I would have first. I'd never settle for just one. I'm past all points of dignity or respectable difference. I'm not a lady anymore—possibly never was, since I can't remember.

I've endured this for over five years.

I've only caught glimpses of the other world they frequent. They're certainly not from America, it seems. No. They live in a rather elaborate place where the colors are brighter, the smells are stronger, and the people are really dark and scary.

Somehow it feels familiar too. Though I'm not sure how.

Hard to explain, since I'm a ghost with no knowledge of my past or other worldly things. I know a lot of useless things.

But I've found myself knowing things that I didn't realize were other-worldly until it was pointed out.

So whatever it is they are, I'm something similar. Though that is all real sketchy. I'm almost certain they're immortals of some kind, but that's all I've gathered. And not vampires; I'm certain of that.

Since I decided to keep eyes on them through all the dirty and the private, my presence has grown stronger. I'm able to stay all the time now. I can even let them out of my sight and not start fading away.

It's still hard to focus in that *other* place, though. And now they're about to start being there a lot more, since they've entered the trials. What trials? Hell if I know.

Since whatever I am doesn't sleep, I even have to watch them sleep.

Ten minutes is the longest I can keep my eyes off them. The

second I feel the warning tingle, I'm practically on someone's lap, pretending he's soothing me as the strength slowly returns.

They're very comforting, though they don't know it.

Needless to say, it's been a long five and a half years.

There are a lot of others in this *other* place they visit. Others who also are possibly immortals. Those people are rather vicious. It's like a forbidden retreat. Ethereal, but full of debauchery and violence.

Seductive as it may be, it's still a very haunting place, and I have no idea why my boys insist on hanging around those terrible people.

Whatever celestial beings they are, they get tested every other year to see if they get some kind of spot on these trials. My boys have finally been selected.

I assume. I'm not really sure.

Things fade to a fuzz around the edges, and I mostly can't hear all the words and stuff when I'm there. So…an academy? Or a training facility? Who knows?

Anyway, they finally finish off the tonight's mushy girl with several more mind-blowing orgasms. She's practically worshiping them now, telling them she thinks she's finally in love.

I hate her. I hate all of them. And yes, I realize it's because of petty jealousy.

They send her on her way the second pizza arrives. I join them at the table, sitting in my seat on the end, pretending I'm eating a piece as well as Two speaks around a mouthful.

"It's my turn to choose the girl next. We haven't had a redhead in a while," he tells them.

I frown, looking at my very dark hair. "Nothing at all wrong with brunettes," I tell him, though he obviously doesn't hear me.

"Blondes are more fun," One states with a dark grin.

"Only because you haven't met *me* yet," I point out. "I'll be game for basically anything with the four of you the second I'm whole."

"Brunettes are the most tolerable," Three says after draining a beer.

"Tolerable is not a very sexy way of describing the women with my hair color, Three" I say on an exasperated sigh. "Do you have to be so rude?"

"Brunettes are the ones who fake it the least," Four says with a smirk, winking over at Three, who pointedly ignores him.

"Yeah, but the blondes I pick out are wildcats. Very little effort in convincing them to try a little bit of anything," One goes on.

"Redheads are wildcats too. And they're fucking vicious in the best way," Two says as he grabs another piece of pizza. "Not to mention they make you work for it."

"I find it rather annoying how you four classify women based on their hair color," I primly state, pretending as though my opinion carries weight, when they can't even see or hear me.

"How about we just get some rainbow-haired girls and call it a tie?" Three drawls.

"I'll change all of your minds on brunettes. Or I'll just figure out a way to finally possess these women and be a little bit of everything," I tell them absently, studying the types of pizza they ordered tonight.

I'll try some of that pepperoni when I can.

The conversation shifts when they start discussing these trials I'm so curious about, so I perk up.

"Manella has something planned if he's finally putting us in the trials. We should be ready for anything," One states conversationally, as though they're picking up a discussion they paused to sex up that very lucky girl.

"He's an idiot if he does let us in. Whatever he doesn't want us knowing will be easier for us to find," Three says flippantly.

That has me inching forward.

"We've played our part. We've done our time. They're running out of reasons as to why we can't be there. They had to do this because everyone else was starting to have the same questions we were. We've excelled at everything, won time after time, yet never get into the trials. They can't cover it up if they make it so obvious," Two—I love his voice the most—says as he pours himself a drink.

Make what obvious? It would be awesome if they'd talk about this stuff here more than there.

"Not to mention the sheer volume of souls we've reaped. Our count is much higher than anyone else's," Four drawls.

Oh, I forgot to mention, they're sort of bad guys. I've been calling them reapers.

I mean, they send the bad souls to the bad place, so obviously they're bad guys if they're working for soul collectors or something.

I still want all four. Told you; you learn a lot about your moral compass when yours is the only opinion that matters. Turns out, I'm an unapologetic psychopath.

Not really. I'd just like to know why exactly they got into this line of work. As I said, they're immortal, which is totally mind-blowing until it's just sort of regular, everyday stuff.

I'm not even wowed by it anymore, but I can't be impressed by a mere mortal now either. Not after being around them so much.

I wonder if I was ever impressed by a mere mortal. I really hope I'm not a virgin—can't even touch myself in this state of being to do an inspection.

I don't want any awkwardness when I finally figure out how to touch them.

And I will figure it out.

They've fortunately had some women over who love their old collection of nineties movies. The ones they have to woo usually get to pick a movie while they get over their nerves of being with four indecently sexy men at once. Some of the ones who've chosen *Ghost?* I love those women. They're totally awesome, even if I still hate them when they get to touch my men.

I've learned so much from that movie though.

It's not done me any good yet, but I hope to get stronger and stronger until I can possess every girl who walks through that door. Don't judge. You'd do it too.

Four's phone rings, and he answers it, cutting off the conversation. "Yeah. We're on the way," he says before hanging up.

"Job?" Two asks.

"Big one. Meet me at the cemetery," Four tells them, and I try to reach him in time to grab on.

Did I mention they can do this freaky disappearing thing? I learned if I'm close enough, it drags me with whichever one is doing it.

I miss Four, so settle for hopping a ride with One, managing to catch him before it's too late.

Just as we land in the cemetery, I see a horde of black souls escaping, trying to go back out into the world.

Four slices through the air with his silver bo staff, and it glows as it sucks in soul after soul.

The others use their own respective weapons, and I watch them as they storm the city, chasing all the deserters. I have no idea where they come from, or why so many come at once.

But every time I'm here in this cemetery, I feel something familiar about it.

It almost feels like home.

And I don't even know my name to check for it on headstones.

CHAPTER II

As always, I walk from room to room, telling them all good night. They can't hear it, but I do things like that. It makes me feel a little more normal.

Whatever that is.

I always sit down with them when they eat, and I listen to them talk about random things and soul breaks—like the one tonight—that they have to clean up. I often offer my two cents on the conversation, but they talk over me, of course.

But my favorite part of the day is going room to room, making sure everyone is in bed, and telling them good night before I watch over them. Sounds less creepy than just *watching them.*

A creak so light I almost miss it manages to snag my attention away from Two—the one I've decided to watch tonight.

He sleeps so fitfully that I usually choose him just so I can feel like I'm consoling him, even though I can't do a thing.

Another barely-there creak has me on my feet and moving down the hall as Two wrestles with the sheets.

Rounding the bottom of the stairs, I expect to find Three, since he has trouble sleeping. He has full days where he crashes to make up for all the times he's been awake.

But it's not him.

I catch a glint of silver as a man passes right through me, the dark house hiding his face before I can even process what's going on. I turn to see him moving silently up the stairs, sans the occasional light creak that won't wake them.

They sleep heavier than that, even if they don't all sleep soundly.

The silver glistens again, and my heart catches in my throat when I realize it's a sword. I have no idea if a sword will kill them, but I sure as hell can't watch them die.

This house is enormous, and yet he's on the exact wing where they all four sleep? He knows his way around.

I pass right through him again, and he doesn't even blink. Walking backwards up the stairs to stay in front of him, I study his face, trying to see who he is. I have to find a way to stop him, and his identity won't help, but at least I'll know who to curse.

"Stop!" I shout.

He keeps walking, not seeing me or hearing me.

"Wake up!" I shout to the guys as I turn around. The man passes through me again, and my non-existent heart beats that much faster as it thumps in my ears, echoing the sound of a ticking clock.

Panic seizes me when I make an attempt to block him again, and almost scream when he barely cracks open the door to One's room.

He peers inside, and I rush through him and the door, looking around for anything I can find. I strain, needing something to happen, feeling completely useless and terrified as that door starts opening wider, the shred of hallway light spilling into the room more with each inch.

One doesn't even stir, even as I pass through him over and over, running through the bed and his body.

"Wake up! Wake up!"

Nothing.

Just as the man snakes into the room with the silence of a seasoned killer, he raises the sword.

I react without thinking, screaming as I launch myself at the man, putting every single bit of my fear into that one action as desperation chokes me.

His eyes widen seconds before the first thing I remember ever feeling comes in the form of blunt, mind-searing pain. Then just as quickly as it appeared, it's gone, as the man and I topple to the ground. I pass right through him, barely managing to stop myself from passing through the floor.

It took me a long time to get the hang of not falling through floors.

Then I dart to my feet, gasping. I just knocked him down! Holy shit! I did that!

The man is staring at me in wide-eyed horror, fear and recognition in the depths, until his throat suddenly starts bubbling blood from a slice I never saw.

One is standing over him, sword in hand, as the man's head starts to slide away.

I jerk my eyes away, not keen on watching a head fall off, even though I've seen them do this before. I've never actually been so close.

It figures the one person who I was able to touch, and the one person who has ever been able to see me, would be a monster who wanted my boys dead.

What a waste.

There's suddenly a sword swiping through me, and I look down, seeing it swipe thrice more before I peer up in confusion at One.

He stares at me like he's confused, and swipes again with that sword. I notice it's his weapon, the one he reaps souls with.

"What the hell?" he asks on a breath.

It's then I realize it's me he's trying to hack to bits, and my eyes widen as my heart thumps a little harder.

"You can see me?" I ask on a choked breath, cautious hope and tempered excitement bubbling inside me.

"What the fuck are you?" he snaps, swiping at me again.

I fling myself at him, ready to finally touch one of them! And, much to my dismay, pass right through him. I should have known that since that sword was doing the exact same thing to my middle, but I got a little excited. Understandably so.

But it's the weird tingle I feel when I pass through him that has everything on me stir to attention.

I whirl around as his eyes glimmer with flakes of gold for a second, and his sword falls to his side as he cants his head.

"What are you?" he asks a little calmer, sounding more curious and less hostile.

"I don't know," I tell him, still entranced by the fact he can see me. Hear me. "You can really see me?" I ask, stepping closer.

He lets his gaze dip, and he bites down on his bottom lip. "I can definitely see you."

So much relief floods me at once that it's a little dizzying. After spending five years being completely invisible, I can finally be seen? I can talk to them?

Tears cloud my vision. How am I crying?

I never knew ghosts could faint.

At least not until it all goes black.

Chapter III

"They sent one of their own assassins. This guy's sword? It's made from much better fire-metal than our weapons. It disappeared from sight the second he lost it. I barely saw it in time to know it was even here at all," is the first thing I hear as I slowly come out of whatever just happened.

I didn't fade. Otherwise, I'd hear that terrible buzzing sound for days as I came back. This is more of a drowsy feeling.

"And she saved you?" Three asks.

I can feel the weight of his gaze, and I swear, if I could have an orgasm, just the weight of someone's gaze would give it to me.

I wonder if I've ever had an orgasm. I know it's got to be amazing. I've heard the real moans, and I always feel warm when those moans are teasing me. It's not a physical feeling like the one I had when I hit that man, but it's a—

I hit that man! How did I forget?!

"Yeah. But she's not a soul. It's like she's a being with a soul, but not alive or dead. I've never seen anything like it," One tells them.

Oh, they're talking about me. Because they see me. Because this is really happening.

On the verge of doing another ghostly faint, I open my eyes, and they all go stiff as they stare down at me.

"That's fucking creepy," Two says, eyebrows up as he studies me with wary eyes.

I guess, since I don't breathe and I'm just staring at them with wide eyes in my transparent-ish form, I am creepy. But they can still see me, even if I am still mostly invisible.

I've always been able to see my reflection, though no one else could, but staring at the wall mirror across from me lets me see more of me. Less transparent than before, but still nowhere close to whole.

Somehow, I just leveled up. And now I need to figure out how to level up again.

"Someone needs to try and die again, so I can see if I can get whole," I tell the four guys who are staring at me as though I've sprouted a tail.

I check, since I feel like anything is possible these days. Nope. No tail.

"What the actual fuck?" Four asks.

"Those weren't the first words I ever planned to say to you, but seriously; someone try to die so I can save you and see if that helps me level up," I state again.

"Who the hell are you? What are you? And why the hell are you here?" One asks me, crossing his arms over his impressive, still bare chest.

They're all bare chested. That's not even distracting me, because I'm too excited about finally making progress.

"No clue who I am. I've been here for five years, and I just sort of appeared here. I have no memory of anything before that. I have no idea why I'm here, other than the fact I need the four of you to exist."

They give me a blank stare, all of them bristling. It's hard to see things from their point of view. I know so much about them. I've been watching them for years.

It feels like it's just finally my turn to talk and that they should be as comfortable and close to me as I am to them. When in reality, this is the first time they're meeting me.

One looks at Four, and Four shakes his head. "I've heard of every type of creature out there, and she's nothing like I've heard of. Her soul is intact and fused to this…state she's in."

"*She* can finally be seen, and would not like to be referred to as though she's not in the room," I say, holding a finger up as a small smile curves my lips.

Three's eyes dip down my body, and he takes an unconscious step closer.

"Is she an illusion? Because if they wish to distract us, this would be the way to do it," Three states absently.

"I can assure you that I am a real person. I'm not sure why I'm like this, or if I'm even alive or dead, but I'm definitely real. Until One was almost killed, you've never seen me. But I freaked out and had to save him, and somehow I leveled up to this. And I've been watching you for five years, but only recently have I been able to stay here for longer and longer periods of time. These past couple of years, I've been able to stay all the time."

"One?" One asks me with an arched eyebrow, at the same time Two dubiously inquires, "All the time?"

"*All* the time," I say with a little too much sassy enthusiasm. "Now I need you to try and die, so I can level up again. Then you four can do all those really fun looking things to me, though I think Three needs to sit out and just take notes for the first few times."

Four's lips curve in a grin. Three looks like he's not happy, though I did just state he was out of the game, but he doesn't know he's Three. Two looks like he's trying to figure me out. And One looks like he wants to lock me in a lab so they can study me from a safer distance.

"She's certainly been watching us all the time," Four says with a smirk and a dark glint in his eyes.

"I'm not sure a pretty apparition should win you over so easily," One tells him. "Not when someone clearly wants us dead. They're upping their game."

"She saved your life," Four reasonably points out.

"Yes, I did. And it was epic. Except for the part when it hurt to crash into that guy. You have no idea how good it feels to finally be heard and seen. So who's going to put their life at risk so I can see if it'll propel me into the flesh state?" I ask, looking between them. "If we have a vote, I think it should be Three. He's quite lazy and lets you three do all the work in the bedroom, while he just has his fun and moves along. He'd bring less to this relationship."

Two's lips curve in a reluctant smile this time, as Four's grin spreads wider. One's lips barely twitch, and Three tilts his head.

"Why are you calling us by numbers? If you've been watching us, why haven't you learned our names?" Three asks.

"And who's three?" Four asks with a knowing grin.

"Jude is Four," I tell *Jude.*

I suppose it is rude to continue calling them by my pet names now that they can hear me. They don't realize it's a term of endearment.

I think I've sprang enough on them today.

I stand and walk over to Four, lifting my hand. The other three spread out, their weapons clutched in their hands, and I slip my fingers over Four's chest, not allowing them to pass through.

There's no actual feel or true physical contact, and I can press against him but he'll feel no pressure, since I can't move objects. I can only rest my fingers on the surface, just as I learned to rest my feet above ground.

Before then, I had to find iron to be around to keep me anchored enough to do it.

A little hum of electricity seems to pass between us, though it's so watered down I can't be sure. He tilts his head, his dark grin still fixed to his face.

"Four's my favorite," I decide to say honestly.

He releases a rumble of a laugh, as Two snorts derisively.

My eyes flick to Two, savoring this moment. I'm finally introducing myself to them. And I'm actually introducing who they are to me, since I know them and don't know myself.

It's sort of pathetically sweet.

"And Two is Ezekiel," I go on, eyeing him as I move closer.

His eyes run over my face, flicking to my lips once, as that steady hum of electricity changes just a little, and buzzes differently with him.

This is new. I like it.

"He loves nipples," I add. "He's the one who gets to touch me first, because I've spent a few years perfecting my fantasy. You're doing everything out of order," I go on.

Two finally smirks, his eyes lightening just a little as a hint of gold glistens in his eyes the way they did One's earlier.

On a whim, I step through him. He sucks in a surprised breath, and I feel some weird tingles this time, something much stronger than the hum.

That's interesting. I felt the same thing when I passed through One.

"Your eyes just did something," Three tells him, moving closer and frowning over at me. "What'd you do to him?"

"Do it to me," Four, my fearless boy, says to me, moving closer.

I pass through him, and I shudder at how good those tingles feel. It's like they're growing stronger.

"His eyes did it too," Three states seriously.

Four looks serious now too when he turns to face me, which is not a look I see on him too often.

Three stalks toward me, his little Rafael things in his hands. Sai, I think they're actually called. And it's one of those words where that's the plural and singular way to say it. I think.

Not the important part. The important part is that he's wanting to use one of those sai to gut me. I can tell by that familiar murderous look in his eyes.

I've seen him use those weapons many times.

"Stop!" Four snaps, stepping in front of me before Three can pointlessly use those weapons.

"What's she doing to you? You're taking her side over mine?" Three growls.

"It's not like that," Four explains, as Two steps closer.

"I can't sense an ounce of threat on her," Two tells them. "She passed right through me, and you know I can feel a threat if I'm in close contact with it."

"That's why that guy went for One first, most likely. He sleeps the soundest, and you sleep like you're at war," I tell him.

"You watch us sleep?" Three asks incredulously.

"Don't look so creeped out when you share a woman between the four of you."

Four turns around to face me, his lips twitching again. "How often do you watch our *activities?"*

"Always, lately. The more I have eyes on you, the stronger I feel. I can stay longer that way. I fade away when I'm cut off from you for too long," I explain.

"Fade away?" Two asks. "Where do you go?"

Sighing, I take a seat, though the bed doesn't even dip or anything—again, I can't put pressure on anything. "Into nothingness," I answer. "There's nothing until I return. Then there's you. Since I can't do anything but talk to you, and I've wanted to do that for a while, I'll tell you all about it."

CHAPTER IV

"I've told you all this countless times, but this is obviously the first time you've heard me," I decide to inform them at the end of my long monologue.

After recapping my walk down memory lane, telling them how I watched them, when I watched them, how I enjoyed it…I sound like a total crazy girl in the bushes with binoculars and a rabbit. Not that furry-friend kind of rabbit.

I'd like to be able to use that battery-operated-boyfriend I've only seen them use on other women. I bet it would be awesome.

But, fortunately, they seem to not give a damn about the creepy aspect.

"If you can't remember anything, then how do you even know English?" Three asks me skeptically.

Shit. I need to start calling them by their *actual* names.

"I just know things. They're not like memories. There's no recalling a certain thing like that. It's just like *bam;* the information is there like it's been there all along, but I didn't know I knew it. Sort of like having an emotion and knowing what it is, without having a single memory of when you experienced it before. Things like that."

They exchange a look.

"She could be another piece of the puzzle," One says thoughtfully.

"Or she could be here to sabotage us," Three, the prick, volleys.

"If she was here to sabotage us, she wouldn't have saved my life," One, my third favorite, reminds him.

Three has no retort to that.

Damn it. No more numbers.

"You never told us who was who. Just Two and Four. That story was hard to follow with all the numbers," Jude says, smirking a little.

I told them who One was; they just weren't paying attention when I referred to him, obviously.

"Are you in my head?" I ask him, since he sort of echoed my thoughts just now.

He frowns. "No." Then he looks at them.

Then they all look at me.

"What?" I prompt.

"Why would you ask that?" Jude asks me.

"Because I was thinking I needed to start thinking about you with your names instead of your numbers. And you asked that."

He bristles.

"Anyway, Two's—I mean, Ezekiel's room is where I usually stay at night, but I'll start keeping watch in the hallway instead. Now that you can hear me, I'll wake you up if I hear anything."

Now I feel like I can finally do something for them. Protect them even.

"Who's One?" Gage asks.

"You are," I say without hesitation, causing his smile to grow as they all give Kai a look.

"I'm Three?" Kai asks dryly.

"The selfish one, yes," I agree, even give him a little nod.

His eyes narrow, but I ignore him as I go on. "I'd ask you why you all need to share a woman when you have needs to sate, but I don't really want to question my good luck. As soon as I'm whole, I'll have you and see if it's worth all the hype."

Jude laughs quietly, his eyes raking over me.

"Any particular reason why you're wearing that? Think it might be what you were wearing when this happened?" Kai asks me, gesturing to my skimpy little lingerie.

It's been so long since someone could see me, that I forgot they could see what I'm also wearing. Or barely wearing.

"That's actually one neat thing I learned early on. When I think of something I want to wear, it seems to just be there."

I imagine a long, elegant silver gown, and it appears, making me look a little classier, if I do say so myself.

Kai takes a step back, and Jude takes a step closer, his eyes hungrily raking over me.

"It's been my one constant source of entertainment, because I can do it all day and never get tired. I usually dress in something very sexy, just in case my dreams came true of being whole. I wanted to be ready. You know."

I shrug a shoulder, and Ezekiel lets his eyes wander over me.

I remember that time he bought a girl a red lace slip, and I imagine it. The second it appears, he grips the chair he's in hard enough to cause it to whine.

That's certainly a confidence booster.

Jude is more into leather, so I imagine a saucy little leather underwear set that has some straps attached to the lace-trimmed thigh-highs I'm suddenly in.

He instantly grabs for me, cursing in frustration when his hand swipes right through me, and those tingles just tease me all over again.

"Something less alluring would be appreciated right now. If we get worked up, you'll have to watch us with yet another girl tonight before we even finish this conversation," Kai tells me flatly.

"I'm okay with watching," I say with a shrug. "Once you get over the indecency of it, it's actually pretty hot. Though I admit I won't be okay with watching once I'm able to be a participant."

Jude groans. "We have to figure out a way to make her whole."

"Just because you want to fuck her that doesn't mean we need to be focusing on her right now. That's probably what they want," Kai growls.

"She has nothing to do with them. Whatever she is, it's linked to our own mystery of who we are. Something is going on, and you know it. Everyone knows it."

"I don't know it," I decide to point out as a pair of flannel pants and a T-shirt appear on me. "I'm actually a little fuzzy on the details of what it is you guys do and what you are. I see the souls and stuff that you take—"

"You see the souls but they don't see you?" Kai interrupts, sounding more curious than hostile for a second.

"Yes. It's why I have no idea what I am. Clearly I'm not the same as them. And I know you go to this other place, but I have no idea where it is. I just hop a ride when you do your disappearing thing."

"You can trail our siphons?" Jude asks, interested.

"You call it a siphon? Then yeah; I can trail that. I just have to be close enough when you do it."

He moves toward me. "Then hold on. We can just ask someone who might know what's going on."

My fingers go to his body without hesitation, and Kai snaps at him not to do it just as we disappear.

The wind whirs in my ears much louder than before, and we appear in the back of an alleyway.

"We're seeing your pawn shop friend, aren't we?" I ask him.

He doesn't even bother asking me how I know that.

"Yes," is his only reply as the other three join us.

Kai stalks forward. "Until we figure out what's going on, we can't risk our very important friends by exposing them to a possible threat."

Jude ignores him, leading the way, and Ezekiel trails me as we walk out of the alley.

I move through the wall of the pawn shop, causing Ezekiel to curse. "She's going to draw attention. It's not late enough for this," he hisses.

Only a few people are on the street. I forgot I could be seen.

They, fortunately, seem too inebriated to notice an apparition passing through walls.

Jude doesn't say a word, just walks to the back counter where the familiar older man with a broad grin greets him.

"Need another pint of the good stuff?" Harold asks, lifting a bottle of the clear liquid they buy a lot of from here.

Apparently it's the only way they can get drunk.

"I'll take two of those and some quick answers about what she might be. We'll pay good," Jude tells him.

Harold immediately looks around like he's searching for something. His eyes pass right by me without so much as a second glance.

"Who?" he asks.

My heart stutters. Have I gone invisible again?

My four boys look at me, then at each other, then back at me.

"You can't see her?" Jude asks, causing me to relax a little.

Wait, why can't Harold see me if they can?

That man I crashed into certainly saw me. I swear he looked a little horrified. I must have had a seriously pissed-off expression on my face if he felt that threatened.

"See who?" Harold asks like he's crazy.

Harold can see souls…

But he can't see me?

"No one," Jude says tightly. "Just had too much to drink, I suppose. But I'll take two more," he goes on.

The other three guys go along with it, even though I can see the way Kai is frowning at Jude and me.

Harold rolls his eyes, but sells him two bottles. We leave without a word, and Jude steps into me again. I feel the tingle of our electricity, and I breathe him in like I can touch him if I try hard enough.

Doesn't work.

Next thing I know, we're back in their monstrous home, and he's stepping away from me. The other three appear behind him, and all four study me.

"The assassin who broke in saw her," Gage, *One*, says. "He was so distracted by her that I was able to kill him before he even realized I was awake."

"The assassin was a high-level royal mercenary. The crest was on his skin before the body vanished," Kai says quietly, his eyes raking over me like he's seeking answers in my appearance.

"She also hit him. Maybe that had something to do with it," Ezekiel suggests.

"Maybe," Jude answers, no one sounding too attached to any particular theory.

"I need more sleep tonight. I'm not sure how well I'll sleep knowing we're being haunted by a possible threat," Kai says as he turns and walks out. "We have orientation for the trials tomorrow, and her as a distraction is going to get us killed," he adds on his way out.

"I'll stand watch while you all get some sleep," I tell them, burying my own selfish desire to talk to them until I can't possibly say anymore.

If the trials are that dangerous, I sure as hell don't want them distracted. I'll even wait until after they're rested to ask what the hell these trials are and why they need to do them. But not tonight.

Ezekiel yawns, but he turns and walks out next.

Jude and Gage just stand there studying me.

"You're able to follow us into purgatory?" Gage finally asks.

Frowning, I tilt my head. "Purgatory is where you go? It's way nicer than I expected it to be. It has some seriously bad PR. But the people there seem horrible, so that much now makes sense."

Jude's lips twitch, and even Gage appears amused.

"Purgatory is a little bigger than the section we've visited. That's for special events. The inhabitants of purgatory who are forced there against their will wouldn't agree that it's just bad PR."

I swallow down the lump in my throat. It didn't seem as real before as it suddenly does now.

I have no idea what they even are.

"Tomorrow, you can explain what that means. It's always very hard to focus there for me. But tonight, you need to sleep. I don't want anyone getting hurt because I kept them awake to talk."

Jude steps forward as Gage slowly starts walking backwards, moving toward the door, but holding my gaze for a moment longer. As soon as he's finally out, Jude reaches for me.

His fingers pass right through me, but that strong tingle has me close my eyes as the pleasure washes over me. He moves in closer, lowering his head until his face is near mine, and I sway a little.

"There's something about you that feels far too comfortable. But if you hurt my brothers, I'll end you, somehow or another. And it'll be painful."

Now he's not my favorite anymore. I thought we had

something special going on.

He steps back, and I ignore the painful tug at my heart. He's the one I just knew would be in my corner, though I have no idea why I thought such a thing.

They're not quite as awesome as I'd hoped they'd be if I ever got the chance to finally be seen and heard. I also thought touch would come with that, but now I'm glad it didn't.

I think they'd kill me.

Feeling like the air has just been sucked out of me, I don't say a word. Instead, I pass through the wall to go stand guard.

As long as I'm close, I can peek in and get my fix every ten minutes to keep from fading.

Jude really hurt me. I'm not sure why, but they all hurt me, if I'm being honest. I was amusing and then disposable.

I've waited five years to be able to speak to them, stupidly thought there'd be an instant friendship between us.

And no one even said good night.

CHAPTER V

Nothing happens during the night. I mostly peeked in on Gage, since he sleeps the hardest and I knew he wouldn't notice me. I was afraid one of the others would wake up and be annoyed with my presence.

My confidence from yesterday to today is nilch, thanks to Jude bursting my little bubble and no one even being nice enough to say good night.

I can hear them all in the kitchen, but I'm sitting on the steps. I've spent so long wishing they could hear me and see me, and now that they can, I just want to be invisible again so I can go back to feeling like I'm part of the group. Instead of the weird interloper who needs them to even exist.

Ezekiel rounds the corner to find me, and he stumbles to a halt, eyeing me. "Where's all that spunk from yesterday?" he asks.

Like a petulant child, I don't answer. I pretend they're invisible to me now.

"Ah, this game? I'm good at this game," he says as he takes a seat by me. "Used to play it when I was three or something."

Dick.

I pointedly ignore that dig and him, and I continue staring at the wall like it's fascinating.

He rolls his eyes and stands.

"Whatever. I tried."

I'm being irrationally emotional over this. It really makes no sense.

Maybe it's because my emotions have heightened since leveling up. Everything seems twice as crucial as it did before.

I'll deal with sorting it out later. For now, my fantasy of these four guys being mine is done. I just want to be whole so I can exist without needing them.

He blows out an annoyed breath before finally walking away, rejoining his brothers in the kitchen. I can barely see them if I poke my head out.

Which I'm doing. Every nine minutes and fifty-eight seconds.

"What the hell did you say to her last night after I left?" I hear Ezekiel asking.

"I went to bed too," Gage says to him in confusion.

I should probably tell them my hearing is exceptional. I hear whispers I don't think I'm supposed to be able to hear all the time. No one else seems to be able to hear quite so well.

But I keep that secret to myself.

"What did *you* say?" Gage asks someone, who I assume must be Jude.

"Just gave her a friendly warning," is Jude's response. "I was fine with everything until I realized it's just us who can see her. There's something going on here, and now I think Kai is right. It feels like a trick, and it's certainly something Manella would do to put us off our game."

Kai is next to jump in and start talking. Of course. "I vote we ignore her like she's not around until we get through the first round of the trials. Then we'll deal with her during the month long break."

"Her timing *is* suspicious," Gage says on a sigh.

Tears prick my eyes, though it's just transparent mist. Unlike the real tears I felt last night before fainting. Those stupid tears were happy tears, because this was *not* how this was supposed to go.

They're so nice to all the women who come and go. I assumed they'd be nice to me too.

"There's something about the way it feels when she tries to touch us. It's just...I don't know. I don't feel like ignoring her is going to do anything but hurt her feelings, and what happens if she's somehow linked to the answers we're trying to find, and we piss her off enough that she—"

A phone rings, cutting Ezekiel off, thankfully.

Jude answers, and I hear the shuffling like they're about to leave. Shit.

Just as I stand and go to chase them down, I see Kai turn and smirk at me. They all disappear before I can reach one to hitch a ride with, and a sick feeling creeps in my stomach.

They just left me here.

I told them I'd fade if I went longer than ten minutes without them in my sight, and they left me here.

I let them know I hated the fade. That it was nothingness.

And, still, they left me here.

The lights flicker, and the house vibrates as tears cloud my vision and anger simmers close to the surface. Things rattle off the counter, and it distracts me enough that everything stops at once.

The lights start shining solidly, and the vibrations cease.

My breath catches in my throat as I look around at everything. From Casper to Poltergeist, it seems. Just didn't have the proper motivation until now.

But as time dwindles on, the stabbing pain catches me off guard. It's never hurt before. Why does it hurt so much now?

It feels like knives are being dragged from my toes to my thighs before a lancing pain shoots across my back like a whip has been cracked.

A scream is torn from my throat as my vision dims, but before I can fade into nothing, I suddenly feel myself moving. My breath comes back in a harsh rush as I suddenly find myself in a huge tree. At the top of it, actually.

Right above the four assholes who left me in pain.

Glaring down at them, I watch as Kai takes out his sword. "You two get the Falker twins into the gulley, and we'll herd the juggernauts in behind them. It's the only way we're going to get out of this with the highest times."

I thought they were coming for orientation.

I'm only half listening as I gather back all my strength that they ripped from me. Apparently this new level I'm on comes with a perk.

It takes me a long second to realize that there's more than one perk.

Looking around, I can see…everything.

And my stomach sinks when I take in the prehistoric looking land that surrounds me, along with various hideous creatures that are lurking about.

Gage slashes his sword through a stringy corpse as it tries to grab him. The stringy corpse falls away, its head rolling off, as they go on like it never happened.

Why did I think these sociopaths were so great before?

We're in the middle of this forest or whatever you want to call it. I half expect a dinosaur or dragon to come barreling through the massive, elaborate trees that stretch on for as far as I can see.

The quad splits up, and I watch as Jude and Ezekiel dart to the right, running instead of siphoning. Kai and Gage are moving slower, so I follow them, sticking to my trees. They're so big and tightly interlocked together, that I can move effortlessly from one tree to another.

And I can jump really far when I need to. One perk of being weightless. Another is the fact I don't have any pressure under my feet when I walk, so they never hear me up here.

They crouch low just as two identical men move in from another angle. Taking a seat, I watch as the two men near them.

Just as they reach the canyon, Gage and Kai spring from their positions, and tackle them with so much force the twins barely have time to yelp before they're flying over the edge.

"That was easy enough," Kai mutters.

"We knew this would be easy to us. Everyone knew it. I told you that you've been stressing too much."

A scream reaches the tip of my tongue, and I swallow it down just before it escapes.

A four-headed beast is running down that gulley, as the twins tumble down the side, finally landing in a heap on top of each other. One barely gets the sword drawn in time before the thing strikes at them. Right behind it, two more of those beasts with four heads are running down, almost as though someone rang the breakfast bell.

Kai and Gage start sprinting, and I have to turn away before I know if those guys survive, because I have to keep up with the two dicks instead.

One of my leaps tests me, because I'm airborne for a little longer than I ever have been and stretch my usual limits before landing on another limb and racing after them still.

The four of them are suddenly all together, and I have no idea where Jude and Ezekiel just came from. All the while, I race behind them. Staying close but not close enough to be seen.

Nothing eventful happens after that.

They've got blood all over them, so I'm assuming more eventful things happened before I got here. I'm not sure how. It was just over ten minutes when I ended up here behind them.

Before I can ask too many questions, a blast of light hits them, and they're suddenly gone.

Cursing, I drop out of the tree, looking around aimlessly. Shit. Not again. What if I get stuck here? It's not like I know how I even zapped myself here to begin with.

Just as I turn around, I meet a set of huge eyes. Eyes as tall as my body. And scales. And fur. There are scales and fur. It's a hideous combination right on the nose that is between the eyes that are in front of me.

A scream tears from my throat before I can remind myself that I can simply pass through the scaly fur best. It reels back like I've slapped it, and it leaps into the air before diving down.

All several hundred feet of it.

The entire earth moves and shakes as it burrows below, taking forever to get that entire, worm-like body down the hole. And I say worm-like instead of snake-like because worms don't scare me as much.

My legs are shaking even after the ground goes still again, and I stagger around, looking for a way out of here.

Just as the pain starts to form in my chest, I feel it happening again. Like a rubberband has been snapped, an unseen force violently yanks me away from monster land and tosses me back inside the quad's home.

"Think she faded?" I hear Gage asking.

He doesn't sound too torn up about that.

"No clue, but Neopold just called. He said since we easily crushed everyone else's times, they'll make the next trial harder."

Gibberish. It's all gibberish.

I poke my head through the wall just a little so I can see them. Fortunately, I pick a spot where no one is looking.

"Which means we can deal with the girl now," Jude says as I lean back before they spot me.

"Deal with her how? We can't touch her. We don't know what

she is. And it's very likely we're the only ones who can see her if she's meant to be a hindrance to us," Gage states flatly.

They better be glad I can't hit them. I'd totally do it right now.

Without a word, I sit down on the stairs and listen to them dissect a hundred nefarious theories about my existence, while I peek in on occasion to get my fix.

Never once in all those fantasies did I see them trying to figure out a way to get rid of me.

It makes me hate them a little.

CHAPTER VI

A week of trying to sneak around the house has left my stomach in knots. Every time I accidentally run into one of them, I quickly pass through a wall.

It's tense and awkward.

They're reading books on what I might be so they can evict me from their lives.

I'm mostly hiding because I'm worried they're going to succeed.

If I can go next level, I'll be whole. Surely my soul or whatever won't be attached to anything then, and I can run like a motherfucking freed animal who just escaped the cage of impending doom.

I've worked too hard to survive to die now by the hands of the ones who once gave me purpose and a reason to want to survive.

Fortunately, they've all gone to bed now. Like a bad habit, I go from room to room, muttering a 'good night.'

Tomorrow is apparently the gauntlet or whatever, so they turned in early. Even Kai is snoring for a change.

In fact, they're all sleeping heavily tonight. Ezekiel is also snoring.

He never snores.

I move to the bed, my hand scrolling over the side of his cheek as I study him in confusion. Never once in five years has he snored. He never gets that deep into sleep.

And Kai went to sleep really fast. Which is very unusual.

I move to Jude's room, finding him to be just as dead to the world as the others. He always sleeps on his back. Tonight he's on his stomach, and he's still in his clothes.

I know for a fact he can't stand sleeping in clothes. He always gets naked.

Backing out of his room, I look around.

Maybe they want to kill me, and maybe I hate them a little, but I can't stand the thought of someone hurting them.

Which is clearly about to happen.

I jog down the stairs, checking the doors and such. I spot the bottle on the counter they picked up from Harold today, and I freeze.

They only had one shot apiece. Not that I was watching. I just heard Kai telling them only one to douse the nerves and take the edge off.

My eyes hone in on the little swirls of green that I can barely see. It's almost like my ghostly reflection used to be—so transparent that only the best vision could catch a true glimpse.

Shit.

That's never been in those bottles before.

The smallest breeze stirs the paper on the counter, and I whirl around, seeing the window open.

Oh no.

I race up the stairs, not seeing anyone around. Then I quickly start shoving my head through the doors, peering in on everyone.

When I get to Jude's room, though, my heart almost flips out of my chest.

A man with a sword draws closer to Jude's bed, as another man grips his own sword by the door, holding it in front of him like he expects Jude to stop snoring and start fighting.

I run through the man, not feeling any of those tingles, and race to the bed, passing through it and Jude as I stare at the one who is warily approaching the sleeping Four.

"Stop!" I shout at the man, but he can't see me.

My eyes dart to the one by the door, but he seems unaware of my presence as well.

The second he draws that sword, I prepare to level up, diving at him just as I did the other one, as every ounce of fear propels my lunge.

But instead of me hitting him with my hand, something flies out of me, and it slams into him. I have no idea what invisible force just zipped through my fingertips, leaving a cold, familiar feeling behind.

His eyes widen as a yelp leaves his mouth, and he crashes into the other man. The other man who…was holding a sword in front of him.

That man looks too stunned to move, while the one with the sword sticking out of his chest opens his mouth in a silent scream. My stomach goes queasy when the veins in his body start turning black. The sword glows brighter and brighter, sucking whatever life is inside him out.

The not-dying guy jerks the sword out of the dying guy, and stares at him in horror as he darts a panicked gaze toward the sleeping man, looking right through me.

With a growl of frustration, he lunges, sword slicing down before I can process. That same familiar feeling crosses through my body and bursts out like an explosion.

The man's breath catches as he freezes midair, and I keep my hand out as I step closer, feeling whatever foreign power is radiating from me.

It feels like it takes forever, but it all really happens within a matter of seconds. He's launched across the room just like the other man, but when he collapses, he doesn't move.

I quickly rush over, fully prepared for him to throw that sword out at me. Instead, my breath hisses from me and I stagger back.

It looks like he has chemical burns all over his face and body. Like his insides were dipped in toxic waste, and now they're all oozing out of every orifice possible, and burning him away from the inside out.

The burns just get worse, and I have to turn away.

Mr. Dark Veins is on the cusp of death, and he stares directly at me now, when he couldn't see me earlier.

His lips curve in a slow grin as he coughs and laughs. He opens his mouth like he's going to speak, but his head falls to the side instead as he goes lifeless.

Dead.

In less than a few minutes, I managed to kill two people. One of which couldn't see me and then could.

I glance down, finding my hand still mostly transparent, even if my breaths do feel warmer as they stagger from my chest.

Maybe I was an assassin before I was this, because this was too easy. And it felt really right.

Which is seriously freaking disturbing.

I wish I could have a drink right now. I think I deserve it.

Glancing back, I look over at Jude and hear the light sounds of his snores as he sleeps peacefully.

"You're welcome," I grumble.

The sound of footsteps approaching sends a chill up my spine. Apparently this night isn't over.

Somebody really wants these boys—no longer *my* boys—dead.

My fingers tingle, ready for action. Just because I can, I change out of my normal attire and go for a more badass look, even though they can't see me.

Because priorities are important.

CHAPTER VII

I'm very annoyed with whatever show this is supposed to be. Fortunately, there seems to be a marathon of it.

That sounds like two odd sentences to press together, doesn't it?

While I can apparently toss grown men around when in panicked, protective mode, I still can't put any pressure on a TV remote to change the channel.

There were a lot more zombies when this show started. I'm quite confused by this entire second season. Admittedly I'm only watching because one of the side characters is actually a very badass woman.

Keyla saves these people time and time again, yet gets zero respect. It's like they take her for granted.

I sort of like the blood and gore though, so I continue to watch, learning a little about fighting for survival. These people do impossible things when their lives or other lives depend on it.

I suppose that gives me a kindred sort of feeling, especially with poor, underappreciated Keyla.

I had a very busy night, but I've still managed to watch this in between bouts of psychotic men who wanted to kill the boys while they slept.

Not that they'd ever believe such a thing. After all, the bodies seemed to disappear shortly after their deaths.

Either the guys will think I'm making it up to get them to like me—*I'm not that pathetic, thank you very much*—or they'll consider me even more of a threat for being able to achieve such heinous things.

I'll just keep it to myself.

The door beside me flies open, and I startle a little.

Usually they try to sneak in with stealth.

My eyes dart to it to see a haggard looking Harold as he collapses inside, his veins black, much like that one man who I knocked into that sword.

I'm on my feet and moving toward him, wondering if he's the one who dosed their bottle of liquor last night. It doesn't look like it, since it seems as though someone wants him dead as well.

His eyes fall on me, but I can tell he doesn't see me as he shakes his head, struggling to get up.

Leaning over, I stroke his arm, trying to comfort him, since it looks as though he'll be dying like that other fellow who disappeared.

His muscles strain as he curses, and the veins throb as he fights so hard to beat this poison. Whatever it may be.

Stroking his arm is silly, since he can't be comforted by my non-existent touch. But I feel like I know him, since they've been visiting him for years, and I can't just let him die alone.

Little by little, the black in his veins seems to lessen as he continues to fight it somehow. So Jude might have survived? Doubtful.

They've said Harold is very important and powerful numerous times, though I have no idea what exactly that means. Most of the time, they speak in what sounds like code, and until recently, I couldn't ask them to explain what that code meant.

And now they talk in even more code since learning of my existence.

Harold sits up suddenly, the black still present but not as fiercely roaming his veins as before. Struggling back up to his feet, I hear him shout a curse so loud the whole house nearly quakes.

I'd like to help him up the stairs, but you can't use a crutch you can't touch, so I follow him instead. As soon as he rounds the top of stairs, I hear a door fly open, and I decide my job with Harold is done.

I'd like to go finish my show if they're going to take care of him.

"Harold?" I hear Gage ask in confusion.

"You're alive," Harold says in sweet relief, collapsing. "Thank fuck for that. Where're your brothers? Are you the only one?"

I hear a lot of scurrying after that, and Gage shouting at them. They're all fine. I've kept a close watch on everyone during the night.

I take my seat on the couch, as Jude and Gage begin helping Harold back down the stairs.

Why isn't there any romance in this show? That's what's missing. A good ol' fashioned romance where the girl can only be rejected by *one* guy she's fantasized about instead of four.

Why do I know that's ol' fashioned romance? Hell if I know. It's just one of those things that is pointless for me to know, so I know it.

"What the hell happened to you?" Ezekiel asks as they get Harold situated in a chair near me.

Gage darts a suspicious glance at me, but I pretend not to notice as my attention seemingly stays fixed on the screen.

"Manella," Harold bites out.

I just keep hearing this Manella fellow's name. I think I'd like to kill him if he's the one behind this.

"Lamar came to the shop last night, stuck a Decay Dagger in

my gut, and took over my identity long enough to pass you along some tainted spirits."

Jude goes to the kitchen, which is next to us and easy to see. He snatches the open bottle of liquor that left them so vulnerable and sniffs it.

"This is why I slept so hard," he growls.

"I've never slept as hard as I did last night, but it was like I was locked in a nightmare and couldn't escape. What the fuck is it?" Ezekiel asks him.

"It's noctem root found only in Purgatory. But's it's hard to find," Harold says, snarling. "I had to watch Lamar put it into my spirit drinks. That dagger left me paralyzed. Then Lamar shifted to look like me, and you dicks didn't know the difference."

Kai takes a seat on the end of the couch, far away from me, as he faces Harold. "You're in neutral territory. You're supposed to be untouchable by law. We never thought we had to question if it was you," Kai points out.

"Apparently Manella isn't concerned with law right now. Whatever is going on, he wants you four out of the trials. Those questions you've been asking are definitely getting more interesting. How are you even alive right now? I had to listen to him call in a hit to any being with the balls to come after you. Once I managed to get that dagger out of my chest, I learned of at least seven who took the opportunity."

Eleven men tried to cash in on that hit, to be exact. But who's counting?

I feel the weight of four very intense stares swing toward me, but I pretend as though I find my nails to be fascinating.

"What are you looking at?" Harold asks, confusion in his tone.

"Nothing," Kai grumbles, which digs that little knife of theirs a little deeper into my gut.

I spent my night killing men to save their lives, but I'm *nothing*.

Awesome guys I've somehow been tied to, huh?

Pricks.

"No one managed to kill us," Gage states vaguely.

"Then I guess you were lucky, since you didn't drink the root," Harold says in a relieved breath, even though he knows they were lucky because they're not dead. "I've spent the night trying to get that damn dagger free from my chest. I'm sure Lamar expected it to kill me on this plane."

Jude lowers himself to a chair right beside me, his eyes raking over me. I continue to pretend as though I'm aloof and uninterested in their attention, my eyes lifting to watch the show again when the commercial break is over.

Ezekiel takes a seat on the couch, his body almost touching mine. But I never lift my gaze from the TV, though I now have no clue what's going on.

"What do you two keep looking at?" Harold asks.

"If Manella is getting this desperate, then we need to do something about our security. Clearly the protection spell surrounding this place has been drained," Kai says to his brothers.

Even his gaze flicks to me momentarily, but I don't give him the satisfaction of looking his way.

"I need something to suck the last of this poison out of me. I've fought it all I can," Harold says on a weary breath.

"Shit. Of course," Gage says as he leaps to his feet and moves through the house.

I hear cupboards banging for a minute before he returns with something. I can't see it from my peripheral, and I'm still making a concentrated effort not to look at them.

As he gives Harold whatever it is, I stand, my eyes averting all of them, even as they all watch me.

I pass through the couch, moving toward the stairs. They'll be leaving for the gauntlet soon, and I'd like to hitch a ride this time, so I'm staying close so as not to get left behind again. I'll hide in the weapons closet, since they aren't wearing their weapons yet.

"I need to call Dominic. He needs to hear about this," Harold says. "Lamar will face consequences for touching an Elder on neutral ground, though I doubt he'll point a finger at Manella. But you boys need to be careful today. They'll come for you in there. Very few survive the gauntlet, and no one will think about it."

"I'll get you a ride," I hear Kai telling him.

They continue to talk about conspiracy theories, as I pass into the weapons closet and wait.

No more than ten minutes later, I hear, "Get out here, nameless girl. We need to speak to you."

Kai doesn't sound overly pleased to be summoning me, and I don't particularly like being summoned. So I stay in my place.

"Where the fuck did she go?" Gage asks, sounding as though he's in the hallway.

"She can pass through walls, so who fucking knows?" Jude growls.

"Come out…We really need a name to call her," Ezekiel states.

Why give me a name when they simply plan to pretend I don't exist?

"She looks like a Mary," Jude deadpans.

The word *virgin* seems to accompany that name, and it doesn't sound quite like me, since I don't plan on being a virgin when I'm whole.

"Something a little edgier would better suit her if she's killing assassins in our sleep," Kai tells him, and I tilt my head, a little more interested.

The prospect of having a name does make my heart beat a little faster.

"Keyla," Ezekiel says suddenly, and my heart all but sputters.

"Why that name?" Kai asks.

"Because of that show she was watching. Keyla is the one who is constantly fending off the worst of the attacks. Maybe our little haunter considers herself our protector. Not a scratch is on us after someone drugged us and left us to die. The protection spell has been drained, leaving us vulnerable in such a condition. We should be dead if Manella dropped a hit."

It sounds like they're moving closer to me.

"If she can't touch things, as she claims, then how did she fend off seven highly trained assassins?" Jude asks skeptically.

Eleven, I silently amend. But again, who's counting?

"She kept saying she 'leveled up' after saving me that first night," Gage answers. "Maybe the same thing happened last night."

"It's doubtful Manella has anything to do with her being here if he just sacrificed Lamar's life to set up this hit on us. Last time he sent one man, and that man died. This time, he sent a small army and attacked an elder on neutral ground. He wouldn't have done that and then asked her to save us, knowing what his failure will cost him. Lamar is his lover as well as his most trusted man."

Well, that's downright intriguing drama. I lean forward, interested in this conversation.

"Maybe so, but her timing is still undeniably suspicious," Kai reminds them.

They move away from the dark romance and back to the subject at hand. I lose interest again, for the most part.

"Regardless, we should at least ask her about the men who came here last night," Ezekiel says quietly. "Keyla! We have you a name," he yells, like he's trying to make sure I hear him throughout the massive home.

Rolling my eyes, I stay hidden, even though I do like having a name now.

"She only has ten minutes where she doesn't have to see us," Kai points out.

My smile spreads. It's been over ten minutes since I laid eyes on them, but I'm still not in pain or desperate to peek out. Just their presence being so close seems to sate my need for them.

How did I not notice sooner?

In fact, it was like that all night, but I didn't notice then either, since I was sort of distracted. Maybe I did level up, just not the way I thought I would. Well, clearly I leveled up with the weird ways the assassins seemed to die, but I'm talking about a personal level-up.

"Well, then, where the hell is she? Because it's been at least twenty minutes since I saw her last," Jude states, frustrated.

When I see the handle of the weapons closet start to turn, I step through the back, passing through that wall, and end up in Ezekiel's bedroom.

Staring at the wall, I continue to listen as the door opens, waiting for my chance to dive through and trail their siphon.

"Found her," comes a voice far too close to my back, causing me to jump and whirl around.

Ezekiel is smirking as he stares down at me with his arms crossed over his chest.

His hair is the lightest, a rich blond hue that highlights his tan. His eyes sparkle with that gold hue that happened when I passed through him.

His broad shoulders lead down to a very impressive chest, and all that leads down to a tapered waist full of ab muscles. Which are easy to count, since he's shirtless.

Why did he take off his shirt?

Before I can slap myself back to my senses—which I can't literally do—three other shirted men are in here with us, fortunately covering up their distracting bodies.

"What happened last night?" Kai asks me seriously, skipping pleasantries.

"You drank some spiked rum; I watched some TV and killed

some men. Other than that, not much," I say with a shrug, averting my gaze.

A hand passes through me when Jude tries to grab me. He curses as those wonderful little tingles slither over my body. Funny how none of that happened with the numerous men I passed through last night.

"What happened?" Gage asks me this time, his gaze on my face.

"I just told you," I say with a tight smile. "But just so you have the facts, it was eleven men. Not seven."

I act like I'm counting my fingers, then lift only middle ones when I give them a cruel smile. Gage's lips do that twitching thing they do when he's trying to suppress a smile.

"You killed eleven men yet claim to have no ability to—"

"Just stop there. I've already heard these discussions," I state dryly, holding a hand up in front of Kai's face. "For whatever reason, my protective instincts are on overdrive with you four. Things I can't do normally come a little too easily when I'm saving your lives."

I take a step back, almost passing through the wall again, and they all four crowd my space like they can stop me.

"Here's the new arrangement," I say to them, crossing my arms over my chest. "You don't leave without me. It fucking hurts when you do," I tell them, certain that will still be an issue if their presence is gone. "Or I'll let the next team of ruthless assassins kill you while you dream of ponies or whatever it is you dream of. You need to give me a reason to want to save you."

"You supposedly need us," Ezekiel reminds me.

"Yes, but what's the point in existing if it's just to feel like an unwanted burden? I need a reason to want to keep from fading into nothing, because honestly? Nothingness is sounding better than this hell you four are putting me through."

They exchange a look, and Jude's jaw tightens as he looks back at me and speaks. "We'll have a new spell up by nightfall. I'm not sure that it won't evict you as well."

"You can try. I'm sure you're dying to get rid of me even as I save your ungrateful lives over and over," I tell him as I pass through the wall.

They appear in the room just as I finish, and I barely stop myself from making some embarrassing noise of surprise.

Jude's eyes darken as his smirk forms. He likes scaring the shit out of me, it seems. He's the one who has cut me the deepest, so I look over to Ezekiel, breaking up the eye contact.

Ezekiel steps closer, his eyes wandering over me. "What in hell are you wearing?" he asks incredulously.

I look down at my warrior princess outfit. It's leather, a little sexy, and downright awesome. It also has the illusion of a bunch of weapons strapped to me, even though they're not real.

"Something a badass wears when she's saving lives all night and about to go to a gauntlet of unforetold dangers," I deadpan.

"Is so much cleavage necessary?" Kai asks, his eyes a little distracted as they continue to trail down.

"And does the leather have to be so tight?" Jude asks from behind me, sending chills throughout me when his hand passes over my ass.

"I prefer to feel pretty when killing. Not sure why, but it seemed to be ideal last night," I state as I look around. "By the way, my terms also include the four of you not ignoring me and not being cruel to me anymore. Either fake being nice and treat me better, or I'll take a spectator's seat the next time men with enchanted swords try to drain you, cut off your heads, stab you, or cut off your junk." They all give me an incredulous look, so I add, "Yes, a lot happened last night."

Jude adjusts his cock in his pants as he arches an eyebrow at me.

"You're asking us to trust you, acting as though we owe it to you. Surely you understand our reservations," Gage tells me, regarding me warily.

Something cold and detached washes over me as I drop my hands to my sides.

"I told you all my story. I explained I've spent five years able to do nothing but watch you. Without you, I faded. Without you, I didn't exist. Only in your presence did I seem to have a purpose. I exposed a vein when I cut open so many vulnerable details of my very lonely existence, laid it all out there for you like my most precious secret. Naively, I expected you all to welcome me with open arms, telling me I was no longer alone. Yet none of you could spare a second to put yourself in my shoes. None of you had an ounce of concern for the fact that I've held on by a thin thread all these years, not knowing anything about anyone else but the four of you—I didn't even know myself, but I knew *you.* You've been all I've had."

My gaze flicks from one set of eyes to another as they all stay quiet.

"Not one of you bothered to tell me good night, or even good morning," I go on, admittedly getting just a little choked up, much to my chagrin.

A few surprised and very bewildered expressions don their faces, but I clear my throat and go on.

"The only thing you're concerned about is how my presence affects you, while I've spent my entire existence thinking of nothing but the four of you. Not one of you could spare me a single thought."

Again, I'm forced to clear my throat of any emotion, refusing to let these assholes see me do my ghostly cry.

"Not everything is about the four of you. I exist too. Now you can see me. In fact, you're the only ones who seem to be able to, mostly. And you treat me like shit. So, no, I can't be bothered to understand your reservations if you can't spare a single minute to view me as an actual person instead of a *thing* you don't trust."

They say nothing, and I grow tired of the intense silence.

"Who's taking me to the gauntlet?" I ask, looking at the four of them. "With any luck, I'll be able to stop someone from killing you when your backs are turned today. And then you can all bypass any gratitude and start wondering how I benefit from that as well."

Ezekiel blows out a breath before he grabs a weapon from the closet, since we're back in the weapons room. Then he steps into me, and I feel the tug of the siphon.

When we reappear, we're in the middle of a huge, gorgeous room full of elegantly dressed people. Meanwhile, I'm next to a shirtless barbarian by comparison.

The other three boys appear around us, and they all start walking.

When I'm certain eyes aren't landing on me or noticing my presence, I follow close behind them.

Today, I learn what the hell a gauntlet is.

CHAPTER VIII

A gauntlet, as it turns out, is an inhumane, monstrous death trap designed to cull the weak from the herd.

Yay me.

This sucks big donkey balls.

It's like a protective spirit's nightmare, since my four ungrateful charges are about to run this thing.

I've decided that's what I must be—a protective spirit who has been cursed to watch over the most self-centered brats in history, who are willingly about to run through this deadly thing.

It's a long, seemingly endless crater. And in it are monsters I don't even have a name for, and they're crawling around everywhere below. It's also filled with blades that swing, fire that shoots out of unseen crevices, and something I assume must be acid, since when the mist sprays, it destroys anything in its path.

We're in a half arena type thing, standing on a platform far above it, as the crowd fills into the stadium seats behind us like they're readying for a show.

"What's the point of this?" I ask, not expecting an answer.

"To see who ascends and gains access to the underworld," Gage answers automatically.

A little surprised, I turn to face him. "Why would you want to go to the underworld?"

"To gain a boost in power and find out what we really are," Jude says from beside me.

"You don't know who you are?" I ask, confused.

They continue to talk quietly so as to escape the ears of others, surprisingly answering some of my questions.

"A while back, we found each other by accident, all of us ending up in the same place at the same time on the same day like we were compelled to go there. When we did, our souls bonded, and we gained access to our powers just before someone tried to kill us," Kai tells me as he moves in from behind.

Ezekiel picks up where he left off. "Whatever we are, no one ever wanted us to find each other, because they've been trying to keep us out of the underworld ever since. And we're different from all of them."

"How so?" I ask, confused.

"To become one of them, you have to die first and endure the underworld from the less privileged side," Kai explains.

"Demons? They're demons?" I whisper-yell, acting like someone other than them can hear me.

Jude's lips twitch. "Demons have no mind or capacity for reason, emotion, or even individual thought," he goes on. "These are upper level dark angels. There are hundreds of varieties, but they fall into two categories: Righteous and Damned. We're of the damned, yet we never died," Gage whispers softly, his eyes shifting as though he's seeing if anyone can hear us.

His lighter brown hair is so smooth and sexy with the way it spikes up. The piercing in his tongue is always a fascinating focal point for me. Maybe Ezekiel should get one of those, since he's the nipple lover.

"Purgatory is where ascension is decided. We've had access to purgatory for almost a decade, but we haven't been able to get chosen for the trials until this year. They've tried to keep us away from here, because they're terrified we'll win. If we get below and get our power boost, we'll also have access to people who might can tell us what's going on," Ezekiel states quietly.

"We'll discuss this more later," Jude says quickly. "Manella just arrived."

My eyes swing up to find a set of fully black eyes glaring down at my boys. Thank goodness he's unable to see me. I'm thankful for my spirit-body right now.

"Stop staring at him," Kai tells me.

"It's not like he can see me staring. His eyes have passed over me a number of times so he can glare at you assholes. I'm wondering if I can channel some of that protective mojo to kill him."

Before they can say a word, I'm suddenly behind Manella, dizzy with how fast that just happened.

I'm up in the stands, my legs passing through the body of a man who has no idea I'm standing *through* him.

Manella turns like he feels me, his eyes searching briefly behind him, trailing past me without an ounce of recognition.

I can see the guys below staring at me with wide eyes before they school their features and look away. When Manella turns back around, I hold my hand out, straining, feeling…nothing.

No great power surges from my hand to make toxins appear inside him and burn him inside-out the way it did the others.

"Several groups of quads survived the night, I see," a woman with bright red hair states in an almost muted tone as she joins him at his side, smiling graciously at the people around.

I smell a snake.

I hate snakes.

"It appears so," Manella says with a cold smile. "I heard there was a hit for some of them."

"Lamar has been taken into custody. Rumor has it he attacked an Elder last night."

Manella stiffens, his hands closing into fists.

"One said he might be recycled," she goes on.

I'm assuming their version of recycling is a little less green and a lot gorier than the human definition.

My eyes keep moving to the guys, worried they'll leave and I'll lose sight of them.

Before I can hear Manella's response, I'm suddenly surrounded by the quad once again.

"What the hell?" Kai hisses.

"Seems like I can move places if I think a little too hard about it," I tell them on a shaky breath. "And it makes me dizzy, just for the record, so I'm going to try really hard not to do it again until I can work my powers and kill him. But he's definitely the one who wants you dead. I think."

"That much we already know. Manella has been the one holding us back from the trials for some time," Gage states in a whispered tone.

"What happens if you win the gauntlet today?" I ask.

"We go back home, continue to reap souls, and wait for the last of the trials," Jude answers with no emotion.

"And the soul reaping is your job?"

"We're surface guardians," Kai tells me as more and more people crowd in, the stadium getting louder as the obstacle course goes eerily silent, a slight fog creeping over it to hide things.

"What just happened? And what are surface guardians?" I ask, staring uneasily at this unnatural fog.

"They're moving the obstacles around and don't want us seeing where they're going," Kai explains.

"And surface guardians stop the breaches so the damaged

souls can't possess a human and run around freely. When demons expose us, then we run into a lot of issues between us and the other side."

"I'm going to pretend you don't mean heaven," I say with a nervous laugh, looking up at Gage.

He just stares blankly at me.

"There has to be a balance. Yin and yang. Good and bad. But there are rules constantly being broken by both sides to keep things tilted instead of balanced. It's something that happens from time to time, but never this often. Lately, more and more souls are breaching the surface. The escapes are becoming so frequent that we're possibly on the verge of being purged."

"Purged?" I ask, looking at Jude since he's the one who said that.

"It means someone is setting these breaches to force our hand. If it looks like Lucifer can no longer control the underworld, he'll lose his crown and his six heirs will battle to see who takes control."

I swallow thickly as my gaze shifts to Ezekiel. "Lucifer? As in the devil?"

He smirks. "They're breaching from hell's mouth. We're the main thing holding the purge at bay, because we're sending the souls back before they can possess a human or before they can expose us if they do manage to possess one. But if we can get underground, we can get closer to proving Manella is the one doing all this. He knows we're trying to out him to his father, so he's trying to eliminate us before we can get below and meet the devil."

"Life goals, I guess," I state uneasily.

"Better the devil you know than the one you don't," Jude says with a shrug.

"In this case, quite literally. If Manella takes the crown, he'll release the souls into the world himself, and life as we know it will cease to exist. Hell on earth will become very literal, and from what I've heard, the non-royal areas of hell are quite distasteful," Gage goes on conversationally.

A hand passes through my hip, like Ezekiel is trying to get closer but can't.

"Now you know why we're questioning your timing," Ezekiel says so close to my ear. "Are you part of the problem or the solution?"

Rolling my eyes and not letting him know how much his proximity affects me, I answer, "Considering I've kept you jerks alive, I'd say I'm helping you save the devil. Though I admit, now even I have reservations. I didn't sign on to save hell. Maybe we should discuss you lot finding healthier life goals."

CHAPTER IX

"The first twenty to emerge will go onto the final round in one month," the weird little troll guy announces.

If he's the same thing as my guys, he has to be hating life, because life has certainly not been fair to him in the attractiveness department. His face looks like the inside-bend of an elephant's leg. I'm not even sure where his eyes are, if I'm being honest.

"He's an angel?" I ask dubiously.

"He's a form of angel," Jude states absently as the man drones on.

"He totally got gipped," I say on a sympathetic sigh.

Gage chokes down whatever sound just tried to escape him.

"The rules are written in the devil's blood. No competitor may use lethal force against another competitor while in the gauntlet," the elephant man goes on.

I glance around, seeing a lot of really hard, nasty people also around us, all of them glaring at the four guys surrounding me. Apparently they don't like that rule, since it looks like they want to break it.

The guys don't notice the angry glares or just simply don't care.

"No competitor can use any form of teleportation to get from one area to another. Doing so will have you immediately disqualified," the man states, facing one woman in particular before dropping his eyes—well, the area where I think his eyes are—to the scroll he's holding.

"No competitor may leave the gauntlet until they've completed it, or they forfeit their chance at ascension and go back to the surface to complete their tasks until someone comes to reap them."

"What?" I hiss, jerking my gaze to Jude.

"The trials are to thin the crop of the weaker links, so that only the strongest guard the surface," Ezekiel answers at my back. "Getting reaped puts you back at the throat to grow stronger again."

I'm not sure I want to know what the throat is.

"Your teams, as you know, can change, should you decide to shift alliances. But only if the other team accepts you."

There're only two other four-man teams. Judging by the groupings, everyone else is solo or in twos, I notice.

I suppose if you can change teams mid competition, it'd be hard to trust someone who might stab you in the back. Unless you're as close this quad.

"If one member of your team is left behind, your team forfeits the thirty bonus points, and that member is disqualified for not crossing the line with you."

"Glad I'm not part of the team," I grumble. They'd totally leave me behind if they could.

Kai snorts when he hears that.

The man rolls the scroll up very slowly, staring up at the stands over our heads as he does so.

I follow his gaze, seeing him look up to the box where there are six people in ornate, golden chairs, set up like royalty. Manella is among them.

"Is Lucifer here?"

"Never. It's too risky for him to leave the underworld. He's untouchable there. Not so much here," Jude answers.

So those must be the six heirs.

The woman with red hair who spoke to Manella is sitting down, her hand on her chin as she smirks down at the world with her red-painted lips and scarlet red dress.

Manella is beside her in a black suit, his long black hair tied back.

A blonde woman is dressed in a sparkly silver dress on the other side of Manella. And to the right of her are two men dressed like they're here to slay. And lastly a man with such dark hair and eyes that *black* isn't black enough to describe them.

All of them are stunning. All of them look pure evil too.

Which, obviously they're the devil's children, so that makes sense.

"Manella, you already know. He's the one who has evaded history, and has the most discretion. Hence the reason he's the trickiest to deal with and the reason we need to get underground to learn more about him," Jude explains.

"The redhead who looks like she can't wait to see blood being spilled is Lilith," Gage tells me.

"As in the vampire?" I hiss.

"As in the devil's firstborn," Jude tells me as though he's exasperated. "After announcing herself to the world as Lilith, she made a few other appearances as women you might have heard of."

"The twins are the Gemini twins—Collin and Marcus," Gage goes on. "They prefer the second round of the trials, since that's when mortal combat comes into play."

I hate these damn trials.

"There are two hundred competitors here today," the man goes on, his eyes staying fixed to the evil royalty in the stands. "The horn of Jericho will blow every time the gauntlet claims a life."

"The blonde is Hera," Kai tells me, resuming the interrupted conversation, and when I open my mouth, he adds, "Yes, *that* Hera, and yes, she posed as a Greek Goddess for a while. She's vain like that. They all are."

Just…mind-fucking.

"And the last guy is Cain. The same Cain who killed his brother—Abel. The same one born to Eve, after Lucifer deployed his plan to corrupt humanity and prove he was right all along, sending his own son into the womb of Eve, just before he was cast from the heavens," Ezekiel tells me.

They don't even have to look back to see these people. They just know them, probably have them memorized.

The elephant man looks away when all six heirs give one nod of approval in eerily timed unison.

"The day of the gauntlet begins now!" the man shouts.

Without a second of hesitation, everyone on this platform starts racing through me, rushing toward the drop. My guys are the first to drop off the side. That's at least a hundred feet worth of drop zone!

I dive to the edge, even as people continue to pass through me en masse.

I watch as they land on their feet, and I curse when they propel themselves into the thick fog cloaking the gauntlet.

The horn is already blowing, signaling a death so soon, and my heart beats in my ears as panic consumes me. Was it one of them?

Before I can even think about it, I'm suddenly dizzy, and I'm spinning around, seeing all four of my guys cut through the fog as they charge right toward me. Shit. I somehow ended up in the gauntlet.

In front of them.

I turn and run with them, easily keeping up, since my spirit body happens to be very fast and nimble. It helps that I can run right through many of the obstacles they're having to avoid.

The blades shoot out, nearly decapitating Jude before he can dodge it like it's no big deal. If protective spirits can suffer cardiac arrest, then it damn near just happened to me.

The acid spray mist takes out several of the men behind us, their screams of agony piercing the air as that horn of death blows twice.

Fire shoots up into the air, and Ezekiel barely stops in time. Another man can't stop so quickly, and a bloodcurdling scream rises into the air as the skin melts from his body.

I cut my gaze away, unable to watch. "That's hellfire instead of fucking eternal flames," Jude growls. "That's supposed to be outlawed."

"Hell on earth better not happen if I turn whole," I grumble as I leap through it, trying to find a way to let them pass.

I finally find a boulder and stare at it, because it would be perfect to create a path. It's just big enough that it would take it a minute to melt, and they're fast enough to use it before it's gone.

Now…how do I get it to move?

Ghost girl problems.

Several more screams erupt when more people dive into it. I hear someone shouting, "It's hellfire! Not eternal flames!"

They came to the conclusion a little later than my guys, it seems.

"They're trying to kill us all. How are we supposed to break through hellfire?" a woman shouts.

Meanwhile, I'm back to staring at the boulder, wondering if I concentrate hard enough, if it'll move into the flames. The fire has gotten closer to it, and it doesn't seem to be affected by the flames.

The ground rumbles under me, and I whirl around and sway a little as I see that giant, scaly, furry worm thing leap out of the ground, a blackened soot color giving it an all the more ominous appearance.

It roars into the air as a spiraled mouthful of teeth protrude from its huge mouth.

Holy deadly centipede.

But the creepiest part is when three more heads suddenly appear, popping out of its neck with gooey strands attached to them. And the new heads are carrying the same razor sharp teeth.

"Hydra!" someone shouts just as the centipede from hell—*huh, that might be literal*—dives and swallows a mouthful...of people.

My heart almost kicks my chest when I see Ezekiel fly over the top of the centipede's back, now that it's blocking some of the flames, and his eyes widen on me.

"That thing seemed a lot more skittish the last time I was here," I say on a shaky breath.

"You walked through hellfire," he tells me, but before I can remind him that nothing can touch me, the centipede rears back, and Ezekiel draws his sword.

"E! Just go! We'll catch up when we find a break in the fire," Jude shouts.

Ezekiel smirks as he pulls his sword back. "I'll make you a break in the fire."

I hear Gage cursing, and Kai calling him a string of names, as the centipede roars again.

But the giant monster thingy suddenly reels back, much like it did the last time it saw me. Three of the four heads slink back inside its body so fast that I almost don't register the action.

Then it turns and dives into the ground, just as it did the last time, running like it's fleeing.

"What the hell?" Ezekiel asks incredulously.

"The boulder!" I snap. "The fire is touching it but it's not burning it, so I assume it's something special and can block the flames."

He stares at it, glances at me, then goes behind it. Like he has all the strength in the world, he shoves that boulder hard, and it rolls, cutting through the flames.

Jude is the first to fly over the boulder, but when Gage starts to follow, I see the glint of a red sword as it swings down. My hand flies out so fast as fear pumps through me, and the woman holding the sword is launched backwards.

Her back slams into the wall, and the head of that giant centipede bursts out, snatching her and dragging her inside it as she screams in vain.

Gage's eyes are on mine, and right behind him is Kai. They've made it past the boulder, and they're just staring at me as others pass them by.

"If you idiots keep staring at me like I'm the centipede monster, you're going to lose this life-and-death race, and then you'll get your shot at seeing hell from the wrong side of things."

Jude's dark grin slowly grows, resembling the man I met on that first night before he was a total dick. I turn and start running ahead before I forget he threatened me later that night.

"You're lucky I must be some type of giant bug repellent," I call over my shoulder.

None of them say anything in response to that. Which they are a little busy dodging more of those blades that I just run right through.

"Right now, I wish we had her ability," Jude growls as he slices through one of the blades just before it can take his head off.

By comparison his sword is tiny, but it has no trouble splitting the giant saw blade in half. He dives and rolls, putting his sword up and grabbing his two piece bo staff out like he's about to fight something.

The rest of the people who aren't them are lagging way behind, struggling with the reemergence of that giant bug from hell.

Again, that might be a literal reference.

I turn around just as Jude leaps into the air. A true giant beast—not exactly a man—with one eye and veiny skin is bringing his fist down.

Jude spins in the air, coming down with just one part of the bo staff, hitting the monster in the face so hard he flies backwards. Dirt scatters into the air, causing some of the fog to lift and make room.

Tingles spread over me as Ezekiel runs right through me, launching himself into the air and coming down with his sword. It slashes the cyclops's chest, spilling blood everywhere, and then Jude shoves his hand into the fresh hole.

My mouth goes slack as the giant's eye bulges, and his body turns to ash that Jude breaks through. He walks away like it's a common occurrence.

They slice through about five more of those, and Jude keeps turning them to ash.

A shot of fire launches out, almost connecting with Kai's head, and my hand flies up on instinct. The fire diverts, shooting backwards. I hear screams in the background and grimace, but I drop my hold on the fire the second Kai is out of the path.

The fire shoots through me, and I run out to see Kai's jaw hard while he studies me.

"Feel free to start sharing some gratitude when I save your lives," I grumble, passing through him and the wall behind him.

It's all dirt and bugs and holey canals where creatures live, as I run through the wall they'll have to go all the way around. Surely they can survive while I scout ahead.

Just as I burst through to the other side, my stomach sinks. I can't see them at first, but I sense their dark presence. Things become more obvious as I stare at the walls, seeing the subtle differences in the rocks.

Ten men at least.

I turn and run back, catching the guys before they're about to come around the corner.

"Stop!" I shout, and the four of them come to an abrupt halt.

It surprises me so much that they listen that I almost forget they're waiting on me to tell them *why* I just screamed stop.

"At least ten men are waiting to ambush someone, likely the four of you because of that conspiracy stuff you were spilling on about."

The horn to announce deaths blows four times, as though it wanted to make this moment more ominous.

"They blend in perfectly with the walls. There could be more that I didn't see," I go on.

"Chameleons," Jude says to the other guys.

"There's only one reason why upper level assassins would be in the gauntlet," Ezekiel groans.

Jude puts his two pieces of his bo staff together to create the long, shimmering metal stick, and he spins it in his hand as a dark smile curves his lips.

"I think we can handle ten of them," Kai says as he pulls out his swords, not his sai.

"There could be more," I remind him.

I'm ignored. I guess they're done listening to me.

"On one," Ezekiel says with a grin that matches Jude's.

"One?" I ask, confused.

They all dart through me or by me, and my breath rushes out as I turn to chase them. Apparently I said the magic word.

Jude is already throwing the bo staff through the chest of one as he breaks away from the wall, coming after him.

His eyes widen as the staff breaks through the skin, and he drops to the ground, a look of pure disbelief on his face. Then his gaze lands on me as the life drains from his eyes.

He holds my stare, and I freeze, certain he sees me. But as he collapses to the side, lifeless, I return my attention to the guys. An awed breath escapes me at how they seem to fight like they can read each other's minds.

Jude ducks as Kai swings a sword, decapitating two of the men rushing Jude from behind. Jude snatches his bo staff out of the other guy's chest, and spins it, putting it through the neck of one guy who is still hidden against the wall.

Ezekiel takes a hard hit to his side, but he immediately slams a sword through the guy's chest and twists it as the guy screams in pain. His head dips as Gage's sword swings by, catching the throat of another attacker.

The four of them work like their own well-oiled army. I prop up and watch, unable to look away.

A man runs right through me, charging Ezekiel from behind, but Gage throws his sword, catching the guy in the face.

He drops, and I frown.

"I thought these were upper level assassins," I state as the final one lands in a heap. More than ten. Definitely more than ten.

"They are," Ezekiel says as he jerks his sword out of a man's body that is pinned to the rocks.

The body drops lifelessly as he wipes the blood off his sword.

"The reason they want us dead so badly, is because we're far stronger than we should be. And if we can get into the underworld, we might be able to stop the coup before there's a purge," Jude answers as he starts stalking down the gauntlet again.

We're now way ahead of the other competitors.

"There's a moment between life and death when people seem to be able to see me. Other than that guy I touched. Clearly upper level royalty can't even see me unless that moment occurs, since the heirs couldn't. So I'm assuming my touch had something to do with that one guy, because aside from the four of you, he's the only one who has seen me outside of the in-between moment of life and death," I state more to myself than anyone.

I'm used to talking aloud to them, expecting them not to answer because they can't hear me.

I'm surprised when Kai speaks. "It would make sense if you're suspended in the same state. But it doesn't explain how you're getting stronger instead of weaker."

"Maybe I'm just really hard to kill," I suggest.

A sword slices through me as if summoned by that brazen proclamation, and my eyes widen as a man charges by, that sword aimed at Jude.

He dispatches him quickly, and my heart slows down again.

"Eyes open in case we missed more," Kai says, rotating his sword in his hand as he looks around, still walking.

I move way out ahead, growing queasy when I see a massive pit of moving lava blocking the path. The volcanic river that floats through probably isn't very inviting.

The guys join me at the ledge, viewing the hundred or more feet in front of us.

"Can't go around this," Jude curses. "We'd have to leave the gauntlet to do that."

"How the hell do they expect us to cross this? What if it's more hellfire instead of eternal flame?" Ezekiel growls.

I can just walk on top of it, since I'm weightless. I move out onto it, trying to study it better. As I tap my foot, I find all four of them studying me.

"What?" I ask, feeling uncomfortable being the subject of all those intense stairs.

I guess that shows I was an idiot to think I could handle an intense foursome. Well, *five*some—whatever that is.

I still want to try it. Just not with these assholes. I saw some other quad teams up there who looked fierce but still high on the list of sexy. Maybe I can attach myself to them and grow whole enough to finally get my fantasy.

I bet their Three wouldn't even be selfish.

"Is it hellfire or eternal flame? One we'll survive. The other we won't," Gage states dryly.

I look down and back up. "How would I know? I can't feel anything physical."

Ezekiel runs a hand through his hair. "They'd have had to put hell stone up here to hold all this lava. The fire beds would have taken a while to prepare, but something of this caliber would take much longer, and it would have drained the individual a large amount. How badly do they really want us dead?" he asks the other three.

"They knew there'd be no way across without running out of the gauntlet or siphoning. Both would disqualify us and likely cost us our lives. What happens when dark angels who never died before finally do die? What if that's what all this is about, and they *need* us to die?" Gage asks.

"If anyone cares, I vote you stay there while I try to channel enough protective mojo to knock some of this away or something."

They ignore me, since they likely know that's a last ditch effort.

"I doubt anyone could want us dead this badly," Kai says, deciding to risk it.

"No!" I shout too late as he steps onto the fire.

It happens so slow and so fast, all at once. The fire rushes up his leg, and a feral sound of agony explodes from him. The guys rush to grab him, just as the lava evaporates, a path around us quickly being carved out and stretching across the fiery lake.

The fire is still licking up Kai's leg, and I dive, landing on him. The flames extinguish along his leg, and he roars that same inhumanly sound again as his body tenses and contorts with excruciating pain.

I push off him, my eyes tracking the lava that continues to retreat as though someone is peeling it away now.

None of that power is coming from me. That's way above my

fear-induced, what-will-happen-this-time, beginner's level. It's an intricate and complex power that hums through me and makes me envious, almost covetous.

I have to blink a few times to keep from going into a rage about it. It makes no sense, since I'm really grateful someone is helping out.

I whirl around, finding a familiar redhead perched on a rock like it's her favorite seat in the house, as she chews a piece of gum around a smile.

Lilith.

Why the hell did she just save them?

The guys start carrying Kai, rushing across before the devil's eldest daughter changes her mind. I watch her, even as she never sees me. She stands and spins in a circle, twirling her hair around her fingers as she walks away with an exaggerated hip shake.

I turn around, watching as the lava starts closing back in, slowly at first, but steadily growing speed the longer she's away.

My gaze snaps back to see them running faster now. Jude turns and grabs Kai, putting him over his shoulder and running behind them, but losing a little too much ground.

The other two turn to grab them, and launch them way ahead. By some miracle, they manage to make it across just in time, and all of them collapse a great distance away from the lava.

"Energy sucking fucking rocks," Jude groans, arching his back like he's in pain.

"They don't just want us dead; they want us fucking tortured too," Kai bites out, his leg still charred and slow to heal.

"I've seen him slice a thumb off with one of his soul sucking blades, and the damn thing healed back immediately. What's taking it so long this time?" I ask aloud, again forgetting they can hear me now.

"Hellfire," Ezekiel answers, kneeling to rip the jeans up and away from the worst part of the leg. "It'll take days for this to heal.

We still have to cross over the last ridge, that will likely have lethal monsters, and dragging him up there is going to take a lot more energy than those rocks left us with."

"Lilith never bestows a gift without offering a curse with it. It's how she maintains balance," Jude says as he tears his shirt off and starts putting more pressure on Kai's leg when he bleeds through the first one.

"She wants us to have to choose to attempt to make it by dragging him to the line, knowing there are only twenty places available. We might all die if we're slowed down too much. Or we could leave Kai behind so we can occupy three of those spots and ensure we survive, even if it means sacrificing his life," Ezekiel goes on.

My heart sinks.

"Is there a way to speed up the healing?" I ask, getting closer and kneeling beside his leg.

He hisses out a sound that tells me he really doesn't want me this close right now. Since he hates me and all.

"No, not in here, and we can't waste anymore time. Tie it off and cut it off. It'll grow back in a couple of weeks. We have time before the second trials. It'll make it easier on him that way. The hellfire hurts worse than amput—"

Gage's words cut off as I run my hand along the wound, tears in my eyes for no reason at all. I really don't like Three. He doesn't like me. But it still feels like my heart is breaking.

So much pain.

It's almost like I can feel it too.

I look down as the skin tries tugging together under every swipe of my hand, and my spine stiffens. My hand freezes against his leg, and he hisses out another sound as the skin starts to slowly pull together, the charred pieces breaking apart like brittle fragments hiding new skin.

It's a little slow, but it keeps going, and he sucks in a breath of what sounds like relief as his body relaxes. It's not completely healed, but the burns are gone, and the skin is healing faster on its own now.

He darts a gaze to me—a mix of wary curiosity and guarded appreciation, but it's gone before I can be sure.

"She put the fire out, and she healed his leg. I'm starting to think she really is a damn protective spirit to balance out the scales that have been tipped against us," Ezekiel says as he studies me with narrowed eyes.

One corner of my mouth tugs in a grin.

"Let's run then discuss what she is or isn't," Jude says as he helps Kai to his feet.

Kai is able to run now, not slowing anyone down. I look around for the woman in red, curious if she's still watching. Fortunately, no one is.

I don't really want anyone knowing they have a protective spirit.

That'll mean more people than them trying to figure out a way to get rid of me.

I look back and quickly cover the same ground they just made in half the time. Kai looks over at me as I run beside him, but I don't meet his gaze.

If he's nice right now, I'll rant about what a jerk he's been. If he looks at me like I'm still gum on his shoe, I might just let them all die the next time and not give a damn.

Either way, it's not a good time for either.

Running through Ezekiel and stealing some of those tingles, I keep going until they finally stop, heaving for air.

"What're you doing? We still have to climb over the ridge," I remind them.

"We're lucky we haven't come across any hell beasts yet, but we're about to go up a ridge that is notorious for them. Those stones stole a lot of our energy, so we need a break before we climb that thing."

My eyes lift, seeing the lava evaporate, and then sensing lives before I see them. A massive spiel of people who were likely trapped there are being let through, but this time it's the Gemini twins who are atop a rock and grinning.

"I'm not sure how many are going to survive, but I strongly suggest running again just in case it's more than twenty," I point out.

"Shit," Kai groans, turning to start climbing.

A surprise burst of tingles happen down below, and my eyes dart down to see a hand poking out of my pubic bone.

"What are you doing?" I ask Jude, knowing without a doubt those dark tingles are his.

"Seeing if you somehow offer a power charge too. Unfortunately, the answer is no."

"Then can you withdraw your hand? At the rate I've been saving your lives, I'll be powering up anytime now, surely. I'd rather not turn whole while your hand is in my vagina."

Gage grins, and Jude laughs under his breath as he withdraws his hand. I stare at the ridge before us. It's really like a thousand feet of mountainside that mostly goes straight up with a few ledges where you can hike instead of climb for a bit.

Already I see something scurrying into a dark cave on the side, a long tail whipping behind it a second before it darts out of sight.

A chill runs along my spine. Not cool.

That looked way too snake-like.

"What kind of monsters are we talking about?" I ask them as they start ascending, looking for footholds and such.

The horn of death wails loudly in the background, announcing a lot of fallen competitors. I suppose the Geminis are a little crueler than Lilith.

"What are the point of these trials? Other than to cull the weak? To show everyone how cold they can be?" I ask, turning to start scaling the mountain beside them.

"It's another balance system. They can't have the weak. The weak will betray far faster than the strong. They want to know who sticks with their team. They want to see how many will cheat. It's called hell for a reason. Not the most trustworthy applicants are applying for these jobs," Kai explains through strain as he hauls himself up.

It's way easier for me to climb. I'm not pulling a muscled body up the oddly angled side.

"But some will always have favorites they want to succeed, because they usually already know the ones they don't trust," Ezekiel adds.

Another long tail whips over my head, and an embarrassing squeal shoots out of me before I can help it. It's just a tiny lizard. In my head, that tail was forty feet long.

"Good thing you look like a leather-wearing badass today," Jude says from above me.

"Fully equipped with unusable weapons," Kai adds.

"Fake it until you make it. I've saved your lives more than once. Speaking of which, why was that girl going to stab one of you? That's breaking the rules."

"Like we said, they want to know who will disrespect tradition. Bad applicants don't make it past purgatory."

The clang of a sword has my gaze darting up, and I get a little queasy when I see the huge lizard snapping at Jude, raising a scorpion-like tail like it's about to strike.

"No!" I shout, just as Kai launches his sword into the air.

The beast screeches and darts away, scurrying into a hole as the sword flies up.

"Yelling brings more," Kai growls.

My eyes dart around in a panic, and I look around, worrying the entire climb where the rest are.

Screams from below me have me looking down—terrible idea, by the way.

I get dizzy as I stare below, watching the monsters pile all over the men and women, ripping things to shreds.

"At least it called them down there instead of to us," Gage says, a hint of sadistic delight in his tone.

I'm busy staring down still, unmoving. I never knew I had an issue with being on the side of the mountain until this moment. Then again, it is the first time I've found myself in this predicament.

For a moment, I don't realize I'm falling until the world is whirring by me. My eyes come up in a panic as I see Kai grab for me, his hand slipping through my body on my way down.

In the next breath, I'm suddenly clinging to the wall again like a wet cat dangling above water, my whole body shaking as I clutch it for dear life.

Jude's chuckle comes right beside me when I see it's him I've just landed by. I really like this being able to move without actually moving thing right now, even if it does leave me a dizzy and disoriented.

"A protective spirit who's afraid of heights," Jude mutters under his breath, still laughing a little as he pulls himself over a ledge.

I zap there too, happy that I seem to have that down pat, at the moment.

"It's more of an aversion to being on the side of a mountain than it is the actual height," I correct.

"We're almost there. The second we reach the top, stay close. They kick us out when we cross the finish line," Gage says as he leaps over the edge, joining us.

The other two join us as well.

At least they gave me a warning.

The mountain turns into more of a hiking trail that I managed to glimpse from the ground earlier, but it's a lot higher up than I realized.

We cut through a huge forest I never would have known was up here, keeping a quick pace. I warily cast a glance in the direction of every sound.

I follow closely, since I have no idea what a finish line even looks like. I doubt there will be a bright red ribbon to run through.

May have to jump through a fire hoop or something.

Something loud roars, and the guys start moving a lot faster as the trees behind us start shaking fiercely.

It's like a spike of adrenaline hits them, and they move twice as fast, causing me to struggle to keep up.

I see trees flying up as something massive barrels through the forest, a hint of dark fur peeking through the top of the tree-line as we start hiking a steep incline.

That's not good.

A hellacious roar almost deafens me even in spirit form.

Just as it crashes through the trees and I get a glimpse of a mouthful of teeth, tingles shoot through my hand, and a white light blasts.

Chapter X

Stumbling into Ezekiel's bedroom, I look around. I'm not sure how I just ended up here, but a sense of panic hits me when I don't sense the boys.

Then their presence washes over me, and I relax.

"Where'd she go?" I hear Kai ask.

"Did she make it?" Ezekiel this time.

"I grabbed her hand," Jude tells someone.

I start to go to them, then realize I'm actually a little drained. Emotionally drained that is.

I'll wait until tomorrow for the inquisition into all I did today and what nefarious reasoning might have led to it. Or maybe they think I'm their protective spirit now, but doubtful. Jude even mocked it himself.

I'll save the verbal sparring for tomorrow, because saving their lives has quite honestly exhausted me. I've never been exhausted before.

I move through the walls until I reach the third staircase that takes me to the west wing.

Humming softly, I walk down the beautiful halls that go unappreciated. I'd planned on making my bedroom one of the ones on this side, just to show this side some love.

There's one with a beautiful view of a rose garden so lavish that it's fit for a king. It was going to be my room if I ever turned whole. They could visit me and sleep there when they wanted.

Back in fantasy land.

In hindsight, it was rather silly to think I'd just be part of the group and fill all their needs.

It's the first time I've been able to stay in this room past ten minutes without revisiting them to put my eyes on them. I soak it in, giving into the illusion once more of having the four of them in here.

All of us a tangle of naked limbs and whispered words…

Still sated with just their presence nearby, I spend the rest of the evening in my fantasy room, kept company by the dust and occasional creepy spider.

By the time it grows late and I assume they're all in bed, I make my way through the quiet house.

Unable to help myself, I poke my head in Kai's door, and mutter, "Good night."

Just as I almost get my head pulled back through, I hear, "Good night."

I'm not sure why my heart acts like it's way more excited than it should be. I withdraw completely, trying not to read too much into it.

Moving to Gage's room, I stick my head through the door, and say, "Good night."

"Good night," finds me before I get my head out of his door, and a small smile curves my lips.

They're a little late, but at least I don't feel as miserable about being tethered to them at the moment.

Poking my head in Jude's door, I whisper, "Good night."

I wait for a moment, unable to see even an outline of him in the jet-black room, and then blow out a breath. I guess two out of three is better than I realistically expected.

When I turn around, I squeal a little, because Jude is leaned against the wall in the hallway, his hands in his jean pockets as he studies me.

His black T-shirt smells like it just came out of the dryer, and his hair is still damp like he's just left the shower.

"The spell has been replaced. It should last a while before someone manages to drain it," he tells me.

"Guess you couldn't get rid of me like you hoped, huh?" I ask through a dark smile.

"Didn't try. It's to keep out harmful intent. Not actual beings. It's a much more costly upgrade," he tells me with a shrug.

I say nothing, just stand here awkwardly for a moment.

"You can stay away from us longer now, can't you?" he asks.

"Seems to be a major perk from my last level-up. All I need is the comfort of your presence to stay anchored now. Major bonus for you guys with your privacy." I walk by him, and he laughs under his breath.

"Is it necessary to prance around in outfits you know we like to see on women, when you know we can't touch you?" he calls to my back.

I walk a little higher in my tall boots and go-go dancer skirt that shows hints of my ass with each step.

"I've learned I'm an unapologetic tease when men are assholes," I retort, moving toward Ezekiel's room.

My outfit changes into a thin, pretty nightgown that stops at my knees.

Before I can poke my head through Ezekiel's door, Jude is suddenly behind me, his tingles riding all down the length of my back as his lips make my ear tingle.

"Good night," he whispers, then he's gone, and I breathe out shakily while fighting a smile.

Instead of poking my head into Ezekiel's door, I pass through it. Maybe I shouldn't care that he's violently thrashing in the bed like he's in physical pain. But I do.

I move to the bed, planning to lie beside him as I have hundreds of times. As soon as I'm on the bed, my hand goes to his side, resting there.

Those tingles are more pronounced than usual, and he goes instantly still, his body relaxing as he seems to drift off into a more peaceful sleep. My lips curl in a grin.

I never see him sleep peacefully. Even under the influence of that drug, his face was scrunched in agony. Peering over him, I see a calm, serene look on his face as his breathing evens out.

I start to pull away, and his face hardens. Curious, I place my hand on him once more, and he falls back into a peaceful sleep.

Since there's a new spell in place for protection, I'm a little less on alert, but I'm still wary. Each sound captures my attention until I can isolate what exactly it is.

"Good night," I whisper to Ezekiel.

I shut my eyes, pretending I can sleep as well. I wonder what rest would feel like.

Those tingles continue to spread when he rolls over, his arm crossing through me.

The longer I feel those sweet sensations, the more relaxed I become. So relaxed, that when I close my eyes again, they almost feel heavy.

CHAPTER XI

The sound of a groan startles me awake. Awake? I don't sleep, so why am I jerking awake to sunlight when it was clearly dark just a second ago.

My head aches a little as something tickles my cheek. I dust it off, feeling the swipe of my fingers, and jerking my hand back to stare at it in horror.

Eyes widening, I study the very whole hand in front of me, then take in the very new sensations surrounding me.

Warmth. Softness. Hardness. A slight chill in the air. The whisper of wind rushing over my skin. But I concentrate primarily on the warmth, because a large, heavy hand is spanned across my stomach, the heat of it carrying through the thin gown that is actually real now.

Soft. Silky. Smooth.

I moan before I can stop myself because of all the sensations washing over me at once.

I can fucking feel…

And I had no idea what I was missing.

My legs glide over the sheets, feeling the exquisite softness beneath me. It's absolutely amazing. Almost overwhelming.

The hand on my stomach tenses, slowly squeezing just enough to wrinkle my gown. Then Ezekiel's head pops up, his eyes widen on me, and those gold flakes almost dance with excitement.

That warmth floods me, and something akin to a dull ache moves between my thighs as I try to get my rapid breathing under control. I only thought I knew what arousal was until this moment.

It's a consuming, burning desire that swarms you, making you desperate for touch like I never imagined possible. And if he doesn't touch me *everywhere*—every inch of my skin—soon, I'm afraid I might actually cry.

His eyes do a quick sweep of my body, and a dark, daring grin tugs at one corner of his mouth before his eyes come back up.

His hand darts out, and I scream, just knowing he's about to kill me on my first day being whole. Instead, he grabs the front of my gown and rips it down to my waist, baring my breasts to him.

Sensation washes over me, stealing my scream as my nipples harden almost painfully, and that ache intensifies as my body continues to heat.

I suck in a breath as he suddenly comes down on top of me, and shoves the rest of the gown up. Without warning, his lips come down on mine, hard and demanding as my eyes cross and I arch against him, needing contact. It feels like a jolt of electricity shoots through me when his daring tongue slips in and starts doing incredible things, electrifying every dormant nerve so that it wakes up and soaks in every feeling for the first time.

I'm moaning like an idiot just from him kissing me, grinding against nothing as I try to get as close as possible, touching everything at once. My hands glide over his strong, smooth back, and he reaches between us, his hand brushing my pussy as he rips down the front of his boxers.

The door flies open, and I jump, panicking a little as it crashes into the wall. A squeal pops out of me like a surprise hiccup, and I drop through the bed, the floor, and almost drop through the next floor before I remember how to stop.

I lie on the ground, panting heavily, Ezekiel's touch still ghosting over me as a teasing reminder of what it's like to actually feel. The thunderous sound of rushing footsteps come barreling down the stairs. I'm still dazed and confused, staring at my mostly transparent hand as my entire body throbs with need I can't sate in this form.

I never had any idea just a kiss could be so drugging.

"Fucking get off me," I hear Ezekiel bark.

"What the hell was going on? How did she turn whole?" Jude is snapping.

They all swing their gazes to me the second they finally reach the room where I am.

"What the hell is going on?" Kai asks, his eyes narrowing on me.

"I…I don't sleep. Somehow I fell asleep next to Ezekiel, because he quit thrashing around when I touched him," I babble.

Ezekiel shoves through Kai and Gage, moving toward me with eyes so gold it looks like his natural color.

He makes a grab for me, but his hand passes right through me, igniting those tingles that only serve to tease me more now.

The gown is still ripped down the front, and Jude is staring very obviously at where it's still hanging above my hips as well.

"Just what the hell were you going to do with her, E? You know you can't fuck her without us. All that bonding stuff or whatever," Kai drawls.

"I could have fucked her," he growls, looking over at them.

Confusion crosses their faces.

"First morning wood of my entire life," he says, his eyes moving back to mine as frustration creases his brow.

"What's going on?" I ask, imagining a pair of leggings and a long T-shirt that appears on my body, reeling back their distraction as I jump to my feet, still a little high on the rush of feeling so much at once.

"We can't have a woman unless we share her," Kai says, his jaw grinding as he looks at me then to Ezekiel. "We were impotent before—"

"Clearly not the thing to tell a woman," Gage drawls.

"—but after we met," Kai goes on, not acting like he was interrupted, "we felt the bond form. We've learned it's a quad thing. There are several groups of four throughout the trials every year, and they experience the same little issue. They also always have the worst obstacles thrown at them before they can make it into the trials. We want to know why."

"Sidetracked," Jude butts in. "The point is, we can't enjoy a woman, unless we enjoy her together. It's part of the bond. None of us have ever had a woman on our own."

"So if you were a boy band, you'd be One Erection," I state, rambling because they have me nervous.

They don't even acknowledge that. Kai eyes Ezekiel, who is straining to refrain from touching me, while the other two just glare at me.

"You're sure?" Kai asks him, not sounding convinced or concerned.

"Fucking positive. Turn whole again," Ezekiel spits out, turning that last part on me like an order.

"Gee, with that attitude, I'll hop right on it," I grumble, moving over to a couch. "You're really ruining the first time I've felt touch like that by freaking out so much. All of you."

"Touching him all night might have had something to do with it," Kai suggests, his eyes raking over me differently for once.

"If we get her whole, I'm going first. You have no idea how worked up I am right now," Ezekiel says, running a hand over the back of his neck as he starts pacing. "It's never been this bad before."

Well, that makes me a hint smug. Especially since he prefers redheads. But he's also a little too scary now.

"Or you could fuck your hand," I point out, frowning as I take a seat on the ground again. "I'm not sure I want you unleashed on me with all your strength while I'm whole. What if you break me?"

Ezekiel stops pacing to turn and arch an eyebrow at me.

"Touch us. Just try it," Gage says as he kneels between my legs and looms over me.

"We'll give you everything you've been fantasizing about if you get whole," Jude says next to my ear.

When did he get behind me? And why does it sound like he is most certainly using his liar-voice?

Hands move over me, through me, stirring all those tingles to life. Nothing happens though. I feel like these savage beasts are trying to lure me out so they can kill me, which has my self-preservation skills likely hosing up my new level-up.

"Shit," Gage groans when nothing happens for a while.

"I'm worked up and I didn't even get to have my damn hands on her," Jude says with a huff as he walks off.

"No erections without each other? So how do you get worked up?" I ask, trying to distract them.

"Usually, we want sex but can't get aroused on our own. A date with the hand only works in the presence of each other, and it's not as much fun without a—"

The doorbell rings, which is a first for me. No one ever rings the doorbell.

I didn't know we had one.

Gage jogs out of the room, and Ezekiel stalks out behind him. Jude takes a seat beside me, his arm going behind my head. I lean back on it like he's doing it to offer me comfort, though I highly doubt it.

When they return, Ezekiel walks over, holding two envelopes. Gage has two as well, handing one off to Kai.

Ezekiel hands over the other one, and he sits down really close to me, our sides touching and creating that tingle.

Jude and Kai exchange a look before casting a glance at our connection. Slowly, Jude withdraws his arm from around me, eyes still suspicious as he opens the envelope.

"So it's official," Jude says, closing the envelope as a calculated grin plays on his lips.

"What's official?" I ask, confused.

Frankly, I need a distraction so I don't sink into a depression about finally being able to feel something and having it ripped away. It's much better to not know what you're missing than to be tortured with just a teasing touch.

"We've been invited to the royal palace of the underworld. We'll be collected in one month," Kai answers, putting the invitation to the side.

"Why a month?" Still needing that distraction.

"Because it takes time to set up the next obstacle, and they make it as hard as possible for the twenty competitors based on how well they did in the first two rounds," Ezekiel answers, not budging an inch from my side.

Gage studies Ezekiel, the way he's unconsciously drawing so close that I'm passing through his body.

"Two other quad sets made it through to the next round as well," Gage says as he closes his invitation and puts it aside.

"So twelve out of twenty are part of a quad group? Why is this done by teams? Someone needs to start at the beginning and explain all this to me," I grumble.

"It's done by teams because you're going to be a part of a larger team," Ezekiel says immediately. "You'll become one of the elite who has access to Lucifer on occasion, and—"

"And there are some things that don't need to be told," Jude interrupts, arching an eyebrow at Ezekiel.

Ezekiel's jaw tightens, but he doesn't say anything else. I roll my eyes, because that means I'm still not trusted. I half suspect they find my vagina to also be evil now.

"Okay, so what can you tell me? Since my level-up, I can see and hear things in Purgatory, unlike before when I didn't even know where we were going because focusing was so hard. And you guys never really talk about any of this here," I go on.

"We used to. There's no reason to discuss things unless we have new developments now," Kai says with a shrug.

"We've been working toward this goal for a couple of centuries now," Ezekiel goes on.

"Centuries?" I ask, my eyes widening.

"Really? Little much information," Gage tells him, narrowing his eyes.

Ezekiel flips him off. "We told her the highlights in Purgatory."

"Highlights and details are two very different things," Kai points out.

Ezekiel looks at me. "A few centuries ago, we were all four born to different mortal families involved with the underworld in some way—imps, lawyers, and some media—"

"For fuck's sake, E, not that much information," Jude says incredulously, looking at Ezekiel like he's lost his mind.

Ezekiel ignores him, and my gaze returns to him as he continues.

"By twenty-six, we were all going a little crazy. Actually crazy. Hearing things, seeing things, always paranoid we were being targeted or watched. I was ahead of them by several decades, and though I'd stopped aging, I wasn't really immortal."

"Ezekiel!" Kai snaps.

Ezekiel doesn't even glance in his direction. His eyes stay fixed on mine.

"That's the reason my dreams are the worst. The madness tries to return when I let my guard down. When we sleep, the bond is the weakest for some reason. It's why Kai struggles to sleep. It's why Jude is so pissed most of the time. Gage may seem to sleep soundly, but he's frozen in the places his mind visits, and he becomes a prisoner until his eyes—"

Gage is suddenly grabbing Ezekiel by the shirt and ripping him up from the couch. "That's enough!" Gage barks in his face.

Ezekiel shoves him off, and then suddenly they're tackling each other, fists flying.

"Stop!" I snap, jumping up from the couch.

An ache lances through me when Ezekiel takes a hit to his face. And sickening dread surges when Ezekiel hits Gage so hard that blood flies.

Kai and Jude take their sweet fucking time coming to break them up, both of them glaring at me as they struggle to pull them apart.

"You don't get to fucking tell her *our* secrets. That's a group decision!" Gage snaps at him.

Ezekiel shrugs Jude off him, and without another word, he turns and stalks out of the room.

Three pairs of accusatory eyes turn and narrow on me.

Ah, great. Well, having them be semi-nice was fun while it lasted.

"What'd you do to him?" Gage growls.

"I told you she was singling him out because he didn't find her to be a threat. Now she's tearing us down by using our connection against us," Kai states.

"How's your leg, Kai?" I ask with a tight smile, my eyes dipping to the fully healed leg that *I* helped heal. Somehow. "Was I a threat when I was scrambling to save your life so you all wouldn't die? I certainly wasn't trying to separate the four of you then or pit you against each other. Wouldn't it have made sense to do it then?"

"You'd know you couldn't be so obvious about it. You've been studying us for who knows how long?" he growls.

"Five-and-a-half years I've been studying you. It's not like the four of you told me before today that you couldn't get it up without each other in the room. As you stated, there are some things you don't feel the need to discuss after so much time together. I only heard what you shared with each other. It was usually dark jokes, women, and some killing I witnessed. That's about it."

He starts to speak, but I hold my hand up.

"You know what? Forget it. You can't touch me. None of you can. Whatever happened this morning was probably another form of torture to show me what I've been missing, because it's become clear to me that whatever I am is a punishment of some sort. Why else would I be stuck with the four of you?"

I turn to walk up the stairs, but Gage is suddenly in front of me.

"Leave Ezekiel alone. The last thing he needs is you tearing him away from us when our lives are at stake. You want to prove you care? Fucking care by staying away from him."

I pass through him without another word. Just to be spiteful, I almost walk through Ezekiel's door, but I stop myself.

For five years, I've stalked their lives. Today is the first time I've ever seen them fight.

A sick feeling forms in the pit of my stomach, and I bite back an angry curse as I spin and stalk away, moving toward the west wing and my self-proclaimed bedroom.

Right now, I really wish I could touch things, just so I could slam a freaking door.

I could hang out in my room, but instead, I zap myself back, swaying a little but not as bad as usual. Like the stalker I used to be, I hide out in the room beside them as they argue.

They all, of course, went to Ezekiel's room.

"I get it. I get the temptation that would present. But remember what makes us the way we are," Kai is saying.

"You don't have a clue what it felt like, and I don't know how to explain it without sounding completely fucking insane," Ezekiel grumbles.

"You turned on us. Do you see the problem here?" Gage asks.

A harsh breath follows that. "Fuck!" Ezekiel shouts before something crashes to the ground.

"I don't know if she's here to sabotage us or just here with some really bad fucking timing, but I do know we can't risk her severing our bond," Jude tells them.

"So we keep our hands off her. We let her hang around, since she has saved us a time or two. Until we really know what the hell is going on and why she's attached to us, we have to be more cautious," Kai says on a long sigh. "Trust me, I get wanting to trust her. When she took away the pain left behind from the hellfire, all I wanted to do was fuck her, kiss her, touch her. Never wanted anything so bad in all my life."

"But usually the things we want despite the consequences is a trick straight from hell," Jude goes on.

Great.

Absolutely terrific.

One step forward, eighty steps back. It's the status quo for my relationship with them.

This time, when I return to my room, I don't wish to be able to slam the door. Because I'm starting to think they may be right.

They fought. Because of me.

Maybe I'm not the blessing to them I thought I was. Maybe I'm their curse.

Perspective is a real bitch.

CHAPTER XII

After a week of avoiding them, even though they've remained at the house, I've gotten used to not having my eyes on them. It was a rough withdrawal, but I still managed.

The media room TV was accidentally left on when they watched a movie a few nights ago. As soon as they left, I quickly occupied a seat and watched the next movie on.

I've never gotten to watch a whole movie without them in here, because they always remember to turn it off, usually. I'm liking my newfound freedom a little.

But for two days, I've been counting down the minutes for the movie that is on right now.

I'm even dressed for the occasion, sitting in the front row, wishing I could eat popcorn. That's the first thing I'm eating when I'm whole.

Just sayin'.

I've been on the edge of my seat the entire movie, glued to the screen like my life depends on it.

Just as the sad, lonely little fella gets screwed over by the ones he thought were his friends, and they get turned into literal jackasses, the door to the media room is thrown open, and the sound of laughter fills the room.

Speaking of jackasses…

I look behind me as all four of them come to an abrupt stop, all eyes on me like they knew I was in here. Ezekiel's eyes have lost their golden hue over the week, and he looks away from me like he's making sure not to fall into my sticky trap of doom and manipulation or whatever.

My *feminine wiles* have these guys on cock-block overdrive.

Considering I was here first and have been dying to watch this movie since I saw it advertised, I turn back around and concentrate on what's going on

"What the actual hell are you watching?" Jude finally asks me.

Damn bipolar, annoying, self-centered, arrogant, distrusting pricks.

All of them.

Now they're just being rude for talking during the movie.

Ignoring them, I try to focus on the movie and nothing else. I've waited too long to—

"And what the fuck are you wearing?" Kai asks as he walks to be in front of the huge screen, his head cutting off my view.

I try to peer around him, but he deliberately steps into my view again.

Blowing out a frustrated breath because I'm near the big climax, I glare at him. "What exactly do you want? And can you hurry up and say it so I can get back to my movie before it ends?"

The screen pauses, and I look back as Jude's lips twitch, the remote in his hand.

"Seriously...what are you wearing?" Kai asks again, his eyebrows up as he stares at my dressy, blue bow tied at the top of my yellow shirt that is buttoned all the way up.

Jude steps forward, his eyes scanning over my red shorts and red suspenders. Don't forget the wooden Dutch shoes.

When Gage joins the gawking fest, he focuses primarily on my yellow hat and bright red feather that is proudly sticking out.

"This is a movie that is resonating very deeply with me, and it needed the proper outfit to enjoy it with," I dutifully explain, hoping they just leave me in peace.

"Pinocchio is a movie that resonates very deeply with you?" Ezekiel asks from far behind me, probably cautioned not to get too close so I can't whammy him with my evil vagina powers.

Evil. Isn't that ironic, considering they're literally trying to save the devil. Take away the D in devil and what are you left with?

"Does your nose grow when you tell a lie? Because that would be helpful to us," Gage states dryly.

"He wants to be a real boy. I want to be a real girl," I point out, even though it really should be obvious.

They exchange a look that makes me feel like they might believe I'm crazy. Of course I'm crazy. Five and a half years of not being seen or heard, then getting treated like a disease when I can be seen and heard…anyone would be crazy.

"Is the outfit supposed to make all your dreams come true?" Kai asks incredulously.

"I have no idea," I say on a long sigh. "I've never seen the movie. I've yet to discover what, if anything, turns Pinocchio into a real boy."

"Spoiler alert, it's the blue fairy," Jude states with a smirk.

I cut my eyes on him, imagining the ways I'd like to kick his ass right now.

"Any chance you can help me find the blue fairy equivalent now that you've ruined my movie?" I ask him through gritted teeth.

"There's no such thing," he answers with a shrug, seeming to enjoy the fact he's pissed me off.

Their phones all start going off, which means a job.

Pulling my knees up to my chest, I silently fume.

"I'm not taking her anywhere in that outfit," Jude says as he disappears from sight.

Kai rolls his eyes and steps in front of me. I just glare up at him as I reach out my hand, feeling the tips of my fingers swipe through his shirt just before he siphons.

We land in the middle of the graveyard, and the others start trying to catch the black shadows of souls that are racing away. Me? I decide to be a pain in the ass tonight, since they're assholes who ruined my movie for no reason.

Jude is my first target.

One of the souls dives for him, trying to invade his body, and I turn around in a Little Bo Peep outfit, sheep hook in hand and obnoxiously large bonnet on my head.

He stumbles, his eyes widening as his mouth twists in a cringe. The soul runs through him, and he curses as he doubles over. The soul is forced back out, and he swipes his bo staff, absorbing the soul until the metal lights up.

My next outfit is a cheerleader outfit, with my hair in pigtails. Midriff showing and short skirt barely covering my bare ass, I lift my pompoms in the air and start exaggerating a cheer.

"J! U! D! E! What's that spell?! Major dick, yes, sir-ree!" My cheer involves a one-finger salute.

Kai snorts, then curses me as he struggles to recover from his accidental burst of laughter.

I chase them through the streets, as they diligently avoid the humans, trying to capture the souls without being caught on film.

The humans can't see the souls, obviously.

"U-G-L-Y, you ain't got no alibi, you ugly, yeah, you're all ugly!" I cheer, appearing just in front of Gage, who runs through me, cursing me the entire time.

Switching to referee attire, I go to where Ezekiel is fighting hard against three particularly crafty souls that keep evading him. He takes a run and leaps to one side of the building, then flips to the building beside him, before pushing off the second building when his feet hit, and finally lands on the first building's roof, managing to snag a soul in the process.

I zap myself up there, finding the dizziness fading with each time I do this. "Foul on the play!" I shout, startling him so much he trips before crashing through me.

"Damn it! What the hell is your problem?" he shouts to my back, before I zap myself back down to where Jude is.

I change my attire into a very skimpy bikini. Big sunglasses frame my face as I lie down and pretend I'm sunning under the moonlight, putting myself directly in the path of Jude.

He almost trips himself up, trying to avoid stepping on me, before finally remembering he can't actually step on me.

His foot swipes through my vagina as he races on, and I don't think that was an accident.

I give a little wave to Kai when I catch him staring for a minute. When a soul crashes into him during its attempt to escape Jude, I smirk.

Then I outright laugh a little when Jude also crashes into him while chasing the soul.

"What the fucking hell are you doing?" Gage snaps, standing over me.

"Careful, pretty boy. It looks like you're talking to yourself," I say as he looks up, seeing the homeless gawking at him and the others like they're all insane.

Grown men with weapons they're swinging at air and yelling at a girl no one else can see? Now who looks crazy?

A little triumphant grin toys with my lips.

Last year, he bought a very pretty girl a black, sheer slip of lingerie, and he had her wear it with some really sexy high heels.

That's what my next outfit is, and he stares down at me with intense, hard eyes. There's almost a palpable energy between us when he reaches down and adjusts himself.

My lips curl in a knowing grin. He can get aroused easily with the others so close.

Why haven't I done this sooner? They've been cruel. So I should be as well.

"This just got interesting," I say to myself as Gage stalks off.

Score one for the phantom girl with no memory.

CHAPTER XIII

"Are you trying to get us killed?" Gage snaps, throwing his swords to the ground as he stalks toward me.

I'm already dropping to the couch of our house, wearing nothing but some more sexy lingerie. I'm calling it their hit-list. All the things they requested girls wear is all I'm wearing from now on.

"Even when I'm saving your lives you apparently think I'm trying to get you killed, so I had an epiphany," I state, shrugging.

"Your epiphany involved stupid outfits and distracting tactics when we're chasing souls that could have escaped us tonight because of you?" Jude snaps, getting right in my face.

"No," I say as I stand and pass through him, ignoring the tingles as I strut through the room with the lacy ensemble showing off all the goods.

As I pass through Gage, I notice Kai's eyes hungrily raking over me, his breathing coming a little quicker. This was one of his favorite outfits on a girl, because when it was his turn, he bought this one several times for several different women.

"Over the years, I told you I perfected my fantasy," I remind them.

"We've decided we're never going to—"

I interrupt Kai, since it's my turn to talk. "There are two types of people," I say to him, and he narrows his eyes on me. "Those who listen, and those who merely wait for their turn to talk."

My eyes move around the room.

"None of you are listeners. None of you care that I can't change the channels on the TV, nor do you ever ask me if you can do something for me."

"You never ask for anything," Kai points out with a roll of his eyes.

"Exactly! I ask for nothing! And you inconsiderate assholes never bother to take that into consideration. I don't even have a light on in my bedroom. I've been dying to watch that movie, and *you* ruined it," I rant on, darting an annoyed gaze at Jude.

His lips merely twitch because he's an unapologetic dick.

"And therefore, my epiphany has been that none of you deserve me. You can look. You can fantasize. Like I've had to. Try to bring home a woman, and I'll make farting noises while wearing a dolphin costume and acting like I'm humping each of you. See how long you can hold an erection then," I carry on, feeling a little proud of that threat as they all eye me like the psychotic girl in the room. "But even if I get whole and you beg, I'd never give in. In fact, I'm going to see if I can't figure out how to attach myself to one of the other quads the next time we're around some."

Ezekiel turns and stalks out, not saying anything.

As I take a seat, Jude leans over me, caging me in as I stare up at him, unafraid.

"You're trying to fuck with us again right now, aren't you? See if you can make us jealous?"

I snort derisively, then outright laugh. "Make you jealous?" I ask around my laughter.

He backs up, a confused expression on his face.

"Why in the hell would I attempt to make you jealous? You don't even like me! You play head games. Three of you finally tell me good night, only to act like I'm the devil's advocate the next day just because I had a fluke where I finally got to feel someone, and surprise surprise, there was almost sex involved. That was apparently me trying to break you up, even though I've been quite shameless in voicing what I want the second I get whole, and I've been voicing it from the very beginning."

They all look a little confused for a second.

"Now, if you'll excuse me, there are a few books open in the library where you guys were trying to research me. I'm going to go see if any of those books hold the secrets to getting myself hitched to four guys who appreciate how awesome I really am. Ghost girl out."

I should have left off the *ghost girl out* part. My speech was epic until then.

Hands shaking and heart thumping in my chest, I stalk up the stairs, ready to commit to this new plan of action. I've been toying with the idea since the gauntlet, but until now, I didn't have the lady ghost balls to go through with it.

As soon as I pass through the door in the library, I see a book shutting. Jude is smirking, his fingers closing another book.

Kai closes a few as well, since they apparently siphoned in here.

Gage props his feet up on a few open books, before shutting a few more beside him, challenging eyes on me the entire time.

"Real mature," I grumble. "If you want me gone so bad, then why would you shut all the books?"

Gage toys with an ink pen, smirking and not looking at me.

"All the better to annoy you with, my dear," Jude drawls.

"We're not letting you go until we understand what it is you really are," Kai goes on with a shrug.

"Fine," I bite out with a fake smile on my face as I cross my arms over my chest.

My outfit changes to the sexiest one yet. It's a little Egyptian Princess in style, gold and alluring. Ornate gold sleeves wrap up my arms, and the laces of the sexy shoes go all the way up to my thighs.

The bodysuit-ish outfit has a neckline that dips all the way to my stomach. The bottom has a touch of long, light, gold chains that hang to the knees, but is spaced apart so you can still see all the way up.

I'm not sure why it's the one that I choose, but it pops into my mind, so I go with it.

Gage falls out of the chair.

Guess I have a winning outfit for him.

Kai sucks in a sharp breath, and Jude is suddenly in front of me, trying to snatch me. All of their eyes light up gold, and I take a wary step back as they start coming toward me like mindless drones.

"Okay. Not funny anymore. What's wrong with—"

I squeal when Kai lunges, but when he passes through me, I roll my eyes at myself for being an idiot. I whirl around just as Gage tries to tackle me.

Shit.

For whatever reason, they really like this outfit, or they seriously hate it.

Because they look feral. Ruthless. Savage even.

I'm suddenly in that dolphin costume I threatened them with for a whole new reason, my head poking out the dolphin's belly, and they all blink like they're waking from a trance.

"What the hell is wrong with you idiots? It was just an outfit. And so help me, if you blame me for that, I will—"

They all disappear from the room at once, and I curse, losing the dolphin costume and donning some normal, very respectable clothing.

I almost don't go look for them, because I know they're going to be doubly suspicious of me. But unfortunately, I'm worried about them, because that clearly wasn't natural.

I really need to detach myself before my attachment gets me killed.

My hurried steps slow when I hear them talking in the kitchen.

"You saw that," Jude is saying.

"I saw that she freaked out and turned into a dolphin to snap us out of that shit. She definitely didn't want us in that trance. Whatever in the hell it was," Kai grumbles.

"She's all I could see for a minute. It was…not the outfit. It was something else. Something in the air," Jude goes on.

"Why a dolphin?" Gage asks.

"Really not the important part," Ezekiel says. "What happened?"

Before the guys can explain to him that once again I did something suspicious, the door swings open.

Five men come walking in, and my heart stutters. Why isn't the spell keeping them out of they mean them harm?

Leaping off the rest of the steps, I race to follow them.

"Hands on your heads," one of the men shouts.

Running up behind them, my hand comes up reflexively, but Jude's eyes meet mine, and he gives me a subtle, but still distinguishable, shake of his head.

His hands go to the top of his head, jaw tensing as he holds my eyes for a minute longer. I barely manage to stop the power on the tip of my fingers, because it knows something is wrong. And it only works when they're in trouble.

Life threatening trouble.

And I really want to use the power. It almost hurts not to when it's so close to the surface and begging to be set free.

Kai gives me the same barely-there headshake, also telling me to stand down.

My hand falls to my side, and I ignore the annoying prickles that spread over me, punishment for denying whatever this power inside me is.

Ezekiel's gaze meets and holds mine as the men start walking behind all of them. They pull out cuffs, and Gage glances my way before speaking.

"What are we being taken in for?" Gage asks.

I wish they weren't all staring at me like they're worried I'm about to save them—as though it would be the worst thing ever. Don't they want to be saved?

When no one answers him, Kai speaks, even as they continue to pull their hands into some weird black cuffs one at a time.

"Under the guardian's privilege rules, you're required to tell four guardians who've entered the trials the reason they're being taken in," Kai tells them dryly.

"It's protective custody," one of the guards tells him flippantly. "There's still a hit out on your names, and as contenders in the second round of the trials, we're required to offer you protection under the crown."

The guys all stare at me, until Ezekiel finally makes a subtle gesture with his head for me to join them. Right. They're about to be zapped out of here, no doubt.

I barely make it to him in time to stick my hand out, and then we're suddenly inside a cell. The men who cuffed them are nowhere to be seen, and I whirl around, taking in the blackened stones surrounding us.

The iron door will be twice as hard to pass through, so I opt to go through the creepy stone, poking my head through to see what's around us.

Bad idea.

My breath runs out in a rush when a flame shoots straight up into the air like it's trying to take my face off. I reel back, but carefully peer back out to take in the cylinder prison we're in.

All the many pointless cell doors are visible in this large circle tower. Right in the middle of us is an endless pit of fire that shoots straight up whenever it has to hiccup or fart or something.

I'm assuming we're in hell right now.

Just a guess.

Why even have the doors when you clearly can't walk out of them?

"Not even the soul stones stop her from passing through," Gage muses, not sounding even the least bit distressed by the fact we're literally in a hell cell.

"I thought nothing could breach them," Ezekiel immediately adds.

Pulling my head back in, I look at the four of them in all their relaxed glory like they're idiots.

Kai pulls his cuffed hands under his legs and works them down until they're in front of him. The other three do the same—like they've done this a hundred times.

"Just curious if the four of you have figured out Manella has put you in here to kill you finally, since you've managed to thwart his attempts in the other world," I decide to point out.

"Of course we've figured it out. It's also why they've cuffed us, so we can't use our *abilities,*" Jude states with a shrug.

"I'm not even sure what your abilities are," I tell him honestly as I turn around and poke my head through another wall, hoping to find a hallway or something.

No such luck. It's another big pit of fire in the center, cells lining up as high as I can see to a fiery ceiling as well.

So I stick my head beside us, finding another cell and a very gnarly looking occupant.

Both of his eyes are dangling, and he's hunched over like he's looking for his *precious,* while chewing on a mangled piece of meat that smells rancid even from here.

Pulling my head back in, I shudder.

"Doesn't matter what our abilities are," Gage says.

"The cuffs keep them contained. It's sealed with the devil's crest."

"How do you get the cuffs off?" I ask them when they withhold any answers about their abilities.

I turn around as Kai shrugs. "They'll wait a few days before attempting to kill us. It'd be too obvious to kill us too soon, so we have time to figure it out. It's easiest to trick a guard into taking them off, since they know the words to speak."

"There are words to speak?" I ask, perking up. I can go find these.

"Not just anyone can say them. They have to be spoken by the chosen guards who've been blessed," Ezekiel calls to my back, but I'm already passing through to Smeagol's cage.

"We could use a protective spirit right now," Jude calls out, acting amused.

I step back in immediately, then see their mocking grins.

"Real funny. Why does this guy next to us look like a Gollum? Are those real?"

"No," Ezekiel says, his eyes dancing with humor. "It's hell, Keyla. If you're cast here after death, your soul starts transforming, morphing into the monster you really are, depending on your transgressions. Once the metamorphosis is complete and a physical form has manifested, they decide what to do with you, based on what you are."

"What's Smeagol's role gonna be?" I ask, curious.

"Likely, he'll be a food distributor to the prison cells. We're in hell's throat right now. It waits until you're finished devolving or evolving before it spits you out or swallows you. The worst of the monsters get sent below or to Purgatory to guard it."

Good to know. I'll be a damn good girl when I get whole. Neither of these places seem like a life choice I want to make.

"She's thinking about being a good girl right now, even though she's admitted she wants a four-way tag from a quad hell squad," Jude says, grinning like the asshole he is.

Rolling my eyes, I leave them to mock me, and scamper past Smeagol to see where this circle leads. Eventually, I have to find a hall. Surely it can't all be pits of flames in the middle of a cylinder prison tower.

I pass through another cell, and stifle a scream. There's a hairy beastly thing that looks like he used to be human. He snarls and tears at the sides of the stone walls. His sharp claws don't even leave a scratch behind.

Hell is so not cool. Which I guess is obvious.

A few cells have these dark shadows bouncing around like pin balls. Apparently they can't pass through the stones as easily as I can.

Don't even get me started on the guy who looks like he has a sledgehammer sticking through his face.

I keep poking my head through the walls on either side, and only keep finding fire.

Several have actual people in it. I suppose they're going to be used like my guys who never died but still turned into whatever these people are once their soul finds a new, mostly immortal body to attach to.

One cell has a fairly attractive man in it, and I linger, trying to see if he can see me like my guys can. But he can't. I'm not sure who he is, but he looks a little broken. For whatever reason, I sort of feel sad for him, and I hang out beside him like I'm commiserating with him.

He curses before running a hand through his hair. He looks exhausted, almost as though he's lost all hope. Not like the other men in here I've seen. His hands are cuffed, just like the guys. I'm assuming he's not a soul in transition.

"I didn't do it!" he shouts suddenly, as though he expects someone to hear him. "I'm being framed!"

Frowning, I study him. For no reason I can think of, I find myself believing him. I don't even know what he's referring to, yet I'm convinced he's innocent just by the compelling look in his tortured blue eyes.

"We have nothing to gain from this! *I* have nothing to gain from this! Why would I risk such a thing?" he goes on.

When I figure out how to free the guys, I'll return to free him as well.

Getting up, I start going from cell to cell again, collecting nightmares for the day I can finally sleep. Again. I only got to experience it that once, and apparently I'm a damn sound sleeper. I didn't even dream.

And I would love to know what the actual hell happened.

Anyway, a few more monsters make me swallow a scream, and idly wonder just how wretched and foul they must have been.

Next thing I know, I'm suddenly bursting back into the cell with all the guys, who are staring at me like they're not surprised.

"How can there be no hallway? Why have doors if there's nowhere to escape to?" I groan.

"The door is to give you false hope," Kai says with a shrug. "You manage to somehow turn into something strong enough to break down that door, iron forged in hellfire, then you find there's nowhere for you to go. It's the moment you're defeated, and they can sink their claws in and own you."

"And you want to work for such a lovely establishment," I state dryly.

Ezekiel shrugs. "We had no say in the matter. Regardless, our special skills require such a thing. They'd be useless elsewhere."

"But I'm not allowed to know what these skills are?"

"Besides being awesome at killing things?" Jude asks, getting comfortable on the ground and putting his hands behind his head as his eyes shut.

I glare at him for a second, though he's oblivious since he's already trying to fall asleep. Instead, I look over at Ezekiel as he rips his shirt off—since he can't just take it off with the cuffs in the way—and rolls it up like it's a pillow as he lies down as well.

With his cuffs still binding his wrists, Kai starts doing awkward pushups in the corner, as though he's trying to tire himself out. No one is going to answer me.

"Don't feel bad, spirit girl," Ezekiel says as his eyes close as well, our special connection severed since that one moment. "They don't know either."

"We don't fully know ourselves," Kai adds, grunting as he starts adding a hop in on every other push up. "Hence the reason we want the power boost. We figure it'll open us up more."

"How do the monsters get out if there's no way to them?" I ask.

"The same way we got in, Einstein," Jude retorts. "Escorts. They have the ability to send you anywhere once you're restrained."

He lazily lifts his cuffed hands as though I need a reminder, then drops them back down, never opening his eyes. "And they can send you anywhere if you were originally a soul here."

Gage is studying me, his hand rubbing his jaw as though he's thinking of something. "You aren't even reacting to being in hell," he finally says.

"Five years of talking to yourself when you don't even know yourself, what you are, or even how you came to be will make you quite impervious to essentially everything. Even the four-dick monster twenty-two cells over if you start that way," I tell him, gesturing the way I started.

His lips curve into a slow grin.

"Four dicks and only one monster to deal with. Sounds like you've found your perfect beast," Kai says through short breaths.

"Keep being an ass to me. I'm this close to saying fuck you all and hanging out with another fellow I found interesting." I pinch my fingers really close together for demonstration. "Maybe I'll help him instead, and leave the four of you in here to turn into something hideous."

Jude just grins, eyes still closed.

Ezekiel snorts while smirking.

"What?" I prompt.

"We're not souls in need of a form. We're not going to turn into anything," he answers flippantly.

"And we don't need your help," Gage adds. "Because you won't be able to get us out of this one."

"So why are you so calm?" I ask as I take a seat in the open corner where none of them are.

"Because we've gotten ourselves out of some really shitty predicaments in the past," Ezekiel tells me with a shrug. "It's amazing what you can do when your survival instincts kick in."

The way he says it makes it sound like it's pointed at me. His eyes hold mine for a moment, and it feels like he's trying to tell me something he's not supposed to tell me.

When Gage darts a look his way, Ezekiel breaks eye contact with me and closes his eyes. I'm now tempted to go lie down beside him, but the other three would flip out.

Just as Kai starts speaking, I shush him, straining to hear something.

"What?" one of them asks me, but I'm too distracted to know which.

Without thinking too much about it, I take off sprinting through the cells all the way back down to the mystery man that I feel an odd sort of sympathy for.

"I told you it wasn't me!" he shouts.

"You're getting a moment with your prince. Be thankful for that," a guard with a solid black leather mask over his face says. How can he even see?

Whatever is about to happen, I hurry myself over to Mr. Mysterious, hoping it works the same way, and really hoping I don't get too far out of range from the boys.

A feeling of something powerful flashes through my core the second I touch him, and in less than a blink, we're standing in what looks like a marble hall.

Glass chandeliers hang above me, and I spin in a circle, taking in all the gold and lavish surroundings.

Mr. Mystery drops to his knees, bowing his head as soon as a familiar face comes around the corner. My breath catches in my throat when I see who is stalking toward us.

Manella.

CHAPTER XIV

My eyes move between them a few times before a sick feeling sinks inside me. This mystery guy is Lamar…

"My prince," Lamar says, choking back emotion as tears start sliding down his face, but he keeps his head bowed.

Manella turns and looks at the numerous guards behind him. "Privacy. Now."

They all exchange a look.

"When a dark prince tells you to get the hell out, you turn and walk away. You don't look around for someone with more authority, because it *will* cost you a trip to hellfire," he growls.

They all disappear without missing a beat. Manella's harsh expression crumples, and he turns, grabbing Lamar by the shoulders and lifting him until he can hug him.

"I didn't do it, my prince," Lamar says on a choked sob. "I have no reason to."

That's…confusing.

"I know," Manella says, soothing him as he strokes his hair.

I stare, unable to look away, at the clear devotion and genuine concern etched in Manella's tired and exhausted face, as though he's lived days in a tortured nightmare.

He kisses the top of Lamar's head, and pulls back before saying, "*Un Bracco.*"

The cuffs fall away, and suddenly Lamar is shoving his hands into Manella's hair, dragging him down to kiss him the most passionately I've ever seen anyone kissed.

I turn away to give them privacy, since this feels far more intimate than anything I've ever witnessed the guys do. And I've seen them do far more scandalous things than simply kiss.

Since I can still feel the comforting presence of the guys, I'm assuming we're still in hell, even if this side of hell is a lot more glamorous.

When I hear the kiss break, both of them panting for air, I turn around to see their foreheads pressed together, each clinging to the other.

"You have to run," Manella says, looking over his shoulder before his eyes meet Lamar's again.

My heart stutters.

"I can't," Lamar says with a sad smile. "They'll believe I'm guilty then."

Manella shakes his head. "You don't understand; someone is in my father's ear right now. Whatever is going on with the three remaining quads in the group has him on high alert. He's brought all three sets here to stay hidden in the throat, convinced they'll all be safe. Someone put that idea into his ever maddening head."

I take a seat, because this just got good.

I can't wait until the day I can have popcorn for moments like these.

"Which means someone is setting the quads up to die in here. The guards can't be trusted, if that's the case, because they'll be the only ones able to get in there besides the escorts," Manella goes on, staring Lamar in the eye. "They'll come for you too. This is an attack on the family."

Lamar shakes his head, clasping Manella's hand. "If I run right now, they'll know you set me free. Lucifer will believe you're the one behind all this."

"He already suspects as much. I have no envy and no greed—he knows this when he's rational. I pointed out it made no sense for you to stab an elder and not ensure his death *while* wearing your true form. Why wouldn't you conceal your identity? I've asked all the obvious questions to my father, and still he insists it was you, and no doubt he believes you were acting on my behalf. I'd rather him banish me than allow you to be killed," Manella continues.

Those are actually good questions. If he could change into anyone, then why wouldn't he just look like someone else in front of Harold, in the event the elder survived? Especially since he didn't stick around to see if Harold died.

Another shape shifter would have a lot more to gain by framing Manella, who was already a suspect.

"I have no clue who is doing this, or they'd already be dead," Manella continues, a growl to his words.

"It doesn't matter," Lamar says, his jaw tightening as determination steals his features. "I'll continue to proclaim my innocence until they silence me. I'll never let them take you down with me. I've already proven I never confessed as they tried to claim I did."

Manella whispers some words, and a small grouping of words appear on Lamar's forearm.

"Use that. Get out of here if they come for you. *Do not* die. That's a direct order from your prince," Manella says, clearing his throat as though he's trying to rein in his emotions.

I bounce out of my seat, seeing the weird words. I'm not sure what language this is, but I hope I can say those words close enough to get the guys out.

Lamar bends, picking up his cuffs and begins putting them back on.

"Say you understand me," Manella snaps.

Lamar gives him a watery smile.

"My time is up, my prince. I'll see you soon."

Before Manella can argue, the doors open, and Lamar disappears, even though another person never comes in here. Well, shit.

That's not good. How the hell am I supposed to get back to the throat?

Then again, I found the answers to escape, discovered Manella and Lamar look to be getting framed, all in less than ten minutes of being down here. It's likely I could discover so much more down here if I had more time.

That explains why the guys want access to this area so badly.

The doors slam shut, sealing me inside with Manella. And I watch as the dark prince sags to a chair…and cries. He seems far less evil when he's a man weeping with a broken heart.

No way would he send his love to go after the guys if the price would be his life. He's not willing to sacrifice anything so important to him.

Manella stands, slinging a lamp across the room. It passes through me and shatters on the wall at my back. Then he breaks.

He drops to the ground, sobbing so fiercely that it's impossibly painful to watch. My chest feels like it's going to cave in on itself just to help bear some of the weight of his misery.

"I'm going to help you too," I groan aloud, hating myself as I turn to pass through the wall beside me and give him his privacy in this moment.

I can't believe I'm going to help the son of the devil that my guys are convinced is working against them. I was convinced of it too…until today.

Blowing out a breath, I ignore my own mist of ghostly tears. They're definitely going to hate me once I defend Manella and Lamar.

The sooner I can sever this link between us, the better. Even if it does feel like excruciating fire in my chest to even think about.

CHAPTER XV

So…hell is massive and confusing. I've walked in a circle half a dozen times, haven't seen another soul—ha!—since I left Manella, and even passing through walls seems to get me lost and spin me back around.

It makes no sense.

I have no real concept of time, but I'm almost positive I've been tangled up in this optical illusion of a maze for hours.

So much for this place having all the answers at easily accessible points.

Just as I pass through another wall, beginning my loop again, two guards with the leather masks appear.

One hands the other what looks like a white key card, and the key card holder disappears from sight.

The one still lingering looks around before pulling out some type of compass looking thing.

"It's done," the guy states into the compass. "The prince's lover won't survive beyond the night."

Shit! Now I have to hopefully conjure enough power to also protect Lamar, even though I have no idea how to even access my power. Damn it.

Cursing, I sit down and start concentrating on the guys, wondering if I can zap myself to them even though I can't see them. It wouldn't be the first time I've done it, but definitely the first time I've done it on my own.

I picture Ezekiel first, thinking of how he touched me and let me feel. Then I go through the routine of thinking of each of them, feeling their presence grow stronger in my mind.

"Where the fuck have you been?" I hear Kai snap, causing my eyes to fly open and take in the fact I am most definitely back in their cell.

Whew.

Grinning, I look over, but my smile falls from my face when I see four angry glares on me.

"What?" I ask innocently, as Jude jerks his gaze away, his jaw ticking as his hands stay balled in fists.

Ezekiel gets in my face. "Where have you been?"

"I hitched a ride out of here and into the royal suite to get the release switch for these," I say with a shrug as I gesture toward their cuffs.

Just as Ezekiel opens his mouth to say something I probably don't want to hear, I say, "*Un bracco*."

The cuffs all open and fall off, and four surly men just stare at me like I've sprouted a second head.

"Now that you're free, does that mean you can siphon out of here?" I ask, even though I'm pretty sure they can't.

"No," Jude tells me warily.

"The soul stones," Gage reminds me, eyes narrowing.

"I think Gage's theory on her is definitely the most plausible at this point," Kai mutters, running a hand through his hair like he's frustrated.

No clue what that means, and it's doubtful they'll elaborate.

"Now that you're free, you can take turns watching each other's back and sleep in twos or something," I tell them, turning to walk through Smeagol's cage again.

"Where the hell do you think you're going?" Ezekiel asks as he blocks my path.

My eyebrows go up. "To help someone who doesn't have three others already looking after him. If I can. I'm not really sure if it's because I'm linked to the four of you that I can protect you, or if I'm just naturally protective of anyone I feel an attachment to. Hopefully it's the latter, because he's going to need my help."

I expect him to move aside, but he doesn't. And since I promised not to touch him, I don't pass through him either. When I start to sidestep him, Kai blocks my path, an angry glare on me again.

These guys are so frustrating.

"What'd I do now? Did I make myself look really suspicious because I got those cuffs off even though only guards or escorts or what-the-hell ever can do it? Well, I think you're wrong on that, or maybe—"

"I think you're a gift to us from Lilith," Gage says from behind me, causing me to spin around and look at him like he's crazy.

"The rest of us are leaning toward that now," Jude adds, tossing aside the cuffs.

"What?" I ask, confused.

"The timing, the ability to withstand hellfire and pass through soul stones, not to mention the fact our spell had been drained without our knowledge," Kai states randomly. "It all adds up."

"Then I apparently don't know devil math," I decide to point out.

"Lilith has a special interest in us for whatever reason. But as we've stated, a gift from Lilith is wrapped in a curse. By the time you reach the gift, you've already torn open the curse," Gage goes on.

I just stare at him for a minute, looking over my shoulder at him as I wait expectantly on him to elaborate. When he doesn't, I nod once.

"Right. I'm a curse, and the fact I've saved your lives is the gift." Totally bitter, by the way. But it does line up with the private thoughts I've had since their fight with Ezekiel.

Jude snorts.

"Not what he's saying," Ezekiel says, causing me to look back at him. "The gift is protection and exactly what we want," he adds, his eyes leisurely raking over me.

That gets an eyebrow arch from me.

"One woman able to handle all four of us, and someone who can fit…in," Jude goes on, causing me to look back at him as he stares directly at my ass with a smirk on his lips.

I know what he likes, and I wanted it really damn bad, until…he was a total dick. All of them have been.

"But we can't touch you yet," Gage resumes. "And we can also apparently touch you without each other when you are whole, which could harm the bond we've built over centuries."

I open my mouth to ask how, when Kai takes over.

"Because there's never been any jealousy before. Already you've stirred that. And that's sure as hell not something we can afford. Everything has a price, Keyla. We're trying to determine yours," Kai continues.

"More than you can afford, as you've told me multiple times," I grumble. "Don't worry. I'm almost positive I'll find a way to detach myself from you and become someone else's curse, because I'm about to do something that will definitely make me a hot suspect in your never-ending conspiracy theories."

Just as Ezekiel tries to grab at me, I pass through Kai and start moving through the walls.

"Keyla!" Gage's voice booms.

Obviously I ignore him. I have one of their sworn enemies to protect tonight.

They can spend a night without a cursed gift.

CHAPTER XVI

I never realized the perks to seeing but not being seen until the quad hell squad, as they called themselves, failed to live up to my very dreamy and super high expectations.

Lamar, however, is excellent company.

We like chilling in companionable silence.

Of course, he has no idea we're chilling at all.

Since seeing Manella, he hasn't been shouting for someone to hear about his innocence. It's like he's defeated, resigned to die whatever death is coming for him, just so he can save his love.

Who happens to be a child of the devil.

The devil's son has a more devoted lover than I've ever even dreamed of having.

Regardless of their lineage, I'm a sucker for a good romance, and I'm determined to make sure this one stays put together. Love like this doesn't deserve to be sabotaged.

"Any chance you could tell me how to fall in love? I mean, you chose the devil's son and still have more love than anyone else I've ever come across. Clearly you know what you're doing," I go on, striking up a one-sided conversation.

Lamar glances around, going on alert suddenly. I almost think he's heard me when he stands up and pales a little.

Without any warning, three men are suddenly in the room with us, and my breath leaves in a rush. Lamar straightens, staring at them with his wrists bound by cuffs like he's prepared to die with dignity.

The first one lunges, and my heart hits my chest as I dive in front of him. I'm not sure what exactly flies out of me, but all three men are blown into the cell wall so hard that it thunders with a metallic echo around us.

I stagger back, taking a major hit from that surge.

Lamar's eyes widen, but I barely glimpse him as the first leather-mask-wearing ghoul charges again.

"*Un bracco*!" I shout, and Lamar's cuffs fall away just in time for him to slam his fist through the heart of the man.

His power pulses with an eerie, ominous warning before a dark smile graces his lips. Gone is the man who was willing to accept death. This version of Lamar seems more fitting for an occupant of hell.

"Releasing me might give you honor in death, but it will definitely assure your death," Lamar tells them, not realizing it wasn't them.

I dive out of the way on instinct as a burst of energy booms from him, and three screams of agony tear through the air.

Well, then. I guess he doesn't really need my help. He just needed those cuffs off.

One of the guards manages to disappear in time to save his own life, but the other two are basically roasted, unable to get out.

I take a seat and watch the show.

I'm telling you, I'm going to eat the hell out of some popcorn one day.

As soon as there's nothing left but the dying echo of their screams and some ashes, Lamar reaches down and lifts his cuffs, breaking them with little effort. The crumpled heap is dropped near the door, and he takes a seat, sitting a little higher.

I get the feeling he left one alive for a reason.

I pat his shoulder, as though he can actually feel it, and he goes utterly stiff before looking directly through me. Did he feel that?

His eyes don't meet mine, since they're shifting back and forth in my direction like he's searching for something, meaning he can't see me.

Deciding to test my theory, I reach down and pat his hand. He jerks his hand aside, and growls. "What's in here? Show yourself, demon."

Demon? I think not. I've heard about demons.

After a few minutes of me keeping my hands to myself, I pull my knees to my chest. Not even he likes help from the unknown. I'm the reason he's alive, and whether he knows it or not, he's just like the hell squad.

In the devil's league, no one trusts anyone.

I guess I shouldn't take it personally.

CHAPTER XVII

"Keyla!" I hear Kai shouting a few days later. Or maybe it's been a week. Hard to tell.

There's no sunlight in hell. The only illumination is compliments of the pit of fire that loves to shoot up and hiss a warning to all the occupants. It lights the cells up through the stones, causing them to glow on occasion.

Lamar hasn't had any more visitors. He also can't seem to hear the guys when they shout my name on occasion. And they can't hear me when I try to answer, even though I haven't left Lamar to go to them just because they want to summon me.

I also haven't announced my presence to him again by touching him. I've gone out of my way to stay out of his way.

But now, for some reason, Kai's voice sounds extra urgent.

Lamar is sleeping at the moment, and since he's had a good eight hours, I pat his back. He immediately jerks upright, looking around as he blinks rapidly.

"Foolish, Lamar," he growls to himself. I get talking to yourself. It keeps you from going too loco when you're on your own. "You can live without sleep," he adds, shaking his head and slapping the side of his face to wake himself up properly.

Once I'm certain he's not going to doze back off, I pass through the cells until I'm finally back in with the guys.

"Just curious, how do you guys keep it from smelling like piss in here?" I ask as I step in, seeing them all staring at the wall I normally come back in through. "Not to mention the other gross bodily—"

They all turn as one, and Ezekiel snaps his teeth, eyes feral, as Kai and Gage curse and grapple him back before he can lunge at me.

"What the hell?" I ask, rushing toward him even as they try to keep him back. It's not like he can hurt me.

"He's been getting worse, but today he's fucking lost it. This is what we meant by the damn gifted curse," Gage gripes, struggling to restrain Ezekiel.

His pupils are almost taking up his entire eyes that are normally a blue color when gold isn't speckling his vision.

My hands go to his face, and I hold either side to the best of my phantom ability, even as he snaps his teeth through my face. This is one of those rare times where I'm thankful to not be a real girl.

"You're blaming me for this?" I ask absently.

"No. We're blaming Lilith," Kai says hesitantly, like he's worried I'll bail again if they piss me off. Accurate assumption, at the moment.

"He looks in on you all the time at the house when you disappear. He just does it without you knowing," Jude tells me before he winds up and punches Ezekiel so hard that it lays him out.

It's almost like I feel that punch too, and I go down with him, crashing to my knees at Ezekiel's side as his eyes roll back in his head.

"It's been bad since he was finally able to touch you," Kai says on a labored breath as he sinks to the floor next to Ezekiel. "I think it's dangerous for him to be separated too long for right now."

I mimic the motions of running my fingers through Ezekiel's

hair, even though not a single strand gets pushed out of place.

"Keyla, don't—"

"I've not touched him since you all ganged up on me and told me not to, but right now, I'll touch him if I damn well please. If you don't want me consoling him when he's clearly hurting, don't fucking yell for me to come in here and witness it," I interrupt, glaring over at Jude.

His lips curve into a slow grin.

"I was going to say don't leave for a while. What the hell are you doing anyway?"

"Looking for a new quad," I lie without hesitation.

Kai narrows his eyes on me, and Jude laughs under his breath.

"What are you really doing?" Gage asks seriously.

"Something you'll all hate me for, but I really don't care about your opinions anymore," I say with a cold smile, then return my attention to Ezekiel as his sleeping evens out.

Without giving a damn about their objections, I curl up next to him.

"I think I know how to get you out of here, but you should know Lucifer is the one who put you in here. And his reasoning really is to keep you safe, but it's believed to be because someone else is whispering ideas into his ear that he, in his apparently maddening state, is listening to without fail," I tell them as I prop my head on Ezekiel's chest, making sure I don't pass through it as I lay against his side.

Jude watches me, his eyes running the full length of our contact before his jaw tightens.

"How could you possibly know that?" Kai asks me, taking a seat right next to me, his body so close it almost passes through me.

"I spied on Manella while he was talking to Lamar," I say honestly.

Gage sucks in a breath, as Jude's tight jaw relaxes once again to make room for his smile.

"Lamar is out?" Gage asks.

"No. He's several cells over. Manella pulled strings to speak with him, and I listened to their very private exchange. Manella isn't the one trying to kill you, and Lamar was set up."

Jude's smile disappears so he can groan. "You don't seriously believe that, do you?"

"Unlike all of you, I trust that some things are exactly as they seem. They had no reason to put on a show for a ghost they didn't know was watching them."

Even though it feels wrong to share so many intimate details about Manella and his true love that I spied on, I still do. They don't have the capacity to believe in people, for whatever reason, but even I know love like that can't be faked.

I've watched a lot of romances. Nothing has ever felt that powerful and real. I envied each touch, each caress, and each heartbreaking moment of longing.

After I finish explaining the encounter, Jude runs a hand through his hair.

"If it's not Manella, who else would it be?" he growls, looking at the others.

"How do we know it's not Manella faking it in front of Lamar so that Lamar takes the fall?" Gage asks.

"He put some words on his arm and told him to run if he had to," I decide to add.

"And you haven't told us these words?" Kai snaps.

"I don't know the language, and I also wanted to stick around to make sure Lamar doesn't need more help, since he won't run. And Manella isn't faking it. I watched him sob uncontrollably after they took Lamar away. He'd never put him in this position willingly. Some people have hearts. Even the devil's most mysterious son, apparently."

They all stare at me like they don't know whether they're confused or pissed.

"You've kept us in here so you can keep an eye on Lamar, because you believe him and you've been protecting him, while Ezekiel was going through this internal riot?" Gage bites out.

"I had no idea Ezekiel was hurting. As for the four of you, you owe me. A lot. And you treat me like shit. I don't give a damn if I've inconvenienced you by making sure someone else just as ungrateful for my help stayed alive."

"At least she's proving she's honest," Jude drawls, even as he takes a seat at my feet before stretching out so that his head is passing through my ankles.

Rude much?

Rolling my eyes, I shrug. "I've never had a reason to be dishonest. It's not like you can kill me."

Kai makes a sound of amusement, and Gage shakes his head as he stretches out along the top, his head almost touching mine. We're in an odd, uneven square right now, with me trapped in the middle as I press against Ezekiel.

He's asleep, not just knocked out. I can tell by the steady rhythm of his breathing. It's a lot like the last time I slept with him.

"I don't understand you, little spirit," Kai says on a long breath.

"I don't understand me either," I confess.

A silence falls over us, and though I'm tempted to go check on Lamar, since he's alone, unlike the quad, I can't bring myself to leave. Guess that makes me a masochist.

Tingles course through my body from all four of them as they get more comfortable. I keep my eyes trained on the cell walls. For whatever reason they haven't been attacked yet.

That might have something to do with Lamar's botched attack. Maybe since their cuffs have popped off, no one—or *nothing*—has been brave enough to attack them.

With the cuffs, they should have been easily dispatched, even with all four locked in the same spot at the same time.

A weird sense of peace settles over me the longer the tingles last. Even Kai falls fast asleep. Though I'm sure none of them have slept much.

After all, it's hell in here.

CHAPTER XVIII

The guys have all fallen asleep, and it's another one of those times where I feel sleepy. Last time I felt that, I woke up a whole girl.

My eyes move around the stone cell, and I think about what a terrible idea being whole would be right now.

Something clanking heavily draws my attention, and I sit straight up when I strain enough to hear Lamar through the cells.

"Is that all you got?!"

Looking around, I get in Gage's ear—since he's the one who sleeps the most in this lot—and whisper, "Sorry. I need you awake."

He jerks, his hand rubbing his eyes as he frowns and looks around. "What the hell? I was finally sleeping without the nightmares for a change," he growls.

"Well, good. But do it when I get back. Something's going on, and I can't leave with all of you asleep."

I stand to my feet, and he leaps to his. "You can't leave at all," he tells me, eyes narrowing as he glares at me.

"Actually, I'm the only one who can," I tell him as I pass right through him.

He still tries to grab me, knowing he can't.

"Don't fucking leave, Keyla," he gripes, but I rush through the walls anyway.

Just as I land in Lamar's cell, another man appears. This one is a different kind of guard. His mask is white leather, and his wardrobe is red.

Lamar starts to do something, but the guy holds up his hands as a show of surrender. "I'm here on your prince's behest," the man states, tearing his sleeve up to show some sort of marking. "Lucifer has requested an audience with the two of you."

I quickly pat Lamar's arm, reminding him of the fact he's got those escape words and he's about to go before the devil, who might find that very suspicious if he's so innocent.

Though I feel absolutely nothing, Lamar subtly startles and tugs down his sleeve to cover the markings before the man sees them.

"Try something and I will kill you," Lamar cautions.

The man in the white mask nods, then his mask turns red. Totally creepy.

I reach for Lamar, touching his back, and finding it peculiar he stays relaxed instead of stiffened.

In a blink, we're out of the room, and suddenly we're alone with Manella, who is walking toward us in a brightly lit, elegant red room. He runs a hand through his hair, a small smile on his lips.

"My father has agreed to a meeting, and he seems fairly lucid today. He even called for me himself, and asked me to once again tell him about the night you were accused and your alleged true whereabouts. After I told him, he nodded and immediately sent for you."

Lamar doesn't look as excited as Manella, and that sends a prickle of dread up my spine.

"If he's lucid enough to read lies, he'll release you," Manella goes on.

Lamar gives him a tight smile. "We can only hope, my prince."

Manella jerks Lamar to him in a pre-celebratory embrace, and Lamar hugs him back, though his is a sadder, more desperate hold.

It makes me almost suspicious, but yet there's no guilt in his eyes. Only trepidation.

Manella pulls back, clearing his throat even as he keeps that boyish, carefree smile on his face. He looks like a completely different man.

"They'll send for you when it's your time to join us," he says, then grabs Lamar's face between both his hands and kisses him hard before jerking back again, that smile spreading.

Lamar just returns a smile that's so beautifully tragic it makes my heart hurt. Manella, oblivious, turns and darts out the doors, leaving them wide open as he vanishes from sight.

As soon as he's gone, Lamar clears his throat and straightens his clothing out in front of the mirror. In a blink, he looks clean and pressed, not a wrinkle on the clothes that were tattered only seconds ago.

"I'm not sure what you are," he says, causing me to look around for someone else in the room. It's just me. My gaze swings back as he blows out a breath and continues. "But if you're a gift from Lilith, I can only assume today I pay the price. Lucifer hasn't been lucid in many decades. It'd be much too hopeful to believe it's as Manella believes today."

Is he really talking to me right now?

"If you're my gift, I will pay the price without falter. But I only request that my damnation be his salvation, and you move onto protecting him without penalty."

That really makes my heart hurt.

He believes Lilith's price for protection is now the cost of his life. The true gift was borrowed time with Manella and seeing him happy one last time.

As happy as a man who is certain his true love is about to be his again.

I hate Lilith.

If I'm everyone's gift and curse, I hope a day comes when I'm able to save her, just so she can be damned in one way or another.

But as it stands, everyone I've protected has faced a consequence.

Five men I've saved. Five men have been locked in hell's throat. One of those men may die today.

Now his last wish is that I protect the one he's leaving behind without consequence. And I have no way of telling him that if I could control it, none of them would suffer.

"You will be busy in this trying time, I'm afraid," he says a little quieter.

I wonder if I'll be able to stop the devil from killing him.

Highly doubtful.

Furious and hurting, I follow him when a red masked man comes to collect. I'm assuming these are the royal guards, unlike the hell guards with black masks.

It's like the death mile with all the eerie paintings of the six royal devil spawns hanging every few inches. Paintings of them throughout time. One has Hera and all her blonde haired beautiful glory in front of the Trojan horse with a deviant smirk on her face.

I stop to try and make sense of the plaque underneath, and the weird symbols turn into actual words. Blinking, I hurry and read, in case the words disappear again.

Helen of Troy. A great war between two great countries, and the ruin of two feared or deeply respected kings.

Body count – massacre

Fear factor – little to none

Historical presence – heavy impact

Is this their weird Hall of Sick Fame dedicated to their earthly visits or whatever? Was she seriously Helen of Troy at one point?

I jog down the hall, but halt when I see another plaque hanging under a picture of a very sinister, yet highly sophisticated portrait of Cain in a top hat.

He's tipping the hat with very bloody hands.

Jack the Ripper. Leaving behind a legacy that still lives on even in new generations, and haunting of the minds of everyone once they hear the tale.

Body count – low

Fear factor – deadly hysteria

Historical presence – notorious impact

Considering I'd rather not add more reasons to make a run for it before I meet the maker of those psychotic people, I decide not to read anymore plaques.

I also quit looking at the pictures so that I don't get curious.

Out of place in the otherwise white décor, two massive, coal-black doors that tower over me slowly start to open. *Sure. Not ominous at all.*

Lamar takes a shaky breath, and then he steps inside.

I try not to piss my pants, because I'm about to be in front of the motherfucking devil.

CHAPTER XIX

We move through a short hallway, and Lamar navigates the bit of a maze we're in like he's done this countless times. With one quick inhale, he steps into another room, and I follow him.

My eyes take in the red and black décor, almost feeling cheated with how cliché and obvious it all is. It looks like an office, and the walls are lined with floor-to-ceiling shelves full of books. The room stretches up at least fifty feet, and I spin around, a little overwhelmed by the sheer wealth of knowledge concealed at the fingertips of the devil himself.

Sensing a presence, I look over just as another set of doors open, and in walks Manella, his bright smile still fixed to his relaxed face. Lamar is so rigid he looks ready to break.

Manella doesn't say anything, but he reaches over and grabs Lamar's hand, his excitement spilling over noticeably.

My eyes come up just as a debonair, regal man emerges from the same room Manella just exited. Dressed in black slacks and a white silk shirt, he moves toward us, his hands in his pockets as he gracefully glides across the floor, his steps fluid and effortless.

It's almost captivating how commanding his presence is.

I quickly move in front of Lamar on reflex when he steps toward him. A harsh burn spikes through my arms and chest, and

I suck in a breath, caught off guard, when he passes through me.

He stills, and I jerk away from the painful heat he radiates even in my form. Hellfire was doable. Devil fire? Apparently fucking not.

Whirling around, I see him completely stiffened, unmoving as Manella stares at him with a curious expression.

Oh no. Oh no no no.

The devil knows I'm here. Why did I think he wouldn't be able to at least sense me if I touched him, since Lamar can apparently sense me now?

Lucifer's head subtly tilts to the side. His eyes aren't on Lamar, just staring at nothing in particular, when he asks, "What have you brought to our meeting?"

Lamar clears his throat. "I believe it to be some protective gift, though I'm not sure who pressed it upon me," he says, bowing his head before adding, "my king. I can only assume it to be a gift from Lilith."

Slowly, Lamar lowers to his knees, and he presses his hands to the floor in a complete bow.

"You can stand, Lamar. This is a rather informal meeting," Lucifer states absently, almost as though he remains distracted. By me. The fact I'm in here and the devil knows it.

I'm going to die the second I get whole, because I'm a freaking idiot.

Lucifer rubs his chin pensively as he turns to face my direction. I freeze like a deer caught in headlights, but his eyes pass right over me.

To the untrained eye, he'd look like a refined man in his early forties, with the shine of an old, insightful soul in his eyes. It's not the feral, evil black eyes you expect to find when you meet the devil. It's very misleading.

"Very interesting. I caught wind of some of my guards attacking you in my custody." He says the words like they're of no real importance, and that knot of dread increasingly grows in my stomach.

Lamar frowns, but nods, even though he still hasn't gotten up from the floor. "Yes, my king," he states affirmatively.

"I've told you once to stand. I'd rather not repeat myself," Lucifer drawls.

Lamar slowly rises to his feet, keeping his eyes lowered as his body visibly vibrates with tension.

"I don't particularly enjoy my custody being violated," Lucifer goes on. "If any custody is protected, it most certainly should be mine. Wouldn't you think?"

I can't tell by his tone if he's being rhetorical, underhandedly vapid, or just curious.

Lamar just remains a block of stone, unmoving and silent.

"Well?" he prompts, casting a sideways glance to Lamar.

"Father, what are you—"

"Silence, Manella. I told you not to speak, or I'd ask you to leave," Lucifer interrupts with an eerily calm tone.

Manella swallows his words, casting a less certain look toward Lamar.

"Yes, my king, I would assume your custody would receive the highest protection."

Lucifer nods, clapping his hands together once. "I agree."

With a wave of his hand, ten men appear in shackles, all of them unmasked to show the horrifying faces. They look to have been burned off and scarred over. I have to look away from the hideously disfigured bodies as well, because those burns scrape every bit of flesh.

"These ten prison guards had access to your cell. I granted none of them access," Lucifer says with a bored tone and a lazy shrug.

Five more men appear in shackles, all of them looking just as gnarled and disfigured as the others. Humans wouldn't be able to survive such damage. Did this happen recently? Or is this their form after transition?

I totally get the masks now.

"These five are the ones I gave access to. One of my most trusted escorts, and four of my most trusted throat guards," Lucifer goes on.

He moves closer to the line of ten men. With a dark smirk, he winks, and the men drop to the ground, screams of agony ripping from their throats as they start convulsing. Black liquid oozes from their mouths, eyes and ears as they start gurgling, their screams being silenced as they drown internally.

Lucifer wipes a bit of black liquid away as though it's a cumbersome piece of dirt. The droplet falls from his sleeve and splatters to the ground before it's absorbed and lost from sight.

The ten dead men disappear from the room, an ominous silence falling over us in their tortured wake.

Swallowing thickly, I take a step away from the devil. Then another. And another. Until I'm against the wall.

Lucifer grins wickedly at Lamar. "Now to find out who exactly gave them access. It's been a long while since I had the ability to hear the lies so easily," he goes on, turning his attention to the five men.

The men have no expression as they remain shackled, since their faces are too distorted to relay any sort of emotion.

"What about you?" he asks the first one.

"No, my king," the man immediately says, bowing his head and exposing his throat.

Lucifer smiles broadly. "Truth," he says, moving down to the next one.

The same question and answer are repeated, and this one bows and exposes his throat as well.

When he moves to the third one, I notice a subtle tension spread through the guard.

"And you?"

The guard doesn't answer as quickly. "No, my king. Never," he says, bowing his head and exposing his throat.

"Lie," the devil says seconds before the man's head goes rolling.

Silence again.

There's no spraying of blood. No scream of warning. One second there's a head, and the next second it's bouncing around on the ground and rolling to a stop at Lamar's feet.

The body falls, jerking the line of shackled men around him closer together, since they're all chained to each other.

I follow Lucifer's gaze to Lamar, and the relief on the prince's lover's face is almost instant. The devil can hear a lie, which means he'll know it was never him.

The chains disappear, and the men step away from the fallen body before it also vanishes from sight.

Lucifer shifts his gaze and studies them briefly, before turning his attention to Lamar.

The four remaining men stand at a militant position, likely waiting to be dismissed.

"What were your whereabouts on the night the elder was attacked in neutral sanctuary territory?" Lucifer asks him.

Tears of pure relief cloud Lamar's vision as a smile spreads across his lips. "With my prince, my king. I spent the night in his chambers, and woke with him that next morning," he says, then swiftly bows, his entire body relaxed as he exposes his throat.

Lucifer glances to Manella. "He is cleared of the charges against him and remains under royal protection. An attack on him is an attack on us all," Lucifer adds.

Lamar barely manages to keep from sobbing, remaining in his

bowed state. Manella's eyes glisten as he bows at the waist to his father. "Thank you, Father. Thank you."

Lucifer snaps his fingers, and five men walk in. All their gazes search the room, seeing the four men instead of the fifteen originally sent in here. They stiffen and go to attention.

"Make sure it's recorded that my son's lover is exonerated of all charges. And place a royal inquiry into the true killer of the elder. Lamar is being framed, and I'll not tolerate these games," Lucifer drawls in a bored tone.

They all bow, then turn and swiftly walk out the way they came in. The four remaining fellows stay at attention, still waiting to be dismissed.

"You may return to your chambers with full pardon," Lucifer says to Lamar. "I'm sure Manella will join you shortly."

Lamar moves to his feet slowly, staying bowed at the waist. "Thank you, my king," he says as he darts a look full of relief and pure joy to Manella.

Manella nods subtly, his face remaining a stoic mask in front of the devil, though I know he wants to run out with Lamar.

"You're dismissed," Lucifer says to Lamar.

Lamar bows again, turning to walk out, giving the devil the last word. I quickly follow him out, and watch with a curse as he disappears from sight, likely going to Manella's chambers.

Shit.

Not this again.

Frustrated, I poke my head back through the door just as Lucifer holds a hand up. All four remaining men burst into flames, and their screams have me jerking my head back, unable to watch.

Why did he do that?

I wait until the screams go instantly silent before I peek back in, seeing nothing but ash before it disappears. Lucifer goes to a throne-like chair and takes a seat, getting comfortable as a dark smirk emerges to his lips.

"You knew nothing of the protective gift your lover had. I could see it in your reaction to that conversation," Lucifer tells Manella.

"No, sir," Manella answers absently. "Are you certain it's not something else? Is it still with us?"

Reeling back, I groan. I forgot the devil knew I was there.

Unable to help myself, I poke my head back in, but find the devil studying the spot where I was earlier.

"I'm not concerned with it, so speak freely," Lucifer finally says with a shrug, returning his attention to his son. "Though, if it is a gift from Lilith, you might want to visit with her and have her revoke it before the curse takes effect. If it hasn't already."

He, for some reason, stares absently at my spot again. I swallow audibly.

"You weren't able to read their lies, were you?" Manella asks him candidly.

Lucifer gives him the creepiest smile I've ever seen. "I'm afraid that gift has not returned. Though I did wake up a few months ago without the breaches of darkness clouding my mind. I've been trying to ascertain who has been taking advantage of my weakened state. Certainly none of your lovers. Lamar clearly believed I could read the truth, and was eager to spill it to me. Let's let him continue believing in such, along with all the others. As far as anyone is concerned, these four died for their own failure to see the traitor in their midst."

He claps his hands together as Manella smirks, looking more like the devil's son than I've ever seen him.

"You're finally back," Manella says like he's pleased.

"I certainly am," Lucifer says darkly. "And the devil isn't too happy with the traitors among us. Your siblings should not be suspect, though I'm sure you already suspect them."

"It wouldn't be the first time they've taken something precious from me," Manella growls.

"None so precious as your Lamar. None so powerful either," Lucifer states absently. "And they'd never create a mess such as this for me, especially not in the state I've been reduced to these past few centuries."

He does realize they're devil-spawn, right?

Manella bristles. "Tensions are high between the six of us right now. I'm afraid you'll be disappointed when you see us together now."

He nods, but a grin still stays fixed to his lips. "That's all going to change, my son. Everything is about to change."

The certainty and malice rolling off him sets my stomach into waves. I don't like how sure he sounds of himself. It can't be good when the devil is excited.

"Tell your siblings to look forward to a reunion." Lucifer shifts his gaze toward Manella again, the corners of his mouth turning out like the Grinch's as he adds, "Daddy's home."

A chill shoots through my spine, and I move back. Focusing hard, I find the boys presence, and I start to zap myself there, when they're suddenly standing right behind me.

I squeal a little, and Jude's wide eyes meet mine. Ezekiel looks half dazed, but his eyes clear when he spots me. Gage blows out a shaky breath, shaking his head as he runs a hand through his hair.

Kai opens his mouth like he's about to speak to me, when the two large doors open on their own.

"What are you doing here?" I hiss, freaking out. "The devil is in there."

The suicidal idiots just smirk at me. Jude even winks at me.

"Come on in, boys," I hear Lucifer drawl, and my entire body goes awash with cold.

Ezekiel passes through me, his eyes closing briefly as he breathes in deep, and I whirl around to follow them.

I really will try to kill the devil if he attempts to harm them.

And I'll find out just how good of a protective spirit I really am.

Or have my heart split four ways and set on fire.

One of the two.

CHAPTER XX

Another, smaller throne has appeared, and Manella is lazily lounging next to Lucifer. The devil is casually sipping from a champagne flute that I don't recall him having earlier, as we step forward.

The doors slam shut, and I step up behind them, ready for whatever.

"Rather interesting quad you fellas must be to keep getting so much attention," Lucifer drawls.

The guys all seem a little too freaking relaxed for my taste.

They bow as one, all of them folding at the waist but not dropping to their knees the way Lamar did.

"All the way to the ground," I hiss, worrying about the respect level.

Lucifer's lips just twitch when they remain bowed at the waist.

"This is informal. You may stand," Lucifer says, not seeming disrespected or offended.

They straighten with the same synchronization as they bowed.

They all take a stance with their arms behind their back and their legs spread shoulder-width apart—a militant stance resembling the one the guards used.

"What's so special about you?" Lucifer asks, his eyes drifting from one to the other.

"We never died," Ezekiel answers without hesitation.

It's subtle, but I notice the slight widening of the devil's eyes, as though that surprises him. He darts a look to Manella, and Manella nods once.

Lucifer's grin curls like he's delighted before he returns his gaze to them.

"Yet you're in the underworld, able to breathe, able to move about like all the others. Very interesting indeed. How did you transition?" he muses.

"We're not wholly sure about those details," Jude answers a little too easily. "We were hoping to earn our ticket here and discover those answers from you."

Lucifer grins, swirling the champagne once before finishing it off. The glass disappears once it's empty, and he leans up, steepling his hands in front of his face as he studies them with renewed interest.

"And it took you some centuries to earn a spot in the trials, from what I've learned. I assumed the documents were just lazily prepared when I didn't discover a previous stay in hell's throat," Lucifer says, almost as though he's a little excited.

I glance at the four of them, seeing their faces stoic and unnervingly calm. The devil is excited about them? That's…terrifying. Just what sort of guys did I go and get myself tethered to?

I know they're lethal, unapologetic, certainly psychotic, and inherently dangerous, but I didn't know they'd get the devil giddy.

"We had assumptions we were being kept out intentionally, given our consistently high rankings with the surface guardians," Kai states honestly.

Manella smirks. So does the devil.

I hate this.

I hate this a lot.

The devil cuts his eyes toward Manella, but Manella pointedly ignores him, never losing his secretive smirk.

"I've heard you were under the assumptions Manella was the one doing so," Lucifer tells them.

They say nothing.

Lucifer's grin grows, and Manella rolls his eyes.

"I can assure you that the royal family has no interest in who makes the trials. Our guards are hand-selected, and the trials are just for the lower levels starting out in the underworld," Lucifer goes on. "In fact, the four of you are the first-ever trial runners that any of us have taken an interest in."

That has the four of them stiffening ever so slightly. Me? I'm a fucking mess right now.

If I had tangible fingernails, I'd have chewed them off. I'm pacing back and forth behind them as it is.

"Of course all the quads rouse interest, so I suppose that's not entirely true," the devil goes on, contradicting himself with weird double-talk.

I remind myself the devil is tricky.

"My interests lie in the fact that someone certainly did try to keep you four away from hell. In fact, it was so imperative that you transitioned without death. A feat never heard of before."

He stands, and I go still, my eyes warily on him as he stretches like he's been sitting for too long. Lazily, he fingers the buttons on his sleeve before rolling it up to his elbow. Then does the same to the other.

The devil likes suspense.

"I'm interested in knowing how you came to believe it was Manella who was against you," he says, placing his hands on his hips.

Jude is the one to answer. "He's in charge of the trials."

That's it?

That's their whole point of conjecture?

"If you have a little more evidence, now would be the time to share it," I whisper-yell at them. "You're accusing the devil's son of a crime," I remind them.

They do nothing.

"He's only in charge of the fun stuff," the devil states dismissively, once again not seeming offended. If anything, he's amused.

"I had no idea you even existed until you were entered into the trials," Manella says on a sigh.

"That's a lie. He and Lilith discussed the quads making it through the night, and a hit that was out on you during the gauntlet run." Then I pause. "Well, that was after the first part of the trials, though, wasn't it?" I muse aloud.

Kai gives me a shut-the-hell-up side eye before returning his attention to Lucifer.

Right. Talking aloud is just distracting, since the four of them are the only ones who can hear it.

"Surface guardians, though greatly appreciated, especially in such trying times as we currently face, are not exactly under royal view," Manella goes on. "We rarely know what they're doing up there unless one of us has gone back as a mortal."

The guys exchange a brief look, but their expressions give nothing away.

"Whoever has been trying their damnedest to keep you out of hell has been very influential in the part of the equation we're very lax in," Lucifer goes on. "Perhaps we should pay better attention to the surface guardians after all."

Manella groans like that task has just been pressed upon him.

"Would you rather Lilith or Cain be the ones to oversee it?" Lucifer asks him, eyebrow arched. "Perhaps the twins or Hera?"

Manella curses under his breath. "I'll start it as soon as the trials are complete," Manella relents grudgingly.

When the devil steps down, he's suddenly right in their faces. I pass through the guys immediately, stepping between the devil and them like I'm ready for anything.

Lucifer immediately takes a step back, a knowing smile gracing his lips when his eyes settle on me. He doesn't meet my gaze, so I really hope that means he can't see me.

"There you are again," he tells me, still grinning. "You do like to protect the weaker from me, don't you?"

The guys, for the first time, seem a little worried. At least I think so. I can feel their tension more than I can see it, because I'm not taking my eyes off the devil.

"Just where did you stumble across this thing that guards you?" he asks them.

I'm assuming he certainly can't see me if he's not referring to me as a woman. It'd be rude to call me a *thing* otherwise, and though the devil is evil, he's not overtly rude. At least not from my observations.

Though he did kill a bunch of guys just because he couldn't sense a lie.

I suppose they probably found that rude.

The guys hesitate for too long, and a bit of pride swells in me when I think they're not going to tell him.

"He already knows I exist. Just be honest," I say to them, my eyes still on the devil.

He tilts his head, studying them, that smile lifting more as they all give him their attention again.

"A little over a month ago we discovered…*it,*" Kai tells him.

I turn and glare at him. "It? Fucking really?" I snap.

His lips twitch, but his eyes remain on the devil.

Muttering a few choice words, I face the devil again, only to see him too intrigued.

"Very interesting indeed," he says, stroking his jaw thoughtfully. Manella has sat up straighter, his eyes passing over me like he's searching for me as well. "And has it protected you?" he asks.

Jude clears his throat. Ezekiel answers, "Yes." No elaboration.

"A gift from my eldest, I presume?" Lucifer asks, his eyes on my forehead, though they pass over me a couple of times too.

"Lilith has taken a special interest in us these past several years. It's the reason we assumed the royal family held an interest in surface guardians," Gage answers.

The devil tilts his head. "I suppose I need to convene with my eldest."

He claps his hands together, his eyes flitting over the four of them. "As of now, I don't find it in your best interests to keep you protected in the throat. You'll return to the surface until the trials commence. I'll grant you some parting gifts that will certainly protect you up there." His eyes pass over me again. "Though it's clear you already have one form of protection."

He turns and walks back toward his throne, sitting down with flourish and that same enigmatic grin as the boys neglect to show gratitude.

At least it's not just me they don't thank.

I'm distracted by the sound of a cry of pain, and my breath catches as I strain to listen.

The devil starts talking again, but I tune him out, listening as Lamar shouts.

"Lamar is under attack!" I shout, rushing out, passing through the walls and following the sound of his voice as it grows louder.

"I've been exonerated!" he shouts.

Just as I pass through a room full of black décor, my eyes

widen.

Fifteen or more guards are surrounding a bleeding, weak Lamar who is bruised and battered, staggering as he clutches his wounded gut. I dive to his side, my heart hammering in my chest now.

He's in his boxers, seemingly caught unaware while his guard was finally down.

They all charge forth, and the power shoots from me with so much force that it blows them all back. Some even crash through the walls, and I whirl around, feeling that acidic power rattling around in my veins, hungry to deliver death instead of just disorientation.

Some scatter and disappear, even as Lamar struggles to use his power. His veins are turning the same black I've seen before, and I try to heal him the way I did Kai.

It doesn't work. No tingles are present.

Just as another man charges forward, I send him flying back again with one harsh wave of my hand. The acidic power remains burning in my veins, wishing to be used.

I'm terrified to use it so close to Lamar though, especially with him already in the process of dying.

By the time the rest of them leap to their feet, my guys are bursting forth, and Jude blurs to two of them, his fists hitting them so hard in their chests that the fists go through the bodies. They shake violently and collapse to the ground, their bodies instantly turning to ash.

Kai grabs two by the heads, and their veins turn red as they start to convulse. My mouth dries when I see Jude's and Kai's blackened eyes.

Gage and Ezekiel trot in and prop against the walls, unaffected by the whole thing.

But just as more appear, they all burst into flames. My heart pummels my chest, worried the guys are next, but it's only the traitorous guards who scream in agony.

Lamar is on the ground, and I drop to be beside him as the devil walks in. Manella charges into the room, rushing to Lamar's side. His hands go to him as Lamar starts to shake violently, the poison eating away at him.

Manella whispers a few words, and Lamar's eyes roll back in his head as the veins in his body start to slowly push the black out. It comes out through his nose like it's running away, puddling on the ground as it vacates his body.

Manella blows out a breath of relief as he cradle's his lover's head in his lap.

Lucifer takes in the scene curiously, his eyes flicking to me again like he can sense my presence more.

"I'm afraid it's time for you boys to resurface. I'm going to have to restrict access to these floors," Lucifer announces dispassionately, never looking at them. "It'll cost you your lives if you tell anyone what happened here today."

He gives them a dark grin. "Wouldn't want someone thinking I'm so weak that I can't even control my guards anymore."

The guys all give one nod of understanding.

Lucifer returns his gaze to Manella, as Lamar takes his first easy breath, groggily waking up as his body continues to heal.

"Thank you," Lamar chokes out, looking around like he's searching for someone.

My stupid smile spreads when I realize he's seeking me out to offer gratitude.

Kai arches an eyebrow at me, and I wipe the grin from my face. Ezekiel smirks at me, and I roll my eyes as I turn and pass through the wall, ready to return home.

"Don't forget your spirit when you go," the devil says. "You'll need it more than Lamar will. And apparently there's only one to go around."

Jude casts me a curious gaze as he walks out and steps into me, but I say nothing as we vanish from hell with the devil's blessing.

I'm not sure what the devil's blessing incurs, and I dread finding out.

CHAPTER XXI

The second we're back in their massive excuse for a home, Jude steps away from me, going to the fridge to grab a beer. The other three appear, and he tosses them all a beer as well.

Ezekiel goes to grab his phone from the kitchen island as it appears as well, and he immediately orders several pizzas. The rest of them are already drinking, and I stand off to the side, now feeling like the awkward outsider again.

I can't believe they're not even discussing anything, and I'm scared to be the one to broach the conversation.

They sit down at their table, and I just watch from my spot, wanting to go to my chair, but worried they'll ask me to leave.

They quietly sit in their normal places, elbows resting on the table as they drink their beers. Every time they finish a beer, one gets up and goes to pass out new ones.

Several empty beer bottles pile up in no time, as they just keep on drinking in weird silence.

When the pizza arrives, Ezekiel leaves, going to greet the delivery guy at the door before he can even knock.

I continue just lingering in my spot, watching them even as they elect to ignore me.

Their gazes are all absently fixed on the dining room table as Ezekiel returns with the pizzas, acting as though they're comfortable just resting in peace. They all eat from their own box, still not speaking.

It's all rather underwhelming. I'm tempted to leave, but I'm curious what they're going to say when they finally do speak.

As Jude drains the last of his beer, Gage pushes aside the little bit of pizza he has left. Ezekiel is the one to finally break the silence.

"We really just held a private audience with the motherfucking devil."

Kai's beer pauses at his lips for a moment, then he drinks the rest of it. Jude starts laughing humorlessly, looking exhausted as he scrubs his face with a hand.

I look at all of them when they start laughing with him.

Psychos. I knew it.

"I'm not sure what's so funny about now being on the devil's radar," I dryly point out.

The laughter cuts off immediately, and they all turn to look at me like they just remembered I'm in the room.

Shrinking under their intense stares, I clear my throat. "I think I'll go to my room. Try not to get killed or anything."

They say nothing, and I mutter, "Good night," without turning around.

It's actually day time, but I assume they'll be crashing for several long hours, considering the events that have happened over the course of the last few days or weeks or however long we've been gone.

My room is predictably unchanged, and I lie down on my bed, sighing as I stare up at the ceiling.

The outfit I'm wearing turns into an elegant dress, fully equipped with diamond studded shoes. It's an odd lounging outfit, but it makes me feel important. Dress for the role you want instead of the role you have, right?

I wonder what it's like to be a part of something. To feel as though you know your purpose and have your people.

"How did Lucifer know you were there?"

Ezekiel's voice startles me, and I look at the entryway to see all four of them propped up inside my room, staring at me like they've been there for a while.

Jude is drinking another beer, his eyes leisurely raking over me.

"Lamar could sense me, but he couldn't see me or hear me. Same thing with the devil," I answer automatically.

They continue to stare at me with no expressions on their unreadable faces.

"It was sort of cute how she stepped in front of us when he advanced on us," Gage says with a smirk forming.

I bristle. It was badass. Not *cute.*

"Like she could take down the devil if he saw it fit to end our lives for the trouble he's dealing with," Jude adds, the beginnings of a mocking grin toying with the edges of his lips.

Dicks.

"*It* was even interesting to the devil himself," Kai adds, a taunting glisten in his arrogant eyes.

Lounging comfortably, I give them all a wry look.

"It's been a rather tiring experience. If you're done making a mockery of me, I'll take some peace and quiet now," I retort, eyeing my fingernails like they're far more interesting than the sexy, deviant pricks in my room.

"Why'd you choose the room farthest from ours?" Ezekiel muses, seeming just as entertained as all of them. I suppose he's out of his feral trance for good, at least for now.

"You're smart boys. I'm sure you can figure it out," I tell them, alluding to a lie. But they don't get to hear the truth.

Their amusement dies, and they all level me with a hard glare.

"Bipolar much? Or do you just prefer to dish it, yet have the inability to receive?" I ask idly, smirking like I'm winning this game of tongue.

Jude's smirk returns as a dark look passes his face. "We all enjoy receiving, little spirit."

Admittedly, my temperature rises, but I play it cool, aiming for aloof. How exactly does one achieve aloofness?

Ezekiel looks around my room, stepping away from the wall. It's a rather large room. If I had any toiletry needs, I'd have my own private bathroom as well.

"Why does a spirt need a bedroom?" he asks. "Especially when she doesn't sleep?"

"*She* has never been able to stay away from the lot of you for longer than ten minutes in the past. Now *she* prefers her space while *she* tries to figure out how to attach herself to a new quad."

His eyes darken on me, but Kai just releases a rumble of laughter.

"That threat is getting a little tired, don't you think?" Gage drawls.

"Not sure exactly how that's a *threat.* A threat would be warning you that *it's* going to put the damn lotion on you before hacking you to bits and feeding you to ravenous cannibals," I point out, feeling rather impressed by my creative threat.

They all look amused now.

I give up.

I never know how they're going to react to any given situation.

"Is that all?" I groan. "I would think you'd all be too tired for this pointless banter."

Ezekiel picks up the remote, turning on the TV, and my eyes

widen. I had no idea that even worked. Hell, when did it even get in here? It didn't used to be. It looks brand new.

He pulls up a familiar movie, and my heart beats a little faster as he starts Pinocchio a little before the spot I got to when they interrupted me.

I get ghostly tears in my eyes as a smile stretches across my face. He doesn't meet my gaze as he tugs his shirt over his head, and my smile evaporates.

"What are you doing?" Gage and I both ask him at the same time.

"I'm sleeping in here," he answers absently, coming and beginning to strip the bed out from under me, pulling off the dusty covers.

The sheets and blankets pass through me, as he moves to a drawer and pulls out some clean replacements.

The other three exchange a look, and I try not to let my attention be divided between the jackasses on TV and the ones in my room.

"I'm not so sure that's a good idea," Kai tells him warily.

"I've stayed away from her like all of you wanted, and it drove me mad when I couldn't see her at all. Doesn't matter what's going on or what she is, it's clear I'm already stuck. I'm going to at least get some good fucking sleep while I can," he answers them as he quickly makes the bed.

I never move from the bed, just allowing the sheets to pass through me. They really have no personal boundaries where I'm concerned and take complete, borderline rude, advantage of my translucent form.

"I didn't agree to that, and this is my room," I point out, holding my finger up.

He ignores me, sliding into the bed beside me.

"What happens if she goes whole again?" Gage points out.

Jude smirks as he comes forward. "I'll stick around and make sure he doesn't do anything to make his affliction worse."

Kai rolls his eyes, dragging him back by his shirt.

"Gage will stay to run interference," Kai argues.

"Why the fuck would I stay?" Gage growls as Jude rolls his eyes and turns to walk out.

"Because you're the only one who doesn't want to see what she feels like," Kai says, clapping Gage on the shoulder.

Nervousness wads in my stomach. What if it does make me whole? That's such a double-edged sword. On one hand, it'd be a dream come true. On the other, it's a death sentence with these four.

I'm not convinced they won't fuck me and then kill me while I'm still stuck in that dopey orgasm haze they leave women in.

"No one is sleeping in here. I don't want to turn whole just to make my death easier for you," I gripe. "And I'm not entirely convinced that had anything to do with it."

Considering I was feeling the overwhelming urge to close my eyes and rest in the cells when they were all touching me, I'm almost positive that's how I turned whole.

I've just been in denial.

Damn Lilith. I still hate her.

Ezekiel's arm passes through my waist as he gets comfortable, his eyes already closing as he settles down, not even acknowledging my refusal.

Cursing, Gage shoulders by Kai, tearing his shirt over his head on his way toward the bed.

Kai smirks over his shoulder at me. "If she turns whole, restrain her. Don't kill her. Maybe we can figure out what's really going on once we have a way to pry answers out of her."

I flip him off, and he chuckles as he turns and leaves me with Gage and Ezekiel. Gage strips down to his boxers, like Ezekiel already is, and he climbs into bed on the other side of me.

Gage makes a conscious effort not to touch me, and I roll my eyes. "Just take him out of here after he goes to sleep, and we both get what we want," I tell *One*.

"Do it, and I'll punch you when I wake up," Ezekiel says in a muffled voice against his pillow.

Gage snorts derisively, rolling over to put his back to me.

I stare at the TV, as Ezekiel picks up the remote and rewinds it, not even looking. Somehow, he starts the movie at the exact right part. It distracts me from the fact I really don't want them in my room, and I sit up as my clothes change.

Ezekiel lifts his head, then laughs under his breath before shaking his head. Gage turns his head to look at me, then rolls his eyes as I sit in my Pinocchio outfit.

"Tell me what popcorn is like," I say absently, riveted as poor Pinocchio barely escapes. But I can feel his heavy heart from here. It's like he can't catch a break.

I know the feeling, little guy.

"Salty, gets stuck in your teeth, and not really all that filling, but weirdly addictive," Ezekiel answers in a quiet, almost sleep-rasp voice.

"Sounds perfect," I say with a small grin.

Gage is already sleeping, I realize, when he subconsciously rolls over, his hand slipping through my waist. The peaceful expression on his face has me rolling my eyes and feeling rooted to this spot regardless of the dire consequences.

"If I turn whole and you guys tie me up, I can promise I'll use my protective powers to protect myself. And I won't even feel bad about it."

Ezekiel smiles lazily, his eyes never opening. "If I tie you up, I can promise you that you'll enjoy every fucking moment of it."

Not sure why I feel a wicked little shiver up my spine, considering I've already decided I'm too good for them.

Deciding it's safer to stare at the TV than talk to Ezekiel, I sit rigidly. I'll get up if my eyes feel heavy again.

My mouth opens for a yawn, weirdly enough. But no way will I…fall…asleep.

CHAPTER XXII

My eyes fly open, and I hold really still as the pressure on my waist has my entire body warming up. Two different hands are touching me there, holding me to them, as two very hard bodies press against my sides.

I fell asleep.

Watching Pinocchio.

And now I'm a real girl.

Between two real killers.

And I'm frozen in place, because I don't want to be tied up or killed.

Trying not to breathe too heavily, I start to sit up, careful not to disturb them.

The hands on my waist tighten, as I struggle to do the simple task of lifting my body. This…is not what I expected. Gravity is a real bitch, and I'm not used to feeling it.

It takes more effort to rise up than I expected, and the hands slide to my lap abruptly when I forget about them—and gravity. I go still, not even breathing, as the two men on either side of me stir ever so slightly.

There's a back door on this wing. I can slip down the stairs back here and be out before they even notice me missing. I'm also faster than them, so that shouldn't be an issue.

Except…gravity. I hope that doesn't affect my speed.

Ignoring all the raging hormones in my suicidal, traitorous body, I carefully remove their hands from my lap, gently placing them on the bed.

Just as I'm about to try to slide down the bed, a hand darts out and snags my arm so unexpectedly and roughly that I cry out.

Ezekiel jerks awake, and I turn to look at Gage as he stares at me with wide, wild, hungry eyes, his grip on my arm tightening to be almost bruising.

Our eyes stay locked, as I accidentally stay frozen in horror like a statue. His nostrils flare, and he looks to be visibly straining not to do something terrible.

"Tell me that's bad, and I won't touch her," Ezekiel says, his breath whispering across my shoulder, the heat of it causing my eyes to roll back in my head as a full body shiver wracks me.

Now is so not the time to be a woman. I'm almost certain it's unnatural to forget one's life is in danger at a moment like this.

A groan is pulled from Gage's throat, and before I can blink, he moves in a blur, coming at me so fast I can't stop him.

His lips crash against mine almost violently, and I try to bite him, only to have him shove his hand in my hair, aggressively turning my head to give him better access as his tongue sweeps in and steals my fight.

My hands fly to his shoulders, and two other hands move to my waist, as a set of incredible lips find my neck. Both of them touching me, surrounding me, intoxicating me with sensory overload…is almost too much.

Gage's hand starts tearing open the buttons of my shirt, when reality smashes back in.

Fear spikes my blood, and I shove them both off, stunning them for just a second as I throw myself off the bed…and crash through the floor in my phantom form, falling all the way downstairs.

A scream leaves my lips when I go from ghost to whole again, and land hard on my side in the downstairs library. Pain shoots up my side, and I groan while cursing my luck.

"Did you hear that thump?" Ezekiel says from above me as feet hit the floor.

"She's whole again," Gage answers, dark excitement in his tone.

Feet start pounding down the staircase immediately, as Gage shouts, "She's a real fucking girl, boys!"

Ezekiel's dark laughter follows that. With every ounce of strength I have, I push to my feet, and I…stumble around like a baby deer on one of those nature shows.

My legs feel weak, shaky, and not at all like I expected. Everyone makes walking seem so easy.

I kick out of the ridiculously uncomfortable wooden shoes, since those seem to be wreaking havoc on my flimsy ankles.

I barely catch myself against the desk, and I push my knees back straight, straining as a cold sweat breaks out over my skin. Fear prickles the back of my neck as they near the door, and suddenly I feel the weight leave me as gravity ceases to exist.

Looking down, I fist pump the air, seeing my phantom body is back, and I race through the library wall, darting toward the back door. But then…I'm falling and sliding, pain shooting through me again.

A silent curse gets swallowed when I look down at the useless piece of shit legs that are flesh again.

What the hell is going on?!

I can't tell if I'm leveling up or short circuiting.

When I get my glorious, weightless body back, I push up and race through the walls, getting as far away from the nearing voices as possible.

"Where the fuck is she?" I hear Gage snap.

"What the hell is going on?" Kai snaps, his voice muffled through the many layers of walls between us.

I'm mid-stumble all of the sudden, once again on those baby deer legs. Barely restraining the cry of frustration, I clutch the dining room table, looking at the closet in the living room.

But before I can make it, Kai is suddenly appearing in front of me, a dark smile twisting his lips as he rakes his eyes over me. "Not exactly the sexiest thing you could be wearing, but clothes are always optional."

He's suddenly on me, shoving me against the wall, and becomes the only thing holding me up when his lips find mine. He groans into my mouth as he presses against me, and through his thin boxers, I can feel just how turned on he is.

I kiss him back, my hands sliding up to the back of his neck, as I pull back my knee and shove it up as hard as I can.

With a cry, Kai breaks the kiss and stumbles back, doubling over as he cups his balls and groans.

"Tie me up now, dickhead," I gloat, then squeal when he lunges at me again.

I feel it when my body shifts this time, turning into my phantom phase, and he passes right through me, crashing against the wall so hard plaster falls off in clumps. Then he turns his narrowed gaze at me.

I flip him off with both fingers, then run like hell before I can get cursed with those useless legs again.

"She's down here!" he calls out.

I dive into the closet in the billiard room just before I turn whole again, and I wobble on unsteady legs as I hang out with all the pool sticks and stuff, panting heavily.

Running is tiring when you can feel gravity, damn it. My

phantom form was just dense enough to keep me from floating away, but I was still effectively weightless. I hate gravity. It's a total pain in the ass. And I need more practice with my legs before I have to run for my life.

"Where the fuck did she go?" I hear Jude snap, and Kai laughs darkly.

"I don't know, but she tastes too damn good to be anything less than terrible for us."

"You fucking idiot, you kissed her?" Jude groans.

"My dick still hurts from how good she felt. And from how painful she felt too. Vicious little thing," Kai adds.

"Where'd she go?" I hear Gage snap.

Focusing really hard, I try to single out the feeling of transitioning from one form to another, harnessing the emotions that led to each. If I'm not short circuiting, maybe my level-up includes a package where I can be either or.

I'd really like to be untouchable in this moment.

It's hard to concentrate when they're tearing the house apart in search of me, but when I feel myself go weightless, I open my eyes and breathe out a sigh of relief, seeing right through my hand.

Concentrating again, I manage to turn back whole, feeling the energy surge through me with the awareness and crisp senses that come with it. It feels good to be a real fucking girl, but it's also terrifying.

The door swings open, and my gaze darts up as Jude releases a slow, dark grin. Before the worst of them can get his hands on me, I smirk, and he passes right through me the second he lunges.

I strut out in my untouchable form, now feeling as though I have control, and I grin at them as they all barge into the room. I feel the glares before I see all four of them.

"Guess what, boys? I just leveled up." As soon as the words leave my mouth, I force the flesh to return, even as I wobble a little.

The second they move, I turn back, grinning as my untouchable phase offers me a fuck-you shield.

"What the actual hell?" Jude asks, slinging broken pool sticks around as he angrily stalks out of the closet.

I turn to flash a grin at him over my shoulder. "It's amazing how much survival instincts aide a girl when she needs them most."

His grin slowly forms when I feel the pressure of gravity again, and I curse, wobbling until I crash into a strong body. Two arms come around me, and warm breath fans against my ear.

"What was that?" Ezekiel asks in a taunting whisper as he rips my shirt open.

It takes a lot of effort, but I manage to shift again, and I pass through his hands, blowing out a relieved breath.

"Fucking savages," I accuse, pointing at all of them as I start backing out of the room on my good legs instead of those stupid real legs.

"It's cute the way you act like you don't want it now that you can have it," Gage tells me.

Four wicked grins stay fixed to their devilishly tempting faces. "No," I say loudly. "Not happening. You don't all get to kiss me stupid so that I forget I sort of hate your ungrateful asses."

"We're not going to kill you, Keyla," Ezekiel says, moving closer. "We just want to make those fantasies of yours come true."

"Ha! Worst pickup line ever," I lie, hoping they don't hear that pathetic little tremor of hesitation in my voice.

After all, I did spend a lot of time thinking of little else. I'm starting to realize there are far more important things in life.

I flicker back to flesh before I manage to strain and concentrate on staying untouchable. It's getting harder to do now. It's like my body demands a little time in its new form, and I'm denying it.

"She can't hold it much longer," Jude says with a deviant spark in his eye, just ready to pounce.

A very important thought occurs to me, and I feel like an idiot for not thinking of it sooner. I'm going to blame it on the fact I finally have adrenaline, and it makes you super durable, but hella stupid.

If I've seen a place before, I can zap myself there. Well, maybe not all the way to hell, but definitely to Purgatory and anywhere in range within the states.

A grin curves my lips. And if I'm whole…I might not need their presence to exist. Which means I can go anywhere without them. Seems like the perfect time to test that theory.

"If you really want to touch me, you have to woo me." I say this with a straight face, but I almost cringe when I hear the words aloud in one fluent sentence.

They all give me an incredulous look.

"Woo you?" Jude finally asks, his eyebrows arched in utter confusion, as though it's the most preposterous thing he's ever heard.

"Yes. If I'm going to be sticking around until I know for certain the devil isn't going to strike you dead, then I might as well be getting some perks before I leave the four of you to continue on in your hellish ways. I'll get the four of you, and you'll get my protection. Then we'll part ways, and I'll go find my one true love, while the four of you move back on to your harem of women."

"Harem?" Gage asks, a sardonic curve to his lips.

I flicker between forms again, but manage to hold on a little longer. I need to get this all out.

"Harem is an interesting choice of word, considering you're the one getting four of us at once, while we only get you," Ezekiel points out with a devious twist of his lips.

"Yes, you'll be my harem. Deal with it. I'm the only one who gets access to you for the duration of however short our time left together may be. In return, I get the ultimate experience to start my new life out with a bang."

I flicker again, sucking in a breath as I strain harder.

"Start your new life out with a *bang*. Again, interesting choice of words," Ezekiel states with that same infuriating expression.

"I get my fantasy," I go on, not letting him deter me, since my time is very limited for how much longer I can hold the new form back.

"All the things you've done to coerce a woman—"

"*Seduce* a woman," Gage interrupts, smirking. "Not *coerce*."

"—into bed with you," I continue, not acknowledging the interruption. "I get that. All of it. Everything I've had to watch over the past five years."

"Five years? Before we even get sex? I can't even count the number of women who've been in here in that span of time," Kai growls, as though I'm ludicrous.

I open my mouth to speak, but Jude waves his hand. "No need to recite the number, *comoara trădătoare*," he says, his accent subtly shifting to one I can't pinpoint on the last two words.

"What did you just call me?" I ask, then shake my head when I remember I'm on a timer here. "Never mind. Not the important part," I go on calmly.

"I want five-and-a-half years of seduction, and not just the touching kind. Roses. Jewelry. Fancy dinners. All of it. I want the same amount you did for them crammed into the limited amount of time we have."

"High maintenance little piece of ass, aren't you?" Kai asks with an eyebrow arch.

I point a finger at him. "You'll be lucky if you get to do more than watch. I'm the one getting to be selfish in the bedroom, while selflessly risking my life for you and following around your ungrateful asses."

Another flicker that I force back has me taking a deep breath, that fortunately helps to calm me. Bonus.

The other three guys just grin over at Kai.

"It'd almost be worth it just to see you suffer," Jude states, his grin growing.

Kai snarls at him, and then turns his glare on me.

"You'll change your mind."

"Highly unlikely," I dutifully point out. "If you want to touch me while I protect you, because I'll be protecting you regardless, then you need to remember how very important it is to woo me. The sex will happen naturally and at my speed, while the wooing continues in between bouts of it. And I'll let you do almost anything to me. As long as my fantasies get put out for me as well."

"We've had a taste. What happens if you leave and we start losing our minds the way E did already?" Gage asks, a very scary look on his face that has me questioning my confidence. I'd say it had me questioning my sanity, but that went years ago.

"I thought we agreed we weren't going to touch her for that very reason," Jude points out as though he's being reasonable and accusatory in the same breath.

"You felt it. You went after her too," Gage tells him without looking away from me.

"You were just too slow," Kai adds, smirking as he darts a taunting look toward Jude.

Jude's jaw clenches, and he forces his eyes back to me. "I take it back. It wouldn't be almost worth it. It's definitely worth it. Sign me up. Tell me how many fucking roses or bracelets you want. Who gives a damn if we're stuck with you for all eternity? As long as Kai suffers, I'll sign eternity over."

Kai flips him off, and I give Jude a dubious look, even as I flicker in and out of flesh, working even harder to force it back this time.

"If it is a long-lasting issue, which I highly doubt, we'll find out how long you can be without me, and I'll return at the end of that span. No touching during those times," I quickly add. "My body like this works just fine in reeling you in from that mad edge. We can go on without ever crossing a line again, and I can be loyal to my one true love."

"I'm sure he'd be just fine with you coming to see your real-girl-christening quad every so often so we can get our fix," Kai states flatly.

They truly are exasperating.

"I rescind the offer. You're making it too complicated."

I turn to leave, and Gage darts in front of me, passing through me, and causing me to lose my hold for a moment.

He immediately pins me against the wall, and for the first time, I feel trapped, unable to simply pass through him. His eyes drift over my face as he lifts a hand and fingers a lock of my hair.

His other hand fists against the wall like it's taking a concentrated amount of effort not to touch me in any other way. I finally manage to force the form back, and his hand slips through my body, ghosting those tingles throughout me that has me straining twice as hard.

I stay in my place, even as he continues to loom over me.

"Uncomplicate it," he says, even though it looks like he hates the words.

"I know nothing else about this world than the four of you. Outside of my fantasies, I don't even know what goals are to be had. I'm asking you to take care of me in all ways, and ease me out there. I can't tell you how many times I was tempted to give into the fade, to stop fighting so hard for so little. I didn't survive this long just to fall into the world with blinders on and get myself killed before I get to live. The tradeoff is me and my devout protection, though as I said, you're protected regardless."

"Sounds very meager as far as comparisons go. If you're protecting us regardless, despite the fact we've survived just fine for many, *many* years without you, then all we really get is to sex you up and fulfill your fantasies," Jude states dryly.

A hint of a grin forms on my lips.

"Gage was only with Ezekiel. They could have both taken me, if you know what I mean," I state with dark humor in my eyes.

Kai's smile falters, and Jude's eyes narrow.

"I could have had her too, and there was no one in the room besides me," Kai grinds out, cracking his neck to the side.

I hold Jude's gaze as I remind him, "You can't have any other girl without each other in the room. Except me. You can have me individually, and share when you want to share. *That's* the tradeoff."

His entire expression blanks, like he doesn't want me to see anything in his eyes or his features to clue me in on where his mind goes. Kai shoves Gage away, taking his place as he gets in front of me.

"What's my incentive if you're icing me out?" he asks coldly.

"Work for it, and who knows, maybe I'll let you have me too," I say with a false bravado that wavers on the end.

Sheesh, he's really gorgeous when that intense stare is on you because he wants what he can't have. It has me questioning just how weak I might actually be once this thing gets started.

He pushes off. "I'm not in," Jude finally says with a shrug. "Individually, we'll get greedy, selfish, even combative. Look at what happened to E. I say we stick to how things have been, and you learn not to be in front of us in flesh. Otherwise, we'll ask you to leave permanently. If you stay, that precious life of yours might just end before it truly begins."

It's always Jude who cuts the deepest. I'm not sure why I keep expecting anything else.

It's like it sobers all of them, and I see the renewed determination in their eyes.

"Then we go on as we have been. Stay out of my room," I say tightly.

"Don't tell us where you'll be," Kai groans, raking a hand over his face. "We don't do well with temptation."

"Fine."

I zap myself to the basement where they never go, and finally stagger in my new physical form, collapsing to a couch. I had planned on leaving the estate to keep them away from me. I'm not quite as irresistible in reality as I was in fantasy.

I also had no idea this level of exhaustion could exist.

If I'm a gift from Lilith, that means I lose something each time I earn something new. What if I have to fight this form more and more to keep my untouchable one? Or what if I lose something else that has been instrumental to my survival?

The comfort that encompasses me when I snuggle up with a blanket has me smiling despite the ache they left in my stomach. My life has revolved around them for so long, that I'm truly quite worried I won't know how to exist without them.

And they're never going to do more than tolerate me.

This snuggly blanket really is a miracle cure for staving off stupid tears.

When my stomach suddenly growls, I'm very freaking distracted from all thoughts of guys. It growls again, and a pang accompanies it.

Then a slow grin spreads across my face as I glance to the basement kitchenette, staring at the fridge. Though they never actually come down here and stay down here, they do use that fridge for storing leftovers a lot.

In the next instant, I'm wobbling on unsteady legs all the way to the fridge. As I'm scrambling to pull out a box of pizza, a thought occurs to me.

It might have been a little harder for them to turn down the offer if I had been wearing something sexier than the Pinocchio outfit.

My mind turns to mush when I bite into the pizza, feeling

something so satisfying ignite in my mouth with a touch of surprise and savoring flavor. A little cold on the teeth, which I hadn't anticipated, since I've never felt cold before.

Yet I know what it is, so I can assume I've felt cold and forgotten it. Even the pizza seems familiar, in a unique, sensory sort of way.

It almost startles me when I realize that the moan in the room is coming from me. If pizza is making me moan, then I can only imagine what it would feel like to have an orgasm.

Pizza still in my mouth, I touch my stomach, feeling a grin light my features as a surge of excitement bursts through me.

I can touch myself.

I practically inhale the rest of the pizza, then grab a glass of water to choke it all down as fast as I can. It's not pretty, but it sure as hell works.

I try to make my clothes change, but it doesn't happen. So I just tear them off and toss them aside, still working on unsteady legs.

I drop back down to the couch, my hand trembling as I slide it down my body. Even my touch is almost too much. My memory from the first time Ezekiel was watered down by my mind to keep me from missing it so much.

My mind goes back to all the women they asked to do this so they could watch. It sounds creepier than it is.

It was actually really hot.

And informative.

Half of it is immediate instinct when my fingers brush over the very sensitive clit I completely underestimated. My eyes flutter shut, and those fantasies flash through my mind.

In my head, they said yes, and Ezekiel is already starting me out by sucking my nipples.

I use my free hand to try and mimic how I think it might feel, and it's like a shot to my lower body. Biting down on my lip so as not to make too much noise, I start slow circles, imagining Gage's face between my thighs as he works that glorious mouth of his on me.

My imagination kicks it up a notch by letting Jude kiss me while Ezekiel continues on with his mouth. And I have Kai in the corner, watching me, his hand stroking slowly, matching a rhythm I've requested.

It's so much more intense when I can actually feel the physical touch and the overwhelming sensations crossing over me all at once.

I immediately know what an orgasm is when one crashes into me so forcefully that I'm forced to arch, my toes involuntarily curling as an unbidden, rasp cry is pulled from my throat.

When I open my eyes, they cross, and the sound of my panted breaths resonate in my ears as I try to breathe normally again. A stupid, uncontrollable smile spreads across my lips, and I stretch, feeling remarkably less stressed and addictively relaxed.

If that's an orgasm, I'm going to have as many as I possibly can until the day I die.

It's so much better than I imagined, even though there is a small, annoyingly hollow feeling stealing a little of my high.

That pizza sounds good right now, so I sit up, planning to eat another slice before round two.

But I freeze.

All four of them are perched up on the stairs or walls, staring. Jude's hands are gripping the banister so hard that there are indentions on the cracking wood.

Ezekiel has his hands clenched in fists, and it looks like he wants to strangle me.

Kai is leveling me with a look that is equal parts murderous and captivating as his arms cross over his chest.

Gage is gripping the bar, and he's the first to turn and look away.

Now I know what it's like to have an audience you're unaware of. It's a little embarrassing. And terrifying, in my case.

"Hide better," Jude finally says through a sardonic, annoyed grin before he walks down the rest of the stairs and pushes out through the basement door that leads to the outside on this side of the house.

"Okay," I manage to say on a rasp whisper.

By some miracle, I manage to go ghost and zap myself to the woods. I pick a new outfit while in this form before zapping to the waterfall just beyond here. The new *whole* form takes over as soon as I end up on the smooth rocks.

That are slippery.

A laughing scream is jerked out of me when I slip off the rocks and land in the cool water that feels…amazing. My eyes open in wonder as I look around, taking it all in.

The white silk gown turns out to be a terrible choice. It's clingy as hell and very transparent in the water.

But I don't care.

It's just me out here, and I'm fairly shameless as I pick out a perfect boulder to lie down on for my next orgasm.

CHAPTER XXIII

Fun fact: orgasms don't get old. However, I'm already desperate to graduate to a two-person orgasm.

Yes, I think about more than sex. But imagine discovering sex for the very first time. I've read about teenagers, so I don't feel one bit ashamed about my current obsession.

However, the guys sure as hell haven't come around. In fact, they've made it easy to adjust to my new form this past week because they've avoided me more than I've avoided them.

I tried leaving the house. It was a terrible thing to attempt, since I sort of got lost fifteen times, and kept having to zap back and forth. Ezekiel finally asked me not to leave without them, since I have no idea how easy to kill I may or may not be.

Another fun fact: I heal as fast as they do. I cut open my finger with a kitchen knife, and the wound sealed almost immediately. I wasn't a fan of the pain, but it was a good learning exercise.

Don't worry, I know their weapons won't allow me to heal as fast.

I've seen them in action, so I go ghostly when they're strapped with weapons and off to reap some souls. They've done a lot of reaping this past week, staying gone longer and longer.

Me? I've just been hanging out in my flesh.

They've kept the fridge stocked with sandwich stuff, and they drop me off takeout when they bring home food. It's probably the most thoughtful thing they've done for me.

Ever.

I'm assuming at the rate I heal that I can't starve to death, but it's nice to not be hungry. Downside? Not one bag of popcorn has shown up in either kitchen.

Anyway, as long as I'm in flesh, I don't ache for their presence. Another plus.

Everything evens out, I suppose.

I haven't seen one bouquet of roses show up at my door, so I'm assuming they aren't going to buy me any. And I have no money to go buy my own or decorate my room.

I've also learned to never drink that damn liquor they get from Harold. I choked half a jar of that shit down, and the next thing I knew, I woke up on the bathroom floor.

Not. Pleasant.

So far, I'm sucking my first week of being a real girl. But it's the best week of my life.

A knock at my door tells me they're delivering more food, which is odd, since they only dropped some off less than an hour ago.

I open the door not expecting to find the four of them loitering in the hallway. Ezekiel is the only one who looks directly at me.

"We're going to the club. Thought you might want to come," he says with a smirk.

The other three all give me a look of amusement I don't particularly understand.

Their words finally resonate, and a smile flits across my face. "Are you inviting me?"

He shrugs.

"You've done good not to leave the house without us, so we figured it only right to reward you with something you want to do," Kai tells me, a smug look on his face.

"How thoughtful," I state, draining as much sarcasm into the two words as humanly possible.

Ha! *Humanly* possible. Fairly sure I'm not too human.

His lips twitch, and Jude turns away to smirk at the wall instead of in my face.

"We've been worked up this week, since you riled us up and left us hanging. It's getting distracting, so we'll be bringing you a show tonight, if you're interested in watching, that is," Gage drawls, his eyes cutting toward me.

I've experienced jealousy a multitude of times, but never so much of it that it left my stomach feeling lined with lead and dragging me down. I also have to swallow back a bit of bile, even as I force a smile.

Right.

I prepared for this. I knew this was coming. They've already gone much longer without a woman than I expected.

"Good. Then tonight I can hopefully do some shopping of my own and find out once and for all if I'm a virgin or not," I chirp, trying to sound enthusiastic so they don't see the unfounded way it hurts to know they're choosing another.

They all give me an indescribably blank stare, almost eerie.

"Virgin?" Kai asks incredulously.

"Fairly certain I'm not, but I'm not entirely sure what I'm searching for or if my fingers are long enough—"

"I'll see you guys at the club," Jude grumbles, turning and siphoning away.

They all look freshly showered. I spent two hours in the incredible bathtub in my bathroom today, so I know I'm clean enough. Baths are my favorite thing about skin. The water feels amazing. And I don't have to even bother drying off if I don't feel like it.

One quick flick from real to ghostly and I'm dry and clothed.

Flicking out to my ghostly form, I opt for a sexy pair of leather pants, and a pink crop top that shows just a hint of my stomach.

My hair falls in loose curls around my shoulders, and I check the mirror, smiling at the fresh look.

A groan catches my attention as Kai vanishes, and Ezekiel runs a hand through his hair as he gives me a look of exhausted patience. His gaze flicks angrily to Gage before he's gone as well, and I shrug.

"Can I hitch a ride with you?" I ask him.

He gives me a curt grin and flips me off before he also leaves.

Guess I'm going to them.

Rolling my eyes, I lose my skin. I can't sense them in flesh—only in my untouchable state can I locate them anymore.

It takes me a minute, but I finally feel them, and I siphon myself inside the…men's bathroom.

Yeah, I can only go where I've been before, so this is…awkward.

Five guys lined up at the urinal look at me as I poke my head out of the stall door. One looks away, then his gaze darts back to me as his eyebrows rise.

Clearing my throat, I push all the way through the door, and flash them a grin. "Oops," I say, shrugging. "Wrong bathroom."

I walk like a boss, other than that wobble in my high heels…that will have to go. Heels are way harder to walk in when gravity is involved.

Just as I pass one very tattooed guy, I back up, my eyes dropping to the dick in his hands, seeing four piercings down the shaft of it. Jude has those.

"Can I ask if those are painful when you have sex?" I ask him, peering up to his very blue eyes.

His lips twist in a grin. "Not at all. And it'd probably be the best thing you've ever felt."

My cheeks get hot for no apparent reason, and I'm almost tempted to fan myself. No wonder the girls Jude takes over the edge always act like their dying and going to heaven.

Interesting analogy there.

It's never struck me as ironic until now.

I glance down, wondering if any of these other guys have piercings like the other guys. I see none, but I do get a couple of incredulous gawks.

Shaking my head clear from my inner ramblings, I pat Mr. Tattoo's arm. "Good to know. Gives me more alone-time material."

His grin only grows, and I walk on out the door, and into the chaotic club scene. The music is pumping as loudly as ever, but like never before, I feel those heavy beats in my chest, vibrating through my body as though the music is alive.

My smile practically takes up my whole face.

Before I take another step, I let my feet go phantom, and change my shoes into some cute flats that aren't going to send me face-planting.

Then I walk out into the madness, feeling the heat from all the writhing bodies as they brush against me with varying types of fabric that range from abrasive to divine.

My sensory stimulation has me closing my eyes, absorbing all the contact I didn't realize I could enjoy so much.

Just physical contact is enough to soothe the ache in my chest.

It's so much more empowering and addicting than I realized it could be. I'm dancing before I even reach the crowded dance floor, grinding with anyone and everyone who wants to dance like we're overly familiar.

Moving through the throngs of people, I start to feel eyes on me. I whirl around, and my gaze collides with Jude.

He's standing on an overhead balcony, his gaze burning through me, as Ezekiel and Gage seem to be having an argument of some kind.

Kai is nowhere to be seen, and I break my gaze away, until I finally spot Three on the dancefloor, a pretty blonde curled against him. I thought he preferred brunettes.

His eyes flick to me, and he smirks as the girl presses into him. My heart is pounding in my ears as the sting of betrayal slithers into me.

They prefer a stranger.

Because I'll never be good enough.

Before I can look away, Jude moves in behind the woman, fitting his body against her as they press her between them. Her entire body flushes as she leans back on him, and Jude barely spares me a glance.

The only thing that keeps me from leaving and going home to find earplugs is the guy suddenly blocking my vision, and a drink being put in front of me.

"Hello again," I say to Mr. Tattoo Dick Piercings as he grins down at me.

"Usually by the time a girl sees my dick, I've bought her at least a few of these," he tells me, smirking. "And I can assure you it's far more impressive when I'm turned on," he adds.

"Are you saying this drink is drugged and you only get it up for incapacitated girls?" I deadpan, arching an eyebrow.

He bursts out laughing, shaking his head. He takes a generous sip of the drink, like he's taking a test, then passes it to me as his eyes sparkle with humor.

He's not as freakishly gorgeous as the four of them, but he's still attractive. He's also flirty and fun.

"Just how impressive are we talking?" I ask him, sipping my

non-drugged drink.

His smile spreads. "Never had a complaint in the past," he says, making his voice carry over the music.

"And what's the usual standard. It's only right for me to have all the facts before handing you my virginity," I go on.

He laughs again, quieter this time. "Funny girl. I'm Neal, by the way."

When he sticks his hand out, I slide mine into his, letting him shake it as I savor the feel of someone touching me with skin. It's not as consuming or drugging as when the guys touch me, but it's…nice.

Like him.

"I'm…Keyla," I tell him, though it's a little hollow, since that's not my true name but the one given to me by Ezekiel.

Those tattoos on this guy are misleading, because he looks like a hardened criminal, when really he's a fluffy teddy bear.

My hand moves to his chest, and I take back the fluffy part. His body is pretty damn hard.

His smile falters, and something lights in his eyes as he steps closer. "Please tell me you're not the kind of girl to tease and walk away."

"I'm actually not sure what kind of girl I am, to be honest, but I'm not in a teasing mood," I assure him.

He runs his thumb along my bottom lip, and though those sparks are absent, I still enjoy the comfort in his touch and the dreamy way he's looking at me.

He's totally in the pile of possible true loves.

"I like the way you talk," he tells me.

Weird compliment, but sure. I'll take it. "I like the way you talk too," I decide to say, returning what must be a common courtesy, and his grin kicks back up.

He presses even closer, lining our bodies up as he starts to move to the music. The sexy song sets a rhythm for our bodies to move to, and his eyes stay locked on mine. He's so tall and broad-shouldered that I can't see around him to know if the guys have already taken the girl home, or if they're still luring her into their trap.

It's a welcome distraction.

My eyes flick to his lips, wondering what it would be like to kiss him. Would it be as powerful with him? No. I know that much, simply because I'm not on fire just from his touch.

But it's only because I've fantasized about the guys so long that I've built up everything too much in my head. It's a trick my brain is playing on me, telling me everything is better than it is to keep it from miserably failing to meet expectations.

His hand slides up and slowly pushes into my hair, tugging my head back, and I suck in a breath, because it looks like I'm already going to find out what that kiss feels like.

My eyes flutter shut reflexively, and as soon as they do, I'm stumbling forward as the loss of his body causes my eyes to fly open. Then they widen, because Neal is on the ground, looking dazed as he tries to get up.

Jude is glaring at me as he steps in front of me, and I feel Kai press against me from behind before I see him.

"What the hell do you think you're doing?" I demand, looking up at Jude like he's lost his damned mind.

"We decided we don't want you touching anyone while you're staying with us," Kai supplies, still standing too close to my back.

"Oh? Well, does that mean you four will also refrain?" I ask, narrowing my eyes.

Jude smirks. "No. But we'll let you watch, and you can touch yourself."

"Unbelievable," I mutter, shoving by him.

Neal is just standing up when Gage and Ezekiel shoulder by

him so hard it sends him to his ass again. Gage looks like he wants to kill me.

Ezekiel looks like he wants to kill Neal.

I give up. These guys are impossible.

And super selfish.

I change my direction, heading into the thick mass of people. I'll go back to the bathroom and siphon myself to another club I've gone to with them before.

I shift directions again, staying low so they can't see me, and finally come out to where Neal is. He gives me a surprised look when he almost runs into me.

"Boyfriend or brother?" he asks me, a nervous laugh following.

"Neither. Just a terrible roommate. Actually, four terrible roommates. I'll ditch them if you want to meet me at the club down the street."

His grin grows. "That sounds like a setup."

I shrug. "Your choice, Neal. If not you, I'll find someone else."

He grabs my hand before I can turn away, and he tugs me back. "My place in an hour if you're serious. We'll skip the club and do Netflix and chill. You got your phone?"

I don't have a phone, but I elect to be vague.

"Not on me."

"It's the Martine apartment complex on the corner of Lexington and Pike. 1501B. Just ring me and I'll buzz you up."

"I'll be there," I tell him with a smile, but my smile falters when I see Jude making his way toward us on one side, and Kai coming in from the other.

"Gotta go. I'll see you there," I tell him, then turn and dart away.

I'm looking behind me, checking for the two unpredictable psychos, when I slam into an unrelenting, hard body.

Cursing, I look up with dread, and find Gage as he snakes an arm around my waist and starts dragging me out. I'll let them think they've won.

For an hour.

Then I'll go see Neal and find out if he's my one true love so I can just dive in and start my life.

Gage basically drags me out of the club, even as I struggle a little, putting on a show. He knows I can't just disappear. I'm not supposed to draw attention to myself, and a girl disappearing will definitely raise a few eyebrows.

As soon as we're outside, I jerk out of his grip, and glare at him.

"I'm not really sure you guys ever hear the stupid that comes out of your mouths. I can watch you? But I can't touch anyone?" I ask, shaking my head.

"I didn't say that," he tells me as Ezekiel comes up and tosses me over his shoulder like a barbarian.

I'm going to smother them in their sleep tonight.

"If you don't think the same way, then put me down. I can promise you I have no intentions of watching you four paw all over another woman, all while you tell me how toxic I am for you. I'm certainly not going to let you dictate whether or not my vagina gets christened or not."

"Can't do that," Ezekiel growls, sounding much too angry. "I told you this would happen," he adds, glaring back at Gage.

"This was Kai's idea. We never considered she'd be this fucking annoying and shameless."

"I've told you I lost shame a long time ago. I have the four of you to thank for that," I remind them, groaning as Ezekiel continues to carry me.

As soon as we reach the park, he siphons us, and the next step we take is inside his living room. He dumps me to the couch, dropping me like it burns too much to hold me another second, just as Kai and Jude appear in the room.

"Unless we lock her up, it'll do no fucking good to leave her here," Kai gripes, apparently carrying on a conversation I've already missed part of.

"Can't lock her up, jackass. She can just pass through walls. Not even soul stone keeps her in," Jude growls.

"I can assure you there's no way you can confine me," I decide to interject, earning a murderous glare from Kai before he directs his attention to Ezekiel and Gage.

"I told you it was pushing her too far, but you had to be a dick," Ezekiel says as he starts making a sandwich.

"I find this all utterly ridiculous and a complete double standard. Why is it okay for the four of you to take home another girl but I can't bring home a guy?" I ask seriously.

"Because we're guys. It's allowed," Kai states just as seriously.

"I'm going to pretend you're not referring to archaic social proprieties, considering you have none, and try not to stab you for that completely chauvinist remark."

They don't even glance my way, as they continue talking amongst themselves.

"No girl or her. Those are currently our options if we expect her to stay chaste while we wait things out," Ezekiel tells them.

I nod in agreement.

"She doesn't have to stay with us, then we don't have to see her with other men," Jude bites out, even though he seems to say it with strain.

Kai disappears from the room, and I hear him cursing above us as heavy footsteps stomp around the second floor.

"You want me gone now?" I ask, my voice a little quieter as I look at Jude.

He gives me a look that has me flicking my flesh switch off so that I become untouchable.

"No. I unfortunately don't want you gone. But for whatever

reason, I can't physically allow you to be with another man. At the same time, I can't physically stand to be without the feel of a woman much longer, or I need to kill something to work off the steam. You're driving us all crazy."

Pinching the bridge of my nose, I blow out a frustrated breath. "I honestly don't even know how to deal with you right now. Neal might have been my future true love, and I didn't even get to tell him that I was looking forward to finding out. Instead, I ran off after you four morons barged in like cavemen."

It grows quiet, and I look up to see the three of them just staring at me for a moment.

"You were going to tell him he might be your future true love?" Gage asks, studying me intently.

"Yes. In case you haven't noticed, I like to be honest in my intentions from the start. If things change, I'll inform him," I state matter-of-factly.

Jude seems to fight a smile for no real reason. Their mood swings grew old months ago.

"Then I suppose we should let you do that," Jude says, still fighting a smile. "You can go back to the club."

"He actually gave me his apartment number," I boast, feeling like I accomplished something, considering the very limited time frame I had to meet anyone tonight.

Ezekiel surprises me the most as he takes a seat. "Then I guess we shouldn't stop you. True love is nothing to mess with," he says seriously, though I swear I hear a hint of amusement.

In fact, they weirdly all look a little amused, when only moments ago it seemed like they were ready to kill someone.

"You'll seriously let me go?" I ask, glancing back at the time. It's only been thirty minutes…

"Like E said, can't mess with true love. Even we have boundaries, Key," Jude tells me, his tone very close to mocking.

"Then I have thirty minutes to kill, because he said to be there in an hour."

"You should go now," Ezekiel urges. "Guys prefer for a girl to be much earlier than expected. The more eager you seem, the better."

I don't really trust them, so I siphon away quickly, making sure they don't stow away and ruin my moment with Neal. I land in the cemetery they frequent, then start asking people for directions when I turn whole.

It takes a little while, but I finally find the building and buzz the appropriate apartment. I think.

But he doesn't answer.

"Already here?" I hear him ask, causing me to whirl around to see him as he grins at me from the sidewalk.

I'm actually late, but I know for a fact men hate it when you correct them. I've learned a lot since trying to be a real girl.

"I ditched them faster than anticipated," I tell him with a shrug. "There's something I need to tell you before we go any farther."

His grin only grows. "I can't wait to hear it, as long as it's no freaky secret," he says, holding his hands up, though a teasing glint seems to be in his eyes.

Smiling back at him, I blurt it all out.

CHAPTER XXIV

I appear in the living room, where all four guys are lounging and eating pizza, and their attention turns to me as the TV plays on. Four matching, taunting grins mock me with just their existence.

"I hate all of you," I say flatly, walking up the stairs without a backward glance.

"I guess he wasn't quite ready for true love?" Jude calls to my back.

I flip him off over my shoulder, ignoring the riotous amounts of laughter that heckles me. I've never seen a guy run so fast in all my life, or make up so many excuses as to why he had to get away from me.

Sheesh.

You'd think I offered him a deadly virus. I'm assuming this is a guy thing, and three out of four of them manipulated me into making an irredeemable ass of myself.

Next time, I'll take it a little slower.

People say "live and learn" for a reason.

I change to my ghost form and fashion me some silk pajamas that I know will be comfy, then turn back and collapse to the bed. I notice the rest helps me grow stronger, which helps me transition easier between both forms.

As I get the TV turned on and get situated on my bed, Ezekiel appears in the doorway, holding a massive bowl of popcorn. My mouth waters instantly as the buttery scent permeates the air, smelling so much better than the times I've caught a whiff of it in my phantom body.

"Thought I might could sleep a few hours with you," he says with a smirk.

"In exchange for popcorn?" I muse.

"You've been asking for it. And I've had two good nights of sleep in my lifetime. Both those came with you. I'm willing to barter."

"And the others won't get upset by this arrangement? You know, since you'll be sharing a bed with my evil vagina and all."

He snorts then rolls his eyes, moving farther into the room. He always moves with the same predatory grace as the rest of them, but his movements are lazier, luring one into a false sense of security.

"As long as I don't do anything sexual, I'm not breaking any rules."

I pull back the other half of the cover and pat the bed. He smirks again before coming toward me, and I reach out for the popcorn.

I'm digging in, pointedly ignoring him as he strips down to his boxers. The salty, buttery explosion on my tongue has me closing my eyes and moaning.

Popcorn is totally going to be my favorite junk food.

When I open my eyes, Ezekiel is staring at me, and he clears his throat before he slides into the bed, taking up a lot of room. I scoot over to him, and he curls around me, getting comfortable.

"Neal really hated the idea of love, it seems," I tell him candidly, and he smothers his laugh against my neck as his body vibrates with it.

I shove at his shoulder, rolling my eyes as he continues to grin against my neck. I also pretend that there aren't a thousand little shocks reminding me how much my body loves one of theirs.

It's hard to ignore, but I manage to fake it.

"Life lessons are never fun," he says, though it feels like he's mocking me again.

I open my mouth to speak when Jude stalks into my room, his glare pointed at Ezekiel. "What the hell?" he snaps.

"Not breaking any rules," Ezekiel says with a shrug.

"You said being around her without touching her was driving you crazy, and you think this is a good idea?" Jude growls.

I slip my leg over Ezekiel, pretending it's merely to get more comfortable. Jude's hands fist, and he levels me with a cold glare.

I, being a little pissy about their manipulation, wink at him as I "scratch" my eyebrow with my bird finger.

"Kiss my ass, Jude. I'm getting some sleep and that's it. Hell, I'm too tired for sex with all the extra reaping jobs we've taken just to work her out of our systems," Ezekiel groans.

Jude turns and stalks out, but not before he punches my wall, leaving a crumbling hole in the sheetrock.

"I find that to be a violent overreaction," I state dryly, causing Ezekiel to chuckle against me.

None of the others come in, and when Ezekiel's hand slips down my body, pushing the thin shorts down, I don't stop him. His breaths get shaky when he brushes the bare skin over my pubic bone, and I slowly put the popcorn down, pushing it away from me.

His lips press against my neck, and my eyes flutter shut as he slowly starts working my shorts down farther. Every touch seems ten times more erotic than it really is, and a thousand times more electric than Neal's touch.

I turn my head and find his lips, and I go a little boneless when he cradles my head and kisses me deeper. His body moves over mine, and my legs spread for him to move into the cradle of my thighs.

We stay like that, so close yet so far away, the thin material of his boxers being the only thing that separates us, as his mouth explores mine in a way none of them have ever kissed me.

It's languid and slow, almost as though he's savoring every drop. His erection strains against his boxers, and I slip my hand down, almost reaching him, before reminding myself this would tear them apart.

"We have to stop," I groan against the kiss, which has him pressing against me harder, more desperate. "It'll make the four of you fight."

He breaks the kiss, breathing heavily as he drags his lips down my neck to my shoulder. He stays there for a second, like he's catching his breath, before he finally rolls off me and scrubs his face with both hands.

"Shit," he grumbles. "It's like I can't help myself."

I pat his shoulder. "I'm not even going to tell you how miserable I am right now, but trust that you're not alone."

He laughs humorlessly. "That only makes me want you more, because I know how bad you want it."

"Let's talk about shark week or something. That should kill the arousal. As long as we don't discuss sharks mating or anything. Not saying that turns me on, but it still makes me think of sex."

He bursts out laughing, shaking his head as his fingers twine with mine. I'm not sure what's going on right now, but it feels like Ezekiel and I just leveled-up together.

He reaches down and snags my abandoned shorts, dropping them to my lap. "Put those on before I forget how important that bond is to me."

CHAPTER XXV

The other side of the bed is empty when I get up the next morning, and my shorts are still on. I'm not sure why I smile when I smell his pillow, but I do.

I slide out of bed, moving through the hallway, and start down the stairs when I hear the doorbell ring. My stomach twists in knots, and I jog down quicker.

Why did I just get a bad feeling?

I quickly remember I don't want anyone from their world seeing me, so I shift to my phantom form just as Gage swings open the door to two guys in fancy suits.

He hands Gage an envelope, and Gage takes it before saying something in a language I don't understand. As he shuts the door, he flips the envelope over.

I can see a wax seal on the back before he turns and his eyes collide with mine.

"Just tell me if it's something bad," I say quietly.

His lips twitch as he holds it up, and I quickly hurry to him, turning whole just before I snatch it from his hand.

I tear the envelope open, and skim the contents quickly.

North Tower Quad,

Your attendance is requested for a royal celebration with the king and his heirs.

No weapons allowed.

"The devil invited you to a party?" I ask, my voice cracking a little. "Is that good or bad?"

"It's hard to tell these days," he says dangerously close to my ear as his fingers trail down my arm.

He presses against my back until his hand reaches mine, and he rips the invitation from my hand before leaving me bereft and a little light headed.

I'm getting a "gullible" tattoo.

I follow him into the room with the others, and Jude's eyes rake over me as Ezekiel hands me a bagel. I take it, eating it anxiously as Gage passes over the note.

Jude's eyes leave me as he and the others read it.

"No date or time, so does that mean they're just going to show up and send us there?" Ezekiel asks absently as he takes my bagel away and smears it with cream cheese.

Kai answers as I get my bagel back. "It means they're springing this on us for whatever reason. And I've got a bad feeling about it."

I moan around the mouthful of bagel now that it's been turned into something twice as heavenly as it was before.

I don't realize I've closed my eyes until I open them and see them all giving me an annoyed look.

"We're trying to have a serious conversation," Gage says curtly.

"Sorry," I say around my mouthful, then look over to Ezekiel and add, "That's way better. Thank you."

He smirks when the others all glare at him, and he shrugs as he lazily chews on his own bagel.

"Sleep good?" Jude asks bitterly.

"Real damn good," Ezekiel tells him with an unrepentant grin.

"What are we missing?" Kai asks.

"Notice how she didn't go from room to room telling everyone good night?" Jude drawls.

Shit. They're about to argue over this ridiculousness for no reason.

Looking around for something to distract them, my eyes land on the invitation, and my breath freezes in my lungs.

"What about it? I just figured she finally got tired of not hearing it in return."

"Invitation," I butt in, shoving it forward.

Two new lines literally start writing themselves like an invisible calligrapher is adding them.

Black tie. Be in the closest graveyard in thirty minutes.

"Shit," Ezekiel says, dropping the rest of his bagel.

They all abandon the table and dart upstairs. I ghost out and change my attire to my badass clothes with all my fake weapons. I also wear heels, because they look really good, and I don't actually have to walk in them, because I'm not going to be a real girl in hell.

No thank you.

The guys appear back in the room in no time, and I have to stare a little harder than necessary as they move around in their tuxes. They look like dangerous temptation in designer packages now.

That's really not fair.

Their tattoos are covered by the shirts, making them look devilishly classy and mysterious. Jude shoots me a knowing look and smirks in my direction.

I clear my throat and start looking around like I'm not impressed.

Then I sneak a few discreet peeks as they finish putting their wallets and phones in their pockets.

"Why do you have to go to the graveyard? Why not just siphon down there?" I ask. "We can sneak around and figure out what's going on."

Kai shakes his head. "We can't siphon to the underworld until we're given access. Besides, you only saw a small portion of it. It's endless, much like the universe. We don't even know what section we're going to."

"Can I ask a stupid question?"

They all look at me expectantly as though I have their undivided attention.

"What happens if one of you dies?" I swallow a little more harshly after my voice breaks unexpectedly on that last word.

"We're not really sure," Gage says with a careless shrug.

"Ordinarily, we'd be sent up or down, if you know what I mean. But that was stolen from us when we inherited hell powers and soul responsibilities," Ezekiel states just as casually.

"The other competitors who die in the trials are sent back to hell's throat for a new transition. They may turn out the same, but that's a rare thing. We tend to get a little more vicious when the powers take root. Most end up the monsters you saw while you were in there," Kai goes on.

"Would you turn into monsters if you were sent for transition?" I ask quietly.

They all grin at me.

"We're already monsters," Jude tells me with a tone that has chills sliding up my spine.

They start walking past me, and I blow out a shaky breath as I turn and follow.

"You look ridiculous in that outfit," Kai tells me without turning around.

"Hot. The word you're looking for is *hot*. Or maybe *badass*. Not ridiculous."

To that, I get a round of laughter, but I still strut like a boss until we siphon to the graveyard.

The second our feet hit the cemetery ground, Ezekiel reaches over, his hand passing through me. Light flashes, and we're sucked into hell. I think.

It's hard to tell when we're in the glamourous section that hides all the monsters, hellfire, and screams of agony.

The chandeliers are in abundance, crystal and ornate. The marble floors are a crisp white that contrasts elegantly with the gold accents.

It's a royal party.

"Another set of quads are here," Ezekiel says, leaning closer to Kai as they have a little stare down with the said second set of quads.

"And they're bonded like you?" I ask.

"Just like us. All the quads," Kai says quietly.

"So we didn't just make friends with the devil and get invited to the party. This has something to do with the trials coming up in a week," Jude states just as quietly, looking around.

"Definitely. Just spotted another set of quads and a few pairs as well," Gage says with the same nearly muted tone as he snags a glass of champagne off a passing tray.

"Stick close, little protector. You might come in handy tonight," Kai tells me warily.

My eyes are already searching the scene, but I pause my search when I see Lamar moving this way.

"Incoming," I tell them, moving closer to what I feel like is my friend, even though he doesn't really know me.

Lamar's eyes land on them, and he turns and looks over his shoulder before facing them again.

"I've come to tell you Manella was removed from creating these trials," he tells the quad in a hushed whisper. "Lucifer designed the upcoming course himself."

"Is that why he arranged this party? To announce that?" Gage asks, stepping closer.

"I'm not quite sure what this party is about. I only learned of it thirty minutes ago."

I exchange a look with the guys. Apparently those invitations all arrived at the same time.

"I offer this as a token of peace and gratitude. There will be riddles in this course that could cost you your life, and monsters that don't even have names yet. Lucifer has created the hardest course in history, and I haven't a clue as to why," Lamar goes on.

The guys all bristle. "And I was starting to think he might like us," Jude drawls.

"Lucifer only cares for his children. His opinion of anyone else can change on a whim. Trust me; I know this very personally." He looks around again, then faces them one last time. "I do hope you brought your protective spirit."

I pat his hand, and his eyes drop to the contact as a grin spreads over his face.

"Good," he says, not looking back up immediately. "It may be your best hope of surviving, no matter what Lilith's cost. I do appreciate you loaning it to me, though I'm not sure why you did it. Manella explained it belonged to you instead of me."

Gage rolls his eyes. "We don't really have any control over her, so don't thank us."

His head cocks. "Her?" Lamar asks, his tone going confused as all the guys stiffen. "The protective spirit is an actual being? And you can see her?"

He takes a wary step back as he studies them, and Jude's lips tighten as Gage mutters a curse.

"I should return to Manella," he says, a curious look in his eyes as the expression on his face worries me. "Beware of the riddles. Don't treat them with no importance," he reminds them, then turns and walks away.

He moves through the crowd, and I watch him as Gage runs a frustrated hand through his hair.

"Way to slip," Ezekiel bites out.

"Fuck. I have no idea how I did that," Gage says under his breath.

"What does it matter if I'm a girl instead of an *it?* Is hell sexist? Do they know it's the twenty-first century topside?"

Lamar gets close to Manella's ear, whispering something I can't even hear. Manella's eyes immediately cut toward us, and Kai curses as he looks away.

"And he just told Manella. Guess that gratitude only extends so far," Kai growls.

"Not sure why you're surprised," Jude drawls.

Manella looks wary and surprised as he moves through the crowd like he's searching for someone.

"I don't get it. What's wrong with me being a girl?" I ask absently.

The crowd parts enough for me to see who Manella is talking to, and my heart stumbles when I see Lucifer. He doesn't look this way. He doesn't even react other than to smile like he has a secret.

When his eyes do come up, it feels like he's staring directly at me, though I see no recognition, and his eyes skip over me, searching around the four of them like he's trying to pinpoint my location.

"The devil looks intrigued," I grumble. "Someone please tell me what I'm missing and put me out of my misery."

Jude blocks my vision, stepping in front of me. "Lamar has a lot more knowledge of the heirs and their powers. He figured out something we've been piecing together, but now we're certain of it."

"What?" I ask, confused.

"That Lilith couldn't have created an actual being. I don't even know if Lucifer can create something like you," Gage answers.

A chill slithers over me as I look back over to Lucifer, seeing him moving this way.

"Then what am I?" I ask so quietly that I'm not sure they hear me.

Regardless of whether or not they heard it, they can't answer since the devil is now standing near us.

"I'm glad to see you boys in one piece. I trust there have been no further incidents?" he asks conversationally.

"No."

The four of them bow at the waist, and I try to think of ways to calm down before I kick their asses for not addressing him as king or Your Royal Evilness or something, damn it. He's so not the guy you want to offend.

He doesn't seem to even acknowledge the misstep though.

"You can stand," he says absently. His eyes land on Jude's for a brief moment before flicking between all four.

"He's really good at guessing about liars, and it's not good if he suspects you of a lie," I decide to remind them.

Jude's lips twitch, but it happens so fast that I almost wonder if I've imagined it.

"Oddly enough, I couldn't find any proof of power when I finally managed to find your very thin files. The only information I seem to have on you is your address and your soul count. I'm not even certain how you obtained your weapons."

Gage doesn't even bat an eye as he answers. "We were tested when we were summoned on the day our powers manifested. Damnedest thing happened, though. I think it must have been performance anxiety."

"Why would you be a smartass to the fucking devil?" I groan, wishing I could slap the hell out of him.

Gage's lips tug at one corner, but like Jude, he wipes it away before I can be certain.

"I see," Lucifer, eerily amused. "During forty-seven summons all four of you had performance anxiety?" he adds, returning the smartassery with a touch of fuck-you-little-turds.

"It's a problem. We're working on it," Kai says in an assuring tone.

"Just so you know, I'm almost positive I can't protect you from the damn devil," I point out.

I'm going to kill all of them.

Still, Lucifer manages to maintain his humored expression.

"I only got a glimpse of two of you, and I'm not certain what you did. Care to try and explain it to me? Because I quite feel like you're being underutilized and pointlessly tested in these trials."

"There's not any real way to explain it, since we're not entirely certain what we're doing," Jude says with a shrug. "We just know how to kill. We like it topside, but we'd like to earn access to this plane as well."

"I'm sure you would," Lucifer says, stroking his jaw thoughtfully. "It's the best of both worlds to remain topside with all the perks of hell. Clearly if you had too much power, we'd have to bring you down below, since it'd be against our law to leave that much of the world unbalanced with dark influence."

"We never really died, so we have no dark influence, since our souls are still whole," Jude immediately points out.

Lucifer actually looks both surprised and intrigued by that confession. "Well, that certainly is another kind of imbalance, but not one that breaks any laws. And a very interesting turn of events," he goes on, his grin spreading.

The guys weirdly seem to be tenser now that the devil seems pleased.

"But I'm afraid I do need to learn what your powers are so we can categorize you. If for any reason you're stronger than you should be on the surface, I'll take into account you have no dark influence. I'm sure we can come to some sort of agreement."

They all look wary now.

Lucifer gets closer to Jude, the amusement falling from his face so smoothly, as though it was an illusion all along despite how genuine it appeared. The ease of the transition chills me to the bone.

"The thing is, you somehow penetrated the notoriously impenetrable chest of a guard. Not that you'd know that. Surface guardians aren't privy to such knowledge, which is why you never once thought about exposing yourself."

Jude's jaw tics, but he remains a stone, keeping his eyes on Lucifer.

"Then you turned him to dust. They didn't regenerate," Lucifer goes on.

A prickling blanket of dread slips over me.

"That sort of power is very high level. It rivals Lamar's, and he's a very old immortal who has spent a large amount of time letting his power grow under the influence of this world."

Lucifer gestures around, as though reminding us we're surrounded by very powerful people who've been drinking the hell juice and getting stronger for a long time.

"And you don't even have access to here yet. Makes a person wonder just how strong you'll be if you succeed," he says, then steps back.

His smile returns like it never left, and his face is deceptively light and amused once again.

"I'll eventually learn just how you managed to do that." His eyes flick to Kai's. "And I'll learn what you did as well, since that's quite the mystery that intrigues me even more."

Kai's fists tighten beside him, and I press my hand against his back as though I'm trying to calm him down.

"You can't punch the devil in hell. Get him topside. I heard he can die there," I tell him, patting his back now.

The tingles make me want to turn whole, so I withdraw my hand. My job is done anyway, because Kai's unclenched his fist, and a smirk toys with the edges of his lips.

"Good luck in the trials, in case I don't see you before then. And enjoy the party," he says, gesturing around, his smile growing as he starts backing up. "Hell is known for its parties."

Two girls immediately join him, one for each arm, and he grins as he turns and walks away. Several really stunning women walk by in their lingerie or just completely naked.

I'm not really sure why I'm just now noticing this.

"So help me, after how you jerks treated me over Neal last night, if any of you try to have sex with some really hot hell girl, I will let you die," I decide to point out. "I might even push you into a giant centipede's mouth to see if you turn into one after transition."

Kai shakes with silent laughter, but he ends up voicing a groan.

"Why did we use our powers?" he asks.

"It felt like I had to. I was just going to punch them," Jude bites out.

"I was going to slam them into each other and knock them out. Instead, I killed them," Kai tells him, clapping his shoulder.

"So we can thank you two uncontrollable hotheads for the unwanted exposure," Ezekiel growls.

"How were we supposed to know the guards are that resilient? There was very little information on them available to us," Kai points out.

"I'm assuming you don't want them knowing about your power because it's too strong to be topside? Like the devil hinted at?" I ask.

They give me a wary look.

"The devil already knows. I highly doubt I'm more of a threat to you than him even if I am out to get you," I say on an exasperated breath.

"It's not that," Ezekiel says, looking around us, reminding me we're not exactly draped in privacy.

They start smoothly moving through the party, and they make their way into a bathroom. Ezekiel checks it, and I hop up on the counter as he proceeds to investigate every stall.

He closes his eyes like he's concentrating, and then his eyes open as Kai locks the door.

"Nothing in here to listen in," Ezekiel says.

Gage turns his attention to me. "Partially. We sure as shit don't want to live here full time. It'd get old. And though the parties are lavish and much more fun than the clubs, things are twice as lethal down here than up there. The ones strong enough to kill us are given limited amounts of time when they can be topside unless in mortal form."

"Mortal form?" I ask.

"They can be born into the world as a mortal if they're important enough or blessed by a royal, and they live until they die, then they bypass transition and return to their form that has been preserved in hell," Kai explains.

"Awesome," I state dryly.

"They're not as powerful in mortal form, but it doesn't really matter. They can't legitimately die, so they live a fast-paced, rock star sort of existence until they get sent back to hell," Ezekiel tells me.

"I think we're telling her a little much now. Half of this stuff is among the things we learned from Harold just last year," Jude growls.

They ignore him, much to my surprise.

"If we're topside, we're among the most powerful there on a full-time basis. Better to be a big fish in a small pond than a small fish in a big pond when it's a game of life and death," Gage continues.

"But we're getting stronger, and we have no idea what we're doing some of the time," Kai says quieter.

"Now you're definitely telling her too much," Jude snaps, looking at them like they've all gone mad. "Just tell her the part she needs to know and stop sharing the details we never agreed to discuss."

"Why are you getting stronger?" I ask, even though I think I already know.

"It seems to happen every time you 'level up,'" Ezekiel says, his jaw tightening a little as I take a step away from him.

"That's why you didn't want me gone," I say more to myself than them, looking down at the sink. "That's why you closed the books when I tried to read them, and why you got jealous about Neal, and—"

"Neal had nothing to do with the equation. That was uncontrollable blind-rage jealousy," Ezekiel interrupts, shrugging unapologetically when I look over at him.

"You never really wanted me there. You just wanted the power boost."

They look at me like they expect me to cry, when all I really want to do is just walk out. Swallowing my pride, since I don't have a hell of a lot left, I just nod.

"Alright then. So how big of a boost did you get after I reached this last level?"

"Haven't tried it out yet," Kai tells me. "We've been recovering from our stint in Hell's throat and trying to conserve all our energy for the trials. It drains us to use too much, and the soul stones drained us in general."

Jude throws his hands up and walks out, slamming the bathroom door behind him.

"I'm not hearing anything so top secret right now. What's his problem?" I ask. "I'm the one who should be walking out and slamming a door. The four of you know how much I care about you, no matter how hard you deny it, and you act like it's no big deal you've been using me."

Yeah, that last part comes out bitter.

"First rule of hell: Don't trust anyone you don't share a bond with," Kai says with a sardonic smile. "Yet, as you already pointed out, the devil is already onto us. However, Jude still doesn't want you equipped with the same knowledge we have or admitting our weakness about not knowing our true powers or reach."

"I find it worth pointing out that Jude is the only one who hasn't tasted her," Gage states dryly. "And he's the only one still keeping secrets."

He cuts an accusatory gaze at me.

Ignoring him, I turn toward Ezekiel. "What do I have to do with any of this? What's my connection to the four of you?"

His lips purse. "We don't know," he answers honestly. "It could be a cosmic perfect storm of some sort, and you could have used us an anchor to…fuck, I don't even know at this point."

"We need to get back out there before someone takes notice of our absence and gets too curious," Gage says, exiting.

Kai turns and follows, and Ezekiel exits with me. I even suppress a taunting grin when he opens the door for me.

He mutters a curse under his breath when he realizes what he just did, and he walks off a little briskly.

Prickly they may be, but right now, they're mine to protect. Nothing else matters when their lives are at risk.

CHAPTER XXVI

The party has been going for a while, and we're still waiting on the devil to lower the boom and tell us why we're all here.

Lucifer has been on his throne for the past hour, and occasionally his eyes land on the guys.

Lamar is standing behind Manella, who is sitting in a throne three down from Lucifer. I start to go to him, when a redhead steals my breath as she lands herself right in front of us.

The guys don't react, but I take an immediate step closer, watching her carefully. She smirks as she runs a finger up Kai's chest, and his fists ball at his sides.

"You four seem to owe me a favor after what I did for you, don't you think?" she asks in a voice so seductive that I expect them to shuck their clothes immediately.

Fortunately, they don't.

"Wait. Is she talking about me?" I ask, looking at them as she slides her finger over to Gage's chest.

He looks really tense right now, and his jaw clenches.

"How do you plan to work that off?" she asks, her finger now moving on to Ezekiel's chest.

"Considering you left me for dead," Kai says, drawing her

attention, "I don't feel very indebted," he answers her.

Oh, that favor.

Her finger pauses on Jude's chest, and she strolls back through, dragging her finger over them again as she makes her way down the line to Kai.

I take another step closer.

Her hand slides down his chest, pausing just above his belt as she steps into him. "If I had wanted you dead, I would have let you fall all the way into the hellfire before I saved you," she says with a little too much pep.

When her hand starts moving lower, I can't help but stare at it like it's the most offensive thing I've ever seen.

"So I'll ask again; what do you plan to do for me?"

Just as her fingers start to dip behind his beltline, my anger might boil over a little overly so. In fact, I feel something leak out of me without permission—power, not anything gross. Just power.

She rips her hand back, shaking it out as it sizzles. An actual hiss leaves her mouth as she glares at Kai like he's the one who did it.

He just smirks.

"I'll remember that," she growls, then stiffens as though something just occurred to her. "How did you even do that?" she asks more seriously, her sexy voice gone as a commanding echo chases her words.

"I actually did nothing. I think someone is toying with you, Lilith," Kai tells her, gesturing toward where Lucifer is staring at us.

"Turning the devil's daughter against the devil is so not a sound plan," I grumble.

Her eyes turn to slits as she glares at Lucifer for a moment, then turns and stalks away. Now that I've noticed him staring, his hands steepled in front of his face like he just witnessed all that, I really don't feel too smug.

I feel played.

I almost feel like this party was called to test me. Or maybe it's to test them and I'm just being paranoid.

Cain distracts him when he leans down to say something in his ear. Lucifer nods, a new smile donning his lips as he stands.

Someone taps a glass over and over, and all eyes drift up to hell's king as he stands on his platform in front of his obnoxious throne.

"I've assembled you all here tonight for a very important reason. The trials lately have gotten a little complicated due to outside interference. Clearly we have to clean house, but before we can do all that, the trials must continue."

He takes a step down, and the crowd parts for him as he starts walking.

I lose sight of him, but I can still hear his voice as it draws closer.

"So, in an effort to keep details from leaking out before I was ready for them to be leaked, we've decided to change the date of the trials." The crowd parts in front of us, and Lucifer stops walking as he stares directly at us with a smirk on his lips.

"Tonight," he goes on, still staring, "we have the final trial!"

There goes the *boom* we've been dreading.

Their jaws tense as they part, making room for the devil to pass between them. Lucifer grins like he's delighted to have sprang this on them.

"And since I designed the final course this year, you can be sure it's going to be a very epic event," he says, walking away from us as the crowd continues to clear a path and start following behind him like really bad sheep.

We follow too, and my hand passes through Ezekiel's shirt like I'm trying to draw some calm from him to keep from wolfing out.

Or girling out. Or fleshing out?

Anyway, I'm losing a little control right now.

"This year, instead of one day in the course, it will be three," Lucifer goes on as he steps onto a platform.

The crowd erupts into hushed whispers and surprised gasps. This sounds really bad.

"Three days?" Kai hisses.

"This is a test designed specifically for us," Gage states quietly. "Look at the other competitors."

My eyes flit around as I start noticing the other competitors losing their suits, and attaching weapons onto their bodies.

"The invitation said black tie and no weapons. It didn't say bring a change of clothes and a secret stash of killing devices," I feel the need to point out.

"He wants to see what we can do," Ezekiel says as his jaw grinds.

The devil steps high on the platform, and his grin only grows as the wall behind him starts to slide open. The thing about this mansion? I've never once seen a window.

I'm guessing the view must suck.

A glowing red light starts creeping in more and more as the wall continues to slide open.

"This year's course will take place in the belly of the beast," Lucifer goes on. "Hell's stomach."

More hushed whispers and some audible sounds of excitement comes from the restless crowd. I really don't know if I want to do something that excites this bloodthirsty gathering.

"I'm guessing they're not talking about giving hell indigestion with all of us in its stomach," I state wryly.

Ezekiel steps closer to me, and I continue to try to draw a modicum of calm from him.

"Hell's stomach is literally the place where the throat sends the most vile monsters that are too vicious for purgatory. It's never been used as a location for the trials because it's the hardest spot to survive. In fact, I haven't ever heard of any survivors," Ezekiel says quietly.

My eyes flick back to Lucifer as the wall opens the entire way.

"We were so busy accusing Manella that we never thought to suspect the devil," I say quietly.

Gage bristles beside me, as does Ezekiel on my other side. Jude glances at me like he wants to agree, but has too much pride to take my side on anything.

"And we bought into everything he was saying," Kai goes on.

"Number one rule in hell: Never trust anyone you're not bonded to," Jude states flatly.

All the competitors are allowed to pass through, and I follow the guys to the edge, looking over to see an endless wasteland of savage creatures racing around far below.

Lava runs far and wide, and now Lilith isn't going to gift/curse us across it. Hellfire sprays up much like it did in hell's throat, but it actually looks like acid reflux that would be in the actual stomach—I assume. You know, if the stomach had lava and monsters and stuff.

Some areas look like deserts. Some look like ashy forests. It all stretches and mingles together, making it impossible to miss any one thing.

"I'm afraid that other than the fact you have to survive all three days and cross the finish line, there are no rules," Lucifer goes on. "It's not like you can leave the boundaries unless you swim in the surrounding moat of hellfire and manage to survive," he adds carelessly.

"No rules? What about other competitors killing and all that?" I immediately ask, panic pulsing through me.

Gage's jaw grinds. "It's another first," he finally answers.

This course is designed to kill. Not to test.

He's stripping the rules and making it a kill zone free-for-all amongst thieves, cheats, and murderers who have hellish powers and/or abilities.

I heave out a breath.

"Sounds like she just figured out how bad this is," Jude drawls.

"I'm going to be exhausted when I finish saving you for three days straight without an ounce of gratitude to show for it," I deadpan.

Kai snorts, and the other three just grin as I mimic the motions of running a hand through my hair the way they've all been doing. Even as I joke, I cast another apprehensive look toward the devil, wondering why the hell he wants them dead so badly.

His eyes settle on their backs as they continue to stare out at the death course from hell's belly.

Lucifer's calculated grin stays fixed on his lips as he says, "Let the games begin."

END OF BOOK I

Keep reading for book two.

THREE TRIALS

THREE TRIALS

Book II of THE DARK SIDE Series

C.M. Owens writing as

KRISTY CUNNING

CHAPTER 1

Just a suggestion: When the Devil says, "*Let the games begin,*" see if you can run in the opposite direction. If not, put on your big girl panties. Someone might die.

"First ten across the line will ascend," Cain, the Devil's son, says as he takes over. "Even if everyone else dies, if no one crosses the finish line, then no one wins."

"The Devil wants to see what will happen to us if we die," Jude growls. "Has to be what's going on. All that shit about not knowing our situation was bullshit."

"I'm not really sure what we were thinking by trusting the Devil to begin with," Ezekiel mutters just loud enough for me to hear it.

I turn again, finding the Devil practically excited as he grins so broadly and continues to stare at them.

"Even if we manage to survive a land no one outside of hell's belly residents or royals have ever survived, we have to remember Lucifer built this course. It'll be full of illusions that could send us in circles. We'll never get out of here if he doesn't want us to," Gage states quietly.

It reminds me of that palace and how I kept going in circles even when I passed through walls. I couldn't get out until I focused on them and zapped myself to them.

I'm not sure what happens. Between them talking about the

fact they'll never get out of hell's belly and the Devil laughing like he's enjoying every minute of this, I snap.

A haze comes over me, and I move away from the guys as they continue to talk to each other. Slipping by people and *through* people, I make my way toward Lucifer as the acidic power burns at my fingertips, demanding to be set free as the dull echo of my heartbeat pulses in my veins.

Lucifer's eyes are still gazing toward the left, watching the guys as they talk about their impending doom. Every single ounce of fear and dread rolls through me, becoming a force that has to be released.

My hand flies out without another thought, and Lucifer's eyes widen seconds before he's launched across the room.

He slams through a crowd people before crashing against a wall, dropping to the ground with a heavy clap. But when he starts laughing instead of screaming in pain, my hand wavers then lowers slowly.

A sick feeling slithers up me as a bit of hopelessness joins alongside it. Lucifer just dusts himself off, still grinning, completely unaffected.

The rest of the party has gone silent, all eyes on the Devil as they worry about what happens next.

"Somebody is *really* not happy about this course," Lucifer says loudly, then laughs along with a few other psychopaths.

His eyes narrow even as a smile stays on his lips, and he looks around like he's searching for me.

Feeling a hollowness at the proof I can't take the Devil down, I turn and walk swiftly back to the guys, nervous the Devil will beat me to them. As soon as I'm to them, Jude gives me smirk and an arched eyebrow.

"Any particular reason you just threw the Devil across the room in front of everyone? Or are you just suicidal? He'll know that was you," he points out.

I look back just as Lucifer predictably starts making his way over here.

"You know that acid power I have that eats people from the inside out?" I ask them.

"Yes," Ezekiel says hesitantly.

"I didn't throw the Devil across the room," I say as Lucifer draws closer, his smile scarily widening with each step he takes. "I used the acid power on him."

Jude mutters a curse under his breath, and he passes through me, standing in front of me as the Devil nears.

"Seems like someone is a little riled up. Tell me what *she* is saying," Lucifer tells them.

I thought Lamar was my friend, but apparently his main priority is to the Devil, to hell with everyone else. Even though I never thought the Devil would be more intrigued with me upon discovering I have a gender, I'm sure Lamar knew.

"She's saying she will find a way to kill this evil son of a bitch if anything happens to you guys in there," I bite out, stepping closer to Jude's back.

Kai chokes back some sound, and Jude smirks. "She says she's sorry," Jude lies. "She knows she was terribly out of line, but she has no true gauge of right from wrong, as she's not an actual being."

I glare at the back of his head.

"That's not at all what I said, and a touchable vagina makes me very much an actual being. My independent thoughts and emotions make me a *being* too, but mostly the vagina. And it's a good vagina, by the way. Not an evil one, despite the house vote."

I ramble when I'm stressed out, it appears.

Gage mutters something under his breath that I don't catch.

"I have a feeling that's not entirely true," Lucifer says, that deceptive mask of amusement on his face. "However, the next time she wants to strike me, tell her to make sure I can strike her back. There should always be a balance."

He turns and walks away, and I flip him off to his back.

"Balance my ass. If that didn't even leave a mark on him, then he has a much bigger upper hand than I do," I snap, feeling way too frustrated and struggling to get my temper under control.

I want this entire place to burn to the ground with the Devil in it. Or maybe ice would be the counter to kill the man who can withstand fiery acid.

"You need to calm down. You didn't get this upset when you thought Manella was trying to kill us," Kai says from too close behind me.

"My power wouldn't work on him, yet it flowed through me to hit the Devil. It only works to protect you, so what does that tell you?" I growl, eyes still on Lucifer as he takes a seat in his throne and lazily lounges like he has all the time in the world to watch them die.

My fists ball at my side, and I struggle not to go whole. I almost think he knows what I am and is trying to lure me into some sort of trap.

"You already tried to kill him, and it didn't work. Maybe your power is trying to tell you something still. You forget you're stronger than you were when you attempted to kill Manella," Gage says from my side, moving closer.

They're surrounding me and trying to get me to calm down?

"Why are you defending him?" I ask incredulously, feeling an understandable pang of betrayal.

Gage actually looks a little surprised, then his eyes narrow as anger settles into his features. "I'm not trying to defend him. I'm trying to defuse you before you turn whole and he kills you in front of us."

If he hadn't just admitted they've only kept me around for a power boost, I'd almost think he sounds and looks like he gives a damn right about now.

For whatever reason, the imitation of concern is enough to ice out some of the burning fury, and a weird little contented burn settles in my chest. Without letting them see their effect on me, I turn around and face the course again.

"Competitors, get ready!" Cain shouts, standing in front of everyone.

I have no idea why I do it, but I think of how I burned Lilith, and mimic the same stirring emotions until his pants…burst into flames.

He curses, reaching down to dust the flames away, but then his pants drop like the fire broke the hem. He grabs his pants, jerking them back up, then glares at the Gemini twins before pointing a finger.

"You fucking assholes," he growls.

Their eyes widen, and they vanish from the room when he starts stalking after them. Apparently no one in this room would have a death wish besides the two of them. He vanishes too, and I smirk.

Well, I just caused at least a little sibling drama among their *royal* realm. Sure, it's minor and petty, but at least there's some satisfaction in it.

Hera steps up and takes over where Cain left off, using a tone that makes it sound like she's terribly bored with the entire ordeal.

"Ready, set, go, and blah blah," she says with a dismissive wave of her hand.

A light flashes and momentarily blinds me.

CHAPTER II

We're suddenly alone in the middle of what looks like a fiery canyon. The fire travels *up* in streams, wrapping over the mountains in front of us. On the other side, we have woods full of black, ashy trees and zero light.

The right and left of us fades into both as they touch. We're standing in the only clearing between the two options.

"Do we die in the forest or on the mountaintop?" Gage asks, looking back and forth between both.

"At least we can see death coming if we climb the mountain," Jude answers.

I zap to the top of the mountain, looking around, then zap back down to them. "He didn't say anything about not siphoning. No rules other than to finish the course," I tell them. "Which way is the end? We'll just—"

"Either direction we choose will take us toward the end or in a circle, depending on Lucifer's agenda at this point," Gage butts in. "And I've been trying to siphon since we got in here. He's blocked that ability somehow. Maybe because we're in the belly of hell it doesn't work. Who knows at this point?"

"And I can only do it in this form—the form where I can't touch anything or anyone so that I can siphon them with me, because for whatever reason, each new gift has a downside. Yet I'm not supposed to be a gift from Lilith because that's impossible," I state-matter-of-factly, rambling again.

Gage starts climbing the side of the mountain with Ezekiel right behind him.

Jude and Kai move as well, and I grin when I hear Ezekiel yell down at Jude. "Really glad I got that good night of sleep now."

Jude mutters something as he climbs a little more angrily now. I just hang out, watching them near the ledge, making sure nothing comes at them while they're distracted. As soon as they reach the ledge, I zap up there, and start looking around, inspecting it for dangers that might catch them off guard.

"I wonder if I can create weapons the same way I create clothes," I say to them, moving from spot to spot on the barren mountainside ledge in front of them as they start hiking up behind me.

"Don't risk it," Kai says to me absently. "Lucifer is likely watching our every move. Besides, we need certain weapons to actually be able to do any damage in hell. I don't think you'll be able to materialize those."

"Can the Devil hear you?" I ask him.

"No," Jude answers. "Not unless he comes down here."

I look around, but don't see an obvious hole in the air where the doorway once was.

As we continue to hike up, avoiding the side with the lava spilling upward, I conversationally say, "So they focus on quads, and they're desperate to know of your powers. Even accuse you of being too strong to be topside. Yet he seemed surprise you had a balance."

"I noticed that too," Ezekiel tells me.

"Just curious, but do you think they're searching for the Four Horsemen?" I ask.

Jude snorts.

"We thought of that first. The Four Horsemen were killed

centuries ago during a collision of the two kingdoms, before we were even born," Kai answers me. "We thought we'd access more information on it, but even if that's what we were, they'd be trying to get us in hell; not keep us out."

Huffing out a breath of frustration, I start to say something else, when a huge half-bird, half-snake creature, breaks through the mountain side, passing right through me with its wide, fanged mouth open for food.

A shudder ripples through me as the scaly tail finishes passing through me, and power pulses from me without me even summoning it, sending the bird-snake squawking in pain as its wings stumble their flight and it starts spiraling downward. It catches itself right before the bottom and shoots off in the opposite direction of us.

"That was so not cool," I grumble, shuddering again, feeling like I need a shower. "Did you see its tail?"

Gage chuckles, but we all start warily listening to the mountainside now that we know there are beasts that can shoot out of it.

"I don't know if that thing could see me, but I am curious why the hell some monsters have seen me, even though people—not even the Devil—can do so," I state idly, glancing around.

No one volunteers any possible answers, so I prattle on, adding, "Maybe because they're deader? Mushed up in that soul chamber called hell's throat until they're the abominations they are now?"

"Maybe because the monsters see differently than our kind. The monsters don't see things three-dimensionally. It's another level of vision that has evolved in their state," Kai says through strain as he starts shoving at a boulder.

Gage helps, and they topple two boulders into the lava, using all their strength to interrupt its path. It's safe to assume it's hellfire lava. Quickly, they all jump over those boulders before they sink.

"I wonder if they see me like an ink blob. Psychology would

make so much more sense to me if so," I observe thoughtfully, changing my entire attitude about ink blobs prints on movies now.

"Or maybe they see things in ones and zeroes. Could be the origin of code if one of these was humanoid and got loose topside."

Apparently they think I'm ridiculous since no one is dignifying my very creative musings as conversation starters.

I keep talking, mostly to myself since they've stopped responding. Talking seems to calm me down, and I'm still a little nuclear-level furious from the Devil's betrayal that we really should have seen coming.

There's a reason people tell you to never make a deal with the Devil.

"Why not just get one girl and keep her for those fun times? Is it really because you're too selfish to spend any amount of time on a woman? Do you not find her worth your time between bouts of dirty four-way sex?" I ask, not expecting an answer as I try to distract my mind.

As I open my mouth to keep talking, Kai answers. "Relationships are different than a one-night experience. Attention gets divided when emotions get involved. We've tried. There are always favorites, and none of us enjoy it when there are favorites, not even the favorites."

"It creates jealousy among us, and we always suffer a power loss," Jude says, staring a little accusingly at me.

"Well, favorites change. For instance, you were my favorite in the beginning. Now you're a peg below Mr. Selfish," I dutifully point out.

"You had us numbered, so I'm assuming four was the best?" Gage muses. "Making me your least favorite, despite your animosity toward Kai and his selfish ways."

"Actually, you were numbered based on the order I saw you in," I tell him as I step across a bleeding rock.

Yes. The rock is bleeding. I'm not sure if it's dangerous, but if it's bleeding, I'm gonna say it's not a good rock.

Certainly not sanitary.

Or maybe it's on its period, so I assume stepping on it would really piss it off more than usual.

"When I first started drifting in and out, fading out of existence then back in again, I saw you," I tell Gage. "I realized quickly that the longer I could see you, the longer it took for me to fade. I followed you everywhere for a few days, but I could never see anything around you or hear anything at all. It was just silence and one gorgeously tattooed anchor."

He clears his throat and looks away, and I shrug a shoulder.

"My vision soon started expanding, and I saw Ezekiel next. He was the one with you when it first expanded. Then Kai came into frame moments later. At last, I could see the whole room, and Jude was the final piece. Just one helped my state-of-being grow slowly. All four sped up the progress exponentially."

They exchange a look, but I pretend not to notice. They're likely trying to detect a lie or spot the manipulative web the evil vagina is weaving.

"Then I watched you moderately. Every time you'd take a woman back, I'd fade out because I refused to watch that. It got harder and harder to come back, so I finally started watching. Then berated myself for not watching sooner."

Kai snorts out a laugh.

I continue on with my story, since I never told them the details of my beginning. "Finally, sound came. It was overwhelming at first. Smells were just behind it. Sight. Sound. Smell. Touch took the longest to appear. The last was *taste* that followed quickly," I say, adding the last part a little quietly.

Ezekiel steps a little closer, then makes a conscious effort to put immediate space between us. He was my first taste.

"You got all pissy about us keeping you around just to boost our powers, yet you admit you stuck around with us to power yourself. Double standard much?" Jude drawls, being his typical asshole self.

My usual response would be witty and catty with equal parts menace and humor. Today, it's honest. Might as well be brutally honest and rip the veins open. Death could come by nightfall for all of them, then me by proxy.

"You four were there for every step of my growth, even seemed to aide in it. I grew attached to all of you—infallibly loyal, viciously protective, savagely lustful, and tragically devoted. I genuinely believed I'd seamlessly slide into your lives and fulfill your need for a woman to share. Pathetic and short-sighted as it may sound to you, it was that fantasy that kept me coming back. And because the four of you unknowingly saved me for years, I became indebted to you on a scale that I can never repay. *That* is why I stick around. I could give in and just fade out—could go back when life would have been so much easier and less lonely. I finally get to be the one saving you, giving back to you all you gave to me, despite your rather extreme protests, so I stay."

No one says anything for a while. It's not the first time I've attempted to bare my heart and soul, then have the pieces of it get thrown in my face directly after by them.

It's odd that I'm thankful for the next bird-snake that emerges to break up the awkward tension surrounding us. It shoots out, passing through me again, just like the last one.

"Why do they keep shooting out at me?" I snap as that sickly tail slashes through me, the bird-snake soaring out and away from us.

I think that other one must have somehow warned him I'd kick his scaly ass.

"I'm a badass," I state primly as I walk a little taller in my sexy phantom heels.

"You could at least give us something pretty to look at while we're off to face death," Ezekiel states flatly.

"My outfit is badass *and* hot."

"It's…not our thing, really," Kai drawls.

A sexy little red Devil Halloween costume appears on me, along with red fishnet stockings hooked to the garter belts. The cliché pitchfork, red horns, and little red heels complete the look for hell's belly's deadly excursion.

At first there's silence, then suddenly there's boisterous laughter, and I grin to myself while swishing my ass that is clad with red lace panties.

"May be just a little too distracting," Gage groans.

"You wanted pretty. My ass in lace is as pretty as it can get."

"I think it's her vanity that always catches me off guard the most," Ezekiel says on a rumble of laughter.

"I prefer to hear it called *confidence*," I once again point out.

"I think it's her greed that surprises me. Wanting all the jewelry and fancy dinners we bought the other women," Kai muses.

"Not greed. I'm not really all that greedy, to be honest. I spent five years coveting the gifts you gave these women as tokens of your brief but passionate affection. They didn't even know you, yet you showered them with such things. I still want all that," I go on. "Even if you do deny me the rest of the fantasy, I still want all the sweet stuff. You might have saved my life, but you did it without effort. I've certainly had to exert effort to return the favor. I feel like the tokens of affection could be accepted as tokens of gratitude, and then there could be balance in the debts."

It grows immediately silent, and I turn to look behind me to see they've also stilled.

"It's not like you don't have the money," I say on an exasperated sigh.

"It's just the choice of words you used," Jude says, not giving anything away with his tone or expression.

A screech from below sounds before the earth starts shaking hard, and Kai is pitched to the side. The others shout for him as he falls toward a lava stream below us.

I zap down, landing on the last ledge before the cliff, and I turn whole just in time to grab his hand as he falls by me. His hand immediately clasps mine as my hair falls around my face.

Light beams around me, almost blinding the both of us, and I jerk him onto the ledge before the light disappears and I tumble to the ground in my phantom form, my heart racing so fiercely that I almost can't stand, even without gravity hindering me.

Kai is panting heavily as he drops beside me, and he says, "You're a lot stronger than you look."

I laugh humorlessly, staring up but not able to see anything.

"What the fuck happened?! All we saw was a blast of light!" Gage shouts.

"I'm alive," Kai calls out. "The rest can wait," he adds, though it sounds as though he's just talking to me as he pushes up to his feet.

He groans as he stares at all the lost progress.

"I'll meet you at the top. Don't linger. I don't want to know what just shook the earth that hard," he calls out.

He studies me for a minute, but I turn away and start hiking again, electing to stay with him so that he's not left down here alone.

"Will you be able to make it three days without giving in to the urge to solidify?" Kai asks me.

"No. My level-up has its own form of balance, it seems," I answer on a sigh. "How much can Lucifer see?"

"Not really sure, but I doubt he can see in caves. You can turn whole in those to rest and gain strength," he says to me. "We'll have to break for rest anyway. This place will drain our energy."

"But you're at your most vulnerable when you sleep. I'll just rest an hour at a time. It'll be enough."

"It's obvious Lucifer has an interest in you, possibly even knows what you are. If you go whole, you're at *your* most vulnerable, and you're not a participant in the trials. He can haul you out and execute you. You know he's stronger, and he might know of a way to stop you from escaping."

"Careful. You're starting to sound like you care, and that conflicts with your selfish image," I say, lightening the mood.

The more they act like they care, the more attached my stupid little heart tries to get to them. Like it's starving for all the scraps of attention.

"It gets old," he finally says with a shrug.

"What?" I ask as we move up higher on the mountain, our pace brisk to make up for lost ground.

"It gets old," he says again. "The game. It's always the same. The only time we shook things up was when we tried to tackle relationships. Once we even tried to have a relationship with four women, and they were game for it. Sex was together, one woman at a time. They didn't find out about each other, but when they did, things got bad. It's the only time favorites didn't matter, because we were all someone's favorite. Yet…"

"They didn't like sharing their favorite," I decide to say.

"Yeah. They didn't mind sharing the rest of us, but the favorite was off limits. Even that proved to weaken us. Our bond is the only thing that steadies us. We're a volatile explosion waiting to happen, and the bond is the glue that holds us together both individually and as a unit. Anything that threatens the bond is the worst threat to us."

"What about being all together in the same room with different women?" I muse.

"Tried that too. It's not…I don't expect you to understand, but we bonded when sharing, and sharing only strengthens the bond. We don't feel whole when we're *not* sharing."

I bet the bleeding hell rocks have synced up their mensies

"I think I know why you're all so moody," I say as though it's just dawned on me. "You all have your man-periods at the same time."

"I'm not even sure how to respond to you when you abruptly shift directions and say shit like that, and half the time you take silence as a sign of being moody," he murmurs distractedly.

"Episodes of homicidal rage. Uncontrollable lust. Middle-of-the-night pizza cravings…Yep. You're all totally synced up like these menstruating rocks," I go on.

I get the usual groan.

"I mean, it's right there in the word. *Men*struating. It'd make more sense to define moody men."

"Feel free to talk about *anything* else," he grumbles. "Unless you want to keep hearing silence."

"You're just grunting and groaning, not really staying all that silent," I inform him.

He gives me an impatient look.

Oh, yeah. I need back on the original topic. "For the record, I totally didn't want *any of you* touching anyone else, and that made me feel selfish. If it wasn't for the evil vagina that got you all individual hard-ons, what would the answer have been to my proposal?" I ask mildly, glancing at another bleeding rock.

Kai weirdly walks into a cave, and I follow, warily looking around. He spins once we're deep inside. "Turn whole," he demands.

I do, and the light is absent this time. I guess the adrenaline must have been playing a part on the cliff.

"What's going—"

My words are cut off when he's suddenly on me, kissing me hard as he lifts the flimsy little skirt that doesn't even cover all of my ass and presses me against the cave wall.

He reaches between us and rips away the scrap of lace, and my breath catches, forcing me to break the kiss, when his fingers find my clit. My eyes almost cross, and I clutch his shoulder, amazed by how much better it feels when someone else touches me than when I touch myself.

Ignoring the terribly inappropriate timing, my lips hungrily find his, and I moan into his mouth as he starts working a finger inside me, his thumb still working those incredible circles at the exact right speed and perfect pressure.

I can't even think.

He kisses his way down my throat, and my nails dig into his tux jacket as he drives me insane with very little effort. The orgasm hits me so much faster than it has under my own manipulations.

My entire body shudders and comes alive with sensation, and I kiss him even harder, needing more of him as I clench around his fingers, not feeling that hollow sensation quite as much.

He manages to break the kiss, pulling back as he pants heavily and stares into my eyes. He brings his finger up and sucks it like he's tasting the most intimate part of my body from the one piece of his body that has touched it.

My eyes grow hooded, and that uncontrollable desire spikes even more like I'm caught in a haze.

He closes his eyes like he's savoring the taste, and my hands mindlessly go to his belt, undoing it like now he's mine to have. His hands clasp around my wrists, halting me, and I look up to see his taunting smirk.

"*If* we could have you, I wouldn't be so selfish. I'd make sure you were well sated before taking mine, and I'd make you crave me as often as possible. The fact that I'm not your favorite kills me. But because of that aching need to be your favorite, I know you'd be the end of us."

He pushes away and starts walking, while I try to gather my senses. I shift back to my phantom form, still feeling the aftershocks of my first orgasm that wasn't self-induced.

Who knew there were varying degrees of pleasure like that? Just a taste and I'm addicted.

"Truthfully, you're totally my favorite right now," I tell him honestly as we exit the cave.

He half groans, half laughs, a tortured sound that fills me with a weird sense of accomplishment.

He stares up at the cliff that bypasses the hiking trail.

"I'm the fastest climber of the four of us," he says, excluding me from that grouping.

Obviously, he knows I'm faster.

"It'll be quicker to go up," he goes on, sounding like he's talking himself into that conclusion more than explaining his logic to me.

He starts climbing, and I ask a reasonable question. "What if one of those bird-snakes shoots out and knocks you off? I might have set the bar too high with that fabulous first catch, but I'm not so sure we want to see if I'm a one-hit-wonder or not."

He curses and laughs at the same time, straining his muscles as he heaves himself up quicker and quicker.

"Climb behind me several feet down. They seem to be attracted to your presence the most," he says.

"Did you forget my fear of clinging to a mountainside? I was just going to zap up when you got closer."

The ground rumbles, and I start climbing immediately. The rumbling shifts, and as if cued, the bird-snake shoots through me instead of taking Kai down.

Kai blows out a shaky breath as that scaly tail—*the tails are the absolute worst*—finishes slithering through me.

"Since you're my favorite and gave me my first two-person orgasm, I'll tough it out," I grumble, closing my eyes as I start climbing slowly, not really needing to actually worry about falling so long as I don't look down.

His masculine, reluctant chuckle accompanies his usual groan.

"I'm going to need you to stop talking about that, because I'm hard as stone, and you have no idea the temptation I'm battling."

"My evil vagina is impressed with her powers of temptation," I deadpan.

Two more bird-snakes pass through me before we reach the top. I zap the rest of the way there once Kai tells me he's over the edge.

The other three men stand from their seats on the ground, and Ezekiel grimly gestures to the next leg of the trial.

A hellfire tundra awaits us, stretching as wide and far as the eye can see.

And there's no way across.

CHAPTER III

"We can go back down and into the forest, but it's going to exhaust us, and who's to say we won't find the same thing on the other end of it?" Ezekiel asks, frustrated.

I look out, only seeing the black forest behind us and nothing beyond it. I'm assuming that's the Devil's trick.

"So we wait for a gift from one of the children, in other words," Jude says on an annoyed breath.

I move to the edge of the fiery lake, bending low. My hand merely passes through the flames, and I try to think of the power I envied so immensely that Lilith wielded.

It crashed through me with such an overwhelming presence before it temporarily dried up the lake of lava then.

"I'm not volunteering to step in it this time," Kai says bitterly. "I was the last sacrifice."

Jude curses, moving toward the edge like he's going to do the same stupid thing Kai did at the last trial.

"Stop!" I shout, and he does, but just barely.

"What if I can duplicate what Lilith did? I remember the power. I recorded the feeling."

"Recorded the feeling?" Gage asks.

I nod. "It's how I've learned to do things. I record the processes in my mind—like the clothing issue that started in the beginning. I pick apart the powers later. I even drew out acid on command today because I've been getting better and better since my last level-up."

"Lilith has a lot more power than you," Kai decides to point out.

A wave of envy washes over me again. I'm assuming she did something to me when that power rushed through me, because I've really hated her ever since.

"Just for that, you're no longer my favorite. It goes back to Ezekiel by default."

Ezekiel's eyebrows raise, at the same time Gage asks, "How did Kai become your favorite when he was your least favorite?"

Since I already replaced the ripped panties with an exact replica pre-barbarian Kai, there's no evidence of our detour.

"The most important part of that you should concern yourself with is the fact you're the only one who *hasn't* been my favorite," I tell him flippantly, studying the fire lake a little more intensely.

My eyes close as I recall that day, making it clear. I separate each intricate part of the power, trying my damnedest to see if I can duplicate it.

"Anything you care to explain?" Jude drawls, distracting me only briefly when my eyes open to see him staring expectantly at Kai.

"Kai showed gratitude. The rest of you could really take a lesson," I inform them absently.

Ezekiel just laughs and walks away. Gage rolls his eyes. Jude is the only one acting like he's upset right now.

The ground around us starts to shake, and the guys go silent as it shakes harder and harder.

"Please fucking tell me you're doing that," Gage says on a quiet breath.

Something is pouring out of me, but I sure as hell am not shaking the ground.

"Not me," I groan.

Just as they start to take cover, a massive beetle spews from the lake, spanning at least twenty yards as it floats atop the fiery surface. It spits and foams at the mouth, and it gnashes its crooked, spiky teeth close to Gage.

A beetle that likes hellfire instead of burning? No thank you.

Gage flips back, and in the next instant his hand shoots out. The beetle freezes, and Gage lunges, connecting with the beetle's leg that he grips with both hands.

A scream tears through the air as the beetle's massive body starts to shrivel, the fight slowly leaving the beast.

"Stop!" I shout, and Gage does, looking at me like I'm crazy.

"We can ride it across. It's subdued with whatever you just did that is making it wilt like a rotten piece of fruit, but it's still floating."

The guys all exchange a look, and then they quickly start climbing it. Kai is the only one left on land, and he kicks his foot out hard, knocking the beetle off the land what little bit it was beached.

Then he runs and leaps. Jude catches his hand, pulling him up the rest of the way. I zap myself up there with them, and we slowly float down the fire. The center of the beetle escapes the licking flames, and they stay there, away from harm.

There's just enough of a current to slowly drag us in the right direction.

"How do you pass an impassible lake without a consequential gift from the Devil's children?" Ezekiel asks as he lies down.

"You wound a hell's belly monster just enough to ride it on the premeditated current," Jude answers, looking over at Gage as he clenches and unclenches his fists, still wired from whatever he just did.

"Riddles," Kai states flatly.

"The riddles are subtle?" I ask on a sigh. "I expected a super creepy echoing voice to pop in and ask us questions that we had to get right before we could pass on to the next phase."

Ezekiel snorts as he tosses his tux jacket off the side of the beetle. It turns to ash instantly when it hits the flames, and he adds the tie to the flames next.

"Why must they overcomplicate these things? How do we know when there's a riddle or just an obstacle?" I ask. "Lamar said the riddles would be the most important."

"They will be. They'll be the trick to life or death, clearly," Jude says, gesturing at the beetle under us, and looking at me like I'm an idiot.

"In that case, I really hope you're all old enough to be wise and not just paranoid, so we can see the riddles before it's too late next time," I tell him, a fuck-you grin on my face.

Ezekiel laughs as he lies down, putting his side against mine as he untucks his dress shirt. Fortunately, I feel no overwhelming urge to go whole.

I'm getting better at this.

Gage loses the same unnecessary items, but he also strips off his dress shirt as well, leaving the white tank underneath to outline his very hard and distracting body.

"What's Hera's way of delivering gifts?" I ask them, since there's nothing else to do but chat.

"She takes something from you before she gives you something in return," Kai answers from somewhere. "You have no say in what she takes."

"Lovely. Let's hope she doesn't help out, because I don't think I'd like what she'd want from you."

"That's more Cain's style. It's why he doesn't help us. He prefers to be given something in exchange for his help, and it's usually on the sexual favor side. Have you ever seen us with men?"

Gage points out.

"The twins?" I muse.

"A fucked up version of yin and yang with their own twist," Ezekiel answers. "They could hurt you or allow you to fuck them. It depends on what course of action they used the last time. You're always gambling with agonizing pain or possible pleasure when you deal with them."

"They have no sexual preference, but again, we do," Kai points out. "Which is why Lilith and Hera are the ones to approach us."

"So Hera has approached you?" I ask, trying not to sound as worried as I feel for whatever reason.

"She tried at the beginning of the first trial. Lilith intercepted her," Jude states, staring in front of us like he's searching for an end to come into sight.

"What about Manella?" I ask when it grows quiet.

"No clue. I've never heard anyone speak about him ever aiding anyone before," Gage says with a shrug.

"I know you're all probably not tired, but now would be a good time to take a nap. This lake is big, and at the speed we're going, we're going to be riding for a while. I'll take guard duty," I tell them.

Kai loses the shirts completely, going bare chest as he flops down. I idly wonder how all four decided combat boots were acceptable footwear for a tux.

"Must you touch her every time you sleep? You have a tendency to form habits, Mr. Nipples," Jude says dryly, his eyes on Ezekiel.

"I only get any actual rest next to her, so if I'm going to nap when I'm not really tired, then it's going to be one hell of a power nap to last me," Ezekiel answers unapologetically.

"Point one for the evil pussy," I say tauntingly to Jude, holding up my index finger on one hand and an O with the other to signify the score.

Jude looks like he's trying not to smile, which pisses him off even more, apparently, since he mimes the motion of strangling me before turning around and calling me a few uncharitable, yet very creative, names.

I give him the bird. It's not creative, but it *is* my favorite sign.

"He's only mad because he hates me as much as he likes me, and since he doesn't want to like me, he tries to hate me a little more," I say as Kai stretches out beside me, his body brushing through mine.

Gage and Jude sit across from me like it's a standoff, and they eye Kai like he's a new traitor to their cause.

I hold up two fingers while mouthing the new score.

They both glare at me.

It's adorable, really. At least in this form. I'd find it less adorable and more terrifying if I could physically feel the true power of a racing heartbeat.

Kai just smirks, even as he keeps his eyes closed. Like he knows the silent exchange going on without seeing it. Ezekiel is already asleep, breathing evenly as his face remains relaxed.

Gage stares a little longingly, as though he's jealous of the obvious peace on Ezekiel's usually tortured sleep-face.

He blinks and looks away, his jaw set as he stares out over the lake. Jude continues to burn a hole through me with his glare.

"I'm all of your types, really, minus the preference in hair color. I had no control over that. It was there when I got here. But all your wants, desires, needs, debaucheries of choice…everything. I'm molded to your specifications, because the only thing in the world I knew was all of you. I learned what you liked, and it became a part of me. It shaped me as the person I am now, because I was learning who the hell I was then. Blame yourselves for all the things you don't like."

A sleepy rumble of laughter slides out of Kai as his body begins to relax.

"Kai loves the chase and is always desperate to make someone who hates him suddenly crave him," I say with a shoulder shrug. "He wants to infect them with his heady spell that he can weave when he really wants to."

Another sleepy laugh is the response to that.

"Ezekiel is the most desperate for peace, as though his nightmares are twice as stained as all of yours. Not sure how I did that. I expected his favorite part to be the fact I really want my nipples adored."

Jude arches an eyebrow at me.

"It's true," I go on unapologetically. "Gage wants a puzzle he can't unravel so easily. He wants to be surprised, and he's tired of all the predictable variables. He's starving for a challenge. He'll admit it if you ask him how much he's actually enjoying the fact he doesn't know if he'll die or live at the end of these trials."

Gage's jaw grinds, but he smirks even as he radiates anger.

Jude looks over at him then at me. "This is why you're so dangerous, *comoara trădătoare*. Giving us exactly what we've all always dreamed of, along with a chance to strengthen ourselves? When something feels too good, there's always a really fucking nasty tail you don't see coming until it's too late."

He turns around, putting his back to me before lying down. His eyes are closed and he is purposely staying inches away from me, not touching me.

"I've already told you my *tail* in lace is the prettiest thing you'll ever see," I deadpan.

He makes a sound of frustration, but I'm apparently going to get the last word.

I'm a little curious just how beautiful Hera must have been as Helen of Troy to have inspired a war between two nations, when I couldn't even get one man to crumble before me.

It, of course, makes me envious. Sigh. I'm still blaming Lilith for that.

"Ezekiel was my first kiss," I decide to say, looking down to see Kai sleeping peacefully. "Kai was my first orgasm giver," I go on.

Jude's jaw tics, as Gage grunts and curses. I grin.

"Don't worry, he just used his fingers. He didn't give it up to the nefarious vagina. My point is, it seems I'm going to be running low on firsts pretty soon, at the rate I'm going. You boys better not come crying to me when you missed all the firsts for being completely unreasonable pricks."

Gage does the same petty thing, refusing good sleep offered by the evil vagina holder for no cost of admission.

They both ignore me, because they don't really like arguing as much as I do. I could quite literally point logic out to them all day.

Surrounded by the four guys who easily close their eyes in my presence, willing to put their life in my hands, yet completely unwilling to stubbornly admit they trust me, I stare out over the fiery lake.

It's actually sort of pretty once you get over the dangerous part of it. Also, as long as you don't mind the occasional bird-snake carcass floating by you, or the living ones casting their ominous shadow over you from the red sky.

I take it back. It's not pretty. I'm really just trying too hard to make this not as doom-and-gloom as we know it is.

With all of them quiet, not bickering or bantering with me as a distraction, the reality of our situation sinks in, and it grows heavy pretty quickly.

I can't see land on any side now. The crackle of the lake and spitting fire that hisses when it shoots too high don't exactly give off a comforting melody.

I'm so alert that it's a good thing they can't feel me jostling around to inspect each sound or smell.

Gage suddenly moves into my knee with just the very tips of his fingers, not making a sound or looking at me.

Jude's eyes are open, staring at me before dropping his gaze to the fingers Gage leaves there, his body relaxing as the tingles soothe him. At least I assume it's the tingles.

Jude's eyes narrow in challenge, as though we're in a war and this is a pivotal battle.

Obviously, I mouth the word, *"Three,"* before holding up just as many fingers and waggling my eyebrows at him.

It's clearly the most mature course of action.

He doesn't find it quite as amusing as I do.

"That's twice you've called me *comoara trădătoare.* What does it mean?" I ask him.

He holds my gaze for so long that I think he's not going to answer.

Just as he closes his eyes, I hear the words that are almost whispered.

"Treacherous treasure."

CHAPTER IV

"I swear, I never want to see another fucking beetle for as long as I live," I mutter under my breath.

Which might be as long as an hour from now for all I know.

We've been stuck on top of this foul-smelling thing for over ten hours now. At least. Possibly even longer. Just floating on the fire. If my ass was capable of feeling anything in this form, it'd still be numb.

Bright side, three out of four guys just got a lot of proactive rest before day two starts out the same way day one ended.

Jude is the only one awake. He never really slept as deeply as the other three, and I'm fairly sure he resents the hell out of all of them for sleeping as well as they have. And he resents me for my wicked vagina voodoo.

My milkshake brings all the boys to naptime…Yeah, that's not how that song goes. The song is a lot sexier, but beggars can't be choosers.

They're a tough crowd, so I take the small wins that come along.

"Fucking finally," Jude says, causing my attention to lift.

I spot gray land with nothing but a shadow behind it, almost as though there's a second picture out of frame, and for a second I'm relieved, until I see a girl and guy lifting bows and launching arrows.

"Get the hell up!" Jude shouts as I leap to my feet.

Before I can even react, he flips into the air, snatching both speeding arrows, and lands in a crouch back on the beetle.

He casually tosses an arrow to Ezekiel as he lands at his side, and the two of them throw the arrows so hard they zip through the air in a blur of speed.

Both archers drop to the ground, the arrows sticking out of their throats as their bodies convulse.

"They could have just went on instead of mistaking you to be vulnerable on the back of a beetle, and they'd have survived," I state, as though they need a reminder of the obvious.

"Depending on their ability to heal, they may still survive if we leave them," Jude tells me.

They'd better stay dead.

"Does that mean you're going to do your five-finger-death-punch to ensure they don't chase us down and try to kill you again?" I muse.

He gives me an annoyed look.

"Did you really just do that?" he asks incredulously.

"What? Use your favorite band to name your Hulk Smash and Decay power? Yes, yes I did," I say very seriously, holding his gaze like there's a challenge to see who holds it the longest.

He breaks our stare-down first, and Kai smirks, even though he seems distracted.

"Well. That's certainly problematic," I announce in a huff when I see what has their attention.

The closer we get, the louder the telltale sign is, making us view the optical illusion differently. It's not one stretch of lake we're seeing anymore. There's a massive drop below before it levels out, and we're actually seeing two levels of fire now.

The newest issue is a massive, fiery waterfall that we're fast approaching, and there's roughly a hundred foot gap from the start of the *fire*fall to the land across from us.

Hell really sucks.

"How far can you guys jump? Because that's a little difficult for me even in this form," I say warily, my heart starting to hammer now.

Gage looks around like he's searching for something, as Ezekiel answers me.

"We can't make that jump."

No land is on either side of us, not giving us any other option, since we're surrounded by hellfire lava. And this firefall? It's five times the size of Niagara Falls in width.

The fall isn't that steep—maybe fifty feet—but there's no way the beetle won't submerge with all that weight, even if they manage to all stay on it during the fall. They'll never survive the hellfire burns.

And the Devil wins.

"Now would be a good time to figure out the riddle early," I tell them, frantically waving my arms as though that will spur them into brilliance.

"How do you cross an uncrossable passage layered with flames of fucking death without falling or jumping into the fire, when there's no obvious escape around you?" Jude asks on an annoyed breath.

"I hate that riddle," I point out, not coming up with my own genius idea this time.

"Jude and I can throw the farthest," Gage says, cracking his neck to the side. "And we can jump farther as well."

"Obviously that's Plan Z. What's Plan A through Y?" I reasonably ask, knowing he can't possibly be suggesting that as anything other than a last resort.

They ignore me, and I ignore the *fire*fall's edge that we're getting closer and closer to. Okay, so maybe I don't really ignore it at all. It actually has most of my attention.

This is so not the time for this bug to be speeding up. In fact, this is the worst possible time for it to finally feel like it's motoring along.

When they continue to stare at each other like they're calculating the probability for survival and considering this ridiculous plan as their true course of action, I throw my hands up.

"That can't possibly be the right answer to the riddle," I shout at them.

Remember what I said about the drop being fifty feet? I was very much off on that calculation.

The closer we draw, the more I realize my depth perception has been masterfully deceived.

That drop now seems endless before it levels back out again.

Damn that Devil and his illusions.

I don't find myself any fonder of plummeting from a firefall than plummeting from a mountainside. And I close my eyes, because if I can't see it, then it doesn't exist.

I can also ignore the roar of the falls that only seems to add to the drama of the dire situation.

"I don't see any other option," Kai says like he's frustrated and furious. "You'd better damn throw me harder than anything you've ever thrown in your life," he tells someone. "Because I'm up first."

My eyes fly open as I gape at them, but I don't yell anything because I sure as shit don't want to distract them when Gage is already winding Kai up, spinning him out like a father would a daredevil child for giggles.

I'm not seeing why those masochist children find this amusing right now, because my stomach is in my throat, terrified a hand is going to slip and Kai will be skipped across the deadly surface.

Just the image and fear of this has me convinced children are sociopaths. It's always the ones you least suspect.

About ten feet from the edge, he launches Kai, and Kai sails over the massive divide.

I watch with my mouth hanging open, even as Jude starts winding up Ezekiel, preparing him for the same thing. My heart is divided in halves, watching as Kai sails and Ezekiel is being wound up to do the same.

Kai lands with a crash on the other side, bouncing so hard and rolling out of sight.

Before I can shout for him, my words are stolen as I stand frozen and watch Ezekiel sailing faster across the same distance.

My eyes are bouncing everywhere when Jude and Gage dart to the back of the beetle and get into a launch position as they stare straight ahead.

I glance over as Ezekiel lands just as harshly, rolling into the shadowed land hidden from us amongst the fiery lake that is coming to an abrupt end.

Just as the tip of the beetle starts over the edge of the firefall, I turn in time to see Gage and Jude rushing by me, grit and determination shading their eyes as they pass through me in a blur.

I whirl around with them as they pass, watching as it all seems to happen in slow motion. They run to the last tip of the beetle they can reach before they leap as hard as they possibly can.

For an agonizing ten*ish* seconds, I have repetitive heart attacks.

Jude barely makes it across, and he immediately rolls back up to his feet so he can turn in time to see Gage's fingertips just barely graze the ledge a fraction of a second too late and centimeters too short.

Gage's eyes widen as he falls to his back, reaching for the hands that make it another fraction of a second too late to grab onto him. Resignation is painfully immediate in his eyes, and his hard gaze turns cold as he falls helplessly toward the lake. My heart lurches as I leap over the edge, diving for him, zapping myself closer to make up ground.

Our fingertips just barely touch, and I turn whole, grabbing onto him as that light bursts from me again.

No magnificent strength saves us as I scream as loud as I can, begging for a miracle of some sort to stop this from happening. I stay whole, knowing those flames won't simply pass right through me like this.

But I don't care. I refuse to let him die alone, even as I scream and feel the tears rushing up the sides of my eyes.

A vine slaps against us, and I try to snatch it, having no idea where it came from. Seconds later, a body barrels by me, and Ezekiel turns upside down, reaching out with one hand and grabbing Gage by the wrist.

Our hands are violently yanked apart when I keep falling and he comes to an abrupt halt.

Gage dangles above me, holding on to Ezekiel, and Ezekiel holds onto the vine with his other hand as they swing over the lake.

"Fucking go phantom!" Gage shouts at me as that light continues to beam from overhead.

I immediately lose my flesh, and I zap myself back to the very top of the cliff's ledge where the other two are peering over.

Then I collapse as that weird light vanishes from the sky.

Even though I can't feel my legs in this form, they still give out. I can't possibly stand. I feel like every emotion I have was just put through the wringer then boiled in a sadistic witch's brew. I'd wager said sadistic witch made a deal with the Devil for her power, because I'm blaming him for everything right now.

I look down the length of my body as Kai turns around and relaxes at the sight of me. Jude has a flicker of relief in his eyes before he turns away and stares over the edge again.

"Nobody gets to die. I've decided I can't possibly survive it," I say almost breathlessly, though I have no actual breaths in this form.

Ezekiel hauls himself over the edge, smiling at me like he's amused.

"You solved the riddle," he tells me. "And just in time."

"What? How?" I ask, sitting up slowly as Gage heaves himself over and collapses to his back, breathing heavily as he scrubs his face with both hands.

"Screaming vines," Jude states flatly, gesturing around us.

For the first time, I take notice of the fact there are a lot of black, wide vines all around us, dangling from those ashy trees we saw at the beginning. Most of the vines vary in thickness from one to ten inches. The overachieving thick vines are definitely the creepiest.

"What's a screaming vine?" I ask, wondering how the hell I didn't see a forest full of vines that drape over that edge and hang down the length of the firefall.

You think I'd have noticed an entire freaking black-treed forest.

"The vines grow the largest the closest to a fire source," Kai says as he lifts one of the medium-girthed vines and gives it a shake. "And if you scream loud enough, it forces them to react. You answered the riddle when you screamed like a banshee, and the forest appeared."

"The answer is to scream for the only vines long enough to span the depth of the Devil's bowels," Ezekiel finishes.

"The bowels? We're out of the belly?" I ask hopefully.

"Just being cycled back up," Kai tells me. "We're going in a loop it seems. We're at the top again, just on the opposite side of the forest we originally decided to skip."

Of course we are. Why would we get to skip at least one death option?

"That's a terribly sneaky riddle, because if we can't see the forest before we answer the riddle, then how do we know the forest is part of the answer without prior knowledge of the course?" I ask incredulously. "What we saw through that wall after it opened was a flat, fiery tundra. That turned out to be the small gulley we started in, and not even a big part of the course. It was all an illusion to think we knew the course."

"We saw the forest in the beginning. That was the clue to our answer, because to finish the course, you have to complete every obstacle," Kai says with a shrug.

Ezekiel randomly lets out a loud yell, startling my already traumatized heart, and the vine in his hand slaps forth like an exposed wire full of untethered electricity. He dodges a few slashes it makes.

"The vine closest to you always reacts the wildest," Jude says quietly.

"You sent the entire horde of vines near edge of the forest over the cliff because your screams were so loud and echoed around. It was almost like you knew the answer without realizing it," Kai adds.

"No," I confess, holding up a finger for a correction. "That terrified the living shit out of me. That's why I was screaming. Apparently I'm a panicky screamer when plummeting to a fiery death."

Gage laughs under his breath, still staring up at the sky and lying flat on his back.

"For the record, that was a horrible plan. You're certainly no closer to being my favorite now," I prattle on nervously to Gage.

A little bit of reluctant laughter follows that as we all turn to face the forest. The high we're on from the survival of something that seemed impossible is now eclipsed by the dark forest that grows so pitch black we can't see any deeper than ten feet.

My eyes glance over to the forgotten archers who are now covered in vines and being treated like they're officially part of the forest.

"At least now I know why they were trying to kill us instead of just running along. They needed a beetle to cross a fiery stream.

They could have shot an arrow with rope. But how they planned to paddle the thing upstream is a mystery," I say as I look back to the guys.

I think Ezekiel gives me a pity laugh, but the others just start walking into the forest.

"I'm almost positive this was their starting point," Gage says, gesturing over to the two fallen archers. "The forest ran over them like it considered them collateral instead of passengers."

"I guess they're not too good at riddles then," I state absently.

I'm the only one who can see, apparently, once we get into the thick of it.

My night vision isn't grand topside, but I can see in shades of gray down here, while they stumble their way around. The one person who can't trip is the only one who can see.

Ironic twist, huh?

Jude follows close behind me, as though he can see my outline and is using me for guidance. I pass through a tree, and I hear a loud grunt when he runs right into it.

I grin as he curses me.

He's apparently glutton for punishment because he gets behind me again.

"You can turn whole for a while in here. He can't see you," Gage says as he comes up on my side, stumbling a little.

Instantly turning whole, my hand darts out and grabs his like I'm stopping him from falling, though he doesn't need my help. The physical contact feels so good after watching him almost die the last time I was touching him.

He clutches my hand for a second a little too roughly, almost a desperate sort of cling, then drops it and walks ahead, feeling his way around as he manages to pull away from me.

At least I can see with my own eyes that he's okay. And even in flesh, I still have gray vision. I can't see too far ahead, but it appears to be more visibility than they have.

"We need some light," Ezekiel gripes.

Feeling out the energy stirring in me, I test out my powers in whole form. I haven't been able to do that yet, since I only just started being able to reach for it. Maybe it's all the adrenaline these damn trials are pumping through me after my level-up.

With one hard push, the acidic power bursts into the vine I grab. It sizzles and sparks, then lights up, slowly climbing up the rest of the vine. If these things like fire, then I'll consider this their "watering."

Yes, I contain my laughter for my own joke since they likely won't find it as funny.

The small flames don't put off much light, but I do it every ten feet or so, offering them some visibility.

"That's called a *burn,*" I say jokingly.

I get groans instead of laughter. See? It's like someone cut out their ability to find humor.

"That's not even close to what that nineties line is referring to," Jude, the all-knowing prick, says.

"If I'm using nineties lines, does that mean I'm from the nineties?" I ask.

"If you're using nineties terms wrong and causing those around you to cringe, it's likely you're from a few generations earlier than that. It was always the parents that screwed up the best phrases when they got in on the fun," Jude goes on.

"Says the guy who is centuries old. You could be my great grandparents' great grandparent." I grin as I add, *"Burn."*

More groans. Damn it, I thought that one was awesome.

"It's a good thing we don't need your help insulting people," Ezekiel says, patting my shoulder a little patronizingly.

"Careful not to hit the base of the trees. If they catch fire, it's like tossing a match on gasoline. The entire forest will go up in flames and burn until the screaming vines drink all of it in," Gage cautions.

"Well, I'm glad you decide to share that *after* I've been lighting these thirsty bitches up for a while," I point out.

"You just used *thirsty bitches* wrong as well," Kai states from in front of me.

"I don't think I want to know your definition of that phrase," I grumble, causing all of the chauvinist dicks to chuckle.

The deeper we go, the more suspicious I get. It's been terribly quiet. Nothing has tried to eat us, roast us, or drop us into a fiery pit in quite a few hours. Granted, the beetle ride took a while, and aside from a few bird-snakes flying overhead rather ominously, it was rather uneventful.

I'm sure this is just like that. Something long and dull to break down your guard so you aren't on as high alert when a three headed hellhound comes after you.

"Are there such things as three-headed hellhounds?" I decide to ask aloud.

Gage and Kai shake their heads, and Ezekiel smiles to himself, walking easier under the small bit of illumination.

"Sometimes I wonder how your thought process works, and what all happens from the last time you speak until the next time," Gage grumbles. "That's what I find most surprising."

"Glad my entertainment stock is going up, but I'm actually expecting an answer to that."

"The Devil invited us to a party last minute, ambushed us with an early final round of the trials, set everyone up for failure on a three-day, impossible quest, and then sent us in here unarmed, while allowing all our competitors to carry their weapons of choice. During all that calculated and obvious plotting, he decided to kindly hand over a list of all the possible creatures we may or may not encounter," Jude states, each word dripping with sarcasm as though he's really trying to drive home his point.

Just because I'm feeling petty, I scream loudly, startling all the rest of them.

Three vines whip through me as I go back to phantom mode, and they crash into Jude hard enough to send him flying backwards into a tree. I smile over my shoulder at him as he pushes to his feet, glaring at me the entire time.

"*Burn,*" I say with a saccharine sweet smile.

Third time's a charm, apparently.

Kai bursts out laughing, and the vines stay dormant. They truly do only like a good scream. Not just any noise will do. Makes sense, since it's hell. Screams are probably a part of its diet.

"We're going to have to stop for the night, or we're going to—"

Gage's words are cut off when the light disappears and a cool chill creeps in. I hear thunder, and I worry what it's warning us is to come. Somehow I don't think rain and a little lightning are what's in store for us.

"Black ice," I hear Kai say on a short breath. "Run!"

"Find shelter!" Gage shouts, dashing through the forest as it lights up in neon blue pulses.

Thousands of flying spiders go crazy when the light starts glowing brighter, slithering like an oozing, neon, live entity over the black trees.

I can hear the sound of rain gaining on us, and I'm too scared to ask why it's called black ice. I'm also scared why the forest is turning a creepy, glowing blue, but I'm positive the two are related.

Kai shouts, tumbling sideways with Gage as they roll with the shifting ground of the forest that seems to be breaking apart to drink in the rain.

Jude curses as he gets stuck out in a newly made opening, and he dives for the coverage provided by the thickly vined trees.

But the rain catches up too quick, passing through me as I shout a warning to them.

Ezekiel dives to the same broken hole Kai and Gage fell to, but Jude is swallowed up by the earth much farther away. I zap myself to him, landing beside him as he roars in pain, his back arching as agony steals every feature and twists him in knots while the merciless rain pelts him.

I turn whole, not feeling whatever excruciatingly painful thing he is feeling. The rain slaps against me, pounding relentlessly, and I grab his arms, dragging him over to a small cave. The forest has been full of them, but I don't actually think we're in the forest right now. It's more like we're under it with massive openings over us, exposing us to the surface.

Roots are sticking down all over in this underground world with thousands of large cave holes that I hope aren't occupied with monsters the same size.

The rain pours through the openings that lead back up the large drop to where the forest is, but at least I have Jude sheltered from it now.

Jude is shivering violently, and I hate to leave him, but I have to make sure the others are alive and okay before I focus on what's going on.

"Are you okay? Can I go check on them?" I ask in a panic, even though I can sense all three nearby when I go phantom.

"Go," he bites out. "Check on them."

I vanish, feeling sick about it as I zap myself to the others.

Ezekiel is staring down at his arm, cursing as he makes a frustrated and pained sound. I dive to him, looking around for the other two, wondering why Ezekiel is just in his boxers.

"What happened?" I ask on a gasp when I see his arm.

It looks and smells like decay, and it's visibly spreading through the veins.

Kai and Gage jog over, both of them also down to their boxers, and Kai answers.

"Black ice. If it penetrates the skin, it starts freezing you with certain death from the inside out. It spreads fucking fast too," Kai growls.

Gage starts looking around him. "We need something to cut away the arm."

My hands reach for Ezekiel's arm on instinct, and I turn whole when phantom hands don't seem to be doing much.

"Don't!" they all shout at once.

Immediately, I flinch at the burning cold on his skin, but the pain is brief, and his relief is instant as his eyes flake gold again, his arm warming under my touch.

Then my stomach roils when I think of how violently Jude was shaking.

"I have to go," I gasp, zapping back to Jude.

My stomach completely drops when I get back to see him practically convulsing as he wheezes in pain. His neck has an icy, veiny black coloring, as he continues to shake violently on the ground.

I turn whole and dive to him, ripping open his shirt to reveal his entire torso. The decay is spreading quickly, and it's so much worse than Ezekiel's was.

With panicked, shaky hands, I fumble with his belt before getting it off, then grab his pants and boxers, jerking them both down to his ankles.

The decaying process goes all the way down to his knees, and it's spreading lower.

He starts choking when it reaches the top of his throat, and I strip out of my Devil dress, whipping it over my head before I drop to him. Putting as much of my skin against his as I can, I press my cheek to his, hoping this works as fast on an area five times the size of what Ezekiel had.

The burning cold is so much harsher than it was with E, but I grit through it, telling myself in mantra that it's working. That it has to be working. I'm too terrified to look and see, though.

I don't speak, unable to find any words that sound soothing enough for this situation. It isn't until I feel his shaking start to slow down, that I finally look up, finding his eyes already on me.

His teeth chatter, even as his jaw tics.

"If it's not infecting you, don't move. It's working," he manages to say through a great deal of strain.

I tuck my head back under his chin, sliding my hands over his shoulders that still feel cool, even though the darker color seems to have faded.

After a few more minutes, the shaking stops completely, and he releases a breath that sounds as though it's been held for ages.

His arms slide around me, almost hugging me, while the rain ceases as abruptly as it began. The neon blue light flickers, losing some of its energy, but still lingering enough to offer us light from the roots above.

Lazily, his fingers toy with the garter straps holding up my red fishnet stockings. At this particular moment, they seem very inappropriate.

I lift up, my eyes meeting his as I cup his face in my hands, studying him to make sure he's not still in pain. His hands tighten on my ass when my gaze flicks to his lips.

"Ghost Girl! Jude!" We hear Ezekiel shouting.

"Over here," I say, going phantom and zapping myself up to the forest entry nearest to us.

I see Ezekiel running toward me, still illuminated by the lingering neon blue ooze.

Kai is right behind him.

Both of them stumble to a halt and rake their eyes over my barely dressed appearance. I'm only wearing the lacy panties, the fishnets hooked to the garter belt, and the matching red heels.

It's definitely inappropriate now.

"Jude is down below, but I think he's healed. Just a little tired from almost dying and all. Again. Seems to happen a lot with you four," I say, reminding them this is a time for action as I fashion a more appropriate outfit.

They blink once my bare breasts are covered.

"Only since you came around," Ezekiel tells me before he winks. "Care to go heal Gage's leg? A leak sprung above us just before the black ice stopped, and it landed on him before he could get away. We can't touch it, or it'll infect us."

"I'll go."

"We're going to cover as much ground as possible while the black ice residue is glowing. It won't last long."

"Go on without us. We'll catch up. I can find you," I say before zapping to where I sense Gage.

The second I see the man of the hour, he gives me a tight, pained smile infused with frustration.

"Struggling to catch a break, it seems. Day two is not your day," I tell him as I kneel down and try not to pay attention to the fact his boxers are now gone.

The gray icy pattern is spreading from his knee, and is high on his thigh. Trying to cover as much as possible all at once, I lose my new pants before becoming whole.

Gage's eyes widen marginally, and his nostrils flare as I sit down on him in nothing but a corset. Because while I'm healing him, I'm going to be as sexy as possible just to be an ass.

I almost died for him, and still didn't receive gratitude. Kai set the bar for showing gratitude a little high.

I straddle his lap, sitting back enough to where the bottom of my thigh covers the top of his. The sting of burning ice is once again enough to make me flinch, but it's dulled almost immediately.

Gage's hands go to my hips as we sit here, waiting on him to completely heal. His gaze dips to where he grows harder between us, his very aroused cock teasing me with its proximity.

Slowly, his hands travel up my back and back down to my hips.

"I think you're healed," I say a little too quietly.

When I start to get up, he tightens his grip on my hips and jerks me forward until my chest smashes against his, and his cock rubs against my slit in the most tormenting tease in history.

I shiver embarrassingly dramatic, and he smirks as I press even closer.

"You were going to go into that lake with me, weren't you?" he asks seriously, his eyes searching mine.

I shrug and roll my eyes as though it wasn't quite the big deal he's making it. I wanted gratitude, but now I think it might make me uncomfortable if he actually gives it to me in such an intense manner.

"You were whole. It would have probably killed you too," he goes on, still studying me like he's expecting to see something.

"I thought it'd be a terrible way to die. It'd be even worse to have to do it alone. I just didn't want you to be alone. Can we go now? We're already going to have to run to catch up."

I don't even try to get up, because his fingers dig in harder on my sides. When his gaze dips to my lips, I decide not to delay the inevitable and lose the moment like I did with Jude. He meets me halfway, and our lips clash almost violently.

He groans into my mouth like he's never done before, and he flips me to my back so fast that I'm left a little dizzied from the abrupt swap.

He settles himself between my legs, only teasing me more as he kisses me harder and the tip of his cock toys with the entrance of my evil vagina.

But I know he's not going to have sex with me. None of them will cross that line until they're sure my vagina isn't going to destroy them.

Really, they're so dramatic. I'm apparently just as dramatic, because I've started fretting about it as well.

That glorious tongue ring of his wreaks havoc on my fantasies, spicing them up as I imagine how good it would feel lower. The way I've witnessed him do for other women.

"I hate to point out the obvious," I say when he breaks the kiss and pulls his hips away, kissing a heated path down my throat, "but your timing is positively terrible."

He smiles against my collarbone as he kisses his way down.

"If I don't do it now, it's very likely I'll talk myself out of it once my head clears and I'm thinking logically again." He kisses a path through the space between my breasts, and my back arches, trying to push more of my body against his mouth.

"Do what?" I ask on autopilot, not capable of actually thinking.

This is my favorite feeling.

The intimate contact with one of them. It always reminds me that I'm finally alive instead of just surviving. Especially in the middle of a game of survival.

He kisses a lazy trail at the bottom of my stomach, teasing me with how close he is to where I want him.

"I know I'll regret not taking this first for myself if I do talk myself out of it," he whispers against my skin before he jerks my legs open wider and his head dips between my thighs.

I'm already making ridiculous sounds and squirming uncontrollably the second his tongue swipes across my clit. It's way more intense with a mouth than with a finger.

Especially when he sucks it into his mouth and uses his tongue to add that much more stimulation. When that metal bar in his tongue only adds to the already overwhelming sensations, my fingers tangle in his hair and I make some garbled noise of praise and curses.

I'm pushing him away, and drawing him closer at the same time, and then doing some shameless grinding, as though my body is confused by the pleasure that is so intense it's almost painful. His fingers dig into my legs, dragging me impossibly closer to his face as he grows more aggressive, driving me wilder with each new flick of his tongue.

It's too much.

Erotic sensation crackles over me with so much force that it turns me hot and cold at the same time, and I cry out so loudly a vine slaps the wall near us.

My entire body goes lax after being so tense just seconds ago, as the ripples of pleasure skate over me in ebbing waves of awareness, the orgasm coming so hard and fast that it's just too sensitive when his mouth doesn't immediately relent.

He finally tears his mouth away, then his mouth finds mine again, his hand roughly grabbing my hair as he slides over me. Too far gone to think clearly, I'm convinced we're going to break the rules and finally get answers about that virgin question, when he breaks the kiss abruptly, breathing heavily as his forehead drops to mine.

"We should run so we can catch up," he says instead, pushing away from me as he leaves the abandoned boxers behind.

I'm glad he can abruptly shift gears after something like that, but I'm not built that way.

"I'm going to need just another minute," I say as my legs tremble to punctuate the point.

Damn man is still naked, and my mind is a little feral at the moment.

He smirks over his shoulder, looking really damn proud of himself, as I stare at his incredibly firm ass. He gives me thirty seconds to recover before he reaches his hand down for mine.

I take it, and he easily tugs me up without me even helping him. Since I don't need to be running around in hell's belly naked, I go phantom and redress myself.

The sensations are watered down in this form, and I almost feel robbed of the post-orgasmic bliss once again.

"When we get out of here alive, you're going to do that again to me on a bed," I tell him as we walk out.

"Who's your favorite now?" he drawls as he turns and starts backing away, a knowing grin on his face.

"Definitely you," I say with one hundred percent honesty.

CHAPTER V

"How much farther?" Gage whispers as we stop for a second for him to take a few breaths.

A massive spider bat flies through me, and I screech before I can help myself. It's happened a lot since the lights fully went out about an hour ago.

Two screaming vines lash out, passing through me, and slap Gage right on the ass.

He curses, bolting upright as he casts a glare in my general direction. I can only see with the gray night vision back in place. I doubt he can see at all.

"For the last fucking time, they can't touch you in that form, so stop screaming. I have welts all over my body because these trees *really* like your little shrieks."

"Oops," I say, very little contrition in my tone.

Closing my eyes, I focus on the guys, reaching out and feeling them nearby.

"Just this way," I tell him, turning and moving toward their direction. "They must have stopped for the night."

"With the light down, it's too dangerous to keep going. We're getting toward the other side of the forest, and it'll likely be another battle of survival."

"You're not allowed to jump, fall, or stand in the rain.

Understood?" I ask him, trying to make light of the situation even as I feel the retroactive fear spike through me like it's happening all over again.

Exhausted from denying my other form so much, I'm forced to go whole. I grab his hand and guide him easier, hoping we don't stir another spider-bat.

He releases my hand and slides an arm around my waist, drawing me closer and making walking a tad awkward. I don't complain, though. I'm not sure why he's being affectionate, but I certainly have no qualms about it.

His lips brush the top of my head, and I melt a little, leaning into him. Our steps are slow and deliberate, like he's drawing our bubble-time for a little bit longer.

He'll probably shove me away in front of the others, and that will suck. But at least I'll have this memory. It's a damn good memory. The location of the memory sucks, but the rest is awesome.

"Will more black ice be coming?" I ask warily.

"Yeah. It'll get more and more frequent the farther away from the fiery lake we get. The screaming vines will continue to get smaller away from their main fire source, which aides in giving us direction."

"How did you learn all this stuff if this is your first trip to hell's belly?" I ask him, wondering which books I need to start reading.

"Harold. He's a balance elder, which means he has very little physical power, but an exceptional amount of knowledge, even though he's only been around for about a century longer than us. We call him powerful because he's endured death and came out perfectly balanced—neither good nor evil. He's the reason we have any books at all, because such things are denied simple surface guardians."

"Will any of those books give me insight on why you four seem a little moody?" I ask seriously.

He snorts out a laugh as I guide us through a thick grouping of trees.

Just as we get around them, Gage spins me and pins me against one of the ashy trees. My eyes search his face even as my chest rises and falls rapidly.

Fear and excitement always accompanies their mood swings, but right now, it's just pure unadulterated desire, thanks to his incredible mouth.

The back of his hand ghosts down the side of my face.

"Humans have more balance," he tells me, pressing closer. "Their emotions are watered down and tempered by that balance. Every emotion we experience is too extreme. We fight feeling anything because it can consume us easily."

His gaze dips to my mouth, even though I know he can't really see it. The pad of his thumb brushes over my bottom lip, and his breathing grows heavier.

"And since you came around, we've been forced to *feel* more than we have in a very long time before we leashed those emotions and learned to channel them with Harold's help and guidance."

I swallow thickly, even as he continues to touch my mouth and hold me in place.

"How'd he find you?" I ask.

"The summons," he says as his hand falls away.

He drags me back against his side, and we start walking again, his point now proven. Emotions are definitely more overwhelming when I'm in this form.

They override rational thought and create sort of a primal haze around me. Maybe Harold needs to teach me how to leash my emotions too.

"He was in attendance when we were first called to the graveyard on the day we bonded. We went, even though we were leery. We were so desperate for answers, and we assumed this was going to be that, even if it killed us. Instead, we were given a task. Harold supplied us with weapons and booze, and I guess he felt sorry for us since we had no idea what was going on, so he took us under his wing. In truth, I think he worried someone would kill us if he didn't help."

"Just curious, how would one leash their emotions?" I ask, thinking of how easily I've been distracted from our predicament just because they have awesome body parts.

It's rather inconvenient.

He laughs under his breath, but doesn't answer me. I try to go back phantom to sense the others, but nothing happens.

"I can't sense the guys like this, but I'm too drained to shift back to my other form," I say, trying to remember the appropriate direction. "But I think we're going the right way."

He keeps me against his side, and we continue to walk.

"I smell a fire now, so I can get us to them," he murmurs.

"How do you know it's them? I've seen a lot of fire in hell."

A small bit of laughter spills from his lips. "Hellfire and eternal flames have no scent. This is a handmade, regular, nothing special or harmful about it, fire," he assures me.

"Let's just hope it's not other competitors."

"I can kill them easily enough," he says with a shrug.

A yawn escapes me as I start leaning on him a little. Talking about killing apparently bores me. Maybe I'm the psychopath after all.

His hold tightens, and once again he kisses the top of my head.

I'm going to have to get some sleep to have enough strength to go phantom for the last day. I need to be my strongest. We've already survived longer than any of them anticipated.

"It's not mood swings," he tells me randomly, drawing me out of my tired reverie. Clearing his throat when I peer up at him curiously, he adds, "When we get angry and pull back, it's us reining in emotions we haven't been forced to feel in such extremes in quite some time. You aren't seeing a shift in moods; you're seeing us force ourselves to take a step back and search for rational answers as to why you're penetrating our shields so effortlessly."

"Because I'm awesome and my ass looks good in lace?" I guess.

He bursts out laughing, and I hear three groans from the distance. I stiffen, but Gage drags me in the direction the groans came from.

"Always the vanity," I hear Ezekiel say.

My eyes scan the area, but I don't see them immediately. Finally, I catch sight of a flickering flame inside a cave, and the closer we get, the more distinctly I can make out three figures sitting or lying near it.

"About damn time you two found us," Kai drawls, his eyes drifting over the way Gage is still holding me to him as we near. "I'm guessing you're her favorite now?"

Jude glares at me like I've tarnished yet another one of them, as Gage smirks. "It'll be hard to take my place right now," Gage boasts.

Kai laughs under his breath. Ezekiel grins and shakes his head before stretching out and lying down. Jude looks away from me.

"What are you wearing?" Ezekiel groans.

I shrug a bare shoulder in my strapless black corset, idly glancing down at my really slinky attire. I'm also in a black top hat, and since we're still in hell, I'm also wearing phantom-made body paint that makes me look like the walking dead.

"Admit it. This is the sexiest I've been yet."

I swear, it's like pulling teeth to get a compliment. All I get are more groans.

Here they are bitching about my attire, and they're all still in boxers or naked—like Jude. I'm trying *not* to be distracted, because I have no idea how to leash my emotions like they do, and yet I'm surrounded by a lot of bare skin.

"The clothes haven't dried?" I ask, even though I distinctly remember Gage leaving his own clothes behind.

"Black ice on clothes is a bad idea. It's the reason it has time to penetrate the skin before our natural body heat can melt it back. The fabric gives it time to be absorbed instead of instantly evaporating. It's actually safer to go naked," Ezekiel says as he winks at me.

"So you're all going to be naked or mostly naked for the remainder of this trial?" I muse, my lips curling into a grin, eliciting more groans. "This is going to be interesting." It makes it sound less genuine when I yawn directly after saying it'd be interesting.

"She needs rest. She's strained herself too much these past two days. Her new form is a lot more demanding," Gage says, pushing me toward Ezekiel.

I stumble sleepily toward him, and Ezekiel snatches my hand, tugging me down on top of him. My breath catches when I'm mid-fall, but he quickly grabs my waist and easily—and gently—pulls me against his side.

I practically moan at how comfortable it is to be pressed down the side of his body without worrying he might kill me.

My head settles on his bare chest as my eyelids start fluttering shut.

"I'll take first watch for two hours. I'm still a little wired," Gage says. "The three of you should sleep. Near her. Get the best rest you can, because tomorrow we do the impossible and beat these fucking trials or get lost in here forever."

"Wired from what exactly?" Kai asks with a taunting smirk.

Gage winks at me, flips Kai off, and walks out as Ezekiel and Kai laugh lightly.

"I'm sure none of you will regret those decisions," Jude states dryly, ever the Scrooge.

He lies down and closes his eyes, staying far away from me.

"Just remember you would have died if that black ice had spread all over you," Ezekiel tells him like he's defending me.

I pat his chest even as I yawn again, and his arms tighten around me as I snuggle closer.

Another body slithers up to my other side, and a set of lips graze over my shoulder.

"Sleep, little spirit. We find out our fate tomorrow, and it seems you'll be stuck with whatever decision is made," Kai says against my ear.

"As long as you four are still safe," I say in a sleepy rumble, not really stringing together the sentence I mean to.

Just before I fall asleep, I feel a gentle, almost ghost of a touch at my ankle, but I can't open my eyes to see who it is.

For the first time, I allow them be the ones to look over me while I sleep.

"Goodnight," someone whispers close to my ear.

CHAPTER VI

The loud pattering of rain is what wakes me up, and I lift my head, peering over at the cave entrance where Ezekiel is staring out at the black rain pummeling way harder than it was the last time I saw it.

I'm not sure how long I've been asleep, but Gage is where Kai was, and Kai is now where Ezekiel was, his arms wrapped loosely around me as he sleeps peacefully.

I'm assuming that means I've slept six hours, which would be three guard-duty rotations, but I'm not certain if Jude has taken a shift. I'm currently smirking at him as he lies at my feet, his arm draped loosely over my ankles as he sleeps *hard*.

That small touch on my ankle before I drifted off must have been him, and he subconsciously got even closer in his sleep.

He's going to be so mad that I saw it.

A huge grin splits my face, and I carefully go phantom, letting all their touches pass through me as I stand without disturbing them and go whole on my way to Ezekiel.

I blame the extreme circumstances for my questionable comfort level with Ezekiel when my hand travels over his shoulder, and I step into his side.

He looks down at me, a heavy expression on his face.

"Sorry," I say, withdrawing my hand.

His lips twitch, and his arm goes around my shoulders,

drawing me against his side. Happily, my arms slide around his waist, all domestic-like. We could be mistaken for a couple instead of just a creepy stalker girl chasing after a crush.

"There's someone watching us," he says quietly when his lips touch the top of my head. "Don't change forms yet."

"Why?" I whisper.

"Because they've seen you already, and they don't know you can vanish. It could be a very important weapon when they finally make their move. Just act casual and calm."

Did they see me vanish to get out of the sleep pile?

My breath comes out shakily, because what if it's the Devil watching us? What if he's studying us the way I used to study my quad?

"It's not Lucifer," he tells me like he's in my head.

"How do you know?" I ask, confused.

"Because there's no light shrouding you."

"That makes no sense."

"I don't know for sure, but I think it's the blind tribe. They're rumored to stalk these woods for food. And we might just be on the menu," he says instead of explaining the light.

"Lovely," I state dryly. "At least they're blind. I'm assuming they can hear every word we're saying, though."

"They actually see things in signatures. Hell's belly, as you've noticed, is very fucking hot. They see cooler signatures instead of heat signatures," he goes on. "And they don't exactly speak English. They speak the language of the damned."

"Is *comoara trădătoare* a damned language phrase?" I ask idly, looking out on the very neon blue forest, and wondering where this blind tribe is hiding.

"No, that's Romanian," Ezekiel states as though it should be obvious.

"Why do you think it's them?" I ask quietly. "The blind tribe, I mean."

"Because I've seen glimpse of a couple of humanoid figures since the lights came on, and the only humanoid figures down here would be competitors or tribesmen. We've managed to avoid the other tribes. They prefer to feed on the monsters and stray from any interlopers. But the blind tribe—"

"Are savage, hungry, fearless, cannibalistic barbarians in the mood for some flesh. Got it. I take it they're immune to black ice?" I interject.

He nods, his eyes still on the land in front of him. "Another reason I'm certain it's not the other competitors. They've been in the storm for the past hour at least."

"Just fucking great," Kai says around a yawn, drawing my attention back to him.

Gage and Jude are already awake, and Gage is stretching, looking well-rested.

Jude avoids my eyes.

"How'd you sleep, Death Punch?" I drawl, grinning like the cat who ate the canary.

He doesn't even look at me before speaking directly to Ezekiel. "If the blind tribe is waiting on us to leave this cave, we're going to have to fight our way out of this."

I start to move to the doorway, but Ezekiel tugs me back.

"Save your strength. You have to be able to hold your invisible form. I think shielding yourself from Lucifer in the open is draining you faster. There's no telling how much power that requires."

I look at him like he's crazy.

"I'm not shielding myself. I don't even know how to do that."

"Most of your power runs on survival instincts. You're only starting to gain some control," Gage says, moving closer as he props up and peers out as well.

"In other words, if Lucifer seeing you makes you feel threatened," Jude says, moving just to the rim where the black rain misses his foot by mere centimeters. "The light surrounds you every time you feel his eyes on you when you turn whole. The light never shines under coverage from his watch."

Good to know. I guess.

"So if you're naked, the rain won't hurt you, right?" I ask, suddenly very intrigued by how distracting this fight will be with a lot of swinging equipment.

A small grins curves at my lips, and Kai arches an unimpressed eyebrow at me as he moves around to be diagonal from me.

Clearing my throat and wiping away the juvenile grin, I *pretend* to have some class.

"That's the theory," Ezekiel says absently.

"The theory? You spouted facts about it."

"We knew it would freeze us to the core if it penetrated the skin," he goes on conversationally. "It's liquid when it connects, and if the surface is not hot enough to keep it liquid, it immediately freezes everything, spreading outward. It evaporates immediately into the ground, and turns into glowing blue residue on the plant life. Your temperature has to continuously rise to battle it, but it cools you if it's able to attach. Double-edged sword."

"The clothing provided a cooler layer that it attached to and grew strength, chilling the surface of our skin enough for the ice to find a weak spot to attach to," Gage adds.

"We *assumed* our skin would run too hot for the temperatures, and Kai was shirtless. His pants got wet, but didn't touch skin before he stripped out of them. However, the black ice ran off his body, never freezing on contact. Unlike it did when Jude was drenched and it attached to his middle in numerous spots. Or when my arm was infected under my drenched sleeve," Ezekiel goes on.

"My boxers fucked me," Gage says. "The theory is that none of our skin can get infected if there's no barrier to help chill it before it penetrates the skin."

"Not an agony I'm in any sort of hurry to revisit," Jude inserts dryly, taking a wary step back. "Someone else can play guinea pig."

They keep talking about how hot hell's belly is, but the heat isn't quite so intrusive to me. I suppose that would just sound like obnoxious bragging right now, so I keep it to myself.

"I'm going to go out there and see if I can determine how many we're dealing with," I tell them, stepping behind Jude.

He covers as much of me as possible, understanding what I'm doing without me having to explain.

"What am I looking for?" I ask as I change forms, hoping the phantom version of me is hidden from their cooler-temp seeking eyes.

"I have no idea. I only saw humanoid shadows just as the forest started illuminating. Since then, I haven't been able to spot them. The books we read had no description of them other than what I've already told you," Ezekiel tells me.

"We might have learned more about hell's belly if we had ever foreseen a visit here," Kai drawls.

"Save your energy. We can fight this time," Jude says quietly to me.

"Well, don't any of you go trying to die, and I'll let you be men. But the second I see you not pulling your own, I'll totally emasculate you. Again," I state as I pass through him and start stalking into the woods.

"Her fearlessly wicked tongue is what surprises me the most," I hear Jude huff under his breath.

"You have no idea how wicked my tongue can be," I assure him, putting my sassy Devil costume back on as I strut a little in my red heels.

A few snorts follow that.

"Guess her hearing is better than we realized," Ezekiel muses.

"Finding out new things about me is what gives me all those

bonus mystery points," I call out as I move farther and farther into the neon woods, even as the rain continues to pour through me.

I'm not worried about being too loud, considering these blind guys can't actually hear me so long as I'm in this form.

I'm expecting to find ten or so tribesmen as I continue to move on.

Yet I'm starting to wonder if Ezekiel is just being paranoid, because I can't even see the cave anymore, despite the heavily illuminated forest.

Sighing, I turn around, and halt.

I finally spot one guy slinking through, and an eerie sensation slithers over me.

He's blending in with the streaks of neon blue and the black background of the tree. As he moves, the shades and colors on his skin adjust, changing as well, making him the perfect chameleon.

The dread that's gathering over me scatters into a thousand fragments and creates a sickly insect-crawling sensation across my nerves when I see what I couldn't see before.

Back before my mind knew to look harder, because these guys can blend in with their surroundings. And they're much better at it than those assassins who camouflaged themselves in the last trial, because these very naked guys have skin that actually changes with the landscape.

With the newly educated eye, I can see them almost too clearly.

I can see too many.

Hundreds.

They're on every tree. They're crawling over the ground, moving slowly but deliberately, the shades effortlessly shifting over them to confuse the eye with yet another illusion.

Every surface of the forest that I can see has men stuck to it, and I've been walking right through them.

"They look like the forest!" I shout as I zap myself back in front of the cave entrance, wishing those books had warned us about this. "They blend!"

My eyes widen, seeing all the camouflaged bodies stuck all over the side of the cave's entrance that I remain just outside of, looking in.

"Watch out!" I shout as Jude's eyes finally spot the first one who has crept just inside of the cave.

The man lunges, his skin flaring several bright colors before Jude narrowly dodges him. Ezekiel's hand slams on his shoulder as those bright colors suddenly light up the entire forest, and a wild, throaty set of animal calls ring loudly through the air.

"I really hope that's not a war cry!" I shout, just as the one Ezekiel releases takes off charging toward his own people, a spear appearing in his hand as he launches it through several men.

Well then. That was unexpected.

Another spear slices through me, thrown by a different tribesman from my side, and I watch as it catches the traitor in the gut, sending him to the ground.

"Now would be a good time to prove you can handle this. Momma's not holding back much longer," I caution as Ezekiel grabs two more guys and slings them.

Those two guys charge their men, but the sheer volume of them is not going to be deterred by a couple of new traitors.

The forest is thundering with all of them racing this way.

The guys are fighting, doing whatever they can to hold their place and not retreat.

Power launches out of me, taking down at least twenty of them, but they heal quickly and bounce back to their feet.

Shit! That's not supposed to happen!

"The spears are all that will kill them!" Gage shouts.

I zap between Jude and Ezekiel, grabbing their shoulders as I turn whole. There's no way we can kill them all with some spears.

"If you're all going, then so am I, I guess. I knew you'd all be the death of me," I say, a grim smile on my face.

I turn just as another brightly lit man flies through the cave entrance, his spear raised and poised in our general direction. I shove Ezekiel back, moving in front of the spear and closing my eyes. I'd rather go first than last, because I'm not capable of simply watching them die.

"No!" Jude shouts as he collides with my hand that I'm holding out to keep him away.

I feel a spray of dust against me, and my eyes flicker open as Jude's eyes glow gold. His hand is out in front of him, and I realize that spray of dust is actually ashes as they funnel through the entryway, infecting anyone daring to pass.

My hand clutches his arm that is already touching me, and I hear a few sharp intakes of air as the others startle.

Ezekiel's hand is suddenly gripping my side, and he throws his own hand out.

I feel something dark and daunting slip over me, almost matching the decay and menace I feel pouring through me from Jude.

I hear the sounds of fighting going on at large just outside of the cave, and Jude staggers away from me like he's a little exhausted or on a high—not sure which.

Ezekiel staggers just as quickly, and we look out over the battlefield that is insane. Those racing colors of war rush over their skin as they kill each other, fighting to the death, as though a civil war has just erupted for no apparent reason.

"What's going on?"

"Chaos," Ezekiel says, swallowing thickly. "I've never created it on this scale before, and not without physical contact."

That's not chaos at all. This is two sides at war with the intent to kill each other.

"And Jude just killed beings who can't be killed without a

certain damning weapon, and he never touched them. The decay hit harder and more fiercely than ever," Kai states as though to himself.

He touches me, beginning to lift his hand like he's about to use me as a conduit as well, just as the rain ceases to fall.

"Don't. We don't know what it does to take from her just to amplify our powers," Gage says, causing Kai to blink and release me as we remain forgotten to the fierce battle just outside.

"We can study all that later. With their attention fractured, we should be able to fight our way out now," Jude says without looking at me as he grabs two spears from the ground.

The others spring into action, collecting more abandoned spears. We race out of the cave, rushing out right into the thick of the madness.

Ezekiel slams the spear into one man's throat, as Kai breaks off a hunk of the wood from the spear, and just uses the onyx point as a blade. He slices through ten men without even slowing down.

I'm in phantom form again for obvious reasons. I have no idea how to work a spear, and I decide the learning curve is just too large to deal with right at this particularly fatal moment.

I'm racing behind Jude as he uses his two spears like dual bo staffs, spinning them before slamming them into the hordes of men fighting a battle they don't even understand.

Most of them are still warring with each other, leaving only the stragglers we run into as an issue.

Just as a spear very nearly slams into Jude's back, I launch myself in front of it, turning whole.

My hands slam together on each side of the angular blade, stopping it inches from my stomach.

"I'm totally a badass," I say on a shaky breath, questioning the bladder issue in whole form at this very terrifying second.

Looking up, I see the tribesmen up close as one bumps into me, acting like he doesn't *see me* at all. Ha! I'll tell them my new pun when we're not in peril—should that day ever come.

I quickly spin and jab the spear into his back in one fluid motion like I'm a battle overlord or some shit.

"I really am a badass!" I shout louder.

He drops like a pile of rubble, and I smirk while dusting my hands off. Then end up squealing like a lunatic girl when I'm knocked to the ground.

Another one of the eyeless men trips over me.

I know I just made the tacky blind tribesmen pun about them not being able to see me, but it's like they don't realize I'm here at all, yet have no problem targeting the guys.

"It's wearing off, I think," Jude gripes, slamming his hand into one's chest.

It decays rapidly, proving they certainly can die by means other than the spear.

I grab a spear and stab the one that is wallowing around beside me, still tangled up on my legs.

"How do you beat an army who need cool signatures to single you out amongst the heat of hell?" I shout.

No answer comes until I'm about to unleash the biggest spark of that mysterious acid I've ever felt.

"You set the forest on fire to block out your cold signatures," Kai says on a breath, then turns and adds. "Run!"

Just as the tribesmen all seem to snap out of their disorientation and turn to face the retreating backs of the guys, I smirk.

My fingers snap together, and a spark of that burning acid slams to the very base of the tree beside me.

That's all it takes.

A *whoosh* of fire ignites, spreading like a wall of flame, and the blind tribesmen scream when they try to leap through it. I've already seen them heal before, so I know it doesn't kill them. But it becomes obvious they can't see beyond the quickly growing wall of heat the guys are racing in front of.

"Burn!" I shout, fist-pumping the air.

I'm not sure why my guys insist on groaning at my jokes so much. It's sad they have no appreciation for obvious humor.

I snap back to phantom and zap myself to the guys, gauging the distance between them and my fire.

They're a lot faster than I remember, and I actually have to strain a little to keep up, even in my weightless form.

The fire starts getting swallowed up by the forest, and the tribesmen are nowhere to be seen. We don't slow down enough to be certain.

After a few hours of solid running, they start losing a little steam, and I decide to voice a question that's been bothering me, now that the immediate threat of death is over—at the moment.

"Why do these trials have so many physical elements? Climbing is unnecessary when you can siphon," I tell them.

"Physical and mental endurance is one of the overall studies in the trials," Jude answers, panting for air as he bends over and rests for a second.

"They need to know how strong you are—body and mind—before they decide what to do with you," Gage goes on, straightening from his doubled over position as he seems to catch his breath.

"And you can't siphon all the time. You have to be discreet when you're topside. You can't disrupt the balance by giving too many humans a visual to their unsolved mysteries of the universe," Kai goes on.

"Plus, it's not as much fun to watch people siphon around a course, and these trials are also for entertainment value," Ezekiel adds as we start walking briskly, no longer running as they conserve precious energy.

"Our senses are stronger down here the longer we stay," Gage says. "Hers too."

"My senses only work with you guys," I point out. "The blind dudes almost got one over on me."

"You sense when the Devil can see you. You're also quick to learn and figure out the next step, even though you have no prior knowledge of the trials or the location," Jude states like a mild accusation.

I open my mouth to start our usual banter, but Gage sucks in a breath.

"There! We're at the end!" Ezekiel shouts, and everyone starts running again.

We burst out of the forest, illuminated by the bright red sky that actually has them shielding their eyes. It makes me grateful to be phantom, since my eyes aren't so sensitive in this form. It seemed like such a dull sky before the blacked-out forest.

My heart sinks when I *hear* the ground vibrating.

Then I'm back to dealing with cardiac arrest when I *see* why.

That gulley we started in is now on either side of us. No longer is the forest nor the mountain we faced earlier, in view. All we can see for miles and miles is one huge canyon full of monsters who are all charging toward us like a stampede.

There are so many—no three-headed hellhounds, though. At least none in my immediate viewpoint.

Some make my stomach roil, skin peeling off them as they shed one form for a much more grotesque one. Apparently they need a different form to devour four very tasty looking men.

"Death trap," Jude growls. "We weren't meant to survive all this time just to face this. There's no fucking way to survive it. Even if we all touched her and used her as a conduit, we'd barely make a dent before we were forced to disconnect like I had to earlier…before it consumed me."

I step closer, staring in disbelief. It's like one giant mass of encroaching death creatures, and I whirl around, seeing the same fate coming at us from the other end of the gulley as well.

"Everyone gather around me," I shout, then glance down at my ruby red slippers as they appear.

Everyone does as I say, putting their hands on/through me as just only my feet turn whole and start clicking together.

"There's no place like home. There's no place like home. There's no place like—"

"Are you fucking kidding me?" Jude barks in interruption, causing my eyes to peel open as I grimace.

"Worth a shot," I tell them, furious with all the false hope movies have given me over these past few years.

Beasts still rapidly approaching, and the tops of the canyon being layered with hellfire lava that is starting to drip down, I take a long, resolved breath.

"How do you defeat a never-ending army of hell's most vicious predators, cast to the belly straight from the throat, when there's not enough power to kill them all?" Ezekiel asks quietly from beside me.

Anger simmers inside me as everything dark and tainted swirls within my soul. The Devil doesn't play fair. Every time we turn around, there's one more impossible task.

A storm crackles overhead as dark clouds form ominously just barely above us.

"Now what?" Gage groans, looking up.

"Not like it matters. There's no answer to this fucking riddle," Jude says through a snarl.

"Yeah. There is," I say as the skies dim, now completely covered by the dark storm clouds as lightning flickers inside them. "You make the never-ending army of predators believe you're a much worse predator. Think of the mouse chasing the cat."

"That makes zero sense, and it's not really an answer," Jude argues.

"I know," I say as that very seductive power rolls around through me with such vigor like I've never felt before. "It was a hint."

"Running low on time," Ezekiel growls as the first line of vicious, spitting, snapping-jawed monsters get within thirty feet of us on either side. "We don't have time for hints and guesses. If you know the fucking answer just spit it out."

A smirk emerges on my lips as I turn whole, and the lightning crackles louder.

"You be fearless," I say under my breath as I start charging toward the beasts, ignoring the quad's loud shouts of protests and swearing.

Gritting my teeth, I pump my arms and legs, racing headlong into the fray.

The monsters split, scattering and scrambling to get out of my way when fear and apprehension hits them. They practically trample each other to get as far away from me as possible.

A lot more unsavory words are flung at me from the guys, but I look back to see them following my lead. Though they don't look happy about it. In fact, I'd say they're looking a little murderous. Maybe they're role-playing to add some drama to our game of mouse-chasing-cat.

I put my mega-bitch face on just in case it makes it work better.

The throngs of beasts continue to split, as the guys follow me in a single-file line.

It's parting the monster sea with one crazy girl leading the charge. The monsters don't even bump into me, because they're so desperate to flee the fearless predator I'm pretending to be.

Just as the last set of monsters rush by us, I turn phantom, exhausted and needing a break from my very unfit, gravity-suffering body.

The storm dissipates as though it's finished with us now that the monsters are gone. Honestly, I'm sort of wondering if that storm was mine. It gave me coverage from the Devil's prying eyes just as I decided to turn whole.

The monsters keep running down the gulley, colliding with the others. I look away when they're barely a distant echo.

Gage holds out a finger, shaking it at me, but he's panting too heavily to use his words, which appears rather frustrating if his expression is any indication.

He settles for miming the motions of wringing my neck right in front *of my neck*, then turns and stalks off.

That's two of them who have used the same charade version of that threat against me now.

Ezekiel just glares at me, also not using his words. He takes a step toward me, then back again, then stops and squeezes his fists together. He finally turns and stalks off as though he's forcing himself to do it.

Jude runs a frustrated hand through his hair, collapsing to a rock as the gulley fades from view, the latest obstacle passed and riddle answered. He looks like he wants to five-finger-death-punch me.

Kai slams his fist into a rock wall, looking back at me over his shoulder as he takes a few hesitant breaths, before deciding to advance on me like a naked Gladiator.

He opens his mouth like he's about to yell at me, then instead releases a series of very loud and random sounds to relay his apparent frustration, shaking his head a little worrisomely, before he turns and starts stalking toward the black rocks now in our path.

"You're welcome," I say to their backs as they all walk away from me.

Another chorus of frustrated sounds is my answer to that as they start walking faster in their angry gait, forcing me to zap myself to them instead of all that walking.

"It worked, didn't it?" I point out from directly behind them.

As if they planned it, all four flip me off without ever glancing back.

"Rude," I sigh, stopping for a second to give them an unimpressed stare they don't even see.

I jog and catch back up. "I bet that was easier than dealing with your swinging dicks during the blind dude battle, am I right?"

I pass through them and hold my hand up for a ghost girl high-five…that gets left hanging as they pass back through me.

"You guys totally don't appreciate my amazing personality."

Just as my hand falls on Ezekiel's shoulder to try and get him to loosen up first, a blinding light blasts in front of us.

CHAPTER VII

When we land in the graveyard, apparently ejected from hell without warning, Ezekiel's hand passes through me. I feel the tugs of him siphoning, and suddenly we're home.

The other three follow us immediately, all of us inside the living room, eyes moving between each other like we're a little speechless. Which is a feat for me, if I'm being candid.

I take notice of the fact I'm still in the slinky Devil's costume, and they're all incredibly naked. Immediately, I go whole, just in case they want to physically thank me for my awesome survival skills like Kai and Gage did during that exhausting trial.

Can't be too prepared in these rare situations.

I inch a little closer to Gage, my arm brushing his. His arm absently goes around me, tugging me closer as though it's a reflex, as he looks at Jude.

"He let us out," Gage says.

"So now what?" Kai asks. "We were certain our death was guaranteed when we were dropped in the belly."

"How could he have expected us to pass that course and survive? Even knowing we have her lingering around?" Jude asks, gesturing toward me like *her* needs clarification.

"Was it all an actual test if it wasn't a death sentence? And what does the Devil gain with the knowledge he's now gathered since having a chance to study you?" I ask.

They all give me an incredulous look.

"Sorry," I tell them, not really sorry at all. "Looking at everything like it's a riddle is a hard habit to break once you've gotten the hang of it."

My hand subtly moves to Gage's chest, tracing one of the weird tattoos I happen to like quite a lot. He's still my current favorite, after all.

When I look back over, I see Jude glaring at Gage, and Gage smirking at Jude.

"Maybe we should discuss this with clothes on, since she's easily very distracted," Jude bites out.

I peer around at four very distracting erections that would say their minds have all gone to the same place as mine. They just like to pretend they're not quite so base as I am.

"Life-threatening situations and survival sex go hand-in-hand," I dutifully inform them, looking around at all the variously pierced cocks jutting out.

Gage's cock jumps against my hip, and my eyes almost close, because I'm still getting used to all the really great sensations and experiencing a lot of firsts.

"Not until we all agree," Gage says, still smirking at Jude.

"I'm the only one who clearly isn't infected by her," Jude tells him, then gives me a fuck-you grin that he stole from me.

"I'm positive I'm a virgin, even though I have no scientific evidence. I'd rather not go to a doctor to have him check. I'm not quite certain I want just anyone rooting around in such an intimate place. The point is, I highly doubt I have anything to infect you with."

"How can I argue with her when she makes no damn sense ninety percent of the time?" Jude snaps, gesturing a little wildly at me like I've finally pushed him over that edge.

It's fascinatingly intriguing, and I go to the kitchen as they continue talking.

"You're the only one still convinced she's a threat to our bond. It's felt stronger over the past three days," Gage tells him. "*We've* felt stronger."

"Everything comes at a price," Jude states as though he's the reasonable one. "There's always a balance. We know this. It's why we agreed *not* to touch her, and now you're all giving her orgasms and sleeping with her wrapped around you. She's in your fucking heads like no one else has ever done before, clambering to be her damn momentary favorite, and none of you are even questioning it!"

Finished with step one of my current task, I press a few buttons on the microwave and go to grab a bowl.

"I'm seriously convinced she's done something to the three of you. I'm the only one who hasn't had my mouth on her, and I'm the only one who remembers how it feels when envy starts to rip us apart," Jude growls.

"Is she making popcorn?" Ezekiel asks incredulously as the telltale *pop pop pop* starts its rapid-fire phase.

"*She* is insane. And very fucking distracting for all of us. Tell me you don't see the fact we've just survived the worst third trial in hell's long history, and instead of discussing the Devil's true agenda, we're discussing *her*," Jude goes on as I pull the popcorn out and start pouring it into my bowl.

I quickly wash my hands, even though I can't actually get dirty if I swap from transparent to whole. I'm just magically clean. Lovely little perk.

I don't mind the guys being dirty. They still smell just as tempting, and now they're a little battle dirty, which is actually very hot, since I'm *insane* like that.

"All we can do is speculate where Lucifer is concerned. He's been called the 'Mad King' for quite some time," Ezekiel drawls. "But we can start processing all we learned about *her* right now, while the memories are fresh. It's clear she's something we've been missing. You're the only one not seeing that."

Jude looks like he's about ready for that death punch again when I come walking around, hugging my bowl of popcorn in one arm, while using my other hand to shovel it into my mouth.

I'm so hungry. And this is definitely one of those popcorn moments I finally get to enjoy *with* popcorn.

They all turn to look at me, not saying a word, blank expressions donning their faces.

"What?" I ask around a mouthful, before packing it full once again.

Ezekiel's lips twitch.

"See?" Jude asks, gesturing to all of me as though I've just proven a very valid point. "Insane!"

He does his usual glare-at-me routine, and I swallow my popcorn while rolling my eyes.

"I'm going to my room. I'll leave the door open—metaphorically—to anyone who wants to help me figure out my virginal status. I'm still too good for all of you, but now I like you a little more. Well, not you," I say, directing that last part at Jude.

"You can't touch me until you stop trying so hard to hate me," I add.

I deliberately bump into his side on my way by, and shake my ass much more than necessary as I strut up the stairs, still wearing my ruby red slippers that have no tall heel. No, I don't wear heels in this form. It's not quite as graceful when gravity is a bitch.

"Don't even think about it," I hear Jude saying to someone. "Not until we all agree. Don't let her strip us of that last bit of power."

This time, I'm the one to flip him off without looking back. Then I eat more popcorn, because I really am hungry. Ravenous, actually.

"We need a way to settle this, or we'll stay at an impasse," Kai tells him.

"Then we'll find a way to settle it," Jude says with a chilling calmness that finally provokes me to look back and down at them from the top of the stairs.

He's smirking at me in a way that makes him look even more dangerous than the Devil himself.

Sometimes I forget he really might kill me one day when he tires of trying to figure me out.

CHAPTER VIII

After devouring *two* bowls of popcorn, I get naked and decide to enjoy the perks of a body when it meets an incredible shower.

The water racing down me in hurried rivulets is one of the many welcome sensations.

I don't think about the guys, or hell, or the Devil, or the fact the Devil is still possibly playing a game of death with their lives. In this moment, I'm just a girl enjoying the luxury of sensation I've watched so many others take for granted over the years.

"The sounds you make for the smallest, simplest pleasures is what drives me the craziest," Ezekiel says, startling my eyes open just in time to see him dig his fingers into my hair and roughly tug my head back so his lips can collide with mine.

When the actual hell did he invade my shower?

That draws a few more sounds of pleasure from me, as my arms wind around his neck and I kiss him back. His hand slides down my wet body, eliciting an entire new set of sensations, and he draws my leg up, lifting me with just that hold as he presses me into the back wall.

He's practically devouring me, and that steady warmth travels through me on a tangent. The head of his cock teases the inside of my thigh with how close he is.

"What brought this on?" I ask, grinning up at the air when he starts kissing his way down my throat.

"I asked him to handle that part, since I knew you'd have no objections," Jude says, causing me to choke on air as I dart my head to the side to see he's joined us in the shower.

Gloriously naked and exceptionally hard, he stands just out of reach, his eyes on mine as Ezekiel lifts me effortlessly, and his incredible mouth moves to my right nipple.

I fight to keep my eyes open, as Ezekiel does things to my nipples I didn't know were possible. It's like there's a direct line from them to my clit, as he moves from one to another, showing them both attention.

"You said I couldn't touch you until I wasn't trying to hate you so much," Jude goes on, his hand lowering to his cock as he strokes himself once. "And since you're so desperate for touch, maybe it's the way to freeing up some answers."

My eyes flutter shut on their own, and I grip Ezekiel's shoulders when his hand wraps around me and starts toying with my clit while he's still doing indescribably sinful things to my nipples.

Jude strokes himself harder as Ezekiel pushes me toward that edge, the sting of Jude's glare the only thing holding me back.

Ezekiel groans against my breasts, sounding as though he feels as tortured as I do.

"Something as tempting as you can only be forbidden," Jude says, releasing his cock as he starts walking toward us.

His face gets right in front of mine as Ezekiel works me harder, adding just an edge of pain as he thrusts against me like he wants me as bad as I want him in this moment.

"Tell us the consequences, *comoara trădătoare,*" he says in a seductive lull, his lips centimeters from mine as Ezekiel pushes a finger inside me, only adding to the overwhelming stimulation.

I'm half dazed, as I answer, "I don't know."

In the next instant, my left hand flies to Jude's shoulder, gripping tightly as the most powerful orgasm I've had yet crashes over me with so much force that I cry out, my nails digging into both of them as I cling to them.

My entire body shudders in Ezekiel's hold as he pants against my neck. He releases me and steps back, running a hand through his hair.

"Not going to get answers that way," Jude says on an exasperated breath.

Legs wobbly, I cast a glare at Ezekiel, who is still a little feral as he stares at me like he's straining to hold himself back. It pisses Jude off that this has been a pointless experiment, and that makes me really damn happy.

Ezekiel siphons away, and Jude remains alone with me in the shower. We just have our usual stare-off before he finally siphons away as well.

"Joke's on you!" I shout to the vacant air. "I'm the only one who just got an orgasm!"

A hint of laughter carries to me from the hallway, and I roll my eyes before turning off the shower. Instead of drying off, I go phantom, style my hair, and select an oversized T-shirt with nothing else to walk out of my room in.

I pause and back up again when I see a blue box with a white ribbon resting on my dresser.

My grin grows as I hurriedly open it to discover…a petrified beetle pendant on a diamond necklace.

"Assholes," I grumble, tossing it down as I go phantom and pick a nicer pendant on a silver chain attached to my neck.

None of those women saved their lives, and they got pretty charms and fancy shit.

After turning whole and swapping the new pendant out with the beetle to go on my new diamond necklace, I put it on and strut out in my T-shirt.

They're all in the living room when I find them, minus Gage. Their eyes dip to my shirt that says *Team Comoara Trădătoare*.

What's weird is the fact I have no idea how I knew how to spell it, but I did. Or maybe I should have used a phone to double check. I hope I'm not walking around in a shirt that says *watery soup* in Romanian.

Kai grins as his gaze lingers.

"This is the pendant I prefer," I say, gesturing to the replaced one.

Jude, the bastard, is smirking at me. I'll give him points for creativity. Now I'll have to think of something as equally annoying to do to him.

"You can make your own jewelry?" Ezekiel asks. "Why are you asking us to get you some if so?"

I point a finger at him. "You're not even my second favorite right now. I want tokens of affection. Not tokens of sarcasm."

Kai's lips twitch, and he stands as he comes toward me.

"Does that make me your second favorite?" he muses.

"Are you going to give me more orgasms just because I like them?" I ask seriously.

His grin grows, but the cock-blocker Jude says, "All of us have to agree."

"We can't fuck her. Doesn't mean the rest is off limits," Ezekiel states dismissively.

"Name one time in history we've done well with temptation," Jude groans. "You're all making this impossible."

Kai winks at me, then tugs me close, bending to nip at my lips. "I'll be by later."

I pat his chest. Good enough.

I zap myself up to the top of the stairs, hearing the necklace drop to the floor under the place where Kai is holding vacant air where I was moments ago.

"She's getting faster at changing from one form to the other and siphoning away," he says with a small smile.

I stare down at them. "Give me at least a couple of days, Jude," I state with all seriousness.

The amusement is drained with that one comment, as the three of them stare at me blankly.

"Just a couple of days to recover. All jokes aside, I need a mental break after all that. I was in hell's belly shortly after learning hell is an actual place," I remind them all. "Give me a few days to be thankful I'm alive, to be thankful I somehow managed to see you all home safely, and give my heart a break, before you remind me how very little you care."

Kai clears his throat and looks away guiltily, while Jude holds my gaze for a moment longer. Finally, he gives me a subtle nod, a silent confirmation of a temporary ceasefire.

It's more than he's ever given me before.

I start to go in Gage's room, but change my mind. Instead, I end up back in the kitchen and swiping a jar of the special alcohol they buy.

It sucks that I can't zap back with something tangible that I didn't create with my limited skills. Which means I have to *walk* it up to my room.

It's a little awkward to walk into the room they're all still in after such a dramatic prior exit.

"Don't drink too much of that," Kai calls to my back. "I want you to feel everything I'm going to do to you tonight."

He grunts like he was just hit, and I smirk. Kai's my new favorite.

CHAPTER IX

Gage pokes his head into my room a few hours later, as I drink more of the foulest tasting concoction I've ever tasted in my entire life. But I love how truly stupid I feel in this moment. As though my world isn't a cosmic ball of madness.

His eyes dip to the jar in my hand, as I say, "If you're going to try to seduce me to steal confessions I can't possibly make—" I clear my throat when I start to slur the 's' words. "—please wait. You have no idea how long or hard it was for me to get to this point of inebriation. And don't you dare make a dirty joke about 'long' and 'hard' being in the same sentence."

His eyes flick to the three empty jars on my bedside table, then back to the mostly empty jar swaying in my hand.

"How in the hell did you drink four of those and manage to stay conscious?" he asks incredulously.

"Fun fact," I say, smiling humorlessly. "Since the last time I drank this and ended up miserable on the bathroom floor, I've leveled-up a lot. Now I'm a hard one to get drunk. One of these gets me a little drunk. Two of these get me happy drunk. Well, it took three tries to make this happen."

I gesture to the table behind him to show him a few more jars he didn't notice.

"You guys need to replenish your stash, by the way," I go on, getting sidetracked.

He looks to be battling a grin, but I continue as though it's imperative he hear this evening's monumental struggle. Total spirit girl problems.

"So when I got hungry after the first two-and-a-half bottles, I realized walking was really hard to do. So I went phantom and zapped myself to the kitchen to get food, too stupid to realize I'd still have to *walk* up the stairs with the food. By the way, I can't make food magically appear the way I do clothing and jewelry. I tried. I was that desperate to keep from going downstairs."

He opens his mouth to speak, and I wave him off.

"Anyway, so I realized I was instantly sober when I went ghost. I still zapped myself to the kitchen. My phantom state apparently resets my inebriation levels."

"That's actually pretty useful information to hold onto," he says, appearing genuinely intrigued. Both of him.

I wish the two of him would quit spinning. It's terribly distracting.

"The second time, I had food readily available, more bottles of that heinous tasting drink, and a bathrobe." I point to the bathrobe I'm luxuriating in. "Comfort was a priority."

He just grins broader, as though he's thoroughly entertained. The carefree grin is so rare that it transforms his whole face. And I realize I really want to see him look at me more like that.

He pushes off from the wall, coming to lower himself onto the bed beside me, taking the drink from my hand and raising it to his lips.

"It's like skunk and dead rodents festered in that thing, and I had to choke it down multiple times because of sober-phantom-me. The second time was brought on by my first ever hiccup. It startled me so much I went phantom on accident, and…I have the cure for hiccups now. Phantom girl fixed that too."

He grins behind the glass as he takes another drink, not making a single expression of disgust.

"Just how? How did you grow a tolerance to that? Because I gotta tell you, this might be my only night to wallow in alcohol."

The bed jostles when he moves closer and hands it back to me, and I take it a little roughly. "Taste it now," he says, leaning over.

Rolling my eyes, I turn it up, brace for the inevitable rancid taste, and…moan in pleasure as the taste of cinnamon invades my mouth. My eyelids flutter shut as I turn it up and down the remaining liquid like I can't possibly get enough.

Gage's lips slowly stroke the column of my throat, and I'm so warm and tamed by the liquor that I don't even question his motives.

"How?" I ask, now wanting more and wondering what I did with that last bottle.

"You choose the flavor," he says against my neck.

"And no one found this to be crucial information to share when they saw me carrying that jar back to my room? I've been choking that stuff down for hours and having to start all over again."

"I didn't see you carrying it to your room, or I would have been in here much, *much* sooner," he murmurs against the base of my neck, slowly kissing lower.

I stiffen and narrow my eyes. "Are you in here because of Jude's weird interrogation tactics? Did Kai stand me up as a part of this game?"

He lifts his head, eyebrow arched as he peers down at me.

"I'm in here because you stared into my eyes and clung to my hand, willing to go into the flames with me so I wouldn't have to die alone," he says with no humor or sarcasm. "I'm in a much different place than the rest of them right now, because there's no reason you did that other than what you said. He's still worried about what price is to come. I'm to the point where I say to hell with the consequences."

Confused, I run my finger up his arm.

His lips ghost over mine as he continues. "Jude is playing his game. He secretly needs you to be a worthy adversary, but the more you prove you are, the more he truly believes no good can come from it. We've been burned in the past many times. And you've already penetrated farther than any woman before you," he says, his eyes never leaving mine.

I wasn't expecting so much honesty or candor.

"Okay then," I say on a breath.

"Okay then?" he asks, one corner of his mouth lifting.

"But in all fairness, there hasn't been any *penetration.* Aside from some fingers, and I can do that myself, so I'm not sure how I've penetrated farther than any woman," I add, simply because I don't do well with serious situations, it seems.

His grin only grows.

I shrug a shoulder. "Anyway, the only way I'm ever going to get close enough for him to truly trust me, is to stop trying so hard to get him to trust me. Three to one odds that I can make it happen by the end of the week."

I really shouldn't be gambling. I'm not a betting woman.

That smile stretches even wider than the last one as his eyes flake with gold.

"You're going to play a game to counter his game?" he asks.

"Jude *needs* control. You saw how crazy he got earlier when he felt all that slipping. I'm going to tip him over the edge, and he'll be so mad he won't know whether to kill me or kiss me. He'll choose the kiss. And it'll be brutal," I tell him, holding out my hand like I'm ready to shake on a deal.

Instead of shaking my hand, his lips come down on mine, and the empty jar tumbles from my hand as I reach up to grab the back of his head. He groans in my mouth, a tortured sound, and I realize he's not going to be breaking the bond tonight.

The kiss cuts off, and he snuggles up against my side, his arm going around me, making me feel a little safe.

"There's a question that's been driving me out of my mind, and I need to know the answer before I go find him and kill him," he says as though this is entirely too exasperating for him to deal with.

Kill who?

"Okay…"

"Why did you think Neal—the weasel from the club—would be your one true love or whatever it is you kept saying?" he asks, causing my smile to spread so much it hurts.

"Are you jealous? Please say you are."

"Just answer the question," he tells me pointedly.

Rolling my eyes, I shrug. "All of you seem to forget that I'm still a novice to so many experiences. I was unseen then unwanted for the first conscious years of my existence. He was the first man in my short existence to be nice to me. The first man who wanted to spend time with me. The first guy who smiled at all my jokes. Nothing else seemed to really matter when I felt how good it could feel to just be wanted."

Gage groans, and before I can say anything more, his lips are on mine again, kissing me as he starts pushing my legs apart and sliding up my shirt as my robe falls apart. His grip on me tightens when he realizes there is no underwear under the shirt.

Just as he starts shoving down his track pants, his intentions clear, I push him back, shaking my head.

"I didn't tell you that to make you feel so sorry for me that you'd piss off everyone and give me what I want," I grumble. "And I really don't want to remember losing my virginity to a pity fuck."

"You want me to see if you're really a virgin?" he muses.

"Kai and Ezekiel have already been there with their fingers. I'll just ask them," I state with a shrug, expecting him to show some more jealousy.

Instead, he smirks. "Then I guess I'll find something else to do with you. No need in giving you all the same experiences over and over when there's a whole lot more out there to show you."

Before I can say more, Kai walks in, taking in our intimate cuddle session, and slides in on my other side. My bed is large, but three is going to be the limit.

"You stood me up," I tell him.

"I realized I couldn't be alone in here with you, or I'd end up betraying everyone—"

"—Just Jude," I interrupt.

"I knew it was just a matter of time before someone else came in, and we could be cock-block buddies," he goes on.

He reaches over and fist bumps Gage with laughing eyes.

"You were my favorite earlier. Gage has now replaced you once again," I tell him idly as he passes me the last jar of alcohol.

I'm stunned a little to taste a rich cocoa flavor instead of cinnamon like last time. I guess Kai prefers a different taste, and it's something new I get to learn about them.

"Is she a virgin?" Gage asks Kai as he grabs my abandoned popcorn and starts snacking.

"To be honest, I have no clue," Kai says, reaching over me and grabbing his own handful. "We've never had a virgin before. They tend to freak out over the four-at-once notion when they're that innocent."

"I would think it'd still be obvious," Gage says with a frown.

Ezekiel walks in, and grins at me when I flip him off.

"Don't be mad. I wasn't going to pass up the opportunity to get my hands on you without him guilt-tripping me for once. The tradeoff was that he no longer says anything about my sleeping arrangements," he says, coming closer.

"The bird was for not telling me I could flavor the alcohol. I drank skunk for hours for no damn reason," I tell him before drinking more of the chocolatey nectar.

Both he and Kai burst out laughing, and Ezekiel drops to the end of the long bed, stretching out as he lies on his back and snags some popcorn for himself.

"And I got you a gift to apologize," he says, pulling a gift box out.

"If this has a beetle in it, you'll never be my favorite again," I tell him, leaning down to snatch the box up.

He just grins as I open it up, expecting a more acceptable necklace, given the slender, rectangular box.

Instead, I find a row of nail polishes. All of them have "diamond" sparkles.

"I was hoping for more real diamonds. I don't remember those women getting nail polishes," I state absently, even as I admire the pretty colors and decide to start painting my toenails.

I have no idea what to do, so I put a pin in it until I can Google a tutorial. I'm not sure how I know how to work Google to its fullest extent just yet, but I'm really grateful for that knowledge. Makes life easier.

"I figured we'd start with the basics, since you don't really own anything yet," Ezekiel says with a shrug. "Besides, every real girl needs nail polish."

I'm not sure why it makes me grin, but it does.

"Thank you," I finally tell him, and he rolls his eyes before turning over.

"We don't really like gratitude around here," Kai tells me. "It just makes shit awkward."

"You'd prefer for me to be ungrateful like the lot of you?" I muse.

"Exactly," they all three say with a smile, not looking at me as they stare at the TV.

Just as my smile spreads wider, Jude pokes his head in the doorway, leaning against the frame as he rakes his eyes over the three traitors.

I subtly adjust, closing my robe, trying not to make it obvious

I'm wearing my Team Comoara Trădătoare shirt a little prouder now.

"Harold called and said there's no word on the trial results yet. I didn't give him the details of the new angle we're working on, just in case," Jude says.

I say nothing. I'm determined to make it look like I'm not interested in his attention.

My leg is draped over Ezekiel's waist, and the other two are pressed up against my sides as I grab some popcorn from Gage's lap.

"Lake wants to meet with us in the morning. She says she might be able to sneak us into hell to get a look at what's going on," Jude continues.

"That's a hell of a risk," Gage says on a low whistle.

I swallow my really curious and irrational jealousy down and refuse to ask Jude who Lake is.

"I can do this on my own," Jude tells them. "With just one of us, it'd be less likely for us to get caught once she gets me down there."

"How about I just go and all of you stay safe and sound up here?" I ask them, hoping that is going to be the new plan of action.

"You can't siphon there on your own, and Lake would never take you whole," Ezekiel tells me absently as he starts massaging my foot with one hand.

My eyes almost roll back in my head because it feels incredible. I might even like it almost as much as an orgasm. I didn't even know to ask for this, because I've never seen them do it to the other girls over the past few years.

"Then I'll follow her around until she siphons below, and I'll hitch a ride without her knowing. I'm positive I could siphon *out* of hell," I prattle on, suppressing a moan while Ezekiel makes the rest of my body envious of my foot.

"Too risky. Lake knows how to navigate Lucifer's illusion in the royal wing. Her father has served directly under him for years. He'll sense her if she goes snooping, but he won't know I'm there because I'm not yet pledged," Jude says dismissively.

He glances around at the three of them, a hint of something flashing in his eyes too fast for me to discern what, before he schools his expressions.

"Then I'm coming with you. You're not going alone," I tell him.

"He'll be with Lake," Gage says, grinning at me like he sees me already failing at my attempt to pretend not to care.

"Lake can't snoop, which means he'll be on his own," I say carefully, not admitting to the outrageous jealousy he's weirdly trying to provoke. "I'm going."

Jude doesn't even argue, much to my surprise.

Why do I feel like I'm being played all of the sudden?

"Then be ready by lunch tomorrow," Jude tells me before backing up.

Just to pretend it's no big deal he's leaving instead of joining us, which I know we'd all really like, I lean over and tap Ezekiel's shoulder.

"Mr. Magic Fingers, am I a virgin?"

Confusion crosses his features as he seems to think about that. "I'm not really sure. We've never had a virgin before, so I'm not entirely certain what to look for."

"See? It's not as easy as it sounds," Kai tells Gage.

The entire room dissolves into laughter, and the conversation changes. The dynamic shifts before my eyes as Kai's arm drops around my shoulders, and Gage's fingers twine with mine.

Ezekiel continues to gently hold onto my foot, as the three of them talk and laugh about things I'm not completely understanding.

I glance up, noticing Jude at the very end of the long hallway that I can see, since he left my door open.

He stands in front of an empty room that has no purpose, just propped against the frame like it's his room, as he simply stares at us like he's studying the image and trying to place it somewhere.

I'm distracted when Kai draws my attention.

"Tell us something memorable about the days you were watching us before we knew you were watching," he says casually.

"You don't have to make it sound so creepy. It's really not."

He just grins.

"I always sat at the end of the table. One of you on my left, and one of you on my right. But it always changed, because you never all stayed in the same seats every time. It often felt like you were rotating so you could take turns being the closest to me during our table-dinner nights," I say distractedly, my attention snagged on the weird cat on TV as he tries super hard to get some lasagna.

Why have I not seen this cartoon sooner?

I don't realize they've gone silent until I look around to see them all studying me with indecipherable looks on their faces.

"What?" I ask, worried I've just taken steps back again.

Ezekiel's smile starts slowly spreading.

"We used to always sit in the same spots. For centuries," Kai says, almost as though he's thinking aloud.

"Until about five or so years ago," Gage adds quietly.

There are totally butterflies right now, because it almost sounds like they're saying they sensed me without ever realizing it and gravitated toward me the way I always have them.

Gage sighs as he drops to his back. "Jude better come around soon. I'm not sure how much more I can take. I'm only so fucking strong," he tells the other two.

"Why did you wear combat boots with your tuxes?" I ask, as though this is the perfect time for that forgotten question.

Laughter follows that, though I'm not sure what's so funny

about it. No one even bothers to answer me. They tend to laugh when I'm actually being serious, and stay serious when I'm trying to be funny.

When I remember Jude watching, my eyes dart up to see the vacant spot where he was. My heart squeezes a little bit, because even when he's an ass, I still can't stand the thought of him feeling left out.

With a sigh, I curl up closest to Kai's side, since I haven't had nearly as much close time with him, and let his arm drape around me. He doesn't kiss my head, but his hand stays fixed to my ass.

We stay up late, watching cartoons, laughing at stupid jokes, and drinking more alcohol.

The entire time, I can't even enjoy it as much as I should, and they all feel it too. After all, Jude's a much bigger piece of their lives than mine.

One person is missing.

CHAPTER X

A smear of red polish goes along the side of my toe, and I curse as I wiggle on top of the bar. Apparently, the skill to paint one's toenails is not in my arsenal of hidden talents.

"Damn it, that girl made it look so easy on the tutorial. I'm tempted to find her address and go slap her across the face for misleading me," I growl, streaking the side of my toe again.

"The kitchen bar is usually used for something other than painting one's toes," Kai says idly from beside me as he drinks his coffee and sharpens his sai.

It's almost noon, and I'm supposed to be ready by the time Jude returns from soul collecting with the other three. Kai overslept.

Kai. Overslept.

It was a first for him. So he stayed in bed with me all morning and into noon. I was beat.

"Can you keep a secret?" I ask on a sigh.

He mimes the motion of zipping his lips, never glancing at me, and I go phantom, imagine my toenails painted the exact same shade of red, and all colored inside the lines. Then I turn whole and wiggle my toes in a pair of snazzy sandals that showcases them best.

Kai glances over at my feet and smirks.

"It was actually a very thoughtful gift, but I'm apparently

terrible at such girly things when I have to actually *do* them physically."

"You're saying you're spoiled," he suggests.

"Just don't tell Ezekiel," I say on a sigh as I screw the lid back on the nail polish.

The guys appear in the kitchen, and Ezekiel flashes me a grin when he sees me holding the red polish, while showcasing my pretty new red toenails.

However, he looks a little unimpressed when he sees my toenails, and looks over his shoulder as Jude jogs up the stairs.

I expect Kai to sell me out and tell him I'm a cheater, but he just keeps sharpening his sai.

"How bad was it?" Kai asks absently.

Ezekiel shrugs as he props up beside me. Gage goes to pull out sandwich stuff.

"More than usual but not too many for us to handle, even the day after the third trials. It almost feels like today's task was just to test us and see us after the trials—energy levels and all."

Kai flicks his gaze over at me. "I bet Jude didn't look as well rested as the two of you," he quips, smirking when he hears Jude stomping back down the stairs much harder than necessary.

I'm too busy preening and trying to get Ezekiel to tell me how awesome I did at painting my toenails for my very first time. He doesn't know I cheated, after all.

"You ready?" Jude asks me, his gaze not meeting mine as he pulls a black masquerade mask from behind his back.

"Are we going to a party?" I ask, edging my foot over the counter, pushing it closer to Ezekiel.

"I'd rather no one see my face, and a masquerade mask isn't too uncommon in the royal part of hell," he tells me without ever glancing my way.

Ezekiel is paying him more attention than my freaking feet.

"For fuck's sake, so what if she cheated? She spent an hour trying to paint the damn things just because you bought her the fucking polish. Give her a compliment already," Kai says, confusing me, until I realize he's angrily directing that toward Ezekiel.

"It's that obvious I cheated?" I ask dryly, as Ezekiel's grin grows to take up his entire face.

"First timers make a mess," Ezekiel says with a shrug. "But yours look perfect."

I beam. "Thank you. That's the closest to a compliment any of you have really paid me. I'll take it," I say as I slide off the bar and go phantom, fashioning myself a long, understated sexy dress.

Silver high heels offer the black gown a pretty contrast, along with a silvery mask that makes it look like we're ready for the ball. Even if he is wearing tactical gear with his mask instead of a tux.

I'm actually sick of seeing them in tuxes since the trials. Bad memories are involved with tuxes.

Jude arches an eyebrow as he sweeps his gaze over me. "I can't even right now," he says, batting a hand in my direction before reaching through me and siphoning us before I can tell the others goodbye.

However, I don't complain as we land in a parking lot outside of a condemned shopping mart.

"This is a creepy meeting place," I tell him, twirling around in my phantom form. "And I think I'm entirely overdressed."

"Remember this is a very important contact to all of us, and don't do anything to ruin that relationship," he says quietly, as though he's worried someone may be listening.

"Why would I do anything to ruin it?" I ask suspiciously.

He gives me a look.

"Fine," I grumble, rolling my eyes and deciding not to argue, since I'm supposed to be pretending I don't care so much. "I promise."

We stay quiet after that, for a very boringly long time.

No Lake shows up.

A sizzling sound has me zapping myself across the lot to a wall, and Jude is right behind me, both of us staring at the burning words as they appear.

It's an address in New Orleans. Why is that—

A tingle passes through me when Jude's hand touches my phantom hip, and suddenly we're inside a hotel.

My breath catches, and I race behind him, still in phantom form as he walks to the front desk. The guy behind the counter looks up with a bored expression on his face, despite the numerous weapons strapped to Jude's body like he's going to war.

The guy never speaks to Jude, and Jude never says a word. A key card is passed over without any other exchange, and Jude walks over to press the elevator buttons.

As soon as the doors open, he boards, and I join him.

"What's going on?" I ask him warily when we're all alone on the elevator.

His eyes flick up to the tiny red dot on a panel, and the plaque under it informs us there is indeed a camera watching the elevator. Right. He can't talk to me in here.

When the doors open, he steps off first, but I'm right behind him, scanning the hallway. I really don't like this cloak-and-dagger stuff. It's making me paranoid.

Honest people don't have their friends sneak around like criminals to meet them, right? Clearly, Lake is not as awesome as I am.

"I don't think bringing in new people at this point is the best idea. I know my opinion doesn't matter, but we learned a lot about the Devil's intentions through the trials," I state, knowing he can't argue with me in the hallway.

He holds the key card up to a door, and he pushes through it.

Pulling out a compass-looking contraption that looks oddly familiar, Jude moves to the desk in the room. He opens it, does something to it, and then leaves it open.

As he draws all the curtains completely shut, he pulls off his mask, and I lose mine as well.

"We can speak and not be heard, even if the room is bugged now," he tells me.

"What if someone is pressed to the wall with a glass to their ear?" I point out.

I love it when he looks exasperated with me. It means I have at least some effect on him. The *wrong* effect, but I'll take it.

"That device makes it so that only silence can be heard in this room, unless you're physically in this room."

"I'm not *physically* in this room, but—"

"Just stop talking," he says, his hands up like he 'just can't with me' right now.

"Why did she send you to this place?" I ask him as he pulls out his phone, but doesn't do anything. "Shouldn't you tell the guys where we are?"

He shakes his head. "We never text locations. Phones are too easily traced. My GPS is off, but anyone could be reading our messages. They know Lake is paranoid and would send me to another location to meet," he tells me.

I poke my head through the outside wall, looking down and noting we're on Bourbon Street. I know this because the guys come here on occasion when they're taking a much-needed break from all the reaping.

Pulling back in, I face him as he pours himself a glass of the drink I got shit-faced on last night. I'll pass today. I need to be level-headed.

"How do you know Lake?" I ask him, sitting down on the bed.

"Are you going to talk the entire time we have to wait?" he

groans.

"Does she always keep you waiting so long?" I muse.

He rolls his eyes as he throws back some of the drink and starts removing his straps of weapons with his free hand.

"She's paranoid. She'll watch the outside of the hotel for a while. She'll watch the lobby. Then she'll gradually move up to her own room and watch the door. Then, when she's certain I haven't been followed, she'll come in."

"That's a lot of paranoia," I agree, as though that's what he's saying.

He studies me over the rim of his glass when he sits down—weapon free—and stares at me.

"We met Lake over a century ago. She went into the trials a few decades back, and because of her, we were able to get a lot of information about the process of selection."

Alarm bells go off inside my head.

"Wait, you thought Manella was in charge," I remind him. "And he wasn't. Sounds like she's feeding you bad information."

"Or the Devil lied. Which is far more likely, since he made it sound like he had our backs right before he shoved us into the third trial to die," he points out. "Lucifer is playing with us, and Lake is hesitant to meet with me because she's worried she's next. There was a culling in the underworld shortly before the third trial."

My eyebrows lift.

"He eliminated all his guards—both hell's throat and royal guards. Lake is an escort, and half of her kind have been replaced because the others were already recycled," he goes on. "She thinks it has something to do with everything going on with us. Something big is happening, Keyla."

I wave my hand dismissively. "I've decided that name no longer fits me. While I have some sentimental attachment to it, and might keep it as a middle name, I need a new name to define me now. Something badass."

He blinks at me before muttering something under his breath that I probably wouldn't like, so I don't ask him to repeat it.

"Why'd you agree to let me come with you so easily?"

"Because if you're here, I don't have to worry about the three of them doing something stupid while I'm not there to reel them back," he fires back without even having to think about it.

I knew it seemed too easy.

"Why do you think I'll cause problems for you and this contact?" I ask him, reminding him of what he said in the parking lot.

His lips twitch, but he doesn't respond immediately. "You gave your word you wouldn't, so the reason doesn't matter," he says evasively.

"Why the culling?" I ask him, going back to the matter at hand.

He shrugs a shoulder. "I have no idea. Unless he felt he couldn't trust any of them, given the Lamar deal. Which would mean he had no part in what happened to Lamar."

"Which conflicts with our theory that the Devil has been behind *all* of it. What if he's just behind *part* of it?" I ask him, my eyes not moving from his.

He raps his fingers on the edge of the chair, smirking like he's already figured that part out and I'm slow to the game.

"This is what you were all discussing last night, isn't it?"

"When you stormed through for an alcohol run? Yes. Yes, it is," he states with a bored drawl.

Frowning, I look down at my pretty toenails in my elegant, high-heeled sandals.

"Why didn't the others tell me?" I ask quietly. They spent the night in my room, after all.

"Don't look so devastated," he says bitterly. "They're too busy trying for the impossible to think straight right now. Your fault, really. The evil pussy is just backfiring a little, it seems."

This is what we do. Line our insults with snark, never being real with each other. Jude is quite literally never going to stop wanting to hate me, because he sees me as…impossible.

"Despite what you think, there is no jealousy between the three of them. It is possible," I say on a sigh.

"A few nights does not make the impossible possible, *comoara trădătoare.* It takes longer for such resentments to fester, and they always do. Just like there will always be a price. Just like there will always be a favorite."

That last part makes my eyes roll. "My favorite changes based on who has made me happiest at the moment. I'm rather capricious that way."

He snorts derisively. "Those are superficial favorites. Eventually you'll become attached to mostly one, seek that one out more and more. And it's never been more dangerous before than you, because we can have you individually."

He adjusts himself in his pants like he's proving a point, and I realize for the first time he's actually hard. And we're alone.

"None of us seem immune, and whoever you end up becoming most attached to…I don't know if they could do as we've done in the past when it reached that point and simply walk away," he says seriously. No bite to his tone. No snark infused to turn it into banter.

Just real, honest disclosure.

"Then the bond would likely sever, and three of us will roam with a missing piece and the inability to ever experience that one pleasure ever again. *That* is your treacherous step, even though you won't admit it aloud. All I want you to do is really think about that. Think about what you'll be destroying."

I admit I wanted *real* talk, but now he's just being boringly obtuse, and I can't suffer another moment of it.

"If I wanted just one of you, I wouldn't be here with you right now, worrying to death you're being tricked or trapped by this girl you trust far more than me. My own jealousy stems to you at the moment, even though you're certainly not my current favorite and haven't been since that first night when you opened your mouth to speak and ruined the illusion of the bad boy who might make an exception for me."

His lips twitch before he takes a sip of the alcohol again.

I'm a little curious what his chosen taste is.

"I don't even particularly like you at the moment, yet I'd still stop my heart from beating if it meant saving yours from such a fate," I add, daring him to argue.

I've done nothing but prove that time and time again.

"The ability to persuade a man to question everything he knows is by far the most devious trait about you, *comoara trădătoare.* And you have quite a few devious traits we overlook just to keep you around. Myself included. As I said, I'm not immune. It's because of my fear of you dying that I—"

"Leveled up and turned the blind tribe to ash?" I ask, grinning. "That was really cool. But I still stand by my theory of the Four Horsemen. Clearly, you're Death."

He groans, draining the last of his drink before standing to pour more.

"This is why you're infuriating. The fact you can't even get your feelings hurt long enough to hate me back is—"

"Endearing?" I supply.

"Exhausting," he counters, not sounding one bit happy.

"My feelings were only getting hurt in the beginning. When it was all of you against me. Ezekiel is my special boy because he was the first to gift me with hope. Kai is like a willful drug, because I truly enjoy the attention he pays me, even when he's so surly he couldn't possibly have a gentle bone in his body. Gage is my current favorite because I know without a doubt he finally sees me as what I am."

He turns to me, his brow furrowing.

"And what is that?"

"All of yours," I state as though it should be obvious.

His eyes heat for a second as he swallows harder than necessary, as though I just said some really magical words that he's struggling not to believe.

"It's clear I was designed just for the four of you. Whether or not I'm a Trojan Horse is beyond my knowledge. But even if I am such, I'll destroy whoever wants to use me against you. My loyalties are sealed and undivided. The four of you are my only charge. If Lamar had been truly trying to hurt you, I would have burned his heart in his chest without blinking an eye. And I happen to like Lamar."

We stare at each other, not speaking, just gauging the other like we're back in our usual opposing spots on the chessboard.

Finally, he takes a seat again, his gaze flicking over me like it's the first time he's letting himself appreciate the sexy black gown I've chosen.

"If we're stuck here, you could at least wear red for me. Kai is the one who prefers black," he says as though it's no big deal.

Instead of making my dress red, I change it to blue.

"That's Gage's favorite color," he points out.

"Yes, and Gage is my current favorite. If you want to make requests, you need to at least try to be my favorite first," I state absently, as though I can't be bothered to think about the fact he *doesn't* want to be my favorite.

He fights a grin even as he shakes his head and looks away from me. I think we work best when we're not trying to be too real. Our banter is our medium. Things get too intense too quickly otherwise.

Same for all of them, really.

Gage was willing to risk their bond just to give me a pity fuck when I was so pathetically honest with him. It's a tad embarrassing now that I look back on it.

I'll make sure to withhold such pitiful stories in the future. I'd rather them not pity me at all.

I want their admiration instead.

That's much harder to achieve, but the reward would be much better.

"I was wrong about why you hated me," I tell him as he glances over at me. "Gage had his own theory, and he was wrong too. I was wrong about all of it. I thought I had you all figured out as we floated down that fiery lake on the back of that beetle."

He just smirks.

"Then you tell me why you hate me over and over," I say, shrugging. "But it's all a lie. Not even Gage truly knows you, and he's the closest to you."

"I can assure you that I hate you just as much as I like you. You weren't wrong about that."

"Well, I guess it isn't *all* a lie. But you're not worried about me choosing favorites and riding off into the sunset with one, while destroying the other three."

The confident smirk slips from his lips.

"You know I value your bond. You've seen me preserve it to the best of my ability. Albeit, I have understandable moments of weakness. I don't even want you one-on-one. I'm selfish for wanting all four of you, while expecting to be the only one you want, but I'm not greedy. I don't want more than that. Just the four of you. You know that. I can see it in your eyes," I go on. "It's why you like me."

I can see him guarding himself, careful not to react.

"Maybe one day you'll tell me the true reason you're afraid of even taking this risk, when you're the most reckless of the four. Your menace is half your charm, so it doesn't scare me anymore that you hate me. I just want to know why."

He leans back, swallowing.

"You couldn't bring yourself to go against my wishes when I told you that you couldn't touch me. Not after the trials. You bartered with Ezekiel, knowing I wouldn't even hold it against him."

I arch a challenging eyebrow at him.

"You know I don't hurt the bond," I say, as though hearing it aloud again makes him all the more intriguing. "So what scares Death himself?"

"The answer would be simple if you stopped to think about it," he says so quietly I almost miss it. "You inspire a fear none of us have known before."

He looks away, and silence descends around us for more uncomfortable hours. I stare at the ceiling, idly wondering what the other guys are up to.

"Does she ever plan to show up?" I ask him as he moves to the window to look out.

"Patience," is all he says.

"You really trust her?" I ask on a sigh, needing him to keep me from being on edge right now with the heaps of dread flowing through me.

So soon after the trials, when everything was life-or-death, is not the best time for someone new to come into the picture and wreak havoc on my nerves.

"With my life," he assures me.

He says it to ease my worries, which is the nicest thing he's ever done. But it weirdly feels like a knife to the heart for no reason at all.

I try not to be envious. I really do.

But I sort of want to kill her already, if I'm being completely honest. I think it's best not to inform him I actually am as insane as he accuses me of being.

CHAPTER XI

Jude drops down to the bed beside me, like he's sick of finding uncomfortable furniture to sit down on and crane his neck to watch the TV that only has a good angle from the bed.

The furniture, by the way, is nailed to the floor. Rather peculiar establishment, if you ask me. And Jude says we're not allowed to pry it free because it's an important meeting place for a lot of *surface guardians*—which is still just a fancy term for reapers.

He's careful not to touch me, unsurprisingly. Especially since I gave up being phantom and went whole hours ago to gain control of the remote.

It's almost dawn—the next day—and there's still been no sign of Lake.

"She must know I'm here or something," I say as the light starts glowing through the curtains.

We missed one hell of a party last night. The streets were loud, and I really wanted to join in, but Lake is a very annoying girl who thinks her time is the only time that bears importance. Selfish brat if you ask me.

No, I do not sound petty.

"No. Only Lamar and Lucifer have sensed you. Lamar has a link to spirits, which is part of his power. It's probably why he sensed you when the hell spawns didn't. And Lucifer is Lucifer. I'd be alarmed if he hadn't been able to sense you, especially in hell."

"But only when I was close enough to touch," I decide to point out.

He purses his lips.

More silence and impatient waiting follows that comment.

We watch *Friends* like we're not both waiting to be dropped into hell by an escort he knows but won't really give me many details about, because he's apparently more loyal to her than to me.

Then again, at least I know she exists. She doesn't have a clue about me. Even Jude has become protective of that secret. So that means I'm winning. You know, if I was in a contest with her or whatever.

My mind reverts back to the theories I've been working on silently in my head for the past several hours when we both grew tired of veiled insults.

"I think Kai is Conquest/Pestilence. The thing he did to those two guards seemed like he was infecting them with poison. But it could be disease," I state randomly, causing him to groan again.

"For the last time, the Four Horsemen were killed centuries ago during a collision of the two kingdoms."

"Who told you that?"

He gives me a dry look. "*Plenty* of people, *including* Lake. Like I said, it was the first obvious answer."

"I don't trust Lake."

"You don't know her. Anyway, it hurt the balance significantly, though the details are murky as to why they were killed. *But* if by some chance all of that was inaccurate, and by some narrow miracle we were the special quad who were that powerful, we'd be accepted into hell. In fact, they'd even drag us there if they suspected it, because our presence topside this long would shatter the balance. In fact, we would have already shattered it by now if we were them."

"Balance, balance, balance," I say on a frustrated breath. "I'm starting to hate that word."

"Get used to it. That's all we're constantly trying to do: Keep the balance. Both sides, no matter how differently opinionated they are, agree on one thing, and that is the importance of balance. Good must level out with evil, or the world becomes too corrupt too quickly, and hell spills over."

"Wouldn't the Devil want that?" I point out.

"Fuck no." He looks at me like I'm a total moron. "It would be the end of hell if the world had no good left in it."

"Why?" I ask, moving closer like I'm desperate to know.

"Because without balance, there is no such thing as good or bad. Free will becomes null and void, and so do both kingdoms."

"That makes no sense," I grumble.

He stands quickly and goes to grab an old-timey scale with two small plates on either end.

He puts it down on the table in the center of the room, and I move to the end of the bed, no longer giving the TV my attention as he places a few lead balls on each of the pans on the scale.

"There is a perfect balance to everyone who can be topside. You have an exact amount of purities and impurities," he says, putting a lead ball on each plate.

The scale stays perfectly balanced as he moves his hand back.

"Like you told Lucifer you guys were," I say, frowning. "He seemed surprised by that."

"Because he senses our impure imbalance, yet we have our souls intact and it defies the laws of balance," he tells me, though it doesn't make a lick of sense. "Plenty of our kind is balanced, otherwise, we couldn't be topside. The most powerful of the balanced ones usually become royal escorts."

He puts an extra ball on one side, tipping the scale.

"And the ones with an imbalance of impurities or purities go up or down to maintain surface balance," he goes on.

"Define purities and impurities," I tell him.

"Impure thoughts, emotions, urges…those are impurities. Compassion, loyalty…things like that are purities," he says absently before continuing. "Humans have some far more pure than others, and far more impure than others. It's their actions and reactions that define the topside balance, but an impure balance of one of our kind topside would have too much dark influence, inadvertently affecting free will."

"Would the same be true if a good angel were walking topside?" I muse.

"They follow the rules better than our kind do, so I don't know," he answers.

I snort, and his lips twitch. It's sort of nice how he's just talking and explaining things without looking at me like I'm searching for a way to use it against him.

"People like Lake have that pure-to-impure balance and can be topside. Many do. But we're an enigma," he continues.

"Because you're the Four Horsemen, but you have souls to keep you from being imbalanced. I thought all the creatures had souls."

He blows out a frustrated breath. "The souls choose a new form. We're in our original. Our soul is still mortal with immortal properties and shrouded by an unnatural immortal body. It balances itself against our impurities." He quickly adds, "But we're *not* the fucking Four Horsemen."

"Famine is Gage. I saw what he did that beetle. It was like he drained it until it was shriveling from starvation," I go on, undeterred.

He looks up from the scale, his brow furrowed.

"Why would you say that exactly?" he asks, clearly intrigued.

"When something starves, it starts eating itself from the inside. The beetle was clearly doing that, hence the shriveling. I would think that was obvious."

He starts to speak, but I continue on.

"And Ezekiel is War, surprisingly enough. He doesn't create chaos. Chaos would have them running in a frenzy and spurred by random events. War is a simple-minded thought to kill the opposition at any cost. Ezekiel just confused their minds with who the opposition was and created a civil war from thin air."

He steps closer, tilting his head.

"As I said, you're clearly death. Death can come in any form. You didn't need a spear to kill them, because you were Death itself."

He blinks and slowly shakes his head. "Famine. No one has ever suggested Gage's power being famine. He drains things."

"He starves them and dehydrates them," I correct.

"Famine's power was to kill the land with pests and such," he tells me dismissively.

"Because he drained the land of nutrients and starved it until it killed everything to keep itself alive and not share resources," I go on. "The land is just as alive as you or I. It only makes sense he could do it to a living being as much as a living entity."

He points a finger at me. "Your ability to rationalize your point by twisting theories and half-cocked hypothesizes makes you impossible to reason with. You make me think things I know can't be possible. The Four Horsemen are dead. That is something agreed on by everyone."

"Then why give the quads so much extra attention?" I ask him, arching an eyebrow. "Why not just leave you forever locked in hell's belly if Lucifer truly wants you dead? Why the theatrics for a man so powerful?"

His hands fist, but before he can answer, I hear the door opening. Instantly, I go phantom, just as a very familiar brunette walks into the room, her smile spreading when she sees Jude.

Envy like I've never felt before slices through me so powerfully that bile almost rises to my phantom throat when he grins genuinely back at her.

It isn't because he's smiling at her.

It's because I know this girl.

"Two years ago, the four of you shared her," I say on a shaky breath as Jude goes to hug her right in front of me like she's nothing more than an old friend.

He ignores me, the girl who doesn't really exist, as the one they've touched between them before laughs and pulls back, greeting him.

I remember the way she kissed all of them, savored them with a familiarity I couldn't understand. Most of the other girls always seemed like strangers to them, but she seemed as comfortable with them as they were with her.

It's now I realize why.

They shared her more than once.

I just got to view a reunion.

Staggering back, I watch as her hand slides down his arm with ease and comfort.

Jude clears his throat, and withdraws from her touch as I stare numbly at the scene at hand.

"I really don't trust her now," I tell him, trying to mask the fact my feelings actually can still be hurt.

Admired not pitied—my new goal, remember? I get nowhere with them when I wear my heart on my sleeve.

She moves to the scale, grinning over at him. "Playing with lead balls, Jude? I hardly pictured you as the idle-hands type after knowing you for so long."

"It took you longer than usual to show up," he tells her casually, moving to sit on the end of the bed near me.

Me? I'm trying not to visibly sulk. Jealousy is a powerful emotion. I literally want to kill this girl. I had no issue with her back then. I mean, of course I was jealous, even tried to possess her—like I did many of them—*especially her.*

She was the one they seemed to really enjoy, and she was flirty and fun, not at all timid or apprehensive of the debauchery they showered her with.

And the most beautiful.

Now she walks in here and makes Death himself smile as though it's a simple task.

She looks around, as though she's searching for something. Everything she does is suspicious now, because I'm just looking for a reason to kill her.

"Now I know why you made me promise to behave," I state dryly.

Jude's lips twitch as she faces him again.

"I was waiting for your brothers. I may not can sneak you all in, but I assumed there'd be a little trade for this very deadly risk I'm taking for the four of you," she says, smirking before she winks.

"I'm going to have to kill her," I say on a sigh, then stiffen, realizing I said it aloud.

Jude clears his throat, his humor gone.

"Fine. I won't kill her." *In front of you,* I add silently, deciding I'm really good at negotiating. Seems like a fair deal to me. No need in getting his vote on the matter.

"My brothers stayed home. The soul breaks are getting worse, and we're stationed in the highest concentration of the breaks right now."

He tells her this easily, even though this is the first I've heard that tidbit of information. One more reason to kill her. She makes my place feel threatened, and I don't particularly care for that feeling.

"Would they have *paid* her the way she clearly wants to be *paid* if they'd been able to come here?" I ask, deciding that is very important information I need to know before I decide if I'm an idiot or not for thinking I was special.

I really will leave and find a way to extract myself from them completely if he answers *yes*. Even if it's just to be a snarky dick to me. I will so be gone, just as soon as I return him safely home.

Those three were beginning to make me feel like I was as important to them as they are me, yet they didn't mention any of this.

Jude, of course, doesn't answer me, since he can't talk to a phantom his guest can't see, without being terribly suspicious. Since she seems to be as paranoid as he is with trust, that would be bad.

I decide to make him talk so she doesn't trust him. I'll find a way into hell to gather their information. They don't need her.

"Would they?" I ask him again.

He signs the letters *n* and *o* behind his back. Hmm… I can read sign language? Oh, he's telling me *no!* They wouldn't have. I hope he's not lying.

As she comes to stand closer to him, her eyes raking over him, I move to his side.

"You're turned on without them," she says, glancing at his lap.

That has me scooting away, since that's my effect.

Jude clears his throat as he leans forward, hiding the noticeable erection he certainly shouldn't be having with another woman in the room.

"If I'm a conduit for your attraction to her, I'll be forced to make her ugly very soon," I tell him seriously.

He gives a subtle shake of his head. I'm not sure what he's telling me, but I think he's asking me not to kill her or telling me it's not her effect.

"I mean it. I will not be the little magic gem that offers you an independent boner so you can screw another girl in my presence."

"I'd never betray my brothers by taking someone without them," he tells her.

I really hate the way he calls them his brothers. It's confusing. Which in a sense, they are. But not in the blood-relation sense.

"The Kincaid brothers only share," she says on a sigh, as though she's repeating something she's heard too much. "I remember well."

"All quads share," he says dismissively.

We'll have to circle back to the *Kincaid brothers* thing. That's the first I've heard of that, and again, they're not really brothers.

Her eyes close, like she's relishing a memory. My phantom fists clench.

"You being turned on by her definitely makes you my least favorite," I mutter under my breath.

Pettiness is my new shade of personality lately.

His eyes dart to me as his jaw tics, but he immediately looks away, unable to say whatever it is he wants to say, since she's here.

I like that I'm making him want to talk. I need this siren gone before she sings her song and I lose him completely.

"You four don't have the same last names if you were born to different families. I've not even been able to uncover your last names. So why does she refer to you as the Kincaid brothers?" I muse aloud.

"Are we going to hell or not, Lake? Time is very precious right now, and I've been separated from my brothers too long. You know how quad bonds work," he reminds her.

I'm not sure why my stomach unsettles, but it's not envy this time.

I look back at her as her eyes open, and she gives him a small, sympathetic smile.

"You're hurting for their presence. Sorry. I really did expect them to be here with you, or I wouldn't have made you wait for so long. The truth is that I was trying to get out of my latest assignment, which is the main reason I'm so late."

He cocks his head.

"What do you mean?" he asks as he stands.

She takes a step back, pinching the bridge of her nose.

"This culling is terrifying everyone. Lucifer hasn't stopped it yet. Forty more escorts were killed this morning. He wants nothing but devout loyalty, and you know where I stand on that fence if I'm willing to break the rules to take you under," she says, smiling sadly up at him.

"You think you'll be in the culling?" he asks, sounding concerned.

There's that damned envy again.

"All of the participants of the trials survived, sans the two you and your brothers killed," she tells him.

"Everyone survived those trials?" he asks incredulously.

She nods, a huff of a breath escaping her. "Lucifer retrieved the others before their deaths. They never made it past even one obstacle. But he needed them to start a change. To replenish what he's recycling, because there can be no vacant jobs, obviously. Everyone has a task to be fulfilled to preserve the balance."

"I don't understand. No one gets out of the trials without completing them," he goes on, confused.

Her watery smile doesn't sit right with me.

"I'm afraid you have no idea what you stirred up by surviving that third trial. It was *impossible* to complete every task in the three days allotted. Even in a month, no one could have done that. I never believed them. They tried to tell me, but I refused to believe it could be true, because I really like the four of you."

I step closer, tilting my head. What does she think is wrong with them?

"She thinks something really bad, but she doesn't know I helped. Tell her so she'll stop believing whatever it is," I tell him, not liking the way I'm now worried about her damn opinion of him.

After all, I want her gone.

"What's going on, Lake? Do you know what Lucifer was trying to achieve?" he asks, not telling her about me even though I'm giving him permission.

She nods once, then meets his eyes. I step in front of him, trying to inspect her look closer.

"I'm afraid I do. And I'm sorry I have to be the one to do this," she says.

I see it too late. She's incomprehensibly fast.

The glint of the blade is barely recognized before it's halfway through my body. It's so fast that I barely even register the fact she's slicing through me.

I don't even hesitate to turn whole, pain lancing through me as the blade gets jammed in my upper stomach, slicing through my spine as I shove power out of me.

She's launched backwards, cracking the wall and hitting the ceiling, pinned there but not dying. Because it hurts too much to strain for the acid.

Two arms catch me before I collapse, and I choke on the blood I feel gurgling in my mouth, tasting like acid on its own as the black streams of it trickle down.

It's like a heavy drumming happens in my ears. I can't hear what Jude is saying, but I feel his power flowing through me as ashes flit around the room.

His eyes are feral and wide as he hovers over me, and I cry out when he jerks the dagger out of me. Pain. All consuming, burning, excruciating, agonizing pain has me almost blacking out.

The trickles of a cold sweat break out across my skin as I start struggling to breathe, coughing. I still can't hear much, but I do hear him shouting on the phone.

In the next instant, I'm in our house. He siphoned us…

I try to go phantom, hoping it can heal me, but a scream is ripped from my throat as it only makes the pain worse, leaving me unable to leave this dying form.

All four of them are hovering over me, panicking, working tirelessly to save me. My head lulls to the side just as Ezekiel gets my dress ripped open, exposing the proof there's no coming back from this.

The black veins are climbing up me from the poison on the blade as black blood pumps out through the cracks of Gage's fingers. He presses down harder, and I scream in pain as he tries to keep me from bleeding out.

"Devil's poison!" I hear someone shout loud enough to just barely cut through the continuous drumming in my ears that is increasing in tempo.

This weak, pathetic form I coveted and craved so much is poisoned.

But this form is what saved them when the phantom couldn't.

"Run," I tell them on a gurgle. "She…wanted…to…know…where you…were," I manage to choke out.

Kai is suddenly cradling my head in his lap. I can't hear what he's trying to tell me, but I can see the grief already shading his eyes.

I'm not going to survive this.

Something is getting shoved into my mouth and slathered over me in the next instant, but I choke on it and spit it out when it makes it feel like my mouth is about to explode and pain shoots through my head.

Four gazes swing to me as the veins only slither up farther, stealing my breaths and causing me to convulse.

I never even got to tell them why I'd give everything to keep them safe.

Maybe they know.

CHAPTER XII

Agony.

No, not agony.

Torture. That's what the burning sensation feels like when I open my eyes.

Next feeling?

Panic that overrides the pain, because I'm inside a motherfucking box! A wooden one lined with silky fabrics as though that's supposed to excuse the fact someone has locked me in a box.

I don't care how soft that gray silk looks, this is *not* okay. In fact, it's weird and very unsettling. Even by my standards.

Still whole, I bang on the lid, but no one comes to open it.

"Let me out! This isn't funny!"

And just why the hell am I naked?

A black shard of singed fabric is all I find while searching around for the handle that will let me out of this damned thing. There is no handle. At least not on this side of the box. Why does it still smell like something is burning?

My vision is in gray, so obviously it is very dark in here if I'm using my fancy new night vision…that only worked so well in hell…

Flicking the confusing yet useless piece of singed fabric away, I close my eyes and concentrate, reminding myself I'm a badass and I can fight through the pain. That is not as intense as the last time I was awake.

Frustrated, I start looking around the box again.

Why the hell is the back of this box charred?

Am I actually *in* hell?

It hurts when I strain for phantom, but at least this time I can do it.

Immediately, I sit up, and see...dirt under me where there should be a box like everywhere else around me. But it's just lots of dirt and charred pieces of wood around the edges.

Am I in the ground?! Is the ground smoking?!

I drop my head back down and observe my surroundings with a newly informed eye, as I'm forced to turn whole again and endure the endless pain. This box is not just a luxurious box. It's a freaking casket. And I've been buried.

Naked, for some reason.

Possibly in hell.

I'm *really* not happy with this current situation.

I thought turning phantom would instantly heal me like it made me sober. Though the wound is not quite as grave as it seemed earlier—*I must have been a little dramatic, now that I'm really looking at it*—it still hurts.

The veins are gone. The flesh is pulled back together. Only a very large bruise remains as proof I didn't make the whole thing up in my head.

Yet, the pain is still unbearable. It's as though I'm still burning alive from the inside, and it's weakening my ability to turn ghost girl.

With all the concentration I can muster, I focus really hard on going phantom, but I can barely sense them when I feel myself fighting to stay in intangible form. It feels like I'm being pulled in four different directions at once.

I zap myself seven feet into the air—*calculating an extra foot for human error in depth since I can't see*—and fall the extra *two* feet back to the ground, landing in a crumple as a real girl who can feel that shit.

They buried me a foot short. Dicks.

I can't even go phantom again when I try.

Oh damn. If I can't go phantom and zap myself all the way back to them, then how the hell am I going to find them? It's not as though they've ever *walked* home.

Looking around, I note that it is a very familiar cemetery.

Then, of course, my eyes dart to the headstone to see how they've endeared their fearless, selfless, wonderful, doting guardian, though they never helped determine her virginal status.

No name.

The stone simply reads, *"Comoara Trădătoare."*

There's also a bed of quickly wilting roses I'm sitting in. I don't feel a single thorn.

It reminds of the roses they showered onto those women as a gift to bring them into the folds. They always took care to remove the thorns. I found it so thoughtful. It was one of those things that just reeled me in that much more.

Now that I've apparently died—*again*—one of those assholes finally got me my damn roses. Whichever one it was, they're my new favorite. I don't even care if it's Jude; this one is a win.

"Lovely," I say to myself, grinning at the heaps of roses surrounding me, even though the ones under me smell like they're burning.

Lush, luxurious, red…and faded red/pink. And dried and dead beneath.

For an entire moment, I'm distracted from my pain as I bask in my roses, then bewildered by their varying degrees of decay.

Just how long have I been dead?

It surely took a while to get such an ornate gravestone, though they certainly could have put a little more thought into the inscription I was supposed to be left with for all time.

Where are my awesome quotes? Not even any dates to show my very short time as this version of me. Just that damn *treacherous treasure* crap that is certainly not a sweet term of endearment.

I'll get mad at them later.

The pain will be distracted no longer.

Staggering to my feet, I look around, confused. How do I find my way home in this mess?

I manage to walk, despite the pain, focusing on the guys, thinking of everything about them. It seems to lessen the pain.

Two people stumble over themselves, gaping at me like they've been traumatized.

"It's just a naked body," I tell them with a bitter smile as I flip them off and keep hobbling along.

Dying apparently makes me very cranky. Especially when I come back whole and struggle to cling the form I once despised.

I tell ya, there's just no way to make me happy right now.

I can't even conjure some clothes for myself. And somehow I'm still dirty even though I did go phantom.

"Sheesh, someone get me a cheese plate to go with my *whine.*"

Yeah, my recycled-yet-slightly-altered bad pun doesn't even cheer me up.

The back alley I turn down doesn't look promising. The guys are in a much nicer area.

The three guys who swing their gazes up in shock and very alarming delight has me looking over my shoulder as I pass them.

They're definitely about to piss me off.

Predictably, they cut off my exit and surround me, all of them leering.

"What do we have here?" Mr. Cliché asks from behind me.

"You have a very naked girl who just dug out of her grave—figuratively speaking on the *digging* portion. If I'm a zombie, you idiots will be the first I infect," I tell them flatly. My gaze deliberately dips to one's crotch. "And depending on your intent, the bite wound could be vicious."

The one in front of me looks hesitant now, as though he's not sure if he wants to do terrible things to a girl who might just be crazy enough to bite away his manhood.

I'll do far worse, but they're human and don't know that. Yet.

"I'm in a lot of pain, and I'm a little lost right now. I'm almost suspicious it's because I've been away from my four very ungrateful boyfriends for too long. Care to hurry up and exercise your free will so I can decide if I'm going to kill you or not?" I ask with an impatient smile.

The one in front of me turns and runs when I smirk at him. When I flick my gaze to the right, the guy there sees something in my eyes I'm apparently missing.

Or maybe it's the fact the concrete under my feet seems to be sizzling and burning away without fire the longer I stand here. That's rather curious.

It makes me look back on everything that's been going on since I woke and consider all the burning smells.

He runs as well, while the one behind me jerks me back by my hair and calls them a string of very emasculating names.

My lips tense when the fella jerks me back harder, trying to force me to the ground. But he cries out in pain before I even do anything to him.

"I think that's enough free will for the day," I say before reaching back and grabbing his hand, yanking it away before throwing him against the wall with it.

His eyes widen as I stalk toward him, and I grin as he starts convulsing.

A sick feeling lands in the pit of my stomach, and I blink back, staring at the man who is nothing more than a pile of ash now.

What the actual hell just happened?

Cursing, I turn and start walking again. For whatever reason, I just enjoyed killing him way too much, and I didn't even particularly mean to kill him. I'm not even sure how it happened so fast. One second he was there, and the next he was ash.

Sure, he needed to die. He's not exactly going to be missed from humanity, but killing has always been an indifference of sorts—in the short time I've had the ability. I neither like nor dislike it.

I'm going to choke those bastards for burying me if the distance has made me someone who enjoys killing.

I'm not sure how the two are linked, but all my instincts point to those four assholes.

Sighing, I turn around. Then brighten.

Harold.

I know where that damn pawn shop is.

Hobbling, I ignore the indignant gasps and the four fender-benders I cause as I cross the street and hurriedly move toward the pawn shop.

Any time I stop for too long, the concrete starts burning again. This is new.

Even the casket was burned all the way through in the back where I was touching it. I assumed that meant I was in hell.

Is this a side effect of dying? Or has this been something I never experimented with?

When I pull Harold's door open, I hold on too long, and the handle burns off and turns to ash in my hands.

He's immediately in front of me, the tip of a sword pressed to my neck.

"Who the hell are you?" he growls, even as my feet start burning through his store's floor.

That tip draws closer, pressing into my neck. My last experience with a blade has me freezing in fear for a second.

"If I don't run in place or something, I'll keep burning a hole through your floor."

He looks so puzzled about the words I choose to use when a sword is pressed to my neck. I'm a little confused by my own thought process.

"I realize we've never been properly introduced, and I'm afraid to shake your hand at the moment, but if my quad doesn't come to me soon, I'm afraid I might die again. And I *just* got myself out of a very depressing grave."

He pulls the sword back, still looking terribly confused, and I hiss out a breath while jogging in place, stopping the burning.

His eyes dip to my breasts, given the fact the running-in-place has given them some bounce, but they come back up quickly.

"Sorry," I tell him, not sorry at all, "but you're quite literally the only person I know outside of them. And Lake. But Lake is dead now, because—"

"Who the fuck are you?" he asks on a rasp.

"I still haven't quite figured that part out yet," I tell him, only adding to his confusion. "But I do need your help, Harold."

The sound of my voice is a little off, and it comes out with quite the enchanting echo. He sneezes then glares at me.

"No need in trying to force me. This is neutral ground. No one from hell or anywhere else is allowed to force anything on neutral ground."

"The only thing I'm trying to force is my other form, so that I can quit running and trying not to burn the ground. No such luck.

I need my guys. I think. I'm not sure, but I think. Please. The Kincaids."

The name has his entire demeanor changing. I'm going to ask them what's up with this weird name and why they're pretending to be brothers. After I bitch about my simplistic gravestone.

"You're picking the wrong fight right now," he tells me, his eyes narrowing.

"Oh, I'll be picking a fight about that damn pathetic excuse for a headstone and the fact it took me dying to get roses. But first I need to hug them or something, so call them."

He looks wary. Understandably. He doesn't know me, and strangers are hard to trust.

"Call them and tell them one sentence, and I swear they'll want to see me," I assure him.

He points that sword at me. "If this is a trap for them, it'll do you no good. This place has been sanctioned. No deaths can happen here."

I still haven't figured out why a pawn shop is an ideal location for sanctuary. Nor do I particularly care.

"If I don't find them soon, I can assure you my death will happen right here," I go on. "Just do it. I'm going to walk around so I can quit all this bobbing up and down."

He huffs like he's not sure what exactly to make of me.

So I give him the one line that always seems to help an older guy along with decision-making with a younger girl. "What would you want someone to do if it was your daughter standing before them as I'm standing before you now?" I ask with as much emotion in my tone as possible to sell it.

I'm jogging and not standing, but pointing that out just sounds weird, and it's not the way they say it in the movies.

Movies, please don't fail me this time.

He sighs as he grabs his phone.

He's already dialing someone when he says, "I'll kill you if you make me regret this."

I give him the winning words, and start perusing his store as he dials three different people, cursing them for not answering. I strain to listen, making sure he's not calling someone else to come take away the crazy naked girl burning holes in his shop floor.

"Yeah?" a hoarse voice asks, sounding very unhappy to be answering the phone. The word is so gravelly, I'm not sure whose voice it is.

"Got a pretty little naked girl here looking for you," Harold tells him.

Hmm…that might work too.

"Don't give a fuck," the familiar voice of Gage says with a little more definition in his tone.

Harold glances over at me, and I give him the get-on-with-it look.

"*Comoara trădătoare,* is what she says – "

His words are cut off, when Gage is suddenly in the room and throwing him up against the wall with his hand clutching Harold's throat. Harold's eyes widen in horror, as the phone slips from his hand and he struggles to pull Gage's hand away.

"Where'd you hear that phrase?" he growls, putting his face right in front of Harold.

"From the *treacherous treasure* herself, of course," I drawl, wiggling my fingers at him.

Harold collapses in a heap as he heaves for air, while Gage turns a black-eyed murderous glare on me, his lip snarling as he moves toward me in a less-than-ideal manner.

He looks pissed instead of apologetic for having buried me.

In a blink, his hand is suddenly on my throat as he tosses me against the wall and starts strangling me. "Who the fuck are you?" he snaps.

I shove his chest so hard he's launched across the room, hitting the wall with so much force that he bounces to the ground beside Harold.

Harold grabs his abandoned sword, racing toward me, but a renewed sense of energy is swirling through me after having felt Gage's touch. I sling him across the room without even touching him.

That sword clatters across the ground, and Gage grabs it, his eyes on me as he slowly stands, weapon in hand.

"Have you lost your damn mind?" I shout. "How long did I have to be dead before you assholes forgot me?!"

I see just a spark of hesitation.

"You have a handful of seconds to drop that sword before I sling you like sleeping Harold," I warn him, gesturing at Harold, who is unconscious. "I would rather be hanging on the side of a mountain or plummeting from a fiery lake than be so near a sword. Neither of the first two ever actually killed me. And I hate waking up trapped in boxes now too, by the way. Quit piling on."

The sword clatters to the ground, and he staggers back like he's seeing a ghost. Speaking of…

I change to phantom form easier, but it's still a strain to hold it. Sensing them still proves difficult as well.

"Where'd she go?" Harold groans from the floor, looking around.

Gage continues to stare at me with a stupefied expression. "Keyla?" he asks as though he's scared to say the fake name aloud.

"I already told Jude I desperately need a new, more badass name. Now I'm certain. Not even Keyla could have just climbed out of a grave without freaking out."

The second I go whole, Gage is suddenly blurring to me again, and just as I'm about to defend myself, I stop. Because his lips land on mine, and he pulls me to him in a crushing embrace as he kisses me stupid.

"I've been alive too long," Harold grumbles from somewhere nearby.

Gage's hold is a little painful against my still bruised and battered body, and I break the kiss. But he immediately starts kissing me harder, even as the wall behind us starts to catch fire.

A loud *whooshing* mixed with something high pitched forces us to break apart as Harold goes to using a fire extinguisher on us and the wall. An alarm wails over our heads as though we can't see the fire and need to be squealed at by the infernal contraption.

Still crabby.

"What the fuck?" Gage roars.

"She's going to burn the whole place down. Get her the hell out of here."

Gage snatches me at the waist, and we're gone in a dizzying instant.

His lips are back on mine in the next, and we're backing up against a familiar feeling kitchen island. That also starts burning against my skin.

He rips me away from it, staring at it like he's confused, and I leap onto him, since his clothes are already falling into ashy heaps. The rest of him is clearly fireproof, which is the important part.

Then again, I never questioned if I could hurt him. It's like I knew I couldn't.

"What's going on?" he asks on a rasp whisper, even as I cling to him like a spider monkey. "Am I mad?"

"Mad like crazy or mad like angry? Because I was thinking a little of both, since you threw me against a wall. What the actual hell?"

My legs tighten around his waist, and my arms tighten around his neck, as he reaches up and cups both sides of my face.

"You're fucking dead," he finally says, as though he's trying to convince both of us of this. "And never recycled."

I push away from his hands and start rubbing my cheek against his like a cat starving for affection, because the pain seems to lessen the longer he's touching me, or maybe he's just that distracting.

"I gathered as much when I woke up in a damn coffin," I tell him, still rather unhappy about that. "You could have at least buried me in the backyard so I could find my way home. Or just let me keep the west wing of the house."

He laughs a little too wildly, and I pull back as he starts running a hand through his hair. I'm clinging to him without any help, because his hands are no longer touching me.

"I've gone crazy. I've reached a state of imbalance, and I've officially gone as mad as we all worried we'd become."

"I'm very confused, at the moment," I tell him, looking around to see the house is a little trashed.

Furniture is flipped over. Windows are broken. It looks like they've stopped giving a damn about how pretty their home is. It's always been kept so clean and almost regal.

Now it looks like they've been fighting so hard to stay alive in my absence. How many people have tried to kill them?

"Where are the others?" I ask, worrying about him being alone when I'm possibly too weak to defend him.

"What the fucking hell?" Ezekiel's voice has me snapping my gaze over, and I grin broadly at the man gaping at me.

"You see her too?" Gage asks, his hysterical laughter tapering off as his hands slide around me at last, helping me hold myself up.

"What is she?" Ezekiel asks, glaring at Gage. "What the hell have you done?"

Gage's grin slowly spreads. "It's really her," he finally says, then looks at me again like he's finally convinced.

"Yes, it's me. And just because you're finally acting happy to see me, that doesn't mean any of you are off the hook for that terribly simple headstone. Where were my damn quotes? I've said some very memorable and insightful things that should be shared with the world."

Something crashes to the ground, and I look over as a grin starts to spread over Ezekiel's face, even as he slumps against a table. But it's seeing Kai gripping the edge of the same table that has me doing a double-take. How long has he been there? And why do they all seem *that* surprised to see me?

I mean, we met *while* I was a spirit who'd somehow clawed her way back into existence. It shouldn't be that hard to believe I'm back again.

A vase lays broken on the ground before them, one that used to don that table, and dead flowers are spilling from it without a drop of water.

"Exactly how long have I been dead?" I decide to ask.

"Just over a month," Gage says reverently, his eyes raking over my face as I turn to look at a mirror.

My hair is messy for the first time ever, since I never fixed it in phantom form. As a person who hates a messy appearance, it's rather irksome, but there are far more important things to deal with at the moment.

Besides, I don't look like a rotting corpse, so I'll consider it a win.

"I look damn good for a dead girl no matter what form I'm in," I say aloud, trying to lighten this terribly stuffy air.

"It's really her," Kai says, a hesitant grin starting to form.

My body washes over with tingles as the three of them so close starts to push that pain much, *much* deeper down, almost extinguishing it completely. It's such a different sort of pain than I've ever felt, nothing like the pull of being away from them too long leaves me with.

As the pain ebbs, the reality of the situation slowly starts to sink in.

Gage lets me down when I start wriggling, and I test my theory. The floor doesn't start burning under me. I knew it was linked to all of them, just like the horrible pain.

They weren't together, and I couldn't sense them like usual. I think them being separated from *each other* was what was making me hurt and tearing my heart in four different directions.

How long have they been apart?

Gage jogs off, and I hear him in the kitchen as the other two just silently gawk at me. Ezekiel even startles back a step when I start toward him.

Determined, I strut right up to him anyway, and throw my arms around him. "Either hug me back, or I swear I'll never let you sleep peacefully again," I threaten when he remains still in my grip.

In the next instant, two strong arms almost squeeze me too hard, and a shuddering breath snakes out of him as he trembles just slightly.

I pat his chest, and struggle to get free, but he finally lets me go to Kai.

Kai, unlike Ezekiel, is on me before I can reach him, his hand roughly digging into my hair as he kisses me so hard I feel the bruising power of his relief.

My arms slide around his neck, returning the kiss, as Ezekiel presses against my back again, his lips moving to my neck.

"It's definitely her," Kai groans against my lips before tearing his away as he steps back and adjusts his very happy-to-see me erection.

Ezekiel turns me, his lips finding mine just as hungrily. Now *this* is the reception I expected the first time I came into their lives as a real girl.

Much better than my last experience.

His hands travel down my bare body, pulling closer as the kiss heats. I almost don't hear Gage talking on his phone in such a quiet voice.

"Just get back. I can't…I just can't explain right now. Get back."

Breaking the kiss with Ezekiel is a little hard to do, now that we're back to that survival and sex thing being linked. I'm so relieved to be alive that I want to feel it, but I first need to set some things straight before they start teasing me again.

Gage comes jogging back in, tugging on a pair of track pants as his no-longer-black eyes rake over me like he can't look his fill.

"I'm assuming that was Jude?" I ask, and he nods once.

"Good. While we're waiting on him to come remove the last bit of pain plaguing me, I have something very important to tell you."

They all step in closer. I found it so sweet when I first found all those beautiful roses with no thorns. I didn't have all the details then.

"I died saving you assholes, and you repay me by putting me in a hole that far away from you?!" I snap, watching as their eyes widen and their grins curve up. "Seriously? *That's* all you could come up with on my headstone? And for a solid month, the only thing you lazy asses brought me was roses?"

They all dart a gaze behind me, just as I hear Jude's familiar voice wash over me with surprise and awe.

"It's her."

CHAPTER XIII

I whirl around, tempted to go to him, but not emotionally capable of dealing with rejection at this very trying moment.

"Yes," I say with a bitter smile. "Apparently I'm too stubborn for *Death* to deal with properly."

I give him a pointed look, hoping he gets the little pun.

I expect a snappy comeback or some hostile suspicion. What I don't expect is for him to be across the room in a blur of motion.

His lips crash against mine for the first time, and it's like a storm pulses in my body. All the pain is gone at last, and warmth travels up through me, as though he finally just sealed the last piece of something into place and made me truly whole.

I moan into his mouth as he grips me closer, his hands moving all over me like he doesn't know what he wants to touch the most.

I'm beyond drugged and unable to pull back, as I clutch him closer, kissing him so hard that my lips start to hurt. I knew it'd be violent with him. Just as it is with all of them.

It makes the times they're soft so much more special.

When he breaks the kiss, he's panting, his entire body shaking against me as his breaths rattle in his chest.

"Now *that* is how you welcome a girl back from the dead," I say on a shuddering breath. "Congratulations. You're finally my favorite again."

They all look torn between laughing and murdering someone.

Jude forces himself to release me and take a few steps back, his body visibly straining with the effort it takes. I'm a little lightheaded, if I'm being honest.

It really does feel like the final piece has clicked into place. I feel so much stronger now.

I go phantom with ease and zap around the house several times before landing back in front of them with a grin on my lips.

"Much better. Apparently the four of you still make me stronger."

They don't look quite as amused as I do.

"Great," I groan. "What now? What have I missed in the month I've been dead that has put all of you in such a terrible mood?" I ask on an exasperated sigh.

Given the condition of the house, I've missed a lot.

"Not much," Ezekiel says, clearing his throat. "No one has tried to kill us since Jude killed Lake. Only the Devil's highest appointed generals should have been able to kill an escort. It seemed to send a message."

I look around the house, seeing all of it torn to pieces. Hell, even the chandeliers look like they're warped.

"Then why does it look like a war raged on in here?" I ask, bringing my gaze back down.

"You were fucking dead," Gage says again, coming closer as though he has to touch me after saying those words. "We broke laws, hijacked royal escorts, and broke into hell numerous times to find out what happened to you. Not recycled. Not in hell's throat. Simply fucking dead."

His hand moves to my cheek, cupping it.

Kai moves forward, reaching his hand out for me. I take it and let him pull me away from Gage and into his arms.

"But what happened to the house?" I ask him, since Gage

didn't answer.

"You fucking died," Kai says, and this time…I get it.

With a more educated eye, I look around again, seeing the distress and anger that went into destroying this room. Beyond us is the kitchen in the same disarray, but I notice the dents in the walls and pans, the fury that went into all that destruction.

This wasn't a struggle to survive. This was a grieving tantrum.

They grieved me?

"Oh," I say on a quiet breath. "Didn't realize you four liked me quite that much," I add even quieter, rather shocked, really.

Kai's finger slips under my chin as he glares down at me. Leave it to Kai to act like it's my fault they buried me so far away.

"I might have healed faster if you'd left me in my damn room instead of tossing me out like yesterday's virgin girlfriend," I state primly.

He grips my shoulders as his eyes harden. I don't tell him it actually kind of hurts. My entire body is actually a little achy, if I'm being honest.

One type of soul-burning pain has been replaced with an achy, uncomfortable, and certainly untimely sort of pain.

"You. Were. Fucking. Dead," he says, punctuating each word very unnecessarily loud.

I'm not sure why he's insisting on saying that. I said I get it.

"That doesn't explain why you buried me instead of leaving me in my room," I point out, ignoring the growing ache spreading out from my stomach. "It's not like any of you ever used my room before I took it, so it's not putting you out."

Kai gives me the neck-wringing look before his lips are on mine again, almost punishing me for trying to make sense of their rambles.

As much as I want to keep kissing him, I can't. My head drops to stare at the subtly expanding bruise on my waist, and I slightly curse. I might finally get my virginity taken if I wasn't in too much physical duress to do it.

"Shit," Kai says, almost as though he's just noticing the fact the stab wound isn't there, but it's still leaving a mark.

In the next breath, he's lifting me and cradling me to him, and I give him an incredulous look. "I'm not quite that helpless. I can still stand. Just maybe don't grip me so hard," I tell him, expecting a grimace and an apology. Not an exasperated eye roll. Which is what I get.

He sits down, still holding me like I'm glass, and cradles me to him like I'm precious. To be honest, it's freaking me out.

"Who are you and where is Kai?" I ask him, moving my hand up his chest a little hesitantly.

The really angry glare he gives me can't be duplicated by anyone other than Jude. So I realize it's actually him. And he's being nice. It's still freaking me out.

"I can't be satisfied," I say on a sigh, annoyed with my own self.

Nobody even bothers to ask what that means. It's as though they know it's a private conversation with myself. It's like they *get* me. Finally.

Sort of.

They're still completely disregarding my list of expectancies.

Ezekiel crouches in front of me, his finger tracing over the bruise, and I wince while painfully swallowing back the weak little cry I almost give up from such a little touch that shouldn't hurt so badly.

"Lucifer's poison did this to you," Ezekiel says while grinding his jaw. "Lake was armed with it either by him, or by her father. She was part of a group preparing to overthrow hell, though the facts on that are still murky," he adds.

"But she was also a royal escort—"

"No, royal escorts wear bags over their heads. I've seen what they look like without them," I point out, then smile bitterly. "She definitely didn't have to wear a bag."

"In hell, she's hideous. Topside...you saw. The balance was grotesque in one place, exquisite in another," Gage goes on, cracking his neck.

"Wait, you mean those scarred, charred, and half human guards...she looked like one of them? They made them bag their heads because the Devil thought they were too *stomach-curdling* for him to have to see so often."

Frowning, I try to remember exactly how I know that last part. Did Lucifer say something about it?

"The point is," Gage goes on, drawing me out of my reverie, "she worked for both. She might have done it for the rebellion because Lucifer needs us. She might have done it for Lucifer to spare herself from the culling going on. So we don't know which one wants us dead, and which one wants us on their side. But in the past month since Jude killed her, everyone has gone silent. Not even Harold has called me until today. We've not even been charged with bringing in souls."

"But why would—" My words cut off when I feel something coming, and I go phantom in the next instant.

I also put on the first outfit that comes to mind, like I'm shielding my naked form before someone sees me and pisses off the guys. They like me, so that means they'll be jealous, right?

Seems important they be jealous, though I'm not sure why.

I shake my head, blaming the fact I'm still a little poisoned for my even more random-than-usual thought process. I feel so clean now at least.

"She's back, isn't she?" a familiar voice asks from behind me somewhere.

Kai leaps up, and I end up on the chair alone as he passes through me and turns around, taking a defensive stance.

I poke my head through the chair, seeing Lamar standing there and looking overly excited. Jude swirls a sword in his hand, coming to stand a little in front of my head like he's protecting me.

"I thought so," Lamar says as he takes them in. "We heard of a botched attack on one of you in New Orleans last month. Then I lost the feel of her," he goes on, stepping closer. "Then I felt her again, and knew this time without a doubt it was her. She feels weakened, though."

Jude takes a step toward him, and Lamar frowns at him like he's offended for some reason.

"I'm not sure what's going on right now," he says, sounding genuinely frustrated. "I understand she somehow resurrected you as mortals and gifted you a chance to live with a balance that defies all laws. She never was much of one for the rules, and she broke them quite frequently. But why keep up the charade now that you've clearly been outed?"

"Is he talking about me? I think he's confused," I tell the guys, moving closer to Kai, even though the wound is starting to drain me now that the adrenaline is wearing off.

"She'll heal faster in hell," Lamar goes on. "You know it. They'll never know I gave you passage, and you can continue to keep your secret. I won't tell them, if she really doesn't want them to know. But why keep it a secret from me?" Lamar asks, actually sounding a little hurt. "Especially when she's spent over a month healing from whatever it is she could have healed immediately from with my help."

"Anyone have a clue why he sounds betrayed?" I stage-whisper.

"No," Kai says from beside me, confusion written all over his face.

Lamar looks between the four of them, who are all staring at him like he's just tipped over the edge of the weirdo cliff.

Lamar has a moment of confusion cross his features when he sees it written all over theirs. I'm not sure if he's mimicking subconsciously, or if he's genuinely confused by their confusion.

It's all really *confusing*, if you want my opinion.

Then his eyes widen as though he's just realized something as he takes a shaky step back.

"You truly have no fucking clue who I am, do you?"

"Yes…" Gage's drawl is exaggerated, as though he's talking to a crazy person. "Your Manella's boyfriend."

"Only because the royals don't believe in marriage of any kind," he feels the need to defend. "But at least you said boyfriend instead of lover," he goes on.

Noted.

"That's all you know me as? You're not just playing some game?" Lamar asks as though this is a very crucial question.

The quad exchanges a look of confusion, and Lamar takes a step back. "Son of a bitch. How the hell did she do that?"

"He's not making a damn bit of sense," Ezekiel points out.

"Thank you," I groan. "I was worried that I'm just stupid."

"Is that how you have a balance now?" Lamar says as though he just thought of something that makes him a genius.

"I'm about to go whole and shake him down for answers that make sense if someone else doesn't do it for me," I say on a sigh.

Ezekiel is grabbing Lamar in the next instant, but Lamar simply winks, and we're suddenly in a windowless room full of elegant décor.

"And we're in hell," I say on a sigh. "Again."

But the pain vanishes, and I make the phantom shirt disappear to reveal the bruise is finally gone.

"She's better, isn't she?" Lamar asks, and I quickly make my shirt reappear and dart a gaze up at him.

He's not looking at me. *Whew.* Thought he could see me.

His eyes are on the four guys who are all slowly looking away as though they were studying the healed injury as well.

"Feeling much, *much* better," I tell them. "Don't kill him yet," I add to Ezekiel, whose lips twitch as he takes a step back and releases Lamar.

"She just told you not to kill me yet, didn't she?" Lamar asks with an excited grin.

"You heard her?" Jude growls, as though Lamar has committed a grave offense.

In the next instant, Kai is behind him, a sword pressed to the base of his neck.

"Either you're being very cruel right now, Paca, or they're not the only ones who lost their memories. Which means everything I just think I figured out will be null and void, and you might very damn well let them kill me. Which means I'm an idiot for bringing you all here without alerting anyone."

He clears his throat.

"A big, dumb idiot," he says nervously as he looks around, waiting for someone to crack a grin and tell him we're all kidding.

No grins are cracked.

"I can't hear her. I just know that's something she'd say if she was toying with me. But I'm starting to think she genuinely has no clue who I am. But why would she save me in that damn prison if she didn't know me? She knows my role with spirits and—"

"She doesn't know your role with spirits, but I'm really intrigued, because I'd also like to know," Jude tells him, smiling wickedly as Kai steps a little closer with that sword, bearing in a bit, just barely not breaking the skin.

"You should sharpen your blades some time," I tell him. "Apparently you've all gotten volatile and lazy this past month when I wasn't around to make you awesome."

Ezekiel blows out a harsh breath, as though he's silently imploring me to shut the hell up.

"I think it's time I explain a little better," Lamar says a little less confidently, keeping his hands raised to show he's no threat. But I've seen a lot of power roll out of him.

He could easily knock them away long enough to disappear. Or possibly kill one.

That has me on high alert as I cross my arms over my chest and pay attention to his every movement. Lake taught me to never be caught off guard again.

No wonder the guys are so paranoid. Now I finally get it. You just can't trust people associated with hell. Who knew?

I never trusted her, of course, but they spent centuries trusting her—even caring for her.

I'm so glad she's dead.

"You see, we worked really hard to keep you out of the trials, because—"

"It was you?" Kai growls, at the same time I say, "That's a terribly stupid way for him to start this explanation."

Jude snorts, then looks really angry when he has to fight a grin while he's trying to be really pissed off. It results in him glaring at me as he finally straightens his face.

"For a reason!" Lamar shouts.

Kai barely eases back.

"For a reason," Lamar says again, swallowing thickly.

Then he disappears, and we whirl around as he lands on his desk, sitting comfortably.

"I'm afraid I'll need some distance from you four until Paca remembers me."

"Paca is so not the badass name I was looking for," I tell them. "I'm a Xena, or Phoenix...something like that."

Kai groans as he glares over at me.

"She's consistently saying inappropriate things at the worst possible times, which debunks the very serious nature of the situations around. Am I right?" Lamar asks them. "Is she the same?"

"I think he can hear her," Ezekiel decides.

"No!" Lamar shouts when they start to advance on him. He holds his hands up defensively, then adds, "I can kill you, since you're lacking a lot of information about your power, it seems, but you can't kill me. However, I can swear I won't touch you at all. She'd kill me if I did."

"That last part actually made sense to me, so that's improvement," I tell them.

"She loves hard," he goes on. "Very hard," he adds, smiling like he's proud of that. "She's the most jealous person you'll ever find."

That makes a few of them smirk.

"I'm not *that* bad," I remind them.

"She'll go to the ends of the earth to save you four. And she'll always be serious when it counts. Because while she distracts you from the intensity of the situation, she's cataloguing each new piece of information, filing it away, recording it for later, then she puts it all together with the most reasonable way to approach a situation. Though to us, we often find it maddening or just crazy. But we don't have the same ability to reason as she does."

"He was doing good until the end," I say, convinced he's kissing my ass because he thinks I'm running this show. It's rather empowering, if I do say so myself.

"Let him live. I'm healed, so take me home and give me many orgasms," I state like I'm the queen and they must do my bidding.

Kai snorts, reminding me that's not really the way this relationship works.

Lamar groans, probably because he has no idea what their seemingly random facial tics and amused or disgruntled sounds are in response to.

"The point is, I know her. She's actually my best friend," Lamar adds.

I perk right up at that confession. I've never been someone's best friend before. The novelty of it is quite intriguing in itself.

The others aren't quite as impressed as I am.

"Fine, let's start with the basics. You four don't even know who you are, do you?" Lamar asks.

"The Four Horsemen," I state automatically, acting as though I'll win a prize if I say it first, even though I can't be heard by him.

"No," Ezekiel says, rolling his eyes at me.

Kai presses himself against my back, giving me those tingles I can feel again now that *all* the pain is gone.

"I figured it'd be obvious by now, but you're the Four Horsemen," Lamar tells them.

I fist pump the air, and my outfit turns into the sexy Devil Halloween costume just to bring some rather insensitive humor to the moment, as I start pointing at them one by one.

"See? I knew it! And I was right. It's actually a little anticlimactic because of how glaringly obvious it's been all this time," I say, feeling a little deflated by the end.

The quick burst of adrenaline burns out from the lack of suspense that led into it.

"But they died during a collision of the two kingdoms or something," Gage states as though he's reminding him of that.

"Of course they died," Lamar agrees. "But I'm not cleared for the true details as to how you were killed."

"They couldn't be recycled because they were too imbalanced or something," Gage goes on, dealing with the partial bits of information they've collected about hell over the years.

"Recycling doesn't work this way. We would have been spit out into hell's throat again for a new form. Not reborn topside," Ezekiel is quick to add.

"They were imbalanced, and it made sense to believe that death was permanent. Recycling certainly does *not* end up with a new birth. Yet here you are," Lamar goes on, gesturing at them. "New bodies. New faces. No doubt hand-selected by her. I'm almost positive that's why you're built with bodies and faces that perfect."

I grin, liking Lamar a little more now, as I wink at the guys.

"He's saying you're pretty because I'm shallow." I rock backwards on my heels, clasping my hands in front of me. "You're welcome," I add.

I even sit down in a chair like a dainty little girl in my devilish attire.

"You're saying we died, but she brought us back as mortals, handpicked how we'd come back, *and* somehow managed to offer us immortality without us having to turn our souls over to hell and risk a harsher internal balance," Kai states like Lamar has just crossed a line of nonsense.

I understand none of this, but I keep listening in, weaving together what I can, and quietly threading my own conclusion one piece at a time.

"She kept history from repeating itself. Made you mentally stronger this way. But I don't know how she did it. It's as though your souls were stolen, swiped clean, restrung with the first breath of life, and now you're all back together again. I'm not even sure how you found each other if you didn't know all this," Lamar goes on.

"The bond drew us together," Jude tells him, frowning. "Like all quads."

"Certainly not like all quads. You're the first. The rest are all poor-man's copies—a cosmic echo of sorts. There's never been a bond as strong as yours. Trust me. They've been hoping to find your replacements for centuries. Manella hid you, because we both saw the enigmas you were—no deaths, yet pure immortals? Impossible. And only Paca aimed for the impossible."

He clears his throat, his eyes seeming a little misty. "However, we didn't wholly believe you were them, if I'm being honest. It's painful to get one's hopes up. But we liked the hope it offered, so we hid you, pretending as though we were playing Paca's or your game. Lucifer isn't aware of that, of course. But we knew if you wanted in, you'd eventually let us know…but we thought you had your memories."

No one seems to know what to believe. This time, standing on their side of things as someone you aren't sure if you can trust, even though they're begging you to follow them out onto a treacherous ledge as they twist everything you thought you knew into something impossibly possible…I suddenly get it.

I just finally proved myself to them. It took dying to get all four, but at least I didn't stay dead. Again. I doubt Lamar would be willing to go to the same extremes I have.

"Lucifer knows it's you now, though. Surely you realize that," Lamar tells them. "He's waiting on you to come explain yourselves. He all but called you out before the trials. He designed that course to be identical to the course Paca gave Nicholai on the last birthday she got to celebrate with him," he goes on.

I look around at the four of them. "Which one of you is Nicholai?"

"Nicholai?" Jude asks him, sounding as annoyed with him as he sometimes gets with me.

"I…uh…Famine," Lamar says uneasily.

"Gage," I whisper softly, remembering the way his eyes lit up when I accused him of actually enjoying the danger and unpredictability that course played with life and death.

Everyone in the room stills.

"I've said something that has finally jarred a memory?" Lamar asks hopefully.

"Not one from the life you're saying we had," Kai tells him vaguely.

"Look, there's no way you could have survived that course without remembering those riddles and having a great deal of prior knowledge of hell. Paca was there telling you the riddles and offering hints to the answers when you struggled the first time," he tells them.

My stomach coils with dread.

I started giving hints by the end…

Ezekiel's eyes meet mine as though the same thing pops into his mind.

"And the very last riddle alone is enough to squash any remaining doubts," Lamar continues, not realizing he's finally gotten us all to take him a little seriously.

I'm not even making jokes right now.

"How do you defeat a never-ending army of hell's most vicious predators, cast to the belly straight from the throat, when there's not enough power to kill them all?" Ezekiel says, echoing the question he once asked me.

He actually asked two of the riddles while we were down there like he'd figured the right questions out on his own. His nightmares also happen to be the worst.

"No," Lamar says, shaking his head. "How would *Paca* face a never-ending army of hell's most vicious predators, to the belly straight from the throat, when there's not enough power to kill them all?" he corrects. "She's rather vain that way."

To this, a few snorts sneak out, and I flip them off as they regain their composure quickly.

Lamar grins knowingly. "But the answer is true regardless. She'd set her mind on a solution and faced it as she did absolutely everything in life. Fearlessly."

A little chill slithers up my spine, and I lose my ability to be inappropriately humorous, and allow for a moment of dread to settle in.

As he warned, I've been cataloguing every bit of information, adding it to all of this I've just learned. I don't like the riddle before me, because I hate the answer I've concluded.

It simply sounds crazy, and I can't even bring myself to actually *think* it.

"Tell him I'm terrified of mountainsides, firefalls, and now most definitely swords," I say on a rasp whisper, causing Jude to noticeably flinch with that newest addition. "Which means he's wrong. Tell him that. Now. Or I'll turn whole and tell him myself."

Ezekiel gives me a puzzled look, but it's because he can't hear the thoughts hovering in my mind. The ones I'm forcing to stay back.

"She's terrified of hanging from mountainsides and firefalls," Gage says, moving closer to my side.

Lamar gives him a watery grin.

"She actually has some of the most random, irrational fears. It's the things that actually require bravery that make her serious and fearless. And it's good she's not always that way. The intensity of those moments…the pure, determined, fearless, selfless way she makes the impossible happen…those are the times she made all of you fall in love with her over and over and over again. If she was that way all the time, Hera would lose her title as the world's best seductress, because Paca would be the only one considered irresistible."

"Sounds like I need to be more serious on occasion then," I say too quickly, trying too hard to lighten this moment, and finding it to fall flat because I can't even pretend that I'm not terrified of where he's going with this.

"How could she do all this?" Gage asks obliviously. "What do you mean over and over?"

"In all your mortal lives," he says, smiling grimly. "I'm just realizing she would have taken that gift from you. It was a game to see if you could fall in love in every life, and you always did. All of you fell in love with her, and she fell in love with all of you. It should have been impossible."

I swallow thickly.

"You'd just finished a mortal life—the five of you always died together." He clears his throat, smiling tightly. "I'll tell her more when she shows herself to me."

"To go back and live mortal lives, you have to be royalty or blessed by royalty," Jude argues.

Kai glances down at me, almost as though he's searching my eyes for something.

"To create an obstacle course in hell's belly just for her current favorite's birthday would also imply royalty," Lamar states, causing me to freeze.

"What did you just say?" Gage asks, looking at Lamar. "Her current favorite?"

"Her favorite constantly changed. It was a game you five played. It kept things from going stale. But you were always her favorite on your respective birthdays. After all, she was reasonable, as I said."

Kai's lips tug in a grin.

"This is not a grinning time. You have terrible timing for humor," I tell him, looking back at Lamar.

"She could send you back for mortal lives because she gave you each a piece of her balance and broke every law when she did it. But as I said, she never cared much for rules. In doing so, she made all of you stronger. And she saved your lives back then. Dragged you all from imbalance's insanity and did what had never been done before in accomplishing it. She saved your lives the first time she met you, and you all saved each other over and over. But this last time, she truly died. Or so we all thought. I'm wondering if it was just the bond that managed to pull her together and allow her to defy the impossible once again."

They all just stare at him until they look right at me like they finally understand what's going on.

"He's trying to say I'm the Devil's daughter, isn't he?" I ask them, shaking my head. "But there are only six," I remind them. "Only two of them are girls."

"Yeah, but the twins could count as one," Kai says, as though he's considering it.

"I know they can count as one, but they don't because five would be an imbalance so they have to count as two," I argue, then frown at knowing that since I don't know how I know it, and since it sort of confuses me. Shaking my head, I go on. "Four boys and three girls would still be an imbalance, because there would be seven heirs instead of six, and the gender would then have to be the balance."

"She's right. That would be four boys and three girls even if the twins did count as one," Ezekiel agrees.

Good job.

Though now I'm simply more confused.

"He's my favorite now just because he's got my back," I whisper almost silently. "Like *baby got back* kind of back."

He just shakes his head, cursing as he leans up.

"Did I use it wrong?"

My question goes unanswered as Jude once again huffs. "No one has ever considered the sexes to be a part of the balance before. It's been four boys and *two* girls for a very long time. Pretty sure they're *men* and *women* by now," Jude says in his overly sarcastic tone.

"The sexes and numbers are even. Three females and three males," Lamar says conversationally, as though he's simply reminding us of something. "When all heirs are in hell, the twins count as one person—one male—with their yin and yang balance. They only count as two when influencing, since they have two separate dark influences. All the heirs have their own dark influence—hence the seven deadly sins."

"What?" Jude asks on a breath.

Lamar's eyes widen, and he tightens his lips. "Only the royal family and closest lovers are to know some of that. There's a vow of death. You make a deal with the Devil to be allowed so close to the royals and inner knowledge of their balances."

It's like he's reminding us of an oath we took that still binds today, even though we don't remember taking it.

"He's all gibberish and nonsense," I argue, shaking my head emphatically. "I want to go."

"We can't go until we find out if he's lying or not," Ezekiel states quietly.

"You're having to convince her she's Lucifer's youngest daughter, aren't you?" Lamar asks, grinning like he's amused. "I can't help but wonder what she was thinking when she did all of this. Clearly she planned for a true death to have made this happen. The bond alone couldn't have accomplished quite this much. You're the only ones who can see or hear her."

"Can't he see I'm trying to talk myself off a ledge here?" I ask them incredulously. "I can't be Lucifer's daughter. That would make me way older than the nineties, first off, and the nineties is the main source of my ingrained information. Not hell politics. You guys are centuries old, which means we would have had to die long before the nineties. He's wrong."

"Why would she be rambling about the nineties if what you're saying is true?" Kai finally asks him.

Lamar's eyes water as though Kai's just asked him something very personal that has made him emotional.

"We can see a lot of the future. The human future, that is. We spent centuries perfecting our nineties slang," the watery-eyed man says very quietly.

"Not quite perfected even after all that," Jude says as he looks back at me, smirking. Then gives his serious face back to Lamar.

"She and I made a pact that we'd go mortal in the nineties. She wanted to be a dancing pop singer, and knew you four would end up her backup dancers or a boy band."

I'm so stunned that I can even recycle my *One Erection* joke.

Lamar continues speaking when no one says anything, and the guys just stare at him like he's lost his damn mind for suggesting such a horrible thing. They'd be an adorable boy band.

"She wanted to read about the scandal later when she had all her memories and her body back, and like always, you'd all sit around basking in how you fell in love again, even though you had no idea who you were in that time. I was going to become a politician, because we both knew Manella would go if I went, and we'd fall in love there. He'd never gone mortal before, but promised me he would in the nineties. It would have been a helluva scandal for us to enjoy upon our return."

"Did he go?" I ask, feeling my heart hurt a little for no really good reason.

"Why would she—"

"Did he go?" I ask louder, talking over Jude, who looks at me like I'm going crazy.

"Did you go?" Kai asks him on a sigh.

Lamar's jaw trembles and he clears his throat while blinking and looking away. "It didn't seem right to go without her."

Deflated, I sit back.

"I believe him," I say quietly. "I'm the Devil's daughter with a horribly non-badass name like Paca. Who names hell spawn something that *bubbly*? I'm not bubbly at all."

"What's she saying that has all of you looking at me like you want to do harm?" Lamar asks, frowning.

"We're trying to decide if you're lying or not. She believes you. It's not going to be good if you're fucking with us," Ezekiel drawls, looking at his nails as though he's bored.

"Touching her seems to amplify our powers," Jude goes on, his hand slipping through mine. "Supposedly I'm *Death*."

Lamar slides off the desk slowly, so as not to make any sudden movements.

"Paca, I know you're probably overwhelmed if you prevented yourself from remembering all this for whatever reason. But trust me when I say we'll figure all this out together. You sought me out in hell's throat. I spent five years convincing myself it was not you I kept feeling, because it was impossible. Then I felt you. Then they said *she,* and I finally knew we'd been right. They were yours and you were back."

Just feeling their tingles start to surround me helps. Kai and Gage are also touching me. It's Ezekiel I'm worried about. He's not touching me, and he looks much too calm for the embodiment of war who got used to peaceful sleep, only to have it ripped away from him for over a month.

He's the one who might actually kill Lamar before I can decide how I feel about him.

"Lucifer knows. He knew even before I did. I told you that. The trials were just him throwing it in your face that he knew so you'd stop pretending you all weren't back. He figured it out months ago as his madness continued to lift the closer to hell she got. Manella told me this just after the night Lucifer exonerated me—the night his lucidity completely returned. You know the Devil's games...I would have told you sooner, but I thought I was playing *your* game, even as it hurt my feelings to be left out."

Looking betrayed makes a little sense, if we really were besties.

"Is that why he tried killing us?" Jude asks, a lethal, hard edge to his tone as he takes a step away. "Because of him, she was killed a month ago."

Never mind about Ezekiel. Jude's the one to worry about now. He's the one who watched me die, and then kissed me for the first time when I came back because I wasn't dead.

Very hard man to impress, that one.

"And all along he could have healed her? Did he know she wouldn't really die?" Gage asks with an eerily calm tone.

Shit. Now he's the one who might kill him.

"Kai, please just stay behind me. I need some tingles, and Lamar has enough of—"

Before I can finish the sentence, Kai is holding a sword under Lamar's chin, appearing there in less than an instant. Now *he* really might kill Lamar too. Damn it.

"Move and I'll do worse than cut you. Answer the questions," he growls. "Did he kill her just to punish us for not properly playing a game we had no idea we were even playing? A royal fucking escort killed her."

Lamar glances at him, not moving anything other than his eyes.

"No. There are always rebels in hell. It's hell, after all. Rebellions spring up like weeds. We're stifled by the volume in this particular rebellion, since Lucifer has been decommissioned for so long with your dead girlfriend's father in his ear. At least we assume it's him, due to her involvement in the botched assassination attempt on your lives. You were just caught in the crosshairs. Apparently we're not the only ones who've noticed Paca back. And the Devil's youngest daughter back from a true death and back to reign with her four unstoppable horsemen? I thought the five of you were playing a very dangerous game."

"Rebels. Really? Rebels are trying to kill us and not Lucifer? I don't know what to believe," I grumble. "His timing is just terribly suspicious."

They all give me a look, as though they're exasperated with me for saying that, considering I heard that from them quite a lot when I first popped up, and I held it against them.

"I do believe I'm the Devil's daughter, though. Oh, and in case this was the only thing still holding you back, it's become abundantly clear I'm most definitely, without a doubt, unquestionably *not* a virgin."

Kai turns and tosses the sword down like he's frustrated, while Jude just huffs.

"On a related note, my vagina *is* most decidedly evil, so you win that argument after all," I add.

"For fuck's sake, Paca!" Kai gripes, saying the new name with ease like it's perfectly natural. "Just take this seriously for a damn second. Do you have any idea what he's saying?!"

I just stare at him, feeling my heart beat a little in my intangible chest. Something about him saying this apparent un-badass name of mine feels like a memory, even though there's no real memory accompanying it.

He's breathing heavily, his eyes hooded a little as he stares at me like he's thinking the same thing. His eyes flick to my lips, and Lamar sighs loudly.

"The more things change, the more they stay the same. The air in here just got considerably warmer. You four were always pissed or serious when you used her nickname. And she always loved it when you did. She loved angry sex," Lamar says, smirking.

"I'm really curious about seeing if that's a real thing," I tell Kai, gesturing toward the door like it's an invitation.

He groans before turning his back on me and cursing.

"Wait, Paca is a nickname?" I ask, snapping out of my trance as I look back over.

Jude repeats the question aloud to Lamar, and Lamar nods, eyebrows furrowing.

"Yes. And not *your* nickname for her. Everyone called her Paca. But the rest of the time you all called her various things. Mostly, however, the four of you seemed to call her one phrase over and over in each life. You used it as a caution in every language you ever learned as mortals. Then you used it when you returned home to hell as a term of endearment."

"What was it?" I ask immediately, curious what they called me back when they apparently loved me.

Me. The daughter of the Devil.

Ezekiel repeats my question so Lamar can hear it.

"The last language was Romanian, I think, because you'd just come back from mortal lives there before…" Lamar lets his words trail off.

"Before we were killed," Kai supplies.

Lamar nods, the life drifting from his eyes a little as he gets distant. With a more informed eye, I almost see a reluctance in his gaze to revisit this memory. As though it's painful for him. *My death* was painful for him.

"Romanian?" Jude asks, stepping closer as he visibly tenses.

"Yes," Lamar says with a shrug. "*Comoara trădătoare,*" he says, causing the air to get sucked from the room. "I think that's roughly the Romanian translation for *treacherous treasure*. You always called her that in numerous languages."

Lamar just stares at us as we all remain still and silent. Well, he's not staring at *me*.

"You remember?" Lamar asks, once again sounding hopeful when he reads their expressions wrong.

"No," Ezekiel says shakily.

"Suddenly that headstone sounds much more endearing than it did a few hours ago," I tell them quietly. "I almost forgive you for its simplicity now. *Almost*."

"If you don't remember, then why is everyone reacting to that odd endearment?" Lamar asks.

"Because we just realized we're living a rerun from the longest running show in history, and we have no idea what happened in the rest of the countless seasons before," I say on an exhale.

Lamar doesn't hear this, obviously.

"You said Paca was her nickname. What's her real name?" Jude asks for me, cycling back to that question, since he knows I'll want to know once I get over the bomb Lamar incidentally set loose.

"Oh, I thought that was obvious by now," Lamar says, frowning in my direction. "Especially after telling you that you're the Four Horsemen. Everyone knows you're the Four Horsemen of *The* Apocalypse."

"Say what now?" I ask dryly.

"Are you saying she's the apocalypse?" Gage asks incredulously.

"I'm saying she's *The Apocalypse.* Her name is Apocalypse. She puts *the* in front of it when she wants to remind everyone she's the only one who can truly level the world. As I said, *she's rather vain that way,*" he says jovially as he reuses the one joke that got him a few snickers last time.

No one giggles this time.

It's not funny anymore.

"My name is Apocalypse?" I ask on a hushed whisper. "As in the end of times for the entire world?"

My four guys look at me, regarding me like they're waiting to see how to react.

"Now *that,* I did not see coming at all," I utter on a shaky breath.

I don't realize, until Lamar's eyes widen, water, and clash with mine, that I've accidentally turned whole. And apparently I must look exactly the same, since the recognition in his expression is unmistakable.

I guess that explains the horror on most of the people's faces who could see me in between life and death.

After all, I'm as bad as it fucking gets. I'm sure I have a reputation.

"I take it back," I say as I swallow hard, my eyes tearing away from Lamar to look at each of my guys individually. "I don't want a badass name."

CHAPTER XIV

"Paca," Lamar says on a choked sound, causing me to turn back to him as a lone tear rolls down his cheek.

He opens his mouth to say more, but only a strained sound comes out. I guess believing and seeing are two different things in this case, because he almost looks like he can't believe what he's seeing, when he believed it before this moment with no problem.

"How do you have your own body?" he asks on a shaky breath, his eyes trailing down and…then his head jerking back as confusion creases his features. "And what the hell are you wearing?" he asks, less reverent and more incredulous.

I glance down, remembering I am indeed still wearing the sexy Devil costume.

"An outfit that wasn't quite so ironic when initially chosen," I say absently.

His grin spreads so wide, and tears wobble in his eyes as he laughs so genuinely that it warms me.

"You said Lucifer knew. Who else knows?" Jude asks him, moving closer.

Lamar blinks, returning his attention to him. "Too many people have likely figured it out. Especially since the trials. The second trial always ends up killing the echo quads, even though they put the rumor out there that some survive."

"Echo quads?" Ezekiel asks him. "You keep mentioning that."

Lamar grabs some books from behind him, and he starts putting them on the desk as he talks.

"Echo quads. There are so many echoes. The Gemini Twins were the first *pair*. Their echoed pairs are stronger than echoed quads. Echoes don't have the same fierce bond as the originals—*you*. There was one obstacle to always drive out the posers in case the four of you ever returned home. You'd never leave a man behind."

My mind flicks back to Kai's injured leg, and the terrible options we had at hand. They would have died beside him before leaving him behind.

He hands them a book, and Gage warily takes it.

"That one is everything on your origins," Lamar tells him.

"It's blank," Gage says as he opens it.

"It's the only one. We never wanted anyone else trying to recreate the four of you. If you want to read it, spill your blood and start reading. The words will appear in whatever language you choose," Lamar tells him distractedly as he grabs what looks like a journal.

"These are all my notes on you and several other sets of quads I suspected to be…well, you," Lamar tells Ezekiel, handing it to him.

Ezekiel takes it and tucks it into the back of his jeans, not looking directly at me.

"These will tell you all her purities and impurities so you can understand her better," Lamar tells them as he hands Jude a thinner book.

"Say what now?" I ask, holding my hand up.

Lamar grins over at me a little sadly.

"You have no memories at all?" he asks quietly.

"I have certain bits of knowledge, but no memories."

He nods slowly, as though that's finally sinking in. "Then I should warn you not to trust anyone on the surface. Right now, the ones who remember you want you dead. Again. And they'll kill your boys to get to you. You're all weaker topside."

My stomach tilts.

"If they die, do they heal like I did?" I ask.

"I'm not really sure what will happen to them, to be honest. Their bodies were destroyed, and since you'd given them each a piece of your balance as protection, you made them as immortal and untouchable as you were—back then. Now? You spent a month healing topside for an injury that could have been instantly healed here. I'm not sure if they still hold that piece of you," Lamar tells me honestly. "Because I have no idea how you did any of this."

His eyes stay on mine, seeming to want to say more, but holding back for whatever reason. I'm not sure if it's because he doesn't want to say it in front of them, or because he's worried about overwhelming me, or if he's hiding something.

All three are valid and reasonable options.

"How did I give them a piece of my balance to keep them safe?" I ask him.

His lips curve in a grin. "It figures that'd be the first question you ask. You see, when you gave them that piece of you, you said you started to *feel* more. Soon, the five of you were inseparable. Those pieces pulled your souls into one bond, and it made you all invincible. Or so we thought. But it certainly made you all…better."

"The piece is still in all of us," Gage says quietly. "That's why it was so hard to fight."

"Gee, thanks for making it sound like I forced you into this, when I clearly just saved your lives," I state dryly.

He cracks a grin at me, cupping my chin and letting his thumb roll over my cheek. He leans down, his lips ghosting my cheek as he reaches my ear and whispers too quietly for anyone else to hear.

"I'm not complaining. I'm just glad to finally have answers.

You really are ours," he says, his fingers moving across my neck so sweetly yet erotically at the same time.

"Actually, *you're* really all *mine,*" I counter softly, my eyes fluttering shut when his lips brush softly against my skin.

"Just curious, for the sake of old times, who's her current favorite?" Lamar asks.

"I am," Jude says, at the same time I dreamily say, "Gage."

Gage grins, Jude arches an eyebrow, and I shrug unapologetically.

Lamar laughs like he's delighted and watching his favorite show that just came back for a reunion.

I really need to quit comparing our hell squad drama to TV shows.

"Hera knows, which is why she tossed in the aviary reptiles—or, bird-snakes, as you would probably call them—into the third trials. You always hated their tails for some reason," Lamar says, causing everyone to smirk as they glance at me.

"We're still supposed to be tensing when he says something that resonates. Not smirking," I tell the four of them.

Lamar's grin only grows as he continues to carefully select books, moving from one to another to decide which ones we need.

"Cain figured it out after the twins swore on their harem they weren't the ones to drop his pants and humiliate him in front of the Trials, no less. They pointed a finger at you," he goes on. "They're the reason the other quads got through the second trials, because they were fucking with Lucifer's game. They're smarter because they share a brain."

For some reason, I almost smile, thinking about Cain's rage as he chased those two. I was so proud of something so petty.

"Sibling rivalry always did make you smile," Lamar tells me as he hands Kai a book. "Manella, of course knows."

My face falls. "Yeah, because you're a gossiping little girl who ran off to tell him they said *she*."

It's an accusation with a little too much heat of betrayal that I shouldn't feel. Lamar's grin only grows.

"I'm sorry. Manella didn't ever really believe me when I said I felt you. He hoped they were yours, but it was a faint hope. Only you could have found a way to save them." His smile slips. "For whatever reason, he said there was no way you could ever come back."

Tension spreads through the air, and my gaze subtly drifts over to see my guys all going a little rigid. Manella is back on the suspect list now.

Lamar doesn't notice as he continues to gather books, moving on from the harder topic and onto trying to jog a memory.

"I'm fairly sure Lilith doesn't know, because she'd have never touched Kai at the party if she had. She didn't fear her own sister very often, but one of the guys would have really made her suffer back then," Lamar goes on.

Kai smirks as his hand slides down my back, and he takes a seat on the edge of the chair I'm in, almost as though he's soothing me from the instant jealousy in my gut.

"She's trying to restock her own harem, since the twins just recycled them all a little before the trials. She always keeps four in her harem, same as you."

I freeze. "What?"

The guys clear their throats and try to mask their smiles.

Lamar turns and looks at me. "You always had four in your harem. Before them, you had a series of really underwhelming males who could be seduced and lured away by Lilith, easily killed by Cain or the twins, and constantly trying to get into Hera's harem without her seduction. After all, beauty is her main purity."

A growl slips from my lips, and Lamar smirks like he knew it was coming.

"You, my dear, are made up of a lot of envy and just the right amount of beauty," he assures me. It's not really reassuring.

"That's all?" I ask in horror.

Lamar laughs like I'm thoroughly entertaining him this evening.

"Of course not," he finally says around his chuckles.

"I'm still hung up on the fact we're her harem," Kai tells me, his hand still stroking my back as a grin flirts with his lips.

"That makes it sound far more scandalous than having four lovers," I point out. "I sort of like it."

I finally think of something really important.

"Lamar, why do they go into a trance when I change into this?" I ask as I go phantom and change into the Egyptian Princess outfit before turning whole again.

The guys…don't go into a trance. Not even Ezekiel, and he missed it the first time. It makes me look like a liar. Weirdly, I take offense to feeling like a liar.

It's weird because I'm the *DEVIL'S FUCKING DAUGHTER and THE APOCALYPSE,* but being thought of as a liar irks me. My priorities are so messed up.

"Okay, so last time I had to change into a dolphin because they lost their minds," I assure him. "I'm not a liar."

Lamar isn't smiling. He swallows hard as he snaps his fingers. Something with a tarp over it lands in the room, and he clears his throat as he walks to it.

"It was an echo of a memory. Sometimes, if you don't have the memory, you can still have a strong reaction to the echo of a memory. Like you all seem to have been doing with whatever similar things cross paths from then to now," he goes on.

He tugs the tarp off, and my breath catches as I look at the woman in the painting. It's me. With different hair. And four guys are all crowded around me, looking just as menacing as the four in this room. But that's where the similarities end.

The four men in the image are harder, but just as attractive in different ways. Standing up, I go to kneel in front of the painting, my fingers tracing over each one of them.

The outfit I'm wearing in the painting matches the exact outfit I'm wearing now.

"They were your harem when you were Cleopatra," Lamar finally says. "It was one of your favorite lives. You all loved that life, except for War. He didn't get to be the favorite as often in that life."

Two strong arms come around me, drawing me to a hard body, and I know without looking it's Ezekiel.

I stare at the picture for a minute longer.

"Why is it here instead of in that hall?" I ask him.

Lamar sighs heavily. "The only ones who know you ever really existed are the ones who were alive five hundred years ago when you were killed. *The Apocalypse* stopped being considered a person by anyone younger than your death."

Five hundred years ago.

Five. Hundred. Years. Ago.

And we were already planning for the freaking nineties?

"Because," Lamar goes on, "for the past five hundred years, no one has been able to utter your name. Lucifer made it a law when he started going crazy from suffering the loss of his favorite child. Even Manella didn't dare utter your name, and he's your favorite brother. It hurt him the hardest."

I'm not even asking. I just can't right now. Round and round the conspiracy theories go every time he drops a new bomb that changes the suspect pool.

Ezekiel pulls me closer, forcing me to turn around in his arms and let him hug me.

"Manella will be coming down any minute now. They've been in a meeting. You should go before he comes, or face your father if you're ready," Lamar says a little too hopefully, like he expects me to move back in today and pick up where I left off, when I can't even remember where that is.

"I died a month ago," I say to him. "I just got back today and found out I'm the Devil's daughter, the end of the world, and apparently died five hundred years ago from a mysterious cause that is no doubt linked to hell. I think I'm going home to process for a while. It's sort of been a shitastic month."

He clears his throat, blinking as though he just realized exactly the load he's dumped on me.

"Of course," he tells me, smiling tightly. He grabs something from a bag and hands it to the guys. Jude accepts it as Lamar explains, "That's enough power to cloak the entire home, should you choose to move its location. It'll do that. It's from Paca's own stash."

"Don't ask that question, or we'll never get out of here," I tell Kai as he opens his mouth to ask a question, having already gravitated to my side. He looks at me, his mouth closing as he swallows the curiosity, and I add, "And I'm not ready to meet my *family*."

"I can't give you access to the underworld. Only Lucifer can do that." Lamar stares at me with a smirk. "But she has access already. She's still the same, unlike you four."

Pushing away from Ezekiel, I start backing out. Ezekiel grabs another stack of the books that Lamar didn't even offer, following behind me. Lamar just grins like he expected that.

"See you soon, Paca," Lamar tells me.

In the next instant, we're standing in the middle of the living room.

Jude opens his mouth to speak, but I hold a hand up. "Not now. Not today. Today, I need a drink, a lot of food, and other things that don't have to do with hell."

"I was just going to ask you if we're calling you Keyla, Apocalypse, or Paca?" he asks, sounding way too damn amused.

Why is he amused?

"Paca. It *feels* familiar, and it's not quite as horrifying as the longer version," I decide. "Besides, it's growing on me."

A heavy silence falls over us, none of us really saying anything after that, as we just stand in a semi-circular formation. No one is really looking at anyone.

Ezekiel leaves the room abruptly, and when he returns, a smile spreads over my face. He smirks as he hands me the jar he's holding, and I take it, sniffing it first.

It smells like citrus, and tastes just as good. I file away one of his preferred tastes.

I turn it up and drain the entire jar. Before I can put it down, Jude is pushing another one into my hand.

It tastes like a Bloody Mary. Figures.

I wish I knew how I know what a Bloody Mary tastes like.

"Well," Kai says as he tugs the drink from my hand. "We all wanted to know who we were."

He takes a long drink then hands it off to Ezekiel.

"Yeah, but we didn't expect it to be an ages-old, *apocalyptic* romance story," I state dryly, stealing the jar from Ezekiel before he can get a sip.

My four psychos burst out laughing, and I turn to walk away, taking the alcohol with me.

"You four have a terrible sense of humor," I call over my shoulder as I move to drop down in front of the TV. "Come show me how to livestream movies because I can only work the DVD player. I've apparently been studying Patrick Swayze when I should have been paying more attention to Keanu Reeves."

Kai settles down right beside me, taking the remote. "I'm going to need more to go on than just Keanu Reeves, since I have no idea what that has to do with anything."

Rolling my eyes, I point out the obvious. "I spent all those years learning about a lovesick ghost, assuming that's what I was. When really, I needed to be watching Keanu."

They just look at me like I'm crazy, and I snatch a quarter from the table.

"Heads, we watch Constantine," I say as I flip the quarter. It, of course, lands on tails.

"What's tails?" Jude asks as he drops down to my other side.

I sigh as I lean into Kai's side, feeling some of the inner chaos settle as I soak in his warmth. "Devil's Advocate."

CHAPTER XV

"We were horrible people," I state quietly to myself.

Apparently not quietly enough, since it causes Jude to jerk awake beside me on the floor-pallet-bed the five of us fell asleep on in the living room last night.

He groans when he looks at the time, and his arm tightens around me as he pulls me away from Gage a little.

"What the hell are you doing up so early after drinking all night?" he grumbles around a yawn.

He dozes back off, saving me the trouble of confessing my new obsession.

I flip the page on the book I'm reading—the book I spilled my blood on to make words appear.

It's a very dirty retelling of how we fell in love in the life I had as a Duchess, who didn't know she was quite so into debauchery when she was an innocent virgin the Duke—also known as Nicholai/Gage—forced her to marry him.

My gaze flicks over to Gage, wondering if he'd have a memory echo or whatever if I made myself look like this little drawing. Maybe all of them would.

Count Lavelle, also known as War—aka Ezekiel—was the first one to come in and defile the Duchess after the Duke gave his blessing. She really liked the way he just took her without warning.

The Duke watched, made her think it was him fucking her so hard from behind, when it was really the Count. My legs press together, and Jude tenses from beside me.

"What are you reading?" he asks, rousing from his sleep a little more.

"Go back to sleep," I say in deflection, reading on as two Earls, who I'm assuming must be Jude and Kai, come to take their turn with their friend's new wife.

As mortals, they could have any woman any time, it seems. But even with no prior knowledge of who I was or who they were, we all ended up in our little circle. I say circle, because reading all these has led me to believe we're an endless line that is seamlessly tied together and ever circulating.

The part where the Duke holds his wife down for the two Earls to take their turns is wrongly turning me on. I can get an image of how confused I'd be if I couldn't remember them, yet feel like it was so wrong to easily give into this.

They'd make me take it, knowing I'd want it, even without knowing me. They *did* make me take it. Over and over, and apparently I secretly loved it, even as I fought them as hard as I could.

It's disturbingly wrong, which makes sense. I'm the Devil's daughter.

That thought has marinated during the entire time I've been reading, reevaluating every active thought I've had.

We all fell in love eventually in this story. I skipped to the end, just to make sure, then went back to the beginning.

Well, the guys just have a strong bond in friendship, and they love each other like brothers. Kind of disappointing. I was hoping for some guy-on-guy action, even though I've never seen them cross that line before.

But they all love me. And I love all of them.

Yet we always sort of hate each other to start out with. At least a little.

It's pretty hot when you read about it instead of feeling the frustration when it's actually going on. I really want to slap them while reading the story about the Duchess. At least in the beginning.

Gage mutters something beside me in his sleep, moving closer as I fan myself and continue reading.

I have to quit reading this. Right now, with all that's going on, sex doesn't need to be on my mind. They didn't even kiss me after we returned from hell, so I'm assuming they're prioritizing as well, even though they did give me the night off to watch movies and sink into a silent stupor.

When I woke up at three this morning, I started reading. And haven't stopped.

Do you know who my mother is?

No? Well, that's because the Devil is an overachiever and had me on his own, and not in the way one might think. I was never really a child nor was I born. I was created.

I'm a manifestation of impurities and purities, then given a drop of Lucifer's blood so I could take form. I'm apparently the most successful blending of the children because of my incomparable balance. My presence doesn't hinder the balance topside no matter what day it is.

I'm a neutral entity. A weapon. A being who isn't really supposed to have any personality at all, according to the original plan. I'm supposed to be cold logic and firm dictation.

Epic. Fail.

Lust is one of those impurities of mine. Love is one of the purities. Envy, of course, is an impurity. Greed is unsurprisingly not one of my impurities. I knew I wasn't greedy. I've been telling the guys this, but they never listen.

They still haven't bought me the gifts they bought those other women. Being covetous is certainly one of my impurities.

My entire thought process is making more and more sense the more I learn about my genetic makeup. It's logically sound to dissect myself more now.

Not to mention, I'm inherently easily distracted, like all of the children, it seems. We like shiny things, booze, violence and sex. We don't do serious very well.

Blowing out a breath, I decide to continue reading about the Duchess after all, and blame my easily distracted mind on *Daddy Issues* or genetic makeup.

Unlike in this life, they didn't avoid sex with me in this retelling. They took it. Made me want them as much as I hated them. My body stayed on fire because they were constantly driving me over the edge.

In one chapter, I spent two days tied to a bed as they took their turns, bringing me to so many orgasms that I seemed to float off into a transcendent head space.

"Totally gipped in this life," I mutter under my breath, flipping the page.

This chapter might be my favorite, because in it, I struggle with a conscience, telling myself it's wrong to love all four psychos. Me. The Devil's daughter.

Apparently I only had a conscience when mortal. I'm sure that was quite the annoying thing to suffer through.

Weirdly, I remember expecting to have a conscience when I first started coming about. I knew it was wrong to watch them in their most private of moments.

I thought I just learned not to care. But nope. I just finally crossed a line and never felt guilty about it. Because guilt isn't one of my purities. And a conscience doesn't exist for this hell spawn.

Obviously, the Duchess version of me was also clueless about her origins, and she'd been raised in societal norms where letting four very corrupt men have their wicked way with your body at their leisure while your husband allowed it was not very ladylike.

So she runs, trying to escape them.

My lips curl into a grin when they find her within a day, and they punish her by taking turns as she fights against them, trying to resist, but unable to really do so in her mind.

Spoiler alert: That's when she finally admits she loves them and accepts the fact she's just as dark and twisted as the four of them.

My eyes close as the book comes down to my chest, and I imagine what it would be like for one of them to hold my shoulders down, two of them to hold my legs open, and then take turns on who fucks me into submission.

Everything inside me clenches, and a moan slips out of me.

The book is suddenly snatched out of my hand, and my eyes fly open as I scramble to grab it back from Gage as he jumps to his feet.

Jude snatches me at the waist, dragging me back down and holding me to him, as Kai's mouth goes to mine.

"Hurry and see what it's about while she's distracted," Ezekiel says as Kai kisses me stupid.

Jude's fingers are sliding up my side in the T-shirt I fashioned before bedtime. All the sensations are definitely distracting.

"Damn," Gage says under his breath. "We were twisted fucks in this life, and she apparently really likes it."

Kai breaks the kiss, a dark grin on his lips, and I jerk my head over to where Gage is grinning mockingly at me.

"This could work out with what we planned," Gage goes on, tossing the book to Ezekiel.

Kai is on me again, ripping me away from Jude, and coming down on top of me as his lips crash to mine once more.

I moan into his mouth as he shoves my legs apart, making room for himself.

"How twisted?" Kai asks, biting down on my bottom lip.

"Very fucking twisted," Ezekiel says on a shuddering breath, his voice thick with a reflection of the same twisted desire.

We should probably not be feeling so good about being evil. It probably upsets someone's balance somehow.

In the next instant, Kai is shoved off, and the book is pushed into his chest as Ezekiel takes his place on top of me.

I'm in a haze of sensation, pulling E down to me so I can soothe some of the ache I've been left with.

He kisses me hungrily, groaning into my mouth as he rips me up from the floor. When he starts walking, carrying me in the process, my legs wrap around his waist.

Breaking the kiss, I pull back to look at him, seeing the other guys have disappeared.

"Don't stop, and you'll be my new favorite," I assure him.

His eyes light up with that gold as he siphons us, and suddenly I'm being dropped to a bed.

That has me pulling my T-shirt over my head in an instant, but he just grins instead of coming down on top of me. My eyes get distracted, taking in the room I haven't returned to until now.

My breath leaves in a rush when I realize we're in *my* room, but it's completely redone.

All the magazines that I've idly been tearing apart and collecting ideas for my dream room…it's all here. Even the bed. The bed that stretches from one wall to another, making it the largest bed I've ever seen in my remembered life, and perfectly comfortable for five to sleep in.

"When did you—"

"We went feral like I did in hell's throat. The mindless haze lasted for about four days. After that, we were just miserable," Ezekiel tells me, surprising me.

"When tearing the place apart and fighting with each other got old, we started doing this," Gage says as he appears, smirking.

"One piece at a time."

Someone appears at my back, but before I can turn around to see who is on the bed behind me, a dark, silky blindfold comes down over my eyes.

My breath hitches as my blinder deliberately takes his time tying it into place. I realize it's Kai when he leans down to whisper in my ear.

"It's not fair for you to know who takes your virginity," he says against my ear. "You might favor them for too long."

My heart starts hammering in my chest as heat swarms my body.

"I'm not really a virgin, so clearly that's not an issue. And I want to see."

"No," is Jude's response really close to my ear. "You don't remember having sex. So this is ours to take, yours to enjoy, and all of ours to keep safe by not letting you get too attached to *just* one of us. Promise on our bond you won't go phantom to peek."

I hesitate, because that's totally what I was going to do.

"I'll know who it is based on the piercings. You all have different ones," I remind them.

A deep rumble of mocking laughter comes at my ear as Gage gets close enough to murmur, "You'll be so lost to sensation you won't be able to pinpoint something as trivial as what piercings do what."

A shiver runs down my body.

"Why do you have the piercings?" I ask, rambling at this point when I hear the distinct sound of clothing being shuffled off.

Now that my moment is finally here, I'm freaking out a little, if I'm being honest. I've dreamed of this for so long that it almost seems too surreal and overwhelming.

Understandable, especially given our newly discovered, daunting circumstances.

"Surface guardians get ink or piercings to signify their levels. We have the most," Jude answers, sounding amused.

"Gage, lose the tongue ring so she doesn't figure that out," Ezekiel says.

I groan, and they all laugh under their breath.

But the laughter is gone, and my breath is stolen when someone grabs me by my shoulders and pins me to the mattress. The sound of me swallowing is all I hear when they wrench my hands above my head, only touching me at the wrists.

The huge bed allows for a lot of space, which they're going to take advantage of, it seems.

Two sets of hands shove my legs apart even as I try to press them together, feeling a little exposed when they can all see me but I can't see them.

The grip on my legs firms, and soon another set helps to pry my legs open, which has my back arching seconds before a mouth is suddenly on me.

My startled cry is swallowed as a second mouth finds mine, stealing all my sounds as the mouth fastened to my clit starts wreaking havoc on me.

It's sensory overload already.

I come so quickly that they actually chuckle at me, everyone except for the one still between my thighs and driving me crazy as I clench around nothing.

It's too sensitive, and I fight to get free. They hold me down, and I force myself not to phantom out just to get away from the pleasure that has a fine line of pain. Until I'm almost on the cusp again, another orgasm coming so quick that it's sure to shred me.

Nothing could possibly be better.

The mouth rips away from me, leaving me just on the cusp, and I cry out in frustration. Arms grapple me down seconds before a strong hand clamps my hip, and something smooth and blunt prods my entrance.

I feel a clench down there, desperate to be filled, as two sets of hands roughly force my legs open wider. So many sounds and words escape me in unintelligible fragments.

Then suddenly fire rushes through my veins as someone thrusts deep inside me without warning. Every nerve in my body lights on fire, as an ache like I've never felt before doubles, almost feeling desperate for so much more.

A groan is muffled somewhere above me, before the hips pull back and surge forth again.

The hands on my legs tighten, and I feel the weight of their hungry gazes even as I'm forbidden to see them. The one inside me thrusts in harder, more urgently, and the hand on my hip starts lifting me at just the right angle.

I can't control anything.

They have sole control.

It's as maddening as it is incredible.

A new mouth finds mine, kissing me hungrily, as the man fucking me starts pushing me over yet another edge. My nails press painfully into my own palms, offering me just enough bite to keep myself from floating away when the third orgasm shatters me.

The body above me shudders fiercely, as they manage to hold onto their sounds much better than me, careful to give me no hint as to who is my current favorite.

I'm panting heavily as he clumsily pulls out of me, almost as though he feels as boneless as I do in this moment.

"I want to see your expression," I whisper softly. "It's not fair that you see mine if I can't see yours."

No one answers me as another body moves between my legs, causing a dirty shiver to spread through me when it sinks in just how deliciously wrong this all is.

It's a heady feeling to embrace it and savor it. It's almost worth losing their expressions in this moment.

Another mouth is one mine in the next instant. I always feel them come to me, but I never feel them leave me. They always stop kissing me when I'm too distracted to notice.

My body arches off the bed when the new man thrusts in forcefully, and they hold me open for him, making me take him even as my body still continues to shudder from the last orgasm.

He only thrusts in three times before he's ripping himself away and flipping me to my stomach in one harsh motion. A grunt rushes out of me, but then I'm lifted into the air by two sets of hands.

When I come back down, my skin connects with warm, incredible skin, and I end up straddling one of them as his mouth fuses to mine. I'm so drunk on sensation that I can't even discern the mouths kissing me from one to the next.

My hands are tied behind my back before I realize it, and the man under me thrusts up, pushing inside me almost too easily. Something slick and wet trails around my backside, as the man underneath me fucks me to distraction.

The sensations are different from this angle, especially with someone else behind me, running their lubed-up fingers down the path of my ass. I suck in a breath, breaking the kiss, as the one behind me pushes in just one finger.

A groan passes out of the one under me when I start moving harder against him, desperate to have more of each.

Hands tighten on my hips just before a much broader tip starts pressing into my ass. Definitely not a virgin there either, because virgins probably don't love the bite of pain as someone works their cock into their ass.

"I only feel two of you," I say on a breathy, half-coherent tone. "Are the other two watching?"

Hands come around to my front, as a voice comes to my ear. "Yes," is all that's whispered so softly that I can't discern whose voice it is.

The man behind me slides his hand up my throat as he starts fucking me in time with the man under me. The movements all feel so much more intense, packed inside me as I shudder uncontrollably against the powerful sensations.

We move as one unit, drawing out the most pleasure, easily synchronized as though we've done this countless times. It's like our bodies have remembered what our minds have forgotten, even if they're not all technically in the same bodies.

Such delicate care is taken not to hurt me, and our bodies writhe like sex and filth with a seductive, heady concentration. Their hands get more impatient, and I keep kissing one then another.

I'm almost positive it's Jude and Gage. Then those hands tighten and I'm certain it's Kai. Definitely Kai. I can feel him.

Nope. It's Ezekiel under me. Has to be.

For fuck's sake, why can't I tell them apart right now?

A moan is torn from my lips, and swallowed halfway through when the one behind me wrenches my head back to kiss me, even as both their hips start moving faster.

I can't…It's just too…I just can't…

I'm shattered in the next instant, the most powerful orgasm yet thundering through me with so much crackle and mind-numbing euphoria that I swear it feels like I'm floating.

In all actuality, I'm collapsing into the arms of the man under me as the two of them continue to drive in and out of me with more frenzied, urgent motions.

They come at the same time, both sucking in breaths as their hands tighten on me.

I'm too groggy to really and truly fathom how long we've been at this when the one behind me slides out first. I wince from the sting of pain and sense of loss when he's all the way out.

Someone lifts me off the other one, and his cock is slowly dragged out of me as my pussy clenches from aftershocks, demanding to keep him in.

Some rustling is all I hear as I'm gently laid on the bed, and someone starts untying my blindfold.

"That wasn't four of you, was it? Did Kai do those few pumps and move on like the selfish man he is, robbing me of my fourth experience?" I ask on a shaky, but certainly accusatory, breath.

Four sounds of laughter comes as the blindfold falls away, and an amused Kai is hovering over me with an arched eyebrow.

"Actually, we decided there should be a balance," he says, leaning forward to nip my lips. "You wanted to see our expressions. We needed you not to know the first person inside you. So I'm taking my turn last to give balance."

At my confusion, he tips my chin up.

"I took last instead of first. You now know I'm certainly not the first one inside you, but I'll be the only one you get to enjoy experiencing you for the first time," he says, brushing his lips over mine as he shifts himself to be right between my legs.

My smile spreads as heat blooms across me. I'm covered in all things them, essentially marked forever.

He grips my hip, and I lick my lips as I watch him grab his very hard, very large cock in his hand and strokes it once. It looks angry, almost throbbing with the desire for relief.

Jude's lips brush my throat as he comes onto the bed beside us. Ezekiel's mouth goes to my breasts, and I grip them both, touching them as I watch Kai stroke himself.

Gage moves above of me, bending to kiss me as that warmth continues to spread over my chest.

"So fucking beautiful," Ezekiel whispers against my ear as Gage breaks the kiss and leans back, his fingers trailing down my cheek.

"More beautiful than Hera or Lilith?" I ask automatically, not even sure why I ask it.

Jude snorts derisively, and I start to get my feelings hurt, until he says, "They can't even compare."

A goofy girl grin spreads as I tell him, "Now you're my favorite even though that was so fucking cheesy."

"Enjoy while it lasts," Kai says to Jude, smirking as he draws my attention back to him.

The other four move back just a little as Kai leans over me, lining himself up just right and raking the head of his cock over my very slick entrance.

His eyes flutter shut as his jaw tenses, and I commit every feature to memory. Licking my lips, I watch as he works the tip in, and his muscles bunch as his eyes barely open, a hooded, sexy expression on his face.

Inch by slow inch, he pushes inside me, more and more of that relief, pleasure, and indescribably hot patience on his face.

When he's halfway in, he suddenly thrusts hard, burying himself to the hilt. His eyes roll back in his head as his mouth falls open, and his sexy rumble of approval vibrates against me.

It feels just as good as it has since the beginning, the fourth piece of my heart clicking into place as my soul is fed by the hunger and pure pleasure on his face.

My hands go to his hair, keeping his head up when he tries to drop it. I need to see all of this. I want to drink it in.

None of them ever looked as lost to sensation as he does when they were with the other women. My jealous nature appreciates that immensely.

"Is this how you all looked?" I ask in awe as Kai stays still inside me like he's savoring it.

"Yes," Ezekiel whispers close to me.

"Now I wish I had thought to go last," Gage groans.

Kai is taking it slower, relishing the feel of me and allowing me to relish the feel of him as he draws back and slides in with an effortless ease, despite the snug fit, pressing against every nerve I have in a way that is almost *too* intense.

I pull him down by the back of his neck, eager to taste his kiss while he's lost like this.

The second his lips touch mine, he devours me, kissing me as he grips one of my legs at the thigh and hikes it up. He uses his new hold as leverage to pull back and slam into me.

A startled cry has me breaking the kiss as he raises up and sets a rhythm that has me arching toward him.

Hands grapple me to the bed, pinning me in place as Kai starts working me over, taking me like he's envisioned this hundreds of times and is on a mission to steal all he can from this moment.

My eyelids try to flutter shut reflexively, but I force them open so I can watch each expression as it crosses his face.

His eyes are burning a solid gold as he stares at me, unable to look away. My eyes screw shut, unbidden, when a pleasurably painful orgasm sweeps through, reminding my body I've received far too much pleasure for any one person.

A hand grips my jaw, and my eyes fly open when Jude turns my face toward him.

"Watch, *comoara trădătoare.* Watch him so you know what you did to us," Jude says as he turns my face back to see Kai.

It's like sweet anguish, as though the pleasure is so intense he's straining to drain every ounce of it out. Then his hips slam into me one last time, and his entire body shudders as he grips me painfully.

His eyes open heavily as he pants for air, staring directly at me like he sees me differently but still the same. I get it. Everything about each one of them now feels more intimate.

He drops to me, kissing me so hard, as though rewarding me for my lazy part.

My fingers tangle in his dark hair as I suck his bottom lip into my mouth and bite it gently.

He groans and shudders again, moving inside me like he's ready for another round.

"Enough for now," Jude says, even as Kai's hips continue to move.

I kiss him harder, not wanting him gone just yet. His hands fly to my hair, gripping it as he starts thrusting like he can't slow down, desperate to feel another release.

"I said enough," Jude bites out.

"Let him. She likes it," Ezekiel says from beside me, moving to watch my eyes as Kai fucks me like he can't stop.

"She can take as much as we can give," Gage says, smirking as he steps back, taking in the scene like he wants to watch.

Kai is stilling again, already coming. My orgasm total for the day has been met, so I don't feel gipped that I don't get another one at the end.

Kai's body goes lax on top of mine as he lazily he kisses me with appreciation, his weight crushing down on me.

"If he got two turns, then I vote I get mine later," Ezekiel points out.

"After mine," Jude drawls.

"Or mine," Gage says.

Kai grins against my neck like he's enjoying this. My legs wrap around his waist, and my arms go around his shoulders like I'm hugging him to me.

"Whoever is my next favorite will get me again. For now, I'm sexually sated but completely physically hungry," I tell them, running my lips up Kai's cheek.

If I continue lying here, basking in all this intimacy, I'll blurt out something stupid. I've learned men hate that.

Giving them no warning, I go phantom and zap myself to the kitchen.

From messy to clean within a flip of a switch, I set about my new task.

I grin when I hear them all follow, siphoning in here behind me. And I don't even care whose arms go around me or who kisses my cheek as I start cooking for five.

It's the first time since I started my lonely, anonymous existence that I finally feel whole.

CHAPTER XVI

"Well, this says the Devil's seven children spread their dark influence when needed or when imbalanced. One guess as to which of the seven deadly sins I am," I state blandly.

"Wrath," Ezekiel pipes up, staring over at me like he expects a treat.

"You don't get to be my favorite by answering rhetorical questions," I immediately fire back.

He rolls his eyes and mutters something petulant, and I grin because I think I just embarrassed Mr. War.

"Found the origins book," Gage says around a mouthful as he walks into the kitchen with a burrito in one hand and an ancient, possibly priceless book in the other.

The two look very odd paired together.

He tosses it to Jude, who catches it midair and starts reading from beside me.

"Read it aloud, jackass," I tell him as I eat one of my ten burritos.

Told you I was starving.

Kai snorts. Jude glares at me.

"Please," I add with faux sweetness as I bat my lashes.

He rolls his eyes, working to hide his smile that he really

doesn't want to give me.

Some things never change.

He gave Lake that smile, but I don't bring her up. The house is still in disarray because of my death—which is highly empowering—but clearly they've only started to heal from her betrayal.

I'm just happy she's dead and that Jude killed her for me.

That's better than any smile. I'm the Devil's daughter, so it's okay to be insane like that.

It's the universal excuse to all my issues now. That's the upside.

Jude blows out a breath. "It says we're four parts of one balanced compass, and essentially the metaphorical needle shifts toward whoever is needed the most for the compass holder."

"I'm guessing that's me," I say with a frown. "I forced you all to be my balance or whatever after giving you that piece of my balance?"

Suddenly, the seven remaining burritos don't look as tempting because my stomach starts to sour.

"I don't think so," Jude says distractedly as his eyes scan the next page, apparently reading ahead silently.

"Aloud," the other three all snap at him.

"For fuck's sake, you read it," Jude growls, shoving it at me.

Pushing my unwanted plate back, I take the book, go back to the first page and start reading it where he left off.

"Lucifer needed four soldiers to divide four treacherous, dangerous powers between. Power that, if seduced by greed, could lead to the world's ultimate demise," I read aloud.

The words on the next page take a moment to rapidly shift through fifty or more languages before finally settling in English.

"Since greed was not one of her impurities and she was bored, Apocalypse decided to remove this burden from him and tasked it to herself. As the world grew, she became in need of more power without disturbing her balance, and four soldiers that strong could provide that balance infinitely through time."

I look up, confused. "I thought Lamar said I was balanced and you four weren't."

"Yeah, all the children are—apparently not as well as you, but still balanced. However, they still have to maintain that balance. Needing more power means needing a counter balance," Ezekiel tells me. "Hence the reason Lilith offers a gift with a curse. Cain has his methods, along with the rest. This is saying you found a way to grow stronger and balance yourself with little maintenance."

I push the book away, not wanting to read more, and Gage picks it up to start scanning its contents.

"So I stole you and somehow tethered you to me to help me keep this balance," I say quietly.

This morning's incredible rendezvous now seems…cheapened. And wrong. Even with my new universal excuse for the wrong things I usually enjoy.

"No," Gage says, smirking as he starts reading aloud. "Apocalypse wanted four strong, fiercely loyal men in her harem who couldn't be recycled during one of her brothers' tantrums or stolen when one of her sisters decided to take new lovers."

"Not helping," I say with a tight smile.

"But she chose four of the most damaged men in the underworld who could no longer exist inside a mind without madness," he goes on. "To keep balance."

"That makes no sense," I point out.

"They were already too imbalanced. In other words, you were able to give a gift with no strings attached, because of that imbalance. You were the only one who had to sacrifice anything, because they'd—*we'd*—already suffered too much," Gage patiently tells me.

"I still don't get it, and it's starting to make me feel like an idiot," I say on a sigh while running a hand through my hair.

Kai starts explaining. "When you're a resident of hell, you can't repent. You can hold only a certain amount of impurities—usually it's a very high threshold. But if those impurities tip the scales, you'll start going mad. Much like humans, only on a much more volatile and dangerous level."

"Once you start going mad, there is no turning back," Jude goes on, frowning. "At least not that I've heard of. It's why we try to keep balance. If you preserve balance, you maintain balance within yourself. Affecting the balance of the universe without consideration for the balance will drive you mad."

"Okay..." I draw the word out, looking around at them.

Gage continues reading. "These four were deranged, scarred from hell's black heart where they were kept when they couldn't be recycled."

Kai groans, pushing his own food away. "We were in hell's black heart?" he asks incredulously. "No one leaves there."

"Hell's black heart?" I ask, lifting a finger as though I'm asking a question in class.

I suppose I've never really attended class.

"It's a place where they send the ones they can't recycle. Madness keeps that from happening, because there's no mad monster Lucifer wishes to create. There's a chance the imbalance would just force them to cease to exist, but they seem leery of that option. So hell's heart is where you're left chained, alone, and forgotten for all eternity."

"That sounds terrible," I say as a chill slithers up my spine.

"Hell is not supposed to sound like an inviting kingdom," Jude reminds me. "Unless you're royalty or upper level, it's actually quite the fucking opposite. Some spend centuries being brutally ripped apart as their soul takes a new form. That alone can drive one mad in a different way."

Gage keeps reading, and I try not to interrupt this time.

"The four had been lost to hysteria, left alone, and chained in the dark chambers where the only sounds were their own screams or those of the souls who just wanted to die, but couldn't. Because they were eternal now."

He swallows thickly.

"The nightmares," Ezekiel says quietly.

"We thought they were a vision of the future, when really it was just an echo of the past," Kai says on a groan. "We've been chasing away a fate we've already endured. All that paranoia for nothing."

"What?" I ask, but they ignore me as Gage continues reading.

"Apocalypse found the most damaged men she could. The ones who needed this relief with desperation. The only way to save them was to give them the power that could tear apart the world and shatter the balance completely if anything went wrong."

"That doesn't sound smart," Ezekiel says with a grin, looking over at me. "We were mad."

"Well, apparently I was too. The point is, did I make you slaves as my payment?" I ask, seriously worried just how horrible I truly was.

"No," Jude says like he knows the answer. "It was a truly free gift. Besides, that would have been too easy and you secretly hate easy."

"He's right," Gage says, drawing my attention back to him. "You healed their bodily wounds. You released them from the chains. And you pushed the power into their bodies one at a time. Then you hovered over them, caring for them for almost a century, as their minds and bodies continued to grow stronger. They slept under your watchful eye for the first time since the madness crept in. And they made up for the many centuries that sleep had evaded them. That version of you was enchanted by the effect you—and only you—seemed to have on them—on *us*."

Ezekiel's hands slide around my waist, almost as though he's drawing some of that *peace* out of me. Rather ironic that I provide peace, given the obvious.

"The end of the world offers the four of you peaceful dreams. I'm starting to wonder just how mad you must have been," I state dryly.

Jude's lips twitch as he leans over to my ear. "That means we were really fucking terrible before you."

Suppressing a shiver, I stare at Gage as he grins enigmatically.

"After a century of peaceful rest in her chambers, the four awoke ready to destroy the entire world so it would only be the five of them," he says conversationally.

"Geez, you psychos," I say on a breath. "You even scared the Devil's daughter."

Gage chuckles, handing the book off to Kai as though he's amused. Kai grins broadly.

"Apocalypse, being ever so vain, refused to admit failure. Besides, she'd gotten so attached to the four after watching over them for a solid century that she couldn't bear to hand them over to Lucifer to drain the power from and toss back into hell's black heart."

Kai pauses his reading, meeting my eyes.

"So she gave all four of them a piece of her sacred balance, disrupting her own stability in an effort to save them from themselves," he adds, holding my gaze. "She tied herself to them, leaving her less than whole. When their bond suffered, she suffered twice as much."

I swallow thickly.

I enjoyed killing an insignificant mortal man. I also left a fiery trail behind, burning the world around me uncontrollably. All because their bond to each other was hurting so much in the wake of my death.

"Simply put, you gave up bits of your much more powerful balance and infused it with ours in an effort to restore our stability by stealing from your own," Jude says, brushing a piece of my hair away from my shoulder as he stares at me differently.

"The power did bond the four of us, uniting us in a way that helped stave off some of the madness, but it didn't restore the balance like you'd assumed," Gage goes on, also staring at me a little differently. "You had no idea just how unsalvageable we truly were when you came to care about us."

"And you refused to send us back to our place in the black heart, and instead gave away something you didn't even know if you could afford to give away. And to four men who were still unpredictable and could hurt you at their leisure by simply abandoning you and sending you on to live the fate we'd just managed to escape after the madness took you," Kai continues.

I need a drink.

"Which is really freaking dangerous, considering I'm *The* Apocalypse," I say on a breath. "Not to mention, the four of you are notably ungrateful, so it's doubtful you felt immense gratitude for such an incredible self-sacrifice of my own."

Jude chokes back a laugh of surprise, shaking his head. Clearly they must have been grateful if the world isn't in ashes all these years later.

"*The Apocalypse,* as she often referred to herself, took the most selfishly selfless risk in doing so. Instead of betraying her, as she'd feared, they proved to be the most loyal harem she'd ever invited into her bed. And she was their first taste of pleasure in centuries," Kai reads on.

His eyes flick back over me, raking down my face and to my body.

"It's a wonder we settled for less even without our memories," he murmurs to himself.

I sit a little taller, if I do say so myself.

Ezekiel moves and takes the book away, reading it for us now.

"Lucifer trusted her when she said they were ready, and he granted them protection, power, prestige, and various other things

Apocalypse asked for, in an effort to help keep them safe, since she broke the law and gave them bits of her. Lucifer would never kill them now. He simply couldn't. His daughter would suffer a fate he couldn't spare her from if he did, for she'd shared too much, and only she could take it back."

"Guess that means I'm too stubborn to do so, since you all clearly still have a piece of me wedged in you. That's why I can't be away from you for too long. Even in whole form, I have limits it seems. But how were you reborn with the same piece if we were all killed?" I ask, looking at Ezekiel. "Does it say?"

He shakes his head. "This is just the origins. The rest is a series of equations that make no sense to me to explain proper balance, execution of power, and various other things. If I could understand the equations, I might could understand our powers better."

"Well, what can kill us? Clearly the Devil's poison couldn't truly kill me. What about you?" I ask.

"We've been out of hell this entire time, not getting our power boosts and such," Jude says on a breath. "It makes us more vulnerable than we apparently were in that life. In that life, it would have been impossible to kill us."

"Evidently that's not true," I point out.

"According to some of the notations in the margins, only the Devil himself could have killed us in hell," Ezekiel says absently, still studying those equations.

Daintily, I dab the corners of my mouth with my napkin, then go phantom and put on clothes. No need to be naked right now. We'll not be going for round two just yet.

They're all just in jogging pants that they put on while I was cooking. It's actually a very domestic image of us. Or at least it was.

"Why are you wearing your badass clothes?" Gage asks warily.

"So you finally admit this outfit is badass," I state, becoming whole to see how the weapons fare.

"They're plastic," Jude says as he picks up a knife from my hip, rumbles of laughter following that with more carefree abandon than I've ever heard from them.

I'm almost distracted by the way all of them are laughing, and I don't even mind that they're laughing *at* me and the fact I apparently suck at making my weapons as real as I am.

"Glad we didn't have to rely on these in the trials," Ezekiel says through his guffaws as he throws a plastic ninja star.

It bounces off the wall.

This renews their laughter.

A smile creeps across my face as I take it in, all of them snickering around the brunch table like I've never once—during all my years stalking them like their unseen guardian—seen them do before.

It's not dark laughter. It's not amused laughter. It's surprised, real, hardy laughter that goes on and on, everyone keeping it rolling by lifting another weapon and making a joke.

"Could you imagine if we'd stabbed one of the blind tribesmen with this?" Gage asks, barely choking the words out through his chuckles as he stabs Ezekiel.

It breaks on impact, and it sets them all off again.

I take it all in, unwilling to break up this rare, never witnessed moment between the four of them.

They look…human. For just this brief glimpse in time.

No wonder the old me wanted as many mortal lives as possible with them. It let me see them like this. I can only imagine how'd they'd be now if they hadn't died and come back with cleansed souls that expelled the madness altogether.

"You expect diamonds and lush gifts, when these were the gifts you offered in a land of every form of death?" Gage asks through his own hysteria.

"I gave you a course of monsters and blind cannibals filled with death riddles in hell's belly for your birthday. The fact I'm a terrible gift-giver is quite apparent. Side note, none of you should be encouraged to ever tell me your birthdays."

Because the laughter momentum is already fierce, they finally laugh at one of my jokes the way my joke deserves to be laughed at. I quite literally pat myself on the back.

"So, seriously, why are you dressed like that right now?" Kai asks as their laughter tapers off.

"Because now I realize who killed us, so I'm going to nip the problem in the bud before history repeats itself."

The lingering laughter dissipates with that.

Ezekiel moves toward me.

"What do you mean?"

"It means I'm going to go kill the Devil, of course," I say with a shrug before going phantom and focusing really hard on the underworld.

On Lamar.

On Manella.

On Lucifer himself.

"Shit," Jude shouts, breaking up the silence.

I feel tingles pass through me from four directions just as my eyes open to see I most definitely just siphoned myself to hell.

Looking around at four angry glares, I realize I also brought along some stowaways. How is that possible? I can't siphon them!

"You four can't be here," I hiss, shoving them away from me.

I flick my wrist, expecting them to go back home, but apparently the Devil's daughter doesn't know how to use all her power. Doesn't matter. I know how to use the killing ones.

"You can't be serious," Gage growls as I stay in phantom form.

"Actually, I am. I just need to find a book that tells me how to navigate the illusions the hallways present to keep you walking in circles."

I go whole, walking toward the massive bookcase filled with little details of hell, I'm sure. Seems I landed us in the last spot we left when we visited hell.

Two arms immediately grab me, but I go phantom and roll my eyes, walking on undeterred.

"You can't kill the fucking Devil," Jude growls, getting in front of me.

I pass through him and start looking for the appropriate book. One catches my eye, because the word *PACA* appears on the binding for a split second before disappearing.

"I think I can. After all, I apparently have the power to destroy the world. I'm sure the Devil made me for that reason because he couldn't do it himself. By the way, if the Devil made me, you were wrong about him not being capable of such, back when we had this discussion before the trials."

"Stop talking in circles. Damn it, Paca, Don't fucking do this," Kai snaps, trying to grab me as well.

"I'm phantom," I remind them. "Will one of you be a dear and collect that for me? I think it's mine."

Gage grabs the book and holds it up like it's leverage as he smirks. "If you want it, come and get it."

I put my hands on my hips as I level him with an unimpressed glare.

"If I don't kill him, he'll come to kill us," I point out.

"That makes no sense. He could have killed us in the trials if he wanted—"

"He's waiting for me to appear so he can kill me too," I say, interrupting Ezekiel. "Reasonably speaking, if he's the only one who *could* kill us, then clearly he's the one who *did* kill us. I'm not overly concerned with his motives. I just want to stop him before he succeeds twice and steals all these memories as well."

Gage hesitates, like he's considering opening the book for me instead of leveraging it against me.

"That's insane. You don't even fucking know if you can kill him," Jude barks, refusing to let this lie. Figures. He's always the last to come around, it seems.

Gage is immediately back on his side.

The more things change, the more they stay the same…

"Lamar stated I have the best reasoning even when it doesn't make sense to anyone else," I primly remind them, shoulders back and head held high.

Four incredulous glares meet me.

"So now we're trusting Lamar because it's convenient to your argument?" Kai asks me dryly.

"He's not wrong. I'm undeniably reasonable about everything but the four of you. The heart gets a little too involved there," I state absently, turning back around and looking for more of my books. "The Devil needs to die, and I'll either kill him today or wait until you're asleep to return and kill him later. Your interference only hinders me in this moment."

"What the hell makes you think you can kill Lucifer?" Jude snaps.

"What makes you think *The Apocalypse* isn't stronger than the Devil himself?" I volley.

I grin over my shoulder at them, and they all glare back at me.

"Worst case scenario, I still can't kill him, despite my level-ups, and I scoot out of there before he kills me. He won't come topside, and we'll continue to thwart attacks," I go on.

"I knew you were here." Lamar's voice cuts through the room like a shock to the system. "I assume she is too."

We all turn to stare at him in the doorway as his face lights up like hell's worst aren't literally standing in his room. Alone. With him. After already being undecided on whether he dies or not.

He's not a very smart fellow, is he?

His smile disappears. "Oh shit. You still don't remember."

"We're here because you told her she was reasonable," Gage tells him in accusation.

"It's the one thing she knows for certain is true," Jude goes on, quite dramatically sarcastic, if you ask me.

"Okay," Lamar says, looking confused. "What is wrong with her being reasonable?"

"Because reasonably, it's safe to assume the Devil killed us," Ezekiel says, glaring at him.

Lamar pales. "Oh dear. That's not at all—"

"Don't bother backtracking," I say, turning whole and cutting him off as I gesture toward the journal Gage is still holding. "Open it up and tell me how to find the Devil. Or do you already know?"

"I know how to find your father—"

"Don't try to humanize him or me by calling him my father, when I'm without a conscience," I point out, interrupting Lamar and reminding him of the knowledge I've gathered about my manufactured self.

"You're not capable of guilt or conscience, so when you feel regret, it is true, unpersuaded, heart-wrenching regret," he says seriously, causing me to hesitate for a split second. "And you'd certainly regret this."

"You're not strong enough to kill your father, but he is strong enough to kill all of us," Gage says like he's trying to reason with me. "Let's think this through."

"He can't come topside. That much we know. The longer we delay, the longer he dangles us on his strings whilst he plays the mad puppeteer," I say on a frustrated sigh. "I'm not opposed to killing, and it seems to be the most logical solution to our current problem. I just got you four. I'm not ready to die without at least a little fight."

Lamar pinches the bridge of his nose.

"Just remember you convinced her that she's reasonable," Ezekiel growls, causing Lamar to groan.

"Well, the old Paca was very reasonable, but also very knowledgeable and not running on snippets of information," he finally gripes, glaring at Ezekiel before looking back to me. "You need to read your journals."

"Do they say I'm a daddy's girl or something? We're in hell. He's the Devil. I expect manipulation and tricks. I won't believe words just because they're on a page in a book we got from *hell.*"

"I don't know what the journals say, to be honest. You blessed them so that only your blood would reveal the words," Lamar answers.

"You were going to read my journals?" I ask on an octave higher. "Those are private!"

"Someone else reason with her. I've forgotten how exhausting she can be," he groans.

"If Lucifer didn't want us dead because it would have made his child suffer, I highly doubt he's responsible for our deaths," Jude says, reciting the origins journal.

"That was from the beginning, and a lot of centuries have passed since I spiced the four of you up real nice. I was created to be a robotic weapon. What if I decided I never wanted to blow the world to bits and he killed me so he could replace me, because there has to be six, not seven children, even though there are already technically seven children, regardless of the weird loophole rule?"

Everyone flicks a gaze between them, almost as though that hadn't crossed their minds.

"Oh for heaven's sake—"

"Really, Lamar? *Heaven's* sake? Is that entirely appropriate?" I ask seriously.

He groans and scrubs a hand down his face.

"What on earth are you wearing?" he asks as he shakes his head.

"My ass-kicking, badass attire. Blame Catwoman for making leather bodysuits so fashionable while whooping ass and taking names. Take me to see Lucifer, get me all my journals, and then we'll be on our way."

He just studies me, and I study him right back.

"How about a compromise?" Kai bites out, glaring at me. "You pretend you have your memories and just speak with Lucifer. It'll be you manipulating him to find out the truth about what happened."

"And what if he kills her on the fucking spot?" Ezekiel snaps, shoving at Kai's chest.

"So you admit he's likely the one who wants us dead," I say to Ezekiel, patting his shoulder and ignoring all the sounds of exasperation.

"Lamar, send them home. I'd like to see my father now," I tell him with a smirk.

"Lamar, don't you fucking—"

Jude's words are cut off when the four of them are suddenly no longer in the room.

"They're in the graveyard now," Lamar says, opening his eyes as his jaw tics.

I cock my head, a slow grin forming on my lips. "I just gave you a command, and you totally obeyed."

His jaw grinds more, and my smile only grows.

"Like an actual command instead of a gently worded request," I ramble.

Still, he says nothing, just narrows his eyes on me.

"Dance for me," I say with the same authoritative tone.

He immediately springs into action, and music weirdly starts playing inside the room as Lamar river dances and curses.

"This is humiliating and degrading," he growls.

"Then stop doing it," I say with an even bigger grin.

He and the music stop at once.

"Next time I ask a question, maybe you should just answer it before I make you do it," I say as I move closer.

He gives me a hurt look. "You always admired it when I looked out for you and never made it your duty to remind me of my place as the others did. Well, the way they did before you became my friend, and I became your only friend who wasn't a lover or family."

I move to pick up my journal that fell from Gage's hand before the siphoning. I open it and peer down before staring at my hand.

Just the right thought has the tip of my finger opening up and a drop of blood spills out onto the pages.

My breath goes out shakily, because I have no idea how I knew how to do that.

My eyes flit down to the journal, expecting it to be in English, but it's not. Weirdly enough.

"What language is this?" I ask.

He peers over, studying it. "Romanian," he says with a sad smile, then starts reading the words to me in translation. "War is the one who will always side with you first, because he thinks like you the most. However, don't mistake that for him being weak or sweet. He'll punish you for that. Regardless, his constant championing will keep you from feeling so outnumbered," he reads aloud to me, frowning. "It's almost like you wrote this to yourself."

My lips tense, and my back stiffens. Why would I be writing to myself unless I expected to die?

"The next line is in Egyptian," he tells me. "Old Egyptian," he goes on, gesturing to the hieroglyphics. "Death is his opposite, in that he will push you to the last morsel of your sanity by forcing you to listen to all the facts. Without him, you're too rash."

He points to the next line.

"This is Russian, and I'm rusty, so bear with me," he says, then starts reading. "Conquest will never do as you expect. He's also your best warrior when you need him most. He'll fight at your back even when he wants to throttle you. You need him to be that unpredictable variable."

He flicks his gaze to me, but doesn't bother telling me what the next language is before he starts reading.

"Famine will be your most solid advisor, but he'll likely side with Death more than you, simply because he likes to annoy you the most. He's secretly the most viciously protective of the five of you."

The next words that appear look like gibberish.

"This is your own made-up language for your personal notes. If you wrote this to yourself, then you had no clue your memories would be gone when you returned."

"But I thought I was going to die before I wrote this, and I clearly planned on coming back," I say quietly.

"Which is certainly news to me," he says as he clears his throat. "I thought you were gone forever. But then again, you were always paranoid, so it's possible this was just a precautionary measure."

"If I thought I'd have my memories, why write this at all?"

He shrugs a shoulder. "Maybe you planned for the absence of memories, but didn't expect to lose your knowledge. You coveted your knowledge."

Now I know a lot about the nineties, movies, current events…and not much else. Lovely.

I close the journal and look at him. "How do I find my father? Answer me this time."

It's a command that he follows with sad, kicked-puppy eyes. "You simply stay whole as you walk. Your blood will guide you to whatever location you wish to see."

He sounds…pitiful. I pat his shoulder.

"If I can command people, I'm sure Lucifer can too. How are rebellions even possible?"

"Commanding the loyal isn't hard. It's commanding the disloyal that proves tedious," he bites out, still miffed.

"You forget I don't feel guilt, so you can stop trying to make me feel guilty for not trusting you or for questioning your motives," I say with a bittersweet smile.

Turning, I walk out, moving down the hallway in whole form. The hallways change before me, shifting and moving, and creating a new passage I wouldn't have seen as a phantom.

That makes this trickier. Phantom keeps me safer.

"Guilt is actually a second-generation purity, one of the very few adopted from the impurities," he calls to my back, surprising me enough to turn around.

Usually I drift down a random path, and leave jaws unhinged as I strut away in peace.

"It belongs in neither, and should the scales ever tip back into purer times, it will be passed about again," he says as he moves closer, another of my journals in his hand.

"Guilt is considered a purity for the time, because of the good it does. It forces one to heed their conscious. The guilt forces them to repent, to love unconditionally, to be there for someone who needs them, and to protect. Guilt has been accused of affecting free will on multiple occasions, and it remains one of the biggest debates today. But there's no way to truly eradicate guilt, so they have to balance things."

"I think I've finally found someone more random than me," I tell him honestly.

Now I know what it's like to be this side of someone who is spewing nonsense.

"But you're a being with no conscience and no guilt," he goes on, undeterred as he patiently moves toward me, finally stopping just a few feet away.

"You spent years searching for four boys, exactly four, who could love you and never envy the other. Four boys who could construct a bond like no other since. You searched until you found it, because unlike all the other children, you have patience. You selfishly shirked all your responsibilities until you found them, also, because you knew the world needed them and you wanted them to be yours. And you're the only one who could have created them as they are."

My brow furrows, because I'm not sure why he's kissing my ass and insulting me at once.

"You're a selfish being designed to be so. You selfishly demand things of life as though you're entitled to them. You selfishly break the laws of balance and reason with yourself that you can tweak things to even the scales, despite the fact no one else is allowed to do this without a death sentence." He grins as he says that, though I have no idea why.

"Because you selfishly know that they really can't kill you because of all the balance you provide. So you do as you please with no regards for empty consequences," he goes on.

"That sounds very reasonable if I'm not actually upsetting the precious balance," I feel the need to point out. "But someone did kill me. Likely the Devil."

He grins so broadly, as though this is familiar for him. Me pointing out the logic after him browbeating their version of the story at me.

"Indeed it is. Which is why *they*—the ones who take offense—never pretend to notice. I have *no* idea how you did this without upsetting the balance. It defies every law imaginable, and it worries me of how your fate came to be for this to have even worked. But you were always smart and selfishly selfless. You're Lucifer's favorite."

He's really trying to force this *daddy's girl* thing.

"I don't know whether to thank you or slap you," I tell him, genuinely perplexed by the plan of action I need to take before I sneak away from his randomness. It could be catching.

"You had no conscience, no empathy, and no guilt, but you had reason. You didn't have greed, so your reasoning capabilities kept you from exerting your excess amount of power without justifiable provocation."

"So I won't go *boom* because I'm pissed?" I ask, sincerely interested in this.

It's not easy to make me mad, I've learned. I'm more amused by things or terrified. Not so much of an angry person. Jealous? Hell yes. Angry? Not usually.

But still…

His grin spreads again. "Certainly not. My point to all of this is the fact that you loved so hard, you did the impossible."

He steps closer, pushing my journal into my hand, but holding onto it even as I grip it. His eyes stay fixed on mine as he speaks.

"You're selfishly selfless. Which means there's a reason you started all this. And you prepared to find the boys, but expected to have your memories, or at the very least, your vast amount of knowledge. In those journals, I'm sure you'll find whatever you need. I'll help when you let me. I miss feeling that love like only you could provide," he says, the last part coming out a little quietly.

He releases the journal and takes a step back.

"*That* is why I will earn my way back into your life. That magnitude of love *only* comes from you. Despite what everyone says, *that* is why you are your father's favorite. Because how could you not be?"

He clears his throat and takes a step back as my eyes water for no apparent reason.

"Kill your father if you must, Paca. But you're making a grave mistake if you succeed."

He starts walking off, and I dart out to get in front of him.

"The earth was scorching under my touch. Was it because I was so far away from them, or was it because their bond was shaky."

"Shaky?" he inquires, sounding confused.

"They weren't together, and they've apparently fought a lot since my latest death. I was in severe physical pain, and—"

"You're *The* Apocalypse. Topside, when your balance suffers, so does your control over your very strong, destructive nature. If their bond was *severely* hurting, then yes, you'd be likely to suffer the repercussions, and the world would pay the price."

Great. So I can go kaboom by accident, after all. He's a big fat lying liar.

That'd be a shitty thing to do—destroy the world by accident just because I'm imbalanced. Humans are a lot easier to kill than hell monsters, I've noticed.

"Can you tell me how to figure out my language?" I go on, not sharing my inner musings with him.

"The only one who thinks like you *is* you, Paca. Whatever it is you wanted yourself to know, you'll figure it out. Just try to do it in time."

He pats my cheek and walks away.

In time for what?

"I currently hate being touched by anyone who isn't them," I call to his back.

"I know," he says without turning around.

Dick.

CHAPTER XVII

I spin around and quickly move through the corridors, trying to ignore the ruthless and completely obnoxious heartbeat pounding in my chest. I'm about to have to be really good at acting.

And even better at manipulating.

Manipulation isn't an impurity of mine, so I'm on my own with outwitting the Devil. Just awesome.

Or die. I could always die.

I'm starting to think this was a terrible idea.

Why do I think I can stick it to the Devil, exactly? Am I that arrogant with my vanity?

I start to turn around and abandon my mission until I'm more prepared, when I see a picture. It's the Gemini Twins divided into two segments of the same image.

A dark twinkle rests in their eyes as they both smirk like they ate their teacher's head or something. A shotgun on either hip, they stand proudly.

I read the plaque underneath, even though I should be leaving.

William "Devil Anse" Hatfield and Randolph "Ole Ran'l" McCoy

Casualties – minor

Historical effect – still the most legendary blood feud to-date

Unbelievable.

This is like the Devil's version of hanging his children's accomplishments on the fridge.

I move on, not paying attention to all the rest of the freaky hall of fame paintings. I do notice there aren't any up of me, yet I've clearly led some wall-worthy lives.

After all, Lamar said I was Cleo-fucking-patra.

Changing course again, I end up turning and moving down the hall in the other direction, walking briskly with determined strides. Not destroying the world by accident takes precedent over pretty much everything else.

And I can't help but wonder if maybe my death wasn't to prevent such a thing. Why did my paintings come down? Why can't my name be uttered in hell? What if *I'm* the bad guy? It'd clearly make sense.

We can't keep searching for answers in a home that doesn't have them, when all the answers are in hell. No matter how much we prepare, we don't have enough information to ever truly be ready for what happens next.

Time to stop procrastinating and delaying the inevitable.

The wall in front of me suddenly vanishes, unlike last time when I came through here with Lamar.

There's a room I don't know in front of me. A huge, ornate bedroom with a large bed even bigger than the one the boys built for me at home.

I whirl around, trying to take in my surroundings and wondering how I just ended up in here, but I stop as a cold sweat breaks out over me.

Leaning against the wall like he's been expecting me all day is none other than Lucifer himself.

He's smirking at me, a dark, lethal look to his gaze.

"Hello, Paca. I've been waiting for you."

Silence of the Lambs flashes through my mind. Along with Darth Vader. It's a scary combo.

"That's not creepy at all," I mutter under my breath.

Clearing my throat, I stare at him like I'm not terrified. What a fearless fool I was to think this would be no big deal.

I've stood before him in the past without pissing myself. However, he's a hell of a lot more intimidating when I'm in whole form.

"I came here to kill you," I tell him, smiling darkly as I begin the ruse of pretending I'm really *The* Apocalypse.

"Oh?" he drawls, his lips curving out in a smile, as though that pleases him in some twisted way.

Lunatic.

Or maybe he's just that unafraid of me, which means I likely can't kill him. Damn it.

"But, thanks to last night's movie night, I've *just* decided to take a different route," I tell him, glancing down at my nails like they're fascinating, while secretly watching him with a wary peripheral.

"And what, dear daughter, might that be?"

He's still smirking when I look up.

With a steady voice and a creepy smile of my own, I answer, "I came to make a deal with the Devil."

END OF BOOK II

End of Books 1&2

Thank you so much for reading.

Continue to next book for the remaining books, 3&4. <3

Made in United States
Troutdale, OR
01/08/2024

16813983R00235